THE
SURVIVOR

A PIONEER NOVEL

Also by Bridget Tyler
The Pioneer

THE SURVIVOR

A PIONEER NOVEL

BRIDGET TYLER

HARPER TEEN

An Imprint of HarperCollinsPublishers

HarperTeen is an imprint of HarperCollins Publishers.

The Survivor: A Pioneer Novel
Copyright © 2020 by Temple Hill
All rights reserved. Printed in the United States of America.

ISBN 978-0-06-265809-8

Typography by Jenna Stempel-Lobell
20 21 22 23 24 PC/LSCH 10 9 8 7 6 5 4 3 2 1
❖
First Edition

A12007 391265

For Toni. This isn't our world. It's yours.

ONE

Earth is dead.

That's not my biggest problem right now.

My family left Earth two years ago. Our team's mission was to establish human life on a new, uninhabited world: Tau Ceti e. Unfortunately, it turns out that Tau isn't uninhabited. It belongs to two species who have nothing in common, except for the part where they don't want to share their planet with invaders from outer space.

Which would be us.

We never meant to be invaders. We were pioneers. Explorers.

Now we're refugees.

Wow. It's not often you can use the word *we* and mean every human being in the universe, but we're all in the same boat now. Well, spaceship, if you want to be literal about it.

The ISA Colony Ship *Prairie* is the biggest spacecraft humanity has ever built. Maybe the biggest we'll ever build, now. She's also an unfinished prototype. The *Prairie* was supposed to have years of testing and redesign before attempting this journey. But "supposed to" isn't a thing in the apocalypse.

The actual trip went fine. The *Prairie* survived the twelve-light-year trip from Earth to Tau. Then her computer automatically woke the crew, and they tried to bring the huge ship into orbit.

That's when things started to go wrong.

Turns out the *Prairie's* solar sails are screwed up. Without the power they provide, the colony ship can't maintain a stable orbit. She can't pull out of Tau's gravity well either. If we don't fix her, she'll fall through the atmosphere and crash into the planet, causing a mass extinction event.

But that's not my biggest problem right now either.

My mom knows how to fix the sails because she commanded *Prairie's* last test flight. At the time, I hated her for it. Three years ago, before our team left Earth, a solar flare almost destroyed our ship, the *Pioneer*. Mom ordered my siblings and me to evacuate with the other kids. Instead, I figured out how we could save the *Pioneer*, and our families.

With my brother Teddy's help, my crazy idea worked. We saved everyone, but it cost my brother his life. I almost died too. I was in the hospital for four months after the accident, and then I spent five more in full-time physical therapy.

Mom wasn't there. For any of it. She took command of the *Prairie* and headed for Saturn the day after Teddy's funeral. She was gone for a year. Back then, I figured she left because she couldn't stand the sight of me. I thought she blamed me for Teddy.

I know Mom better now.

I'm pretty sure she left because she blamed herself. And we're lucky she did, which is messed up but true. If Mom hadn't taken that assignment, she wouldn't know what's causing the *Prairie*'s sail to glitch. No one would. Five of the six engineers who designed the *Prairie* died racing to make her spaceworthy in time to get the survivors to safety. The sixth, our chief engineer and my mom's best friend, Penny Howard, died here on Tau. In my arms.

So, basically, my mom's lack of healthy emotional coping mechanisms is going to save the human species.

The catch is, the repairs have to be done on the *Prairie*'s hull, and they require at least two people. Mom and I are alone on our shuttle, the *Trailblazer*, and there's no time to go back to the surface for the engineering team.

That means I have to do an EVA.

As in extravehicular activity. As in go outside. In space.

And I'm afraid.

In order to save the *Pioneer*, Teddy and I had to eject ourselves into space without our suits. It sucked. I can't even begin to explain how much. I never expected to do an EVA again. I never wanted to. Now I have to. The survival of my whole species depends on it, and I'm afraid. I don't think I've ever been so afraid.

My fingers are shaking as I smooth the last seal on my pressure suit closed. The slippery gray fabric vibrates gently against my skin, and the suit's internal computer whispers, "Seal failed. Please reapply."

I'm glad Mom is still up on the bridge and not here to witness this. She's got enough to worry about. She doesn't need to add me to the list.

I shake my hands out, swearing quietly as I rip the seal open all the way down to my belly and start over.

I hate spacesuits. I always have. I hated them before the accident. Now I feel like this thing is a python and I'm helping it swallow me.

With a thin hiss, the suit sucks tight against the body stocking I'm wearing underneath. I breathe a sigh of relief and pull on my EVA utility harness, snapping the sturdy straps around my thighs and over my shoulders. I look like someone melted a wrapped candy bar and let it harden again all lumpy. I can't believe my brain even has the bandwidth to notice right now. I guess worrying about my thighs is one way to avoid having a panic attack.

"Okay, *Trailblazer* is on autopilot," Mom says as she steps through the interior door of the airlock and seals it behind her. "This is as ready as we're going to get."

She keeps talking, but I can't hear her over the remembered roar of explosive decompression. It's more than a memory. I'm drowning in a sound that isn't there. Deafened, even though I *know* it isn't real.

I'm *so* not ready.

"What did you say?" I ask, trying to sound like I'm not shaking.

"I said, 'Cross check?'" Mom is fully suited except for her helmet. Her face is almost the same shade of gray as her gear.

"Right. Sorry."

My voice catches on the words. Mom flinches, like I'm a sore tooth.

She looks away as she raises her arms, holding them away from her sides so I can check her seals. Then she spreads her legs so I can check the seals between her suit and her boots.

Breathing feels harder than it should, like the airlock is already venting atmosphere, which it isn't. I know it isn't. The exterior door is still red. The airlock is still sealed.

So why can't I breathe?

"Check," I say, managing not to gasp the words. "Cross check?"

Mom runs her hand over the seal at my throat, down my arms to the seals on my wrists that bond the suit to my gloves.

Her hands are shaking, too.

Fear arcs between us.

"Mom—"

She pulls me close. Our suits wheeze over each other as we cling.

Then she steps back.

"Okay, Joanna," Mom says. "Run me through it." Her voice, at least, is calm. Like it's being piped into her shaking, red-eyed body from a distance.

I breathe.

In. Out. In. Out.

I can do this.

I can't do this.

I have to do this.

"We are currently matching orbital velocity with the ISA Colony Ship *Prairie* at a range of twenty-five kilometers." The words snag at each other, tangling in my mouth as I yank them into order. "We will tether to the airlock and make a controlled—"

"Skipped a step," Mom interjects. "Sloppy." Her tone strikes my anxiety at just the right angle, throwing sparks of irritation. I glare at her. A tiny smile flashes through her pallor.

"That's better."

"Fine," I say, backtracking. "First, we tether in, then we decompress the airlock. Open the doors. *Then* we will make a controlled jump to the *Prairie*'s hull and tether to the *Prairie*. Once we're secured, we fix her solar sail so she doesn't crash into the planet and wipe out three sentient species in a single, spectacular moment of dumb."

Mom is right. Irate is better than afraid. My words are getting smoother with every phrase.

"How do we do fix the sail?" she asks. This is helping her, too. Color is flushing back into her face, like someone's changing the filter on the scene.

"First, we attempt to reboot the sail deployment app," I say, feeling the words gain velocity. "If that works, we're golden. But what are the chances?"

"Gonna have to brush up on your optimism, kiddo," Mom says, a wry smile coasting over the words.

"All evidence to the contrary?" I say, feeling an answering grin teasing at my lips.

She rolls her eyes and makes a tumbling motion with her hands. *Keep going.*

"Okay, so pessimistically, let's assume the reboot doesn't work," I say, the words building pictures in my mind. "In that case, we would extend the sail by hand. There are thirty-eight joints in total. It should take roughly six hours to manually unfold them all. Exhausting. Boring. But not hard. Just like pitching a tent. On a moving spaceship. In space."

The sarcasm doesn't land. Or at least, not like I intended it to. Mom's gone all pale and gray again.

"Mom, what's—"

"I'm sorry, Jo."

The thin veneer of humor I've managed to paint over my terror evaporates. I wish she'd just put the damn helmet on so I don't have to see how terrified she is. I'm scared enough for both of us.

"You're not the one who put the last survivors of Earth on an unfinished prototype, Mom," I say, grabbing my helmet with both hands. I'm afraid I'll drop it otherwise. "Everyone on the *Prairie* is fresh out of inso and you can't fix that sail alone. That means I'm going outside. Which is fine. I'm okay."

Mom turns away and grabs her helmet from the locker behind her. I still hear the little sob she's trying to hide.

She doesn't think I'm okay.

Neither do I.

I jam my helmet over my head anyway. At least in the featureless gray bubble I can't see Mom looking at me like I'm as broken as I feel.

Maybe I am broken. Maybe we all are.

Earth is uninhabitable.

I know it's true, but I'm still having a hard time believing it. Our home planet is gone. Ruined by the automated systems we built to preserve it. Once the ISA realized the end was literally nigh, they crammed as many survivors as they could into the only-mostly-finished *Prairie* and sent her here, under the command of my grandfather, Admiral Eric Crane.

That's weird, thinking of him that way. He retired when I was a kid. But now he's back in the ISA, and he's here.

Grandpa is here.

I thought I'd never see him again, and he's here.

The thought is like a tiny spark in the darkness.

Grandpa is here.

I get to show him Tau. That makes me feel . . . I don't know, like I'm not just a hollow shell of skin that's about to collapse. I just wish . . . I don't even know where to start wishing. I wish the ISA hadn't lied to our Exploration & Pioneering team about Tau's inhabitants. I wish their lies hadn't caused us to nearly wreck our new ecosystem. I wish that mistake hadn't wrecked our relationship with the Sorrow. And I really, really wish the colony ship wasn't broken.

"Beginning decompression." Mom's voice slips through the speakers in my helmet, bringing me back into the moment.

"Three-sixty mode, please," I say, and the blank gray bubble I've been hiding in flickers into a 360-degree view of the airlock around me, composited from the cameras that wreathe the outside of my helmet.

Mom is standing at the airlock's exterior door watching the hatch fade from red to green. That means the air around us is getting thinner and the pressure is falling to match the airless vacuum that's waiting for us.

The thought makes my lungs burn, so I focus on the *Prairie* instead, on the task ahead of us. Mom has the airlock set to three-sixty mode now, so the view from the *Trailblazer*'s exterior cameras covers the wall, floor, and ceiling.

The *Prairie* blocks out the stars. She's so close. And massive—a golden disk three kilometers across and five stories deep. She should be rolling through orbit like a wheel on a track, the motion creating gravity in the ship's outer ring where the crew lives and works. But the great ship is staggering through orbit, wobbling like a top. That's why we can't just land the *Trailblazer* on her hull. She's too unstable.

We have to jump.

Remembered pain blasts over my skin. I bite my lip, using the real pain to remind my body that I'm in a perfectly good spacesuit. The visceral memory of being frozen and fried at the same time is just that. A memory. It isn't real.

But I can still feel myself burning.

The airlock is almost green.

"We're T minus eighteen seconds," Mom says.

She must have opened a shared channel between our suits and the *Prairie*, because Grandpa answers her.

"I've got eyes on, Alice."

He's still hoarse, even though he's been out of inso for nearly twenty-four hours. But he's seventy-four. Recovery takes time. And his crew has been in deep sleep for almost six months. That's why we're doing this, and they aren't. Going straight from inso to EVA would be way too hard on your cardiovascular system.

A full-body memory of my heart imploding rips through my chest.

Stop it, Joanna.

My heart is fine now. The Sorrow healed it. But my brain isn't convinced. I feel broken.

Stop it, Joanna.

The hatch starts to flash as the last bits of red are eaten up by green light. In case we didn't get the color-coding memo, the computer chimes in, "Decompression in ten . . . nine . . . eight . . ."

Mom taps the autoconnect button on her suit. Black filaments flow from her EVA harness and spin together into a tether line that shoots up and bonds with the frame of the airlock.

"Six . . . five . . ."

I hit my autoconnect. My tether flares out, twisting up to bond with the airlock beside Mom's. The thin black cables look delicate, but they aren't. These tether lines are made of nanoactive Kevlar. That means nanoscopic robots spin our tethers like tiny robotic spiders. This tether could hold our entire shuttle. It's plenty strong enough for one seventeen-year-old pilot.

"Three . . . two . . . one. Lock pressurized," the computer crows. "You are clear for extravehicular activity."

Mom triggers the door release. The hatch swings open. I resist the urge to clamp my eyes shut.

That's a mistake.

The endless view shoots my heart into a racing thud. My legs tense, like they're preparing to run. But there's nowhere to go. Nowhere but out there.

I force myself to breathe. The air is a little musty, like whoever used this suit last had bad breath. But it's still oxygen. My suit works. I have a tether line.

I can do this.

Teddy knew he was going to die when we blew ourselves into space to save the *Pioneer*. He told me to do it anyway. If he could do that, I can do this.

Except I don't think I can do this. The shuttle isn't rotating, but in my head I'm spinning. Tumbling in every direction at once. Remembered cold burns my skin and boils my blood.

"Jo!"

Mom's voice blasts through my helmet at top volume, snapping me back into the present like a verbal tether line.

"Talk to me, Joanna."

"Here." I gasp. "I'm—"

"You're here," she says, lowering the volume a little but keeping her voice sharp. "You're here, now. Be here. Now. In your suit. Next to me."

"I'm here," I say. But my body isn't convinced. It's still feeling the memory, not the reality. No matter what I say, what I see, what I know, it feels like I'm still tumbling through the dark. Still alone. No. Not alone. Teddy is there, dying just beyond my reach.

I stumble back, skittering across the airlock and pressing my body against the sealed hatch that leads back into the ship.

Mom's sigh soaks through my helmet, drenching me in shame.

We don't have time for this.

I need to get over myself and get out there. My species

12

is depending on it. And so is my mom.

But I can't move.

"Situation report?" Grandpa rumbles through the open comms feed.

"It's just a temporary delay, Dad," Mom says. "This is the first time Jo's done EVA since the accident. She needs a minute to get her head around it."

Oh good, so now I'm not just disappointing my mother and putting my whole species in danger. I'm disappointing Grandpa, too.

Mom comes to stand in front of me. Helmet to helmet, like she's looking into my eyes, though all I can see is the octagonal camera lenses that tile over her helmet.

"I wish you were still a little girl," Mom says. "If you were, I could leave you here, safe and sound on the shuttle. But you aren't a child anymore. And I need you. I need the clever, rule-breaking young woman who figured out the ISA's darkest secret. I need the brave young woman who got herself and her friends out of an extraterrestrial city and back to camp in time to stop us from making a catastrophic mistake. I need the daring young woman who faced off with an extraterrestrial king to stop him from destroying his own world. I need *you*."

I know what she's trying to do, but those memories are just memories. Some of them are pretty screwed-up memories. But they aren't enshrined by trauma. Not like the accident.

"What you're afraid of isn't out there, Jo," Mom says. She gently taps my helmet. "It's in here. The only way to escape it is to jump. Trust yourself, not the fear."

I want to. I need to. I'm not sure I can.

I take a step toward the airlock anyway. Then another. And another.

I grab the doorframe. The ship hums under my fingers. The gentle buzz of reality coats the burning memory.

I breathe.

Then I look outside.

The endless glitter swims in my vision as vertigo slams into me again. My body jerks away, but Mom's hand is planted on the small of my back this time, holding me in place.

"Just do it, Jo," she says. "Jump. Once you're out, it'll pass."

I believe her.

I tighten my grip on the airlock. I bend my knees. I tense my belly. Then, just as my toes start to push off the hatch, a suited figure bursts over the golden horizon of the *Prairie* and surfs down the great disk like a little kid sledding a big hill.

"What the—"

"You stay right where you are, Joanna," Grandpa's voice on the comms feed blows through Mom's expletive. "We've got this."

"Dad!" Mom protests. "You're less than twenty-four

hours out of inso and you've got high blood pressure."

"And I'm seventy-four," he adds, chuckling.

"Exactly," Mom snaps. "You are not cleared for EVA!"

"So we'd better get this done quick, eh?" Grandpa counters. "My heart *and* the future of the human race are hanging in the balance."

Mom's sigh is halfway to a growl. She tugs me back into the airlock. "Since he's out, we might as well do the repair and leave you to pilot *Trailblazer*," she says.

"It's not safe to just let your shuttle drift on autopilot, anyway," Grandpa tosses in.

"I know, Dad." Mom grinds the words between her teeth. A red blinking light pops up in the bottom corner of my screen, indicating a private feed has been opened.

"Don't worry, Jo," Mom says, for my ears only. "We'll be fine. And Dad's right, it'll be good to have you at the helm here. You'll be our spotter. When we're done, I'll follow him back into the *Prairie* and you can dock the *Trailblazer* with her and join us, okay?"

"No, Mom, I . . . Yeah," I say, the protest slipping away before I can get it out. "Okay."

Then she hurls herself out of the ship.

TWO

My gaze clings to Mom as she hurtles through the void. Her form is perfect, arms and legs tight against her body like a diver plunging into the vast, golden sea of the *Prairie*.

I hold my breath until she says, "Extending second tether . . . contact!"

That's step one. Mom is tethered to the *Prairie* and the *Trailblazer* now.

A few seconds later she says, "Magnetizing."

Then I hear the *thunk* of her boots snapping down to the big ship's hull.

She made it.

"Releasing, *Trailblazer*," she says. "You can close the doors now, Jo."

I pull the hatch closed and seal it, which takes me

straight from agoraphobia to claustrophobia. I don't want to be out there, but I don't want to be in here, in this impossibly small airlock, either.

I want to help Mom.

I can't.

Instead, my seventy-four-year-old grandfather is out there, doing an EVA he isn't even cleared for because of me. Because I'm too afraid to do it.

"Repressurizing," the computer informs me. "Please wait."

I want to scream. My suit feels like it's shrinking. Suffocating me.

"Atmospheric pressure restored," the computer announces.

I rip off my helmet and pop the seals on my suit. It doesn't help. I still feel itchy all over. Hot. It's like my skin is too small for all the self-loathing stuffed in there along with my uselessly healthy body.

I go back into the main cabin.

It's already in three-sixty mode, so I watch Mom and Grandpa work while I change back into my regular uniform, dragging the soft gray flight suit up over my body stocking and snapping my regular utility harness into place.

They look so small—just tiny dark specks crawling over the gleaming carapace of the *Prairie*. I wish I could help them. Then I immediately feel a billion times worse, because I *could* be helping them. I could be out there right now. I should be. But I can't.

Mom and Grandpa end up having to extend the sail by hand. Of course. Plan A isn't a thing on Tau. The job takes hours, but I hardly notice time passing. I just sit there, watching and listening to them talk over the open feed, like if I pay close enough attention, it'll help them somehow.

I report their progress to Dad hourly. At least he's stuck on Tau and has an excuse for being a useless observer. Jay and Leela and Chris text me, too. They're all freaked out and shocked about what happened to Earth. What's going to happen to Tau.

Dad decided he shouldn't wait for Mom to get back before they broke the news to the rest of the team. The *Prairie* is so big you can see her from the ground, even during the day. There was no hiding this.

I reply to my friends, but I'm not sure what I write. I can't focus on anything but the tiny figures slowly but surely unfolding the last of the *Prairie's* busted solar sail.

"Jo?" Mom says over the open feed.

I reflexively jump to my feet, like I could run to her. "I'm here!"

"We're done," Mom says, exhaustion lowering her voice. "Wait for the *Prairie's* orbit to stabilize before you dock."

"Understood," I say. My voice is small. I feel small.

I watch them clamber back up the golden disk and disappear into the ship.

Then I wait.

I'm hungry.

I'm thirsty.

It's been hours since I last ate or had any water. I should grab a hydration bag and a ration bar.

I don't.

I just sit there, watching the *Prairie*.

After what feels like an eternity, the enormous ship's wobbling progress steadies. It's working. As soon as she starts to rotate, I can dock.

Then what?

There are ten thousand people on the *Prairie*. They're almost all still in inso, but they can't stay that way for long. The human body can't withstand deep sleep for more than a year, and the survivors on the *Prairie* have been asleep for at least six months. We'll have to wake them up soon and bring them down to Tau.

A new strand braids itself through my guilt.

Tarn.

What am I going to say to Tarn?

Tarn is leader of the Sorrow, one of the two native sentient species on Tau. But Tarn wasn't "the Followed" when my friends and I accidentally made first contact with the Sorrow. He was just Tarn. His brother, Ord, was the Followed then.

Ord almost destroyed Tau by weaponizing our Stage Three terraforming bacteria to wipe out the planet's other sentient species, a race of predators we call phytoraptors.

I promised Tarn that humans would leave his world if he stopped Ord. Tarn had to kill his brother to keep his end of the deal. I convinced Mom to help me hold up my end of our bargain. We were going to leave. Go back to Earth. Start over and search for a new planet to pioneer.

We can't do that now. Earth is gone. None of the other planets the ISA has scouted for colonization are close to ready for civilians. We have to settle on Tau. We have nowhere else to go.

Ten thousand people.

That's not just breaking a promise. That's a betrayal.

On the wall screen in front of me, the *Prairie* finally starts to rotate.

Finally.

My hands dart to the navigation app to press the shuttle into motion. But I'm moving too fast. I accidentally trigger the landing thrusters and send the *Trailblazer* shooting off course for about three seconds before I manage to turn them off again.

Thankfully, my mistake sent the shuttle away from the *Prairie*, instead of crashing into it. Wouldn't that be spectacularly ridiculous? Watch Mom and Grandpa fix the colony ship for six hours and thirty-two minutes, then slam the *Trailblazer* into her and wipe out the human species by accident.

I force myself to slow down as I reach for the nav app again. I very deliberately bring up thrust control and just tap the maneuvering rockets. Once. Twice. Then I give the shuttle just a little extra momentum from the boosters. And just like that, I'm on course to the *Prairie*'s docking ring.

So easy, and I nearly screwed it up.

Maybe it's a good thing that I didn't go out there with Mom. Who knows how much damage my stupid, nervous hands might have done?

I put the shuttle on autopilot to dock.

I never do that. Docking is one of my favorite parts of flying. It always has been. But now all I can see are the hundreds of mistakes I could make.

Autopilot is so slow.

I feel like I'm going to crawl out of my skin, waiting for the computer to find alignment and bring us in. But I'm too afraid to do anything else.

So I wait.

The second the *Trailblazer*'s computer announces that it has a hard seal with the *Prairie*, I hurl myself into the airlock, slam the inner hatch, and demand that the computer "Match pressure and release outer door seal!"

"One moment, Joanna," the computer replies. I know I'm imagining the mildly injured tone in its too-perfect-to-be-real voice. The *Trailblazer*'s AI doesn't have empathy subroutines like the educator does. Its feeling can't be hurt.

I add a thank-you anyway.

"You're welcome, Joanna," the computer says. Green light starts to bleed through the red of the exterior hatch. A little stab of fear comes with it. I smack it away. It's one thing to be justifiably afraid of deep space. It's another to be afraid of airlocks. I refuse to be afraid of airlocks.

I don't realize that I'm holding my breath until the hatch goes green and I shove it open. Air explodes from my lungs in unison with the sigh of warm, humid air that rushes in from the *Prairie*.

The ship's docking ring is huge—a two-story-wide tube that runs as far as I can see in both directions. The air is so humid, it almost feels like it's going to rain. The *Prairie* uses the same algae-based purification system the *Pioneer* does, and it must be working overtime now that the ship is back on full power.

I expected Mom or Grandpa to be here, but they aren't. So I wait. I wait so long that I'm nearly in tears again before it occurs to me that *I* can find *them*.

I rip off my flex and press it to the wall screen beside the airlock. The moment it syncs with the *Prairie's* computer system I say, "Locate Commander Watson's flex, please."

"Certainly, Joanna," my flex replies. "Located. Commander Watson's flex is in the ISA Colony Ship *Prairie's* sleep center."

That's weird, but I'm too anxious to be curious.

I just want my mom.

"Please show me the fastest route to the deep-sleep center," I request as I pull my flex off the wall. A glowing green line snakes across the floor tiles, starting at my feet and slipping across the floor ahead of me.

I follow it for what must be half a kilometer. Just when I'm starting to think something's wrong with the *Prairie's* computer, a bulkhead melts out of the seemingly infinite gray ring ahead of me.

The green guidance line runs up to the single door in the center of the bulkhead. I step through it into a more human-size hallway that's bustling with activity. Men and women in dark blue Marine Corps uniforms and pale gray ISA uniforms, calling out requests and dirty jokes as they pass each other and completely ignoring me.

The green line keeps going. I follow it past a locker room and through the *Prairie*'s bridge, which is surprisingly small—about the same size as the one on the *Pioneer*, despite the ship being a hundred times bigger.

The green line leads me past the *Prairie*'s medical center. It's full of people who are fresh out of deep sleep—still bald and covered in insulating gel. I'm surprised they're waking so many people so fast. Doesn't Mom want to at least tell Tarn what's going on before we start pouring humanity all over his planet?

By the time I reach the doors labeled Sleep Center, I can feel my pulse racing against my clenched jaws. My anxiety collection has gotten so big, I don't even know what I'm freaking out about. There are too many things to choose from.

The door to the sleep center slides open as I approach, and I step inside.

The *Prairie*'s insulated deep-sleep center is another long, elliptical tunnel. According to the schematic, it wraps all the way around the ship and spirals inward, filling most of the enormous craft. Row after row of transparent insulated sleep crates are strapped to the curved walls. Each crate contains a single person in a medically induced coma, floating in the opalescent goo that kept them from getting fried by radiation when the ship went superluminal.

"Joanna!"

My grandfather's voice rushes ahead of him as he hurries around the curve of the sleep center. I race up the tunnel and throw myself into his arms.

He's tall and broad, but too thin. I can feel the sinews and bones of his arms and gently bowed chest, even through his uniform.

"Grandpa," I whisper.

He sets me away from him so he can take me in. "Hello, Little Moth. How are your wings?"

The old nickname takes my breath away. I thought I'd never hear his voice again. Or feel his arms around me. I'm so glad he's here. Which is just . . . horrifying. How can I be glad? My grandfather is only here because Earth is dead.

"I . . . I think I'm . . ." I can't even finish the sentence. There are too many thoughts and emotions stuck in my head, trying to get out.

"I see them there," he says, skimming a hand over my head and shoulders. "Still beating."

Tears roll down my cheeks.

"I'm so sorry." I sob. "I should have—"

Grandpa clucks his tongue, cutting off my apology. "Nonsense, Little Moth. Besides, it makes an old man feel useful, being able to take care of his family."

"Commanding the ship carrying the last remnants of humanity isn't enough, Dad?"

I look up to see Mom emerging around the spiral of the sleep center. She's glaring at Grandpa. If she were looking at me that way, I'd apologize. Even if I didn't know what was wrong. But Grandpa smiles at her fondly, like he thinks it's sweet. "Still nice to get my hands dirty, every once in a while."

"In other words, your delegation skills are poor at best," a tall woman in fatigues with a long blond braid says. I didn't notice her before. She's leaning against the wall by the door, reading something on her unfolded flex. There's a pistol holstered on her belt. The sight of it makes my stomach clench.

Grandpa chuckles. "Everyone has a weakness."

"We aren't done here, Dad." Mom grinds the words out between her teeth.

She's furious. What happened between them?

"I realize that, dear heart," Grandpa says, turning away from me to face her. "But until you can present me with a reasonable alternative—"

"Anything!" Mom almost shouts back. "Literally any other plan would make more sense than this."

"Hyperbole isn't helpful, Alice," he says mildly.

For a second, I think Mom is actually going to punch him.

"Jo, Lieutenant, can you two excuse us for a moment?"

"Sure thing, Commander," the blond woman, who is evidently a lieutenant, says. "C'mon, Junior."

She strides through the door without waiting to see if I'm following.

"Mom—"

"Please, Joanna," Mom says. She sounds vaguely frantic, which makes my stomach twist with nausea. "Just . . . go. Okay? I need to talk to Grandpa."

Eight hours ago, she said she needed me by her side. But eight hours ago, we both thought I was something I'm not.

"Okay."

I follow the lieutenant out into the hall.

The door slides closed behind us. The lieutenant resumes leaning against the wall and texting on her flex. The raised voices that immediately hammer at the closed door don't seem to concern her.

I can't hear the words, but Mom sounds angry. And afraid.

"Chill, Junior," the lieutenant says without looking up. "I can feel you stressin' from here."

"Forgive me if I don't find the circumstances relaxing," I snap, more indignant than I mean to be. "And my name is Joanna. Not Junior."

"I know that, kid," she says mildly. "But mocking the admiral's nepotistic tendencies amuses me."

And I'm being a jerk to this complete stranger for no good reason. It isn't her fault I'm freaking terrified.

I take a deep breath and try again.

"Admiral," I say. "That sounds so strange to me. He's supposed to be retired."

"Nobody's retired anymore," she says. "End of the world, remember?"

A sob catches in my throat, even though I'm not crying anymore.

"I can't believe Earth is gone."

"Eh, you'll get used to it," she says.

I doubt that. How can anyone get used to the idea that ten billion people are dead and our planet is ruined?

"What's going on?" I say, gesturing to the door. "Why is Mom so . . ."

"Royally pissed off?" the lieutenant supplies.

I nod.

"Deep-sleep system is screwed," she says. "Apparently forcing the solar power back online fried a circuit some-where. Now the sleep center is sucking in way more juice than it's meant to. We have about eighty-two days, give or take, to get everyone outside before the excess power draw fries the engines and the ship becomes purely decorative."

"That's only twelve weeks!" I cry. "We can't bring ten thousand people down to Tau in twelve weeks!"

"Since the other option is extinction, I'm pretty sure we'll figure it out," the lieutenant drawls.

Ten thousand survivors in twelve weeks. That would

be nearly impossible even if we didn't have to deal with the Sorrow. Or the phytoraptors. We still don't know what triggers their hunting instinct. How many of those ten thousand humans will get eaten before we figure it out?

The lieutenant flashes a sharp grin. "And now you know why your mama's so pissed." She shakes her head. "Commander's got a point. Dropping a gang of civvies on a hostile planet with no training and minimal shelter really shouldn't be plan B."

"Tau isn't hostile." The words pop out reflexively. "It's just—"

"It's just home to two different sentient species, one of which is a dangerous predatory race, the other of which are manipulative bastards with freaky superpowers they've used to turn said scary-ass predators on your people not once, but twice? Killing, what, eighty-three people?"

"Eighty-six," I say. I don't know if it's embarrassment or lingering terror at her summary that's making my heart pound all over again. "And they did it three times. The Sorrow manipulated the phytoraptors into killing the original scout team, too."

"And eating them," she adds.

"And eating them," I acknowledge, sick despair twisting in my guts.

She smirks again. "Sounds pretty hostile to me."

I want to tell her she's wrong, but I know she isn't. I've spent all this time worrying that we'll be a disaster for Tau, but Tau has been just as much of a disaster for us.

As always, my face is thinking out loud. The lieutenant claps me on the shoulder. "Don't worry, Junior." She grins. "We got this."

"We?" I say.

She snaps into a salute. "Lieutenant Emily Shelby, 156th Infantry." Then she slouches out of the salute and adds, "We're as hostile as it gets."

The sleep center doors slide open and Mom storms out.

Grandpa follows, calling after her, "This is no time to panic, Alice."

She spins, stalking back toward him. "I'm not panicking, Dad. I'm . . ." She shakes her head. The next word comes out choked. ". . . despairing. I . . . I don't see a way forward that isn't hideous and so I am shaking my useless, ineffectual fists at the universe."

Grandpa doesn't flinch away from her sadness. "We'll find a way. We have time."

"Eighty-two days," Mom says. "That's not time, Dad. Not to wake up ten thousand people and drop them on a planet that doesn't want them."

"Can't you fix it?" I blurt out the question. Mom tosses me a glare so withering that I can feel my words shrinking as I continue, "You fixed the sail. You can't—"

"I'm a pilot, Jo," she snaps. "Not an engineer. I knew how to fix that sail because I helped Penny fix it during the test flight. But Penny is . . ." She gasps, like the memory of her best friend's death is a punch in the gut. "I can't fix this alone."

"You're not alone," Grandpa says, holding a hand out to her. "We're together. And this family doesn't give up."

Mom squeezes her eyes shut, like she's hoping her vision will clear and she'll see something new when she opens them. But when our eyes meet again, the despair is still there, drenching her amber-speckled brown irises with tears.

She takes Grandpa's hand, letting him pull her close. Her shoulders are shaking. She looks small, wrapped in his long hook-shouldered frame. She and I are the same height now, but I don't think I've ever thought of her as small before.

Lieutenant Shelby clears her throat pointedly. Grandpa nods and then murmurs something into Mom's hair. She shakes her head.

He looks up at me. "Joanna, can we rely on you to pilot the *Trailblazer* for us?"

"We're going down to Tau?" I say.

He nods. "It's time."

Mom pushes out of his arms and strides up the corridor without waiting for the rest of us. I start to follow, but he stops me.

"Give her a moment, Little Moth," he murmurs.

"Half the squad's still bald," Lieutenant Shelby says. "For the record."

"Leave them here," Grandpa says. "For now. They can

30

continue reviving vital personnel while they're growing out their lustrous locks, then follow in shuttle *3212*."

"You're the admiral," Shelby says. Her tone is sardonic, but the sharp salute she offers him is respectful and professional.

"Grandpa," I say as she jogs up the hallway after Mom. "You . . . we . . . Mom is right. We can't drop a bunch of people on this planet and start building. The Sorrow. The phytoraptors. They deserve better than that."

Grandpa smiles gently, enfolding both of my hands in his.

"You're right, Little Moth. But I"m going to find a way to make this work," he says. "Because this is your world now. I don't want you and your generation to just survive. You're going to thrive here. I'll do whatever it takes to make sure you do."

People say stuff like *whatever it takes* all the time. But my grandfather ended the Storm Wars and invented a system to repair a whole planet. When he says that, it means something.

"I'm glad you're here, Grandpa," I say.

His return smile is broad and uncomplicated. Like I've just given him a gift.

"Me too." He wraps an arm around my shoulders and tugs me up the corridor. "Come, Little Moth. It's time to show me your world."

THREE

Shelby and half a dozen other boisterous, heavily armed people are already on the shuttle by the time Mom, Grandpa, and I board the *Trailblazer*. They're acting like a bunch of teenagers on a field trip, but they're obviously marines.

I expect Grandpa to make them stow their weapons. One accidental discharge and we'll all be sucking vacuum.

He doesn't.

As pilot, I could ask them to stow their weapons myself. But maybe I'm overreacting. They're just blowing off steam. If it were a problem, Grandpa would shut it down.

He takes the copilot's chair, beside me. I expect Mom to object—that should be her place. But she just collapses into a chair in the front row and curls into a ball. Her vivid despair makes my stomach clench. I've never seen her this way.

By the time I finish calculating our trajectory, her eyes are closed. But I don't think she's asleep. Her body is coiled too tightly for that, like she's trying to fold up into herself and disappear. Grandpa's hands shake as he takes my flex to check my math. Guilt digs in like splinters under my fingernails. They're both so exhausted.

The flight is long. Our timing wasn't ideal, and we have to do nearly a full orbit before the *Trailblazer* can dive through the atmosphere and into the icy gray evening that's settling on Pioneer's Landing as we touch down.

Most of the Exploration & Pioneering (E&P) team, including Dad and Beth, is gathered on the airfield by the time I get the engines shut down and the ramp open.

I'm the first person off the shuttle. The soaking wet breeze cuts through my uniform as I walk down the ramp. Dad grabs me into a hug before my boots hit dirt.

"Oh, thank goodness. You're okay." He gasps the words, like he's been holding his breath this whole time.

He was worried about me. I was sitting safe and sound in the *Trailblazer*'s passenger cabin and he was down here worrying about me.

Embarrassment flushes up the back of my neck, making my hair prickle.

"Nobody is okay, Dad," I mutter, pulling back. "It's literally the apocalypse."

"According to Mom's message, Earth became uninhabitable approximately five months and seven days ago," Beth says. "Roughly seventeen days after the *Prairie* began its journey. The apocalypse has been over for some time."

My eyes roll of their own accord. "Post-apocalypse, then. Same difference."

"I doubt it," Dad says. His face looks like someone is pulling his skin tight against his bones. Probably because he's empathizing with the billions of people who were left behind to die, not cracking terrible jokes about them.

What the hell is wrong with me?

"Dad," I say, reaching out to him again. "I'm—"

The *thud* of boots on the ramp behind us drowns out my attempted apology. Lieutenant Shelby strides off the shuttle, breaking the tentative connection between Dad and me as she leads her squadron out onto the airfield.

They fall into two straight lines at stiff attention.

"Marines!" she shouts. "Welcome to Tau Ceti e. As always, situation is fubar. But does that bother us?"

"No, sir!" The squad snaps the words out in perfect unison.

Some of them have the same deadly serious look on their faces as Shelby. Some are grinning hungrily. Like they're already spoiling for a fight.

"That's right," Shelby says. "Fubar is what we do best. So get to it. Secure the perimeter, then find the *Pioneer's* squad and make friends. I expect to see all of you assembled outside ground control in thirty. Copy?"

"Sir, yes, sir!" they shout.

"Then move your butts!"

At that, the marines scatter, tearing through the anxious crowd like shrapnel.

"Given the general anxiety level right now, that seemed unnecessarily aggressive," Beth observes, as Dad struggles to answer the questions that bubble from the pioneers in their wake.

"Lieutenant Shelby isn't subtle," Grandpa says, coming down the ramp to join us. "But she's good at her job."

"Not if her job is to keep us safe," Beth points out, her voice coated with ice. "Stress and anxiety make people stupid. We can't afford to be stupid right now."

"Astute," Grandpa says, offering her a smile. "As always. Hello, Beth. It's good to see you."

"Is it?" she says, turning to look up at him. "Under the circumstances?"

"Beth!" I protest. "That's—"

"Where the hell is Alice, Eric?" Dad interupts in an urgent whisper.

"Asleep," Grandpa says, not bothering to keep his voice down.

"Excuse me?" Dad isn't just startled. He's flabbergasted. He knows just as well as I do that Mom would never sleep through this. These are her people. They need her. There's nowhere she'd rather be than taking care of them.

And yet she's still in that shuttle.

"Alice has been awake for more than two days straight,

and spent much of that time in a spacesuit, repairing the ship that holds our survivors," Grandpa says, still talking loud enough for the others to hear. "My daughter saved more than ten thousand lives today. I think she's entitled to some rest."

A little sigh ripples through the pioneers around us, like they're watching a really exciting three-sixty drama and something cool just happened.

"What was wrong with the ship?" someone calls from the depths of the crowd.

"Is it stable now?"

"Is there a list of survivors we can access?"

Dad throws Grandpa a look that's somewhere between a question and a challenge. "They need her."

"I don't care," Grandpa says, pitching his voice low so only we can hear him.

Dad shakes his head. "You never did understand her."

Grandpa grabs his arm. "Nick," he says, "Alice is a grown woman. A leader. There isn't much I can protect her from anymore. So when I see a burden I can carry for her, I will. I need to." His gaze goes to me for a long, pointed beat. Then he looks back up at Dad. "I'm sure you understand."

Dad's eyes jump from Grandpa to Beth and me. He sucks in a breath and then he lets it out, deflating in the process. "Excuse me."

He ducks up the ramp into the *Trailblazer*.

Grandpa turns to face the crowd.

"I am Admiral Eric Crane," he calls, his voice effortlessly quelling the jostling conversations around us. "Some of you know me. All of you will. I'm sure you have a lot of questions. I'll do my best to answer them."

The crowd explodes with anxious demands. Everyone is talking at once. I don't know how Grandpa keeps track of it all, but he does. He supplies answers calmly, one at a time, talking directly to each person but somehow including the whole group. With each new piece of information, the pioneers get a little calmer.

My flex buzzes. It's Jay again. The goofy picture assigned to him in my contacts makes me ache. He's out with Dr. Howard's foraging team. His text says they're still hours away, but they're heading back as fast as they can.

That means Chris's dad isn't here, either. Where is Chris? I don't want him to be alone right now. And what about Leela? She must be taking this hard. But when I search the crowd, I realize I'm having trouble focusing my eyes.

I blink, trying to clear my head. The setting sun stabs at my retinas, throwing off chilly white shards of light as it sinks into the mountains. The sun was midsky when Mom and I took off. Yesterday. No, I realize abruptly, the day before that. I may not have gone on the EVA, but I've piloted two transorbital flights since then, and I've been awake for nearly two and a half days. No wonder I can't seem to focus. My brain is shutting down.

I need to sleep.

I start walking. I don't say goodbye to Beth or look for my friends as I push through the crowd. If I stop now, I'm afraid I won't make it to my bed.

The streets of the Landing are empty. The quiet amplifies the lonely pit inside me, making my exhausted body feel even heavier.

I trip, but I don't fall. For a second, I can't figure out why. Then I realize that there's a hand gripping my arm, steadying me. I look up and find Beth standing next to me. She doesn't say anything. She doesn't even really look at me. She just tugs me forward gently, urging me to keep going.

We get to the greenhouse and she pushes the door open. I walk between the lush rows of Tau plants growing in sample pots, past the little stands of Earth corn and wheat, and into the storage closet my sister and I have turned into a makeshift bedroom. We're supposed to be sharing a cabin with Mom and Dad, but those units aren't really designed for privacy, and four adults, two of whom are happily married, are a lot for one cabin.

I collapse on my cot and reach for my boots, or I mean to. But my arms aren't cooperating. My whole body feels tingly, like it's fallen asleep and my mind has yet to follow.

Beth kneels in front of me and unfastens the bindings on my boots, then pulls them off.

"Sleep," she says.

"Beth."

"Sleep," she repeats, before I can figure out what I want to say to her. "I'll be here."

I don't even remember lying down. I must have. I'm cocooned in my sleeping bag when the whispered sigh of the greenhouse doors opening wakes me up.

I open my eyes. It's dark. Beth is asleep on the cot across from mine.

Then Jay is there, the hover servos in his leg braces whining gently as he kneels down beside me.

I hurl myself at him.

His arms close around me and I dig my fingers into the ropes of muscle that run over his shoulders and down his back. Clutching the sweat-stiff fabric of his T-shirt. He squeezes me closer, burying his face in my sleep-wild hair.

After a while, the tension ebbs from the embrace. I lean against his shoulder. His fingers rub the base of my neck, right at the spot where the muscles always knot together. Mom is the only other person who can find that spot. It weirds me out a little bit that he knows my body that well. But it's good weird.

"Are you okay?" he whispers.

"No," I say.

I feel his chuckle more than I hear it.

"Me neither," he says. "But I'm glad to be home."

Two days ago, one of us would have qualified that

statement. We would have reminded ourselves that this isn't home. But today, it is.

He rolls his shoulders as he sits back on his haunches, his leg braces sighing and shifting as he uses them to lever himself to his feet. He grimaces.

"How long have you been in those things?" I ask quietly as I lead him out of our makeshift bedroom. He follows me between tidy rows of plants to the cluster of orchid tree specimens at the far end of the greenhouse. We have a spare camp bed and some chairs arranged in the private hollow created by the trees. Leela and Chris and I set this up when the weather got too cold to hang out in the square.

Beth complained about it at first, but not in a way that made any of us think she actually minds. Dr. Howard must know it's here, but he doesn't seem to care either. I guess he's just happy Chris has somewhere to be when Dr. Hunter is busy on foraging trips.

"Twenty hours." Jay shoves the chairs aside and eases himself down on the bed, back against the plexiglass wall.

"Jay!" Since he was stabbed during Ord's attack on the Landing, Jay hasn't had full control of his legs. He uses braces to walk. They work pretty well, but he isn't supposed to wear them for more than twelve hours without a break.

He waves off my concern. "We started back right away when we got the news. James had been on the stick for eight already and nobody was gonna wait out a rest period, so . . ." He shrugs, like *that was that*.

"First things first," I say, dropping to the camp bed beside him and pressing the power-down switch on his hip.

"I can tough it out a little longer," he protests.

"Why?"

A little smile sneaks over his lips as he realizes I want him to stay the rest of the night. I think it's the first genuine smile I've seen from anyone since the *Prairie* burst over Tau's orbital horizon.

We work together in silence, unlatching the matte black Teflon bands that encircle his legs at the ankle and above and below his knee. Each one vibrates gently in my hand as it breaks the wireless connection with the nanoreceptors embedded in the nerves of his legs. He winces when my hand brushes a spot where he still has sensation. He's in more pain than he admits.

Once the braces are off, he lays them on the ground and switches them to charge mode. They pulse with gentle yellow light—pulling power from the greenhouse through the floor tiles.

"I'm sorry I didn't reply to your texts," I say as Jay settles back on the camp bed beside me. "I was just . . ."

"A little busy helping save the species?" he says.

More like having a panic attack and refusing to help save the species, but before I can tell him what happened up there, he adds, "My mom and my sister are on the *Prairie*."

"Really?"

I feel the flush of happiness that colors his cheeks as if it were my own.

"I almost didn't check the manifest," he says. "I didn't think . . . but Dr. Howard looked when your grandfather uploaded it, and his sister and her family were there. So are Chief Penny's cousins. That made a couple of the others check. When they all found family members, I decided . . . I had to look." He shakes his head in amazement. "I don't know how, but they're on it. They're alive. They're here." He sweeps me into his arms. "I can't believe it. They're really here. And they're safe, thanks to you."

He presses a kiss to my lips.

Self-loathing stiffens my spine, pulling me away from his sweet excitement. I try to force my clenched jaw to relax, but Jay feels it. His shoulders go up defensively as he turns away from me.

"Jay," I start, but he waves me off.

"No," he says. "I get it. Our home world is gone and billions of people are dead and I'm happy. I don't blame you for being weirded out. But . . . I was pretty sure I was never going to see Mom and Seo again when I came here. And I felt like the worst, knowing that I chose this place over them. But now we're going to be together again. I get to see them every day and they get to meet you and . . . that makes me happy. And feeling happy right now is so . . . confusing. I mean, here I am, babbling about seeing my mom again when almost everyone else is . . ."

"Oh Jay," I say, feeling like a self-centered jerk all over again for letting him think I was judging him when I was

42

really judging myself. "That's not it at all. It's okay to be happy." I duck my head under his arm, curling into him. "I'm glad you're happy. You should be. There's going to be a lot of surviving to do. Our whole lives. I think we're going to have to get used to living at the same time. Does that make sense?"

Instead of answering, he presses a kiss into the top of my head. I turn my face up to his, and our lips meet and mold to each other. It isn't new anymore. We've kissed each other many times. But the shape of it is different every time. Surprising, even when it's familiar.

It feels good. His kisses always do. But this is more. Different.

When I was little, Grandpa made us learn to swim across the lake at his cabin in Geneva. It's almost a kilometer wide. I spent the whole summer trying and failing. The last time, it was nearly autumn and the water was cold. But I was determined to make it, so I kept swimming even though I knew I was too tired. By the time I got close to the other side, I could feel myself sinking a little with every stroke of my arms. I stopped to try to rest, but the waves were like fistfuls of broken glass, tossing themselves into my face. Before I knew it, I was sinking. Drowning. Then my toes brushed the bottom. I'll never forget what that felt like. Kissing Jay right now feels like that. Like I'm drowning and he's solid ground.

I need that.

I need him. Desperately. I feel like I might die if he doesn't kiss me again. Longer. Deeper.

I think Jay feels it, too.

His urgent hands mold over my hips and run up my back, under my thermal. His callused fingers throw sparks as they trail over my bare skin. Our tongues tangle. My breath is coming faster.

It feels good.

I want more.

I pull my thermal off.

His hands stroke up my stomach, fingers grazing the plain gray cotton of my sports bra as I yank at his T-shirt. He drags it off and pulls me into his lap, wrapping himself around me.

We've gotten this far before, but no further.

Tonight it isn't enough.

Tonight, I want to feel all of him with all of me. I need to. Tonight, I want more than sparks. Tonight, I want to burn.

Jay pulls back.

"What are you doing?" I demand, trying to drag his lips back to mine.

He puts a gentle hand on my chest, over my pounding heart. "Wait. Please, Hotshot."

"No. No." To my surprise, the little word catches in my throat. "Please," I whisper. "I want . . . I need . . ."

"Me too," he says, leaning his forehead against mine.

"You know how much. But when we . . . I want it to be about us, Jo. Not tangled up in this." He reaches out and brushes a tear from my cheek. "And I don't want you to be crying."

I lean forward and press my face against his bare shoulder for a long time. Letting his heat evaporate the tears. After a while, the burning need fades, leaving my mind quiet.

Jay stretches out on the cot, pulling me against him on the narrow foam mattress. He's so warm. I let his heat seep into me, easing my muscles and my mind.

His breathing gets deeper. Slower. He's sleeping.

I close my eyes and follow him into the dark.

FOUR

My flex hums softly on my wrist, waking me from dreams I can't remember, except that they sucked.

Something brushes my neck. I reach up to shoo whatever it is away and my fingers come back wet. That wasn't a bug. It was a tear. I've been crying in my sleep.

Great.

I check the text that rescued me from my nightmares. It's from Mom, informing the whole team that there will be a memorial service for the dead at 1100 hours.

For the dead.

How do you mourn a whole planet?

Jay is still asleep beside me. His skin has gone cool in the morning chill, except where our bodies are pressed together.

Neither of us bothered to put our shirts back on last night. The morning light dappling through the potted plants around us paints his bare shoulders, darkening the purple scars that zag down his lower back. You can see the violence that left them there, permanently written in his tawny skin. But you can also see the strength it took to survive in his coiled muscles and the graceful, straight line of his spine.

I feel ridiculous. Lying here mooning over how beautiful my boyfriend is to avoid thinking about the end of the world. It's both cliché and a total waste of time. If we're really going to wake up ten thousand people in the next three months, there's no time for my hormones. Or my grief.

A faint rustle of movement slips through the orchid trees that shelter us. Murmured voices follow. Beth is up, and she isn't alone. A crackling chuckle drifts through the greenhouse. That's Chris. What is he doing here so early?

Embarrassment flushes my cheeks as I fumble on the ground beside the cot for my shirt. I don't want to wake Jay, but I can just imagine the lecture if Beth comes in here and finds us asleep together, half dressed. She'd never, ever let it go. None of them would. They enjoy teasing us way too much already.

I slowly peel myself away and slip my thermal on, careful not to wake him. But when I stand up I almost step on Jay's flex. It was charging, draped over one of his leg bands.

I must have knocked it down when I grabbed my shirt.

When I go to put it back, I realize it's buzzing with an alert.

"Hey," I say, quietly placing a hand on Jay's shoulder. His eyes open immediately.

"What's up?"

"Did you set an alarm?" I say, holding up his flex.

He tries to bolt out of bed and goes sprawling over his unresponsive legs.

He swears. Loudly.

"Are you okay?" I ask.

"Yes," he grumbles, pushing at my hands as I try to help him back onto the bed. "Leave me. I just forgot for a second."

He looks pale under the olive brown that long days with the foraging team have brushed over his skin. He's so good at handling . . . everything. It's easy to forget he's only been dealing with the braces for the last five months. He does okay most of the time, except for these moments when it sneaks up on him. If we were back on Earth, there'd be trauma counseling and weeks of physical therapy to help him through. I know he goes to see Dr. Kao sometimes, but not as often as I think he needs to. Ironic, considering how hard I avoided my own trauma counseling. I guess it takes one to know one.

"Do I need to know?" Beth calls to us.

"No," Jay calls back. "I'm just an idiot." He grabs his flex and slaps it on. "And I'm late for reveille." He shoves

48

one of his bands on, then swears again as it beeps in protest because it's misaligned.

He stops. Takes a deep breath. Then he offers me a bittersweet half smile. "Help?"

I crouch to help him, our hands moving together in a quick harmony that makes my stomach flip. That's been happening, lately. These little moments when it feels like Jay and I are two parts of a whole.

"Joey and Ja-ay sitting in a tree, K-I-S-S-I-N-G," Chris shout-sings from the other side of the greenhouse. His voice cracks across the "n" and he dissolves into laughter.

Jay twists to glower through the orchid trees.

"I'm a marine, you know," he calls back. "They train us to kill people."

"Do you really have time to kill Chris?" I say, not trying that hard to swallow my amusement. "I thought you were late."

Jay sighs. "You're right." He starts for the door. Then he turns back and drags me close for a surprisingly thorough kiss. My laughter dissolves into lust, sliding hot and needy through my veins even as he lets me go and hustles for the door.

"You're lucky I don't have time to demonstrate my skills, kid," I hear him growl at Chris on his way out.

"Timing is everything," Chris fires back, unfazed.

I duck between the rows of plant specimens to the lab table, where Chris is setting out bowls of oatmeal from a tray.

I continue past him, into our makeshift bedroom.

Beth follows me.

"I assume your Academy personal health education was adequate?"

"For what?" I say, shoving my boots on and reaching for a fresh thermal.

"Half-naked marines," she says in the same dry tone.

"Beth!"

"Joanna!"

See. I knew she would never let me live this down.

"Yes, it was adequate," I mutter, tugging my utility harness over my shoulders and around my hips. "But unnecessary, for sleeping. Which is all we did."

"Be that as it may," she says calmly as I stalk back out into the lab, "as your older sister, I have certain educational obligations toward you when you partake in mating rituals."

"Mating rituals?" I spin to glare at her. "Seriously? Not even you are that analytical."

"No." She smirks. "But you're that easy."

I stick my tongue out at her. Then I feel like a terrible human. How can I be joking around with my sister and my friends right now? Earth is gone. Billions of people are dead, and we're about to go to their totally inadequate mass funeral.

"Compartmentalization," Beth says, reading my face like an open flex. "A necessary skill in an ongoing crisis."

Ongoing crisis. Only Beth could make the apocalypse sound boring.

For some reason, that makes me feel better.

"Is it wrong that I kind of don't care?" Chris says abruptly. Then he shakes his head, like he's arguing with himself. "No. That's not . . . I care. It's awful. So awful, it feels like I should . . . I don't know . . . it should feel worse, shouldn't it? Than . . . Mom."

Mommy! I can still hear him screaming for Chief Penny as she died in our arms. I'll never forget the heartbreak in his voice. It hasn't faded. I understand that. Mine hasn't, either.

"It doesn't," I say. Teddy's funeral felt like I was being recycled alive. My body shredded and ground down to its individual components. I thought I might not survive it. But our species has almost been wiped out and our home world is gone and . . . "It isn't the same."

"I'm glad it's not just me," he says.

I nod.

Chris eats. Beth sits across from him, but instead of eating, she pulls off her flex to start taking notes about something. From here, it looks like she's making a list. Probably planning a new research project or something. Trying to lose herself in work.

I pour myself some coffee and make a face. Beth must have brewed this. She always makes it jet fuel.

"This'll help," Chris says, tossing me a sealed paper packet. I look at the label.

"Coffee creamer?" I say, thunderstruck.

"Dr. Kao said the admiral brought a stash from the

Prairie," Chris says, taking a sip from his own mug. He makes a face. "I think it's vanilla."

I dump the white powder into my coffee and swirl the mug to mix it in. The vague chemical sweetness doesn't taste like vanilla, or much of anything, really. But it's familiar. And right now familiar tastes good.

"What are you doing up at this hour, anyway?" I ask Chris, snagging one of the bowls of oatmeal on his tray.

"I never went to sleep," he says, shoving a huge bite of oatmeal into his mouth and chewing around his words. "Chief G started printing cabin parts before you guys even got back from the *Prairie*. I volunteered for a second shift, since I knew I wouldn't be able to sleep anyway. Not until Dad got home."

"You see him yet?" I ask.

Chris nods. "He came and found me at like oh three hundred." Chris takes another bite of his oatmeal and stares down at the bowl as he chews and swallows. Then, like he doesn't really want to say it, he adds, "He cried."

The closed fist of my mother's face flickers through my memory. I swallow hard. "I think that might be better. Than not crying, I mean."

Chris nods, still hunched over his breakfast. "Still."

"Yeah." I agree with the unspoken horribleness of seeing our parents so broken.

"I wish Mom were here," he says.

"Me too," I whisper.

But Chief Penny is dead.

This planet killed her.

Chris sucks in a snuffling gulp, forcing back tears. His voice is still gluey as he adds, "She'd for sure be itching to get her hands on all that raw they're gonna bring down from the *Prairie*."

"They're bringing raw down? Already?" I ask, willfully allowing the distraction to shelter me.

"Sure," Chris says. "Twelve weeks. Ten thousand people. There's no time like the present."

That plunges us into silence again. It's so quiet I can hear Beth's stylus scratching against her flex as she writes.

"They're alive!" Leela's voice shatters the silence as she crashes into the greenhouse, clutching a crumpled flex. "My family is alive. All of . . . almost all of them. My grandparents aren't on the *Prairie*'s manifest, but all of my cousins and uncles and aunts and—" She throws her arms around me. I hug her back. Tight. She's shaking like a leaf. Or is that me? I really can't tell.

"My aunts and cousins are up there, too," Chris says. "And Chief G said her sister's family is on the manifest."

"So are Jay's mom and sister," I say.

"I can't believe he did this," Leela says, pulling back. She's still wearing pajama pants and a tank top under her parka. She must have just woken up and checked the manifest. "In the middle of the freaking end of the world, your grandfather cared enough to get all our families on that ship. I just . . . I can't believe it."

"He always says family is what makes people get up in the morning," I say.

"Ironic," Beth says. The word is like a shard of glass, puncturing Leela's infectious joy.

"What's that supposed to mean?" I demand. My sister just keeps writing.

"Chill, Joey," Leela says. "We're too keyed up right now. Besides, I have to go. I just wanted . . . I needed to be excited for a minute. That's all. And I knew you guys would get it. But I have to get back. Baba is a mess. He was already upset about the idea that his parents were probably going to die while we were here, and now . . . he isn't taking it well."

The thought is startling. I've never even seen Doc anything less than calm. I guess it's only natural that he's upset about his parents dying alone, light years away, but Leela's dad has been my doctor since I was born. He's brick in the foundation of the Project. Of my world, I guess. And now it's all crumbling.

"How do you spell your grandparents' given names?" Beth asks without looking up from her flex.

"S-I-T-A and C-H-A-N-D," Leela says, throwing a *huh* look at me. "Why?"

Instead of answering, Beth writes something out on her flex and then double taps the stylus. The transparent touchscreen tiles that make up the walls and the ceiling are suddenly covered with neatly handprinted columns. Lists of names.

I cross to the wall to look closer at the nearest one.

Sami Farsakh.

Noam Levy.

Malik Jones.

The names are all familiar, but it takes me a moment to figure out why.

"Are these your lab mates at Stanford?" I ask finally.

"And miscellaneous other students and faculty," Beth replies. "Also the sanitation staff."

"Why are you writing a list of names of people you knew at Stanford?"

"Because I've already written down all the names I remember from primary school, Galactic Frontier Project HQ, MIT—"

"And everyone who worked at Jemison Memorial?" I say, my fingers tracing a long list of names I recognize from the medical center where I rehabbed after the accident.

"No," Beth says, going back to writing on her flex. "Only the names of your medical team. I was too distracted by your recovery to properly introduce myself to the rest of the staff. I don't know their names. And I'll forget these if I don't write them down. Everyone will."

"You're making a list of people who died on Earth," I whisper, the realization welling up at the back of my throat like tears.

"Only the ones I can remember," Beth says.

I look around the greenhouse walls again with fresh eyes. There are at least a thousand names written here. Maybe more. Beth's memory isn't photographic, but it's the nearest thing to. Every name she's ever heard, every hand she's ever shaken, is burned into the folds of her brain forever.

And all those people are lost now, except in Beth's head.

"You added my grandparents to your list?" Leela whispers. The quiet words are so dense with emotion that I can almost feel them, like the tactile language of the Sorrow.

"A hollow gesture, perhaps," Beth says. "But remembering is the only thing I can do for them, or for Doc. Or for you."

Leela gasps in a little sob. "It's not hollow, Beth," she whispers.

"I'd prefer we keep emotional displays to a minimum," Beth says, starting to write again. "I've had quite enough feelings of late."

"Pretty sure we all have," Leela agrees, wiping at her eyes again. She swallows hard.

"Breakfast?" Chris asks, pushing a bowl of oatmeal toward Leela.

"No thanks," she says. "I gotta get home. Aai wants to make an offering before the memorial. For Aajoba and Aaji."

"Hey," I realize. "Shouldn't you be at reveille with Jay?"

Leela makes a face. "Nah. I'm still ISA. The admiral killed the transfer."

"What? Why?"

"Says he still needs me as a cadet pilot." She shrugs in a *no big deal* way that makes it obvious it's totally a big deal. "Oh well."

My heart sinks. Of course Grandpa needs Leela as cadet pilot. I just proved I'm still unfit, functional cardiovascular system or not.

"I'm so sorry, Lee-lu," I whisper.

A sharp little laugh stabs through her disappointment. "Only you could take credit for the apocalypse."

"I'm not . . ." There's no way to tell her why Grandpa still needs her as cadet pilot without making her worry about me, on top of everything else.

I hug her again instead. She hugs me back, resting her head on my shoulder for a moment. Then she pulls away.

"See you at the memorial?"

"Yeah," I say.

When I turn back to the table, Chris has his head down beside his empty bowl. A little bubble of memory pops inside my chest and evaporates into a smile. "You used to fall asleep at the table like that when you were tiny."

"What?" He snaps upright, eyes blinking. "I wasn't sleeping."

"Both unconvincing and unnecessary," Beth says. "Sleep in Joanna's bed."

"No, I—"

"You've got a couple hours before the memorial," I say, cutting off his protest. "Go. Sleep."

He gives up arguing and shuffles into our storage-closet bedroom.

Beth keeps working on her list.

I scrape and stack the dishes and clean out the coffee pot. It's only 0600. I have five hours until the memorial. I could sleep more, but Chris is in my bed, and I can't imagine anything but nightmares waiting for me.

I take the dishes to the recycling center. The machines are still running, breaking down yesterday's used dishes and clothes and building scraps and broken tools into tiny beads of raw plastic that the 3D printers can use to make new gear. I toss our plates and utensils into the next set of recycling bins and then dump the food scraps and coffee grounds into the sealed compost tubs on the other side of the cabin.

I take a shower and put on fresh clothes.

Once I'm dressed, I set the wall screens to mirror. I look pale. Deep shadows cup my eyes. I grab a wide-toothed comb and yank it through my hair. It catches on a huge snarl in the fine, curly mass. Then another. My hair is always like this when it's long.

I'm going to cut it. Right now.

There are several pairs of scissors in the first-aid kit. I grab one and scrape my hair up into a ponytail. I'm about to chop it off when I hear the *snap-boom* of a shuttle making atmospheric entry. That must be the *Prairie*'s shuttle, *3212*. That was fast. I thought it would take at least a couple of days before the rest of the marines followed us.

I look at myself in the mirror again. What am I doing? Chopping all my hair off would be so melodramatic. *Look at me! I'm Joanna, and I've got needlessly uneven apocalypse hair.*

Who knew I was so selfish?

I put the scissors back and grab a heavy parka from a supply cubby. Then I walk down to the river to watch the shuttle land. My ponytail drips down my neck as I peer up into the predawn gray.

At first, I don't see anything. Then a bright flash of reflected light snaps against the morning. And another. That must be the shuttle. Weird. Why is it so hard to see?

I get my answer when the Landing's particle shield ripples down to let the shuttle in. *3212*'s skin is mirrored silver, unlike the *Trailblazer*'s black rainbow metallic. It's an older model than the *Trailblazer*, smaller and sleeker, like a stretched-out triangle with twin engines sticking out behind it like a pair of clenched fists. The design dates back to the Storm Wars, when shooting military units into space and slingshotting them around the planet seemed like a good idea. It wasn't part of the *Prairie*'s fleet of shuttles and satellites, last time I looked at her specs. But that was almost two years ago, during Mom's test flight with the enormous ship. The ISA must have decided to add tactical shuttles to the big ship's complement since then. I wonder why.

The fido tree I'm standing next to reaches out to me, stroking my shoulders with a thick cluster of flowers that are fading to white as the weather turns colder. Fidos are hybrids, like a lot of the flora on this planet. They photosynthesize like plants, but they're also carnivores. The pretty clustered flowers are traps, designed to lure in insect analogs. Earth has—I mean, had, I guess—a few hybrid plant species. But nothing like the huge photosynthesizing carnivores on Tau.

Nothing like the phytoraptors.

Of course, the fido trees aren't much like the raptors, either, even though the Rangers classified them as part of the same genus—*Chorulux*, which means "light dancers." Fido trees are rooted, and they look like Earth trees until they reach out and nuzzle you. Phytoraptors look more like a lion crossed with a gorilla and a rose bush, except with way bigger claws. They still draw energy from sunlight, but they aren't really plants anymore.

I reach up and let the tree twine its tiny white flowers through my fingers. I know I shouldn't be assigning emotions to trees, but it feels like it's happy to see me.

Movement lurches through my peripheral vision. Something too fast to be a fido. I twist, peering through the shifting floral branches to see my grandfather wading into the river a few meters upstream.

I shiver just looking at him.

"Grandpa!" I call out.

"Hello, Little Moth," he calls back as I walk up the riverbank toward him.

"Isn't that cold?" I ask.

"Sure is," he says. "Care to join me?"

"No way."

He grins, amused at my vehemence. "Suit yourself. I find that intense sensation is the best way to mediate intense emotions."

"Intense emotions?" I don't mean to sound surprised, but I am. He's been calm, even relaxed, this whole time. Especially compared to the rest of us.

Grandpa chuckles. "Glad to see my old poker face is still operational. I paid dearly for it in my youth. But it helps, when folks are counting on you." He pulls in a deep breath, stretching his curved spine out to its full length for a moment before he releases it, slumping back into his usual slouch as he exhales. "But I try not to let my poker face fool my brain. A good leader feels everything. Only way to really appreciate the consequences of your actions."

The phrase tosses a memory across my brain. My brother's soot-smeared face seconds before I blew us both into space. If I'd known Teddy was going to die, would I still have tried to save the *Pioneer*? I really don't know. Especially after yesterday. I don't know if I would have been brave enough.

"Consequences suck," I say.

"Never truer words," Grandpa agrees. "But a good leader accepts them. That's why groups need leaders. Someone has to be able to look past the moment and plan for the future. Even if that means plotting a harsh course."

Another face I'll never see again fills my mind. *Miguel*. Grinning in triumph, seconds before a massive phytoraptor the Rangers dubbed Sunflower killed him.

How ironic that Miguel died to save Sunflower's species from being wiped out by human terraforming. Actually, Beth thinks stopping Stage Three saved this whole planet, which means Miguel saved humanity, too.

Can I accept his death as a consequence of that?

I don't know if I want to.

"I see we have some catching up to do," Grandpa says, studying me.

"Obviously, I haven't got much of a poker face yet," I say.

"Don't be in too much of a hurry." Grandpa turns to look up at the sprawl of blue-green light spilling over the horizon. "It isn't cheap, and paying for it . . ." He shakes his head. "To borrow a phrase, it sucks."

Mom has always had a good poker face, too. Beth, Teddy, and I used to call it her "commander face." What did she do to earn it? And how did she lose it?

I think Mom answered that question herself when she was arguing with Grandpa on the *Prairie*.

I'm not panicking. I'm despairing.

"Is Mom . . ." *Okay* seems like silly word right now. No one is okay.

"She's fine," Grandpa says. "I made her have a good meal and clean up before we debriefed last night. She's brought me up to speed on the events of the last few months and your interactions with the indigenous sentients."

Interactions with the indigenous sentients. That's one way to think of half our team being torn apart and eaten by phytoraptors followed by the Sorrow demanding that the rest of us leave the planet.

"How are we going to do this, Grandpa?" I ask. "This course . . . it isn't just harsh. It's impossible."

Grandpa offers me a wry smile. "You're not overstating the problem. We're going to be asking a lot from our people. We're also going to be asking a lot from your friend Tarn."

Tarn. Just thinking about him makes my stomach hurt. How will he react to all this? How will his people react?

"Your mother tells me you know more about the Sorrow, and their leader, than anyone else on the team," Grandpa says.

"Not really," I say, flustered. "Beth has spent way more time studying Dr. Brown's notes than I did. Dr. Brown lived with them for years after the rest of the Ranger team died. My friends and I were only with Tarn a few days."

"It is a shame Lucille was killed," Grandpa says. "She was brilliant." He huffs a little laugh. "She never did care for me. Said I was shortsighted and old-fashioned."

"What?" I say. "Weren't you research partners?"

He nods. "That's how she developed such a nuanced

opinion. Of course, she was right."

"No, she wasn't!" I protest. "You aren't either of those things."

That earns me a full-fledged laugh.

"Sure I am," he says. "Or are you too young to remember how much time I spent telling your father that the Galactic Frontier Project was a fool's errand?" His eyes drift up to the crystal mountains to our west, just starting to spark with rainbows in the morning light. "Sometimes, it's good to be wrong."

I follow his gaze. I've been living at the feet of those glittering peaks for months and they still take my breath away. I think they always will. I'm so glad I got to see them. But that doesn't mean we belong here.

"I do remember those arguments," I say. "You told Dad that colonization would be more complicated than the GFP imagined. And you were right. It was more than complicated. Coming to this planet . . . that's what was wrong. And staying here is worse."

Grandpa turns to study me with the same intensity he gave the prismatic mountain range. I wonder if I've offended him. He just crossed light-years to get what's left of the human species to Tau. He probably doesn't want to hear about the moral complexities of that decision right now.

My stomach twists as he sloshes through the water and clambers up the steep riverbank to my side. Should I say I'm sorry? Or will that just make everything more awkward?

"Brrr," he says, shuddering a little. "It's damn cold out here."

"Grandpa," I start to say, "I didn't mean to—" But the apology evaporates as he pulls a pair of silver studs from a pocket on his utility harness.

"Are those ensign insignia?" I almost whisper the words. "How did you . . ."

Grandpa beams. "I found them in your mother's office. She had them made weeks ago." He leans in to fasten them to my collar. "I was supposed to wait. Do this with her. But I'm a selfish man. And I needed to replenish my spirit."

"So you're promoting me?" I say, astounded. "But I . . . .why would you promote me?"

"Because you understand that settling on this planet is wrong, even though it is necessary. That's going to be the crux of every dilemma we face here. We can't pretend this situation is fair to the Sorrow or the phytoraptors. It would be a lie, and they won't thank us for it. You see that. You're willing to say it out loud. I need you to keep saying it. I need to see this world through your eyes. To understand it, so that I can build a place for us here."

"Really?" I say.

He nods. "Really. It won't be easy. I'm going to be asking a lot from you as well."

My fingers go to the tiny metal dots that just transformed me into Ensign Joanna Watson. They're heavier than I thought they'd be.

I meet my grandfather's expectant eyes.

"I won't let you down, sir."

"You never have," he says. "I only hope, when all of this is said and done, you'll be able to say the same of me."

FIVE

By the time we gather for the memorial service, it's even colder, if that's possible, and the world is soaking in fat drops of rain.

Mom isn't here yet. She's probably juggling a million things. I hope she got a few hours of sleep last night. Dad is standing with Doc and Dr. Kao at the front of the assembled crowd. They look worried. I'd be surprised if they didn't. Still, I don't feel like learning any more depressing details about our future right now, so I find my friends instead.

Chris and Leela and Beth are huddled together under a big tree next to the memorial stone.

"Where's Jay?" I ask, as I join them.

Before anyone can answer, a chorus of gunfire smacks through the air. We all turn to see both marine squadrons lined up back to back on the path from the Landing, rifles aimed at the sky. They fire again. And again. And again.

My ears are ringing by the tine they flip their rifles to their shoulders and march down the path toward us. It's so quiet I can hear the rain pattering on the fido tree flowers in between the dull thuds of the boots on the wet ground.

The crowd parts before the marines. They march past the memorial stone and unfold into four straight lines on the riverbank behind it. Jay is in the back row, his rifle on his shoulder, his body stiff at attention. I can't see his face.

"What was that?" Chris whispers.

"Twenty-one-gun salute," Leela whispers back. "I've never seen one, but it used to be a thing at military funerals."

It didn't feel like a salute. It felt like . . . showing off, I guess. A memory rebounds through my head. Ord marching his Takers into the Landing for the first time, bristling with weapons. What was it Tarn had called that?

An honest display of strength.

But why does Shelby feel the need to demonstrate her strength to us, the people her squadrons are supposed to protect? Is this meant to make us feel safe?

Grandpa emerges from the crowd and walks to the memorial stone. Standing there, the two squadrons frame him perfectly.

"Friends," Grandpa calls, "we are faced with an impossible task. How does one mourn a planet? How do we honor such a loss? How do we move on?"

Beth's tidy handwriting fills my brain, her list of names superimposing itself over the scene before me as Grandpa continues.

"The task seems beyond the scope of human imagination. It is certainly beyond me. But thankfully, we don't depend on my wisdom alone." He sucks in a breath and sighs it out. "My beloved wife died when our daughter was still a child. But she taught me a lot before she was taken from us. She always said a big problem is just a lot of little problems swimming together, like a school of fish. So if you want to solve a big problem, you just have to catch one of the little ones and gut it. Then you do it again and again until you're done."

He chuckles, almost to himself. "She was a ferocious woman, my Cleo. Dauntless. I can only hope that piece of her is still with me. Because the task facing us is monumental. But I know that we can accomplish it, one little fish at a time."

He rests a hand on the memorial stone.

"But first, we must honor our loss. Grieve. Then, tomorrow, we will face all those little problems. Together."

"Humanity is not lost. We are found. This planet is a new beginning. A clean slate, untouched and waiting for us to shape a new world. A new future." He raises his arms, encompassing first the crowd, then the gray, soggy day behind him as he speaks.

The murmur of shared tears has faded into a crackling

silence. Everyone is leaning forward like they're metal filings and Grandpa is a magnet.

Everyone except Dad.

He's texting.

What the hell is wrong with him? How can he be texting now, of all times?

My brain answers its own question.

"Where's Mom?" I whisper to Beth, alarmed.

"I'm amazed it took you this long to notice," Beth whispers back.

"I *noticed*," I mutter. "I just figured she hadn't gotten here yet when I showed up."

"Something must be wrong," Leela says, quietly. "She wouldn't just bail on us."

Dad lets his arms drop to his sides like his hands are suddenly heavy. I expect him to slip away and go find Mom. He doesn't. He just stands there, staring dully as Grandpa gives his place at the memorial stone to Doc.

Doc begins the same Hindu prayer that he led us all through at Teddy's funeral. Not all of us, I guess. Half the people there that day are dead now. Their names are written on the stone behind him.

I look back at Dad. He hasn't moved.

"Go," Beth whispers.

Leela nods in agreement, even though she's mouthing the prayer along with her dad.

I slip along the edge of the praying crowd, then pick up speed when I reach the path back to the Landing.

I tap my flex as I jog up the hill. "Locate Commander Watson's flex, please."

The computer promptly replies, "Located. Commander Watson's flex is in the Command Office, Joanna."

The dirt path becomes a solar-tiled road lined with labs and family cabins. I turn left at the school and cut through the community garden to reach the street that runs behind Ground Control.

I burst through the back doors and dart through the empty hallways until I see the door to Mom's office standing open ahead of me.

I call out, "Mom?"

There's no answer.

I peer through the doorway anyway and find Mom standing at the wall screen, staring at an unsent message.

"Mom?"

She still doesn't reply. It's like she doesn't even hear me.

I cross the office to stand beside her. From there, I can read the message she hasn't sent.

This report was classified by the ISA. It contains information you need. I was under orders not to share it with you. The admiral and I have decided those orders no longer apply.

There's an attachment.

A file marked *PSR.Tau.Ceti.e.Classified*. The message is addressed to the full Exploration & Pioneering Team.

No wonder Mom's frozen up like this. This is the top-secret planetary survey report on Tau that she and the ISA hid from everyone. The whole team is about to discover

71

that Mom knew about the Sorrow and the phytoraptors before we came here and kept them secret from the rest of us. That decision cost a lot of people their lives.

The ache of sympathy in the pit of my stomach is curdled by a surprising amount of lingering anger. How much did the ISA really know about the Sorrow and the phytoraptors when they sent us here? Could we have made a better start if we'd known the truth? Or would everything still have gone wrong?

"Computer, please edit message," Mom says in a strained whisper. "Add sentence: *I'm sorry.*"

"My apologies, Alice," the computer says. "I didn't get that. Can you speak a little louder?"

"No," she rasps, tears shredding her voice. "I can't."

She stares at the unsent message. Eyes brimming.

"Do you want me to add it, Mom?" I ask.

She's so startled she almost stumbles, like the unexpected question was a physical blow.

"What are you doing here, Jo?" she snaps, scrubbing tears from her face.

"The memorial . . ."

"Oh." She closes her eyes. "I was just going to share the report and go, but then . . ."

But then she stood here, staring at it for twenty minutes instead of hitting send. The thought is heavy and hot. I want to run away from it, but I can't. I'm not a little girl anymore. I don't get to pretend my mom is superhuman just because it makes me feel better.

"You were just following orders, Mom," I say. "The ISA made you keep the survey report from us."

"Maybe. But I knew it was wrong," she says. "I knew it was a bad choice."

"So why did you do it?"

I've wanted to ask that question for a long time. Now that it's out, I think I want to take it back.

The series of expressions that pummel her face tells me more than any words could. Sadness. Anger. Guilt. And something that looks weirdly like pride.

Then she sighs, breathing out a tiny, sardonic smile.

"It seemed like a good idea at the time."

It isn't an answer, but at least that slice of a smile brought some life back into her face.

She turns back to the wall screen and jabs "send." Then she slumps, like that took all the energy she had.

I wait for her to say something. Or move.

She doesn't.

"Mom?" I try again, finally.

"I don't see a way through this, Jo," she says without looking at me. "I don't know what to do."

My heart hammers against my ribs, just once. A huge thud that shoots fear through my body. Mom always knows what to do. That's just a thing that's true. Like gravity or breathing. Except it isn't anymore.

What am I supposed to do about that? An idea slips into my worry. I don't know if it's the right thing to say, but I have to say something.

"Maybe you don't have to know what to do."

"True," Mom says, flashing her sardonic smile again. "I could just stand here staring at the wall awhile longer."

"No, that's not . . ." I stop myself. She knows that isn't what I mean. Trying again, I say, "Grandpa was just telling this story, at the memorial. About something Grandma used to say."

Her dry little smile drops into a silent *oh*.

"A big problem is like a school of fish," she whispers.

I've never met my grandmother, but I hear the echo of her voice in the words.

"Yeah," I say. "That's it."

She closes her eyes for a long heartbeat. Then she nods, like she's agreeing with herself.

She opens her eyes again and holds out a hand to me. "Come on, kid. This little problem is handled."

She hangs on to my hand as we walk through the empty camp and down the sloping path to the memorial stone. As we approach, Dr. Vega is just finishing saying a Catholic funeral rite for those lost on Earth. Mama Alejandra comes forward and joins her in the final prayer. Then they offer their place at the front of the crowd back to Grandpa and join Doc and Ben Petuchowski, who are standing just behind the stone, having already offered their own prayers.

"Friends," Grandpa begins, but then Chief Ganeshalingam catches sight of us.

"Commander!" she exclaims, cutting Grandpa off as she and her wife turn to pull Mom into a double hug.

"How are you, honey?" Chief G asks Mom. "We haven't seen you since you got back."

"Thank goodness you were able to repair that sail," Ezra Brin chimes in beside them. "My brothers are up there. All four of them!"

Then everyone is talking at once, pulling Mom forward into the heart of the group as they pour out their worries and their joys.

I fight to stay by her side. I want to yell at them to shut up and leave her alone. She's so tired. She doesn't need them putting all this on her.

But I quickly realize they aren't a burden to her. I swear she's getting a little taller with every touch. Every question. Every comforting word. Like the cacophony of need is nourishing her.

I look up at Beth and Leela and see my own relief written in their faces. Dad's, too. But Grandpa has a weird look on his face. Pinched. He almost looks angry.

Is he worried about her? Maybe he can't see the look on her face from where he is. He probably thinks they're putting too much pressure on her, just like I did.

"Come, my dear," he calls, pushing through the crowd to Mom's side. "Join us. You built this team, after all. And that hard work, the choices you made . . . they will build the foundation of human history on this world."

He means that as a compliment, I think, but Mom shrinks at the words, her face going pale again as he pulls her against him. My heart sinks. He said "choices" but she heard mistakes. The choices that went wrong. That seems to be all she can think of.

"I'm so glad to have my daughter by my side as we embrace this new age, on this new planet," Grandpa continues.

Something about that statement feels off. It takes me a minute to realize what it is.

By my side.

That makes Mom sound like his second.

Wait.

Grandpa is an admiral. Mom is a commander. And Grandpa came out of retirement to command the *Prairie*. That means that he's the senior ISA officer on Tau. That means he's our leader now. Mom is his second in command.

"Come now," Mom says, as the realization that just hit me rebounds through the crowd. "It's wet and cold out here, and I bet Mohan has hot coffee waiting."

"Sure do," Dr. Kao calls out.

"Good," Grandpa says. "Come, friends. Join me. Let us face our future. Together."

With that, he leads Mom up the path, the crowd trailing behind them like the spreading tail of a comet.

I stay rooted where I stand. I'm shocked by how resentful I feel. It's not like Mom's had the best-ever track record here. And Grandpa has decades more experience than she does. Having him in command is a good thing.

But Mom has been our mission commander for as long

as I can remember. I hate the thought of following anyone else. Even if it is my own grandfather.

Mom's voice slips through my memory. *I don't know what to do next.*

Maybe she's glad to step aside and let Grandpa take over. But I just don't know who she is, if she isn't the commander. I don't know if she does, either.

A blast of cold wind cuts straight through my parka. I should go with the others. Get some coffee. And food. I'm starving. It's been hours since my too-early breakfast.

As I turn to go, I realize I'm not the only straggler. Dad is slumped against the memorial stone, glaring at his boots.

He looks so angry. No. That's the wrong word. Bitter. Which is strange. Dad doesn't do bitter. He always looks for the positive side of things. Always. It's irritating, and I really, badly want him to do it now.

"Dad?"

His head snaps up. I don't think he didn't realized I was still here. "Sorry, kid. Just letting something get under my skin."

"The apocalypse?"

He makes an odd face. Like he wants to say something he knows he shouldn't. Then he shakes his head.

"Sort of," he says. "But my feelings are the last thing that matters right now. Your grandfather is right. We've got work to do."

"Idle hands ruin plans?" I say, trying for lighthearted.

He smiles.

It breaks my heart all over again.

"Every plan I've ever had is ruined, kiddo," he says.

Then he trudges up the path back to the Landing, without waiting to see if I follow.

SIX

We spend the afternoon together in the mess hall, not grieving but planning. We've got twelve weeks to transport ten thousand untrained civilians to the surface and keep them alive until they acclimate. It's terrifying, but it's also a challenge. We're pioneers. We're good at challenges. You can feel the energy building as the day goes on. We couldn't save Earth, but we are going to figure out a way to protect the survivors.

I haven't seen Jay since this morning. Shelby has both squads out doing drills and target practice in the square, except the teams she has patrolling the shield perimeter. I know the marines need to train, but I wish Shelby had waited until tomorrow. Every time I start to relax, there's a burst of frantically thudding boots or synchronized shouting. Or gunfire. It's nerve rattling. And kind of scary.

I've never felt intimidated by our own soldiers before. I've never really thought of them as soldiers before, actually. Mom and Sarge didn't divide the squad out from the crew. They were just members of the team, like the rest of us. But today, watching them jog through the rain, shouting and shooting and keeping us all on edge, it feels like *us* doesn't include them.

I wonder how they feel, working hard in the wet and cold while we're warm and comfortable inside.

I hang around the mess hall until late, helping with the dishes. I expect Jay to come in, once he's excused from exercises. He always used to, when he knew I was on KP.

But tonight he doesn't come.

The rain has stopped by the time I take the compost and waste down to the recycling center. The moons are both nearly full, silvering the waist-high grass that flows out for kilometers around the Landing. It's beautiful. I hate that we're going to have to plow a lot of it under to build shelter for the survivors.

This is the last run of the day, so I add my load to the bins and start the recyclers and composters. This stuff will be raw by morning—ready to go back into the 3D printers and start over. If only I could do that to my brain. Grind up the guilt and worry and sadness and turn it into something useful.

The recycling center is only a few meters from the

shield perimeter. The lights from the building catch in the force field, turning it into a warped mirror. Like looking out a bright window into a dark night.

I switch the lights off. In the darkness, the shield becomes transparent again. I let my eyes wander through the silver ocean of grass, broken only by the occasional cluster of fido trees.

The Landing looks so small in the wide-open darkness. It *is* small. There's so much more of this planet to explore, so many other places we could live.

According to her notes, Dr. Brown believed the Sorrow only live in the Diamond Range region. I'm not sure that's true—Ord didn't trust her as much as Dr. Brown thought he did. But if she was right, it would be better for everyone if we found a way to move our population elsewhere on this planet.

Dad suggested relocating today, during our planning sessions. Nobody disagreed, but it's not that simple. If we're going to get ten thousand people off the *Prairie* in three months, then we don't have time to find another place on Tau that's safe. It'll take a month just to transport them to the surface, and at least a month and a half to build what we need to feed and shelter them. And that's only if nothing goes wrong.

This is Tau.

Something's going to go wrong.

Grandpa believes the best solution is to build up the

Landing with temporary housing for now and find a permanent location once we've woken the survivors.

He's sure we can convince Tarn to give us the time we need. Specifically, he's sure *I* can convince Tarn to give us the time we need. I hope he's right, but I've got this memory of Tarn stuck in my head, like a catchy tune that's playing on loop:

My world ended the moment Lucille's ship landed on our soil.

I can only imagine how Tarn's going to feel when he sees us ripping into his planet to build all the housing we're going to need. Even if the buildings are temporary, they're going to leave a scar. Tarn has read our history. He knows what we did to Earth. There's a good reason he doesn't want us here, and looking out at the thick grass flowing in the night breeze, I sort of don't blame him.

I should head to the greenhouse and try to get some sleep.

I take one more deep breath, drinking in the pristine darkness before turning back toward the Landing.

A flicker of light catches at the edge of my vision.

I turn back and scan the night.

There's nothing out there. That was probably just a surge in the shield. Maybe one of the little insect analogs flew into it and—

There it is again. And there. It's not just flickers now. There's definitely something bright out there in the grass. Moving fast. Coming this way.

For a second, I think it's a flex in flashlight mode, but it isn't. It's too bright for that. And the yellow is too warm to be artificial.

The realization hits me seconds before the smudge of light resolves into a narrow figure draped in a glowing yellow robe.

It's Tarn.

He's carrying the long, heavy staff he prefers over the swords and battle hammers most Sorrow warriors carry. It looks like a walking stick, but I know it's a dangerous weapon. He's used it against me before. His lantern cloak billows around him, its deep hood hiding his face and multiplying his natural bioluminescence into something bright enough to catch in the shield and cast a warping halo around him.

Damn it. It can't be a coincidence that he's here. He knows about the survivors.

I should have anticipated this. After Tarn helped us defeat Ord and became leader of the Sorrow, I promised him we would leave Tau as soon as we could. But the *Wagon* was a complete loss. We had to start over with the *Trailblazer*, and constructing a new transorbital shuttle from scratch took time. Months. Tarn has been patient, but I know he's been watching us to make sure we keep our end of the bargain. I should have realized that he'd notice when we landed a second space shuttle that we didn't have three days ago.

I'm supposed to be Grandpa's Sorrow advisor, and I'm already failing.

I should text Grandpa. Tarn is the Followed. He should

hear the news about Earth from our leader. Shouldn't he? Or would it be better coming from someone he knows? My new insignia press urgently against my collarbones. I might not be able to space walk anymore, but I can talk to Tarn. He may be the Followed now, but he was my friend first. He listened to me before, because I listened to him.

It saved this planet. It also saved my life. Now it could save my species.

Tarn stops on the other side of the shield.

My hands are shaking. It takes two tries to bring the shield app up on my flex.

I create a portal.

Tarn charges through it.

This was a mistake.

I stumble step backward as he storms at me. My boots catch on something and I go down hard. For a blistering heartbeat I can't see anything but grass and stars; then Tarn is there.

He lets his hood fall back as he looms over me, drilling his round black eyes into mine. The yellow glow of his bio-luminescent blood is bright enough that I can see his bones and muscles through his transparent skin. He doesn't say anything. He just stands there, pinning me into the dirt with the force of his glare.

Finally, I dig words out of my head and string them together into a sentence.

"I'm so sorry, Tarn."

"Meaningless!" His tritone voice turns the flat English word into a chorus. It sounds like a dozen people are standing behind him, hurling their fury at me in perfect unison. "Just like your promises!"

"Things have changed, Tarn!" I protest. "Mom was going to end the mission—"

"And now there are two ships in my skies," Tarn snarls, talking right over me. "One so big it casts a shadow on the moons themselves!"

"Let me explain," I beg, scrambling backward, trying to get enough room to stand up.

He grabs the cross strap of my utility harness, yanking me to my feet and past them, to the point where my toes are scratching desperately in the dirt.

"Tarn!" I whimper, my voice retreating deep inside my throat. "Please—"

"I never expected you to keep your promise." The words thrum around me, sticking to my skin like stinging nettles as my brain struggles to interpret the layers of his voice that go beyond the range of human hearing. "But I did not expect you to *lie*."

"Lie?" The startled question leaps free of my choking terror before I can snatch it back.

"Yes. Lie. Do you really think I don't know how long it takes one of your ships to get from Earth to this planet? Lucille told my brother when your people departed your planet, and when you would arrive. You and I both know that the great ship that now orbits *my* planet left Earth long before you made your so-called promise."

"That's true, I guess, but I didn't know—"

"More lies!" Tarn sings the word into my face, his layered voice discordant with outrage. "But it worked, didn't it? You lied to me, and I believed you. I gave you time to bring more invaders to our soil."

"What?" I cough, gasping for air. "No. No. You've . . . We aren't invaders, Tarn." Once the first sentence is out, the others pour through the space it left behind. "We're refugees. Our world is gone."

"Gone?" He follows the English word with a burst of Sorrow. I *feel* the words, even though I don't understand them. The Sorrow can echolocate, so their language has a sonar element that human brains interpret in some weird ways. Whatever he just said makes my skin flush hot and my stomach twist like I'm about to throw up.

He switches back to English. "How is that possible? Not even humans could destroy a whole planet."

"It isn't gone." I gasp. "The planet itself is there. But humans can't live on it anymore."

I take a deep breath. Another. Another.

"It was just a stupid mistake." I can feel my voice getting louder and firmer as anger mingles with the fear and sadness. "The ISA pushed a software update to all of its computers, including a bunch of tiny robots that float around in Earth's upper atmosphere eating pollution and extra carbon to stabilize the climate. The update had a bug in its calendar system. The atmosphere scrubbers had to reboot, and when it came back online, the nanobots couldn't tell the difference between hydrogen and carbon and . . ."

I cut myself off before I start babbling about the technical details.

"It doesn't matter exactly what happened. By the time the ISA figured out how much damage was being done, it was too late to stop it. We only have a few ships with superluminal drives—the kind that can travel between stars. There was only one in Earth's solar system. A prototype colony ship they built to follow us to Tau. It was already stocked up for its second test flight, so they loaded in as many people as they could and just . . . left."

"And came here," Tarn says, finishing the thought.

"There are a little more than ten thousand survivors," I say. "By now, everyone left on Earth is dead."

My knees give out then, and Tarn lets me fall.

I stay there, sprawled in the grass, looking up at Tarn. He's staring past me at the lights of the Landing and the pair of shuttles looming beyond it.

"I wish . . ." I whisper. "I wish this was just an invasion. You could win that fight. But it's not. It's worse. We can't leave Tau. We don't have anywhere to go."

I slump, resting my head in my hands.

I don't know how long we stay that way, each lost in our own grief and fear.

Then Tarn begins to speak in Sorrow. The words feel like swimming underwater in Grandpa's lake—cold and heavy and suffocating, but in a weirdly pleasant way. Peaceful.

He drops to the first of his two knee joints and plants his forehead against mine, wrapping one hand around the back of my neck. His trijointed fingers are so long, they fold all the way around my larynx to meet his palm.

It happens so fast that I don't have time to object or struggle.

Then he's squeezing. Pressing his fingers into the flesh of my neck. They feel kind of springy—like I'm being throttled by a Slinky. It should hurt, but all I can feel is the dense vibration of the Sorrow words, shuddering through my skin. Somehow, that makes it worse. I try to protest, but my voice has gone back into hiding. My hands fly up to grip his arm, his fingers, anything that might give me leverage.

Tarn grabs them with his free hand, pinning them to my chest as he talks. Or sings, really. The suffocating peaceful Sorrow words are lilting—rising and falling in a thick melody. I can breathe, but just barely. Tears are running down my cheeks, dripping onto his glass-clear skin.

All he has to do is twist and he will crush my windpipe. Or break my neck.

But he doesn't twist.

He just sings.

I can *feel* the sound radiating through his forehead and the implacable fingers around my neck. The buzz is sharply percussive at first, rattling through me in sizzling bursts that leave my body hot, like I've been working in the sun, despite the frosty chill in the night air around me. Then the tactile melody settles into a profoundly unsettling hum. A thick, wet sound that seems to pluck at every nerve in my body. It isn't painful, just . . . I don't know . . . awful. I need to get away from him. Now.

I twist in his grasp, throwing all my weight backward to break his hold. I don't care if it breaks my neck. I just want that sound to go away.

It's useless. He's too strong. I try to scream in his face instead, but I can barely summon a whisper.

"Tarn. Please."

He ignores me. The humming gets more intense.

I'm sobbing now. Racking tears that shake my whole body.

I thought he was my friend.

The crack of a gunshot punches past my left ear, leaving behind a whine so loud I can hardly hear Shelby call out after it, "Leave the kid alone!"

Tarn shoves me down into the mud and leaps over my head, straight at Shelby.

She fires again, but he's moving too fast. The bullet punches past him and slams into the shield.

Then he's on her.

It's so dark that I can only see flickers of movement in the yellow gleam of Tarn's bioluminescence. I want to help, but I know better than to jump into a close-quarters fight between two armed combatants.

As I pull my flex off my wrist and slap the emergency alert, Shelby bucks Tarn off, sending him sprawling. He bellows in pain. I startle and drop my flex. It disappears into the dark grass. I crouch, fumbling frantically to find it again.

There's another scream. I look up and see Shelby leap onto Tarn's back. A stun gun crackles. Tarn shouts in pain and rears up, bending his second elbow joint backward to snatch her off his back and whip her several meters through the darkness.

She cries out, and I hear rather than see her scrambling to get her feet back under her.

Tarn finds his first. He stumbles upright and roars, throwing sound out like shrapnel as he swings his heavy staff down into the small of Shelby's back.

"No!" I cry, giving up on my flex and stumbling toward them. "Don't do this!"

Tarn draws his staff back again. A killing blow.

I scream wordlessly.

Shelby raises her pistol and fires. *Bam. Bam. Bam.*

Tarn throws himself back, bending almost horizontal to evade the bullets. He snaps upright and sweeps the gun from her hand with his staff. Then he whips it back, slamming it into her torso with a vicious wet *thud*.

Something flashes through the darkness and I'm moving even before my mind puts together what I'm seeing. I throw my body between them just as Tarn stabs his narrow black blade down toward Shelby's chest.

He manages to pull back, but just barely. I can feel the tip of his blade pressing into the padded shoulder of my parka.

He pulls, slicing through the waterproof shell of the jacket as he draws the knife across my body, centimeters from my skin.

I don't move.

It isn't bravery. More like terror-induced paralysis. I desperately want Shelby to scramble up behind me, but she's just lying there.

Tarn leans in close, until his black eyes fill my field of vision, the yellow light of his blood burning out everything around me but him.

"Leave this world, Joanna Watson." The words pour over me like boiling water. "Leave this world, and take your people with you."

Then he bellows a blast of sound so loud, it fills my ears with hollow silence and the pounding of my own heart. And even after I can't hear anything anymore, I can still *feel* him shrieking.

Light flares, snagging my eyes from Tarn to the particle shield behind us. Crackling bursts of light are popping over the force field, burning its translucent rainbow to an opaque white.

Then the shield bursts, falling away to empty air.

Tarn just took down our shields with his voice.

He says something then, words my deafened ears can't hear that spatter over my skin. With that, he flicks his hood back into place and disappears into the night.

I twist back to look down at Shelby. She's lying on the ground behind me. She isn't moving. She might be dead.

I can't hear myself screaming for help.

SEVEN

"Wake up, Joanna."

Beth's voice cuts through the deafening silence of my nightmares.

I can't hear myself screaming in my dreams, but Beth can. It's been three weeks since Tarn attacked me, and I don't think either of us has had a good night's sleep since.

"Sorry, Beth," I say.

Beth flops back down in her cot. "Don't be sorry, just be quiet. I'm going out on another raptor survey with Leela in three hours, and I will be more functional if I can spend them in uninterrupted sleep."

"I know," I say. "I'm trying . . ."

I trail off because I don't know what I'm trying to do. Not be so scared at every moment of the day that I scream all night? That doesn't seem like a thing you can try.

"I know," Beth says. "I know, Joanna."

We both lie there in the dark, staring at the hexagonal tiles of the ceiling. She isn't sleeping either. I can hear it in the rise and fall of her breath.

This is so bad. We need rest.

We've all been working 22/7 to prepare for the survivors. What Beth is doing is even more important than constructing new buildings. She's studying the phytoraptors, trying to develop a strategy so we can interact with them safely. Or just avoid them.

But avoiding them has been getting harder.

Ever since construction began, we've been seeing a lot of raptors around the Landing. We don't know why. Beth hasn't found anything that suggests there's a nest nearby or that phytoraptors frequented the area before we started tearing up the grassland.

I wonder if they're keeping tabs on us.

Beth doesn't think so, mostly because these raptors don't use sign language. Dr. Brown and her team taught some of the phytoraptors to sign when they first encountered them. A few have acquired a pretty sophisticated grasp of the language. Especially one the Rangers nicknamed Bob. Bob seems to like humans—he actually saved my life a couple of times.

We know Bob has been teaching the other raptors in his nest sign language, but none of the phytoraptors around the Landing seem to know it. That makes it pretty unlikely that they've organized in some way to keep track of us, or intimidate us. Beth thinks they're just curious. That almost makes sense, except for one thing—if these raptors aren't local and they aren't somehow communicating with Bob's nest, then how did they even know we were out here?

It's Beth's job to find out. The rest of the botany team is hunting for a stable food source, and basically everyone else is on construction duty. Printing and building even temporary shelter for ten thousand people is going to take every second of the next nine weeks.

We've already woken up two hundred survivors—people with useful skills like construction and engineering, and the families of Shelby's squadron. The lieutenant insisted we wake her squadron's families first. She's fiercely protective of her people.

She's also kind of a jerk.

When she found out Dr. Kao had convinced Grandpa that prioritizing the *Prairie* squadron families might cause tension between our team and the newcomers, Shelby left the medical center in the middle of a nanobot treatment to heal her burst spleen. She limped into Ground Control in her patient gown to demand that Grandpa keep his word to her people.

She openly doesn't care if that pisses anyone else off. Shelby told Dr. Kao to his face that she doesn't give a "good goddamn" about anyone she met after Earth was destroyed, because most of us are going to die anyway, and there's no point in getting attached. Shelby and her people don't even live with the rest of us. They've been rebuilding the old Ranger camp. They call it River Bend.

Shelby has both squadrons doing half a shift of combat drills every day, as well as their usual patrol and construction obligations. And she insists on formal military discipline—a bunch of "sir, yes, sirs" and synchronized marching that just intensifies the separation between pioneers and soldiers I felt that first day, after the memorial. I really don't like it. We're all in this together. It should feel that way.

But it's more than that. I feel like the closer Jay gets to his new squad mates, the further he gets from us. From me. I've only seen him a couple of times since that morning before the memorial, and even when we manage to be together, it isn't the same. If he isn't being distant and weird, he's talking about weapons training or battle drills, and all I can hear is the little voice in the back of my head reminding me that this is all my fault. The marines wouldn't have to train like this if I'd done the job Grandpa promoted me to do. He was counting on me to help him negotiate with Tarn, and I started a war instead.

I guess that's hyperbolic. It's not a war yet. We haven't seen any sign of the Sorrow since the night Tarn almost killed me and Shelby, but we will. Shelby insists that it's not a question of *if* they attack us. It's a question of when. Since we can't trust the shields anymore, she's got two-man armed patrols walking the perimeters of both settlements twenty-two hours a day.

As Leela has pointed out, repeatedly, Tarn started this by attacking me. But I'm the one who took it upon myself to tell him about the destruction of Earth. I should have gone with my first instinct and called Grandpa and Mom. They could have formally requested asylum, instead of hysterically telling Tarn that he was stuck with us because we have nowhere else to go. But I just had to do it myself. Now I've done worse than break my promise to Tarn that we'd leave. I've turned us into enemies.

I'll never forget the look on Grandpa's face when he came into the medical center that night and saw the bruises on my throat. He was so angry. I've never seen him like that, out of control, almost.

And Grandpa's not the only one who seems out of control. Dad is angry all the time. He does nothing but argue with everyone about everything. But that's better than Mom. She spends all her time in her new second-in-command office doing paperwork, and when she isn't working, she's sleeping. I don't think she's said more than two or three words at the same time in weeks. It's like she's disappearing, a little bit at a time.

I tried to talk to Dr. Kao about it, but all he'd tell me was that he's working with her and I shouldn't worry.

Don't worry.

Everyone keeps saying that. Grandpa even told me

not to worry about Tarn and the Sorrow, which is just ridiculous.

Tarn fried our shields with his *voice*. If the Sorrow can overload our shield projectors like that, then they can definitely use focused sound to destroy other vital stuff. Like our brains. My eardrums were both ruptured by Tarn's battle cry. Doc thinks Tarn could have killed me with that scream, if he'd wanted to.

We should have realized it was possible. Sorrow Givers used their healing chant to repair injuries that my human doctors thought I'd have to live with for the rest of my life. That means, at a minimum, they can rearrange molecules and stimulate cell growth with sound. Why did we never wonder whether they could use sound to kill as well as to heal? Why did *I* never think to ask Tarn what else they could do with sonic manipulation?

Just another entry on the list of Joanna's potentially deadly mistakes.

I offered to give up my commission after the incident with Tarn. Grandpa wouldn't even consider it. He told me I'd earn my pips in other ways.

I want to earn them. I do. But I keep volunteering for piloting assignments instead. Nobody turns me down—we need to make as many trips up to *Prairie* and *Pioneer* in orbit as we can to get all the survivors and supplies back to the surface. But running endless missions into orbit isn't what I was promoted to do. I'm supposed to be helping Grandpa understand Tau so he can negotiate with the Sorrow, not leaving the planet every chance I get.

The problem is, I feel like *I* don't understand Tau anymore. No. There's no point in lying to myself. I understand Tau. I'm just terrified of it. I remember when the intense strangeness of its beauty was thrilling. It wasn't that long ago. Now everywhere I look, all I see is disaster and death. For the Sorrow. For the phytoraptors. For us.

And I'm afraid. I'm so afraid, and I don't know how to stop.

I roll onto my side and squeeze my eyes shut. I'm taking the *Trailblazer* back up to the *Prairie* at 0530 for another load of raw. I need to be well rested.

I lie there for a few minutes. I can feel sleep tugging at my brain, but my body is still tense. Clinging to wakefulness. I really don't want to dream again.

The nightmares aren't just about Tarn attacking us. My brain comes up with creative new mash-ups every night, mixing and matching sense memories of burning of solar radiation with the sound of Miguel's body hitting the rocks after Sunflower the phytoraptor tackled him off a cliff and the look on Teddy's face, seconds before I pressed a button and sent him to his death. The medley of fear and anger and guilt feels like acid, dissolving me slowly from the inside out.

I'd rather be tired.

I sit up and grab my boots.

Beth doesn't comment as I slide them on and leave our makeshift bedroom. She knows it's better this way. She can sleep and I can avoid my nightmares.

I slip out of the greenhouse. Low clouds are crowded into the sky, blocking out the stars and turning the moons into dull smudges. It's so dark that the pale glow of stand-by mode seeping from the cabins around me seems bright.

I get new clothes and brush my teeth and hair. That uses up twelve minutes. I've got hours before launch, and I haven't a clue what to do with them.

I shiver as I step out of the bathrooms and zip up my new parka. Winter got at least this cold back at GFP HQ on Earth, but I don't remember it feeling this harsh. Of course, I spent a lot less time aimlessly wandering around in the way-too-early-to-call-it-morning back then.

I walk down to the memorial stone. Someone has sealed a flex to the rock, below the carved names. You can use it to scroll through Beth's list of people who died on Earth. Actually, it's not just Beth's list anymore. People have been adding to it. I guess I should, too.

My eyes drift up to the names carved on the stone instead.

Cadet Theodore Watson.

Teddy's name is right at the top of the list. What a stupid honor—first guy on a list of billions of dead people. I can almost hear him laughing at the thought.

The Ranger team's names are carved right after his. *Dr. Rylan Pasha. Dr. Amahle Obasi. Dr. Vitor Sousa.* They should probably come first. We don't know exactly when they died, but it must have been a least a year before Teddy. Maybe we should add Dr. Brown's name to the stone. We never found her body, but Ord shot her point-blank after she changed sides and helped us take the Stage Three virus back. There's no way she survived that.

I check my flex again.

Still way too early.

Maybe I'll go mess around with the *Vulcan*.

Grandpa started rebuilding the wrecked Ranger ship two days after the memorial service. He said it was just a way to keep his hands busy, but I think he knew we all needed . . . something. A goal that wasn't just survival. And he was right. Chief Ganeshalingam joined him, after her shift was up. The next day, Chris and I decided to help them and found the little ship swarming with pioneers and marines. Since then, I think almost everyone has contributed a few hours here and there.

The *Vulcan* is nearly spaceworthy again. It would be nice to help finish her up, but the little scout ship is at River Bend, and the first jeep won't head out there for hours. Before, I would have just walked. It's only half a klick. But with raptors wandering around out there and the prospect of a Sorrow attack hanging over our heads, I don't dare.

I sort of wish the Sorrow would just get it over with. The waiting is killing me. But if—*when* they come, they're going to *actually* kill people. Marines.

Jay.

No. I'm not going to think that way. I can't. It makes me feel too helpless.

I stare through the shield, into the inky night shadows

of the orchid forest on the other side. It would be so easy to walk to River Bend. I could just carve a portal and—

Boom!

The shield flashes and crackles as something big slams into it. I shriek, stumbling back as a massive phytoraptor with a crown of thorns rears up and drags its huge claws over the shield. It hoots with glee as crackling light bursts in the wake of its swipe, showing off a mouthful of fangs.

I clamp down on another scream. There's no reason to get hysterical. It can't get through the shield. But reminding myself of that does nothing to combat the surge of terror adrenaline that thing just sent shooting through my body.

Being, I remind myself. *Being.*

A hand grabs my elbow.

I scream.

"Chill, Hotshot," Jay says, gently pulling me around to look at him. "It's me."

I blow out a shaky breath. "Hi."

Jay's got a helmet and flak jacket on over his uniform, and he's carrying a rifle along with his stun gun and side-arm. He must be on patrol duty. If I'd known, I would have gone looking for him. But I didn't. That stings.

"Hey," Jay says, slinging his rifle over his shoulder and pulling me close. "You're shaking, Jo. Are you okay?"

"No," I say. It comes out almost whiny. I hate that. I shake off the irrational terror and try again. "Yes. I'm okay. Stupid, but okay."

"What were you doing out here?" he asks.

"Avoiding nightmares," I say.

Jay squeezes my shoulders. "Tarn again?"

I nod into his shoulder. "Amongst other things. I don't know why I can't shake them."

"You got hurt by someone you thought was a friend," he says gently. "That's nightmare-worthy."

I rest my head on his chest and stare through the warping lens of the force field. I guess he's right, but that doesn't make me feel better.

"Hey," he says, "I got good news tonight. The LT is putting together a special team to deal with the phytoraptors, and she put me on it."

"Deal with?" I pull back, uneasy. "What does that mean?"

He shrugs. "Not a clue. I just got added to the training group." He grins. "But it's a promotion. Gotta keep up with you, *Ensign*."

"Don't you think you should know? Before you agree to do it?" I snap, unreasonable anxiety whiplashing up my spine.

"No," Jay says, instantly irritated. "Because I trust my commanding officers. The LT knows the phytoraptors are sentient beings, so I am gonna give her the benefit of the doubt. Would have thought you'd do the same for me, since I nearly got myself killed helping you save them."

Dismay crashes over me. "Jay. I didn't mean to imply—"

"But you did."

We just stand there for a moment, looking at each other and not looking at each other at the same time. I hate this. It's like the ground between us is cracking open, pulling us a couple centimeters farther apart every day.

"I'm sorry," I say, finally. "I know you guys are just trying to protect us. But Shelby makes me nervous. I don't know why."

"I get it," Jay says. "Shelby's a really different kind of person than you're used to. Different priorities." He shrugs. "She's also kind of an asshole. But she knows what she's doing." He flashes me a quick little smile. "Raptor training starts today. I'll tell you all about it after we run the gauntlet with your folks tonight."

My face goes hot. Grandpa decided Jay and I need to have dinner with him, and Mom and Dad and Beth. He says he wants to *get to know my young man*. I was embarrassed to even ask Jay, but he seems to find the whole thing amusing. Of course.

"So," he says, gentle mischief sparking in his voice. "You think being on the special raptor team will make the admiral cut me some slack at dinner?"

"You don't have to come, you know," I blurt out.

Jay raises a sardonic eyebrow. "The admiral invited me to dinner with his family. Pretty sure I have to go." He snags my hand then and presses it to his lips. "Besides, I'm looking forward to being grilled mercilessly by your family."

"You are?"

He nods.

"Why?"

His amused grin dissolves into a low laugh. "It's part of the thing."

"The 'Watson family takes time out of saving the species to embarrass Joanna' thing?"

"Nah," he says, rubbing his thumb across my palm in these little circles that somehow manage to untangle all the anxious knots in the back of my neck. "The *us* thing. And I like the us thing."

"Oh," I say, all the fear and embarrassment momentarily evaporating into a cloud of hopeless happy. "Yeah," I say. "Me too."

"It's kinda gross how cute you guys are, ya know."

I twist to see Private Ryan Hart sauntering toward us. Hart is the youngest member of the *Prairie* squadron—just a couple of years older than we are. He and Jay have gotten to be friends. Jay even brought him along to the greenhouse, the one time we all managed to hang out since the survivors showed up.

"Are tough guys supposed use words like *cute*?" Jay fires back, slinging his arm around my shoulders, unabashed.

"Artificial gender constructs are so twenty-first century, bro." Hart chuckles, crouching next to a pylon a few meters up the shield and pressing his flex to its casing. "Power levels ninety percent," he says, taking the reading from his flex.

"Good enough," Jay says.

"Till the glow worms show up," Hart agrees amiably.

The easy warmth of the conversation curdles.

"The what?" I ask, hoping I heard that wrong.

Hart and Jay exchange a look that makes me want to pretend I never asked the question. I think I already know the answer, but I can't let it go.

"What's a glow worm?" I ask again.

"It's just a joke," Hart says. "The LT's way of keeping 'em from being too intimidating."

"You mean the Sorrow," I say. "Lieutenant Shelby calls them glow worms?"

"Yeah," Jay says. "She does." He doesn't drop his arm from around my shoulders, but the comfortable fit of our bodies is gone.

"It's not a disrespect thing," Hart insists.

Jay snorts a *yeah right*.

"No, seriously," Hart says. "I know it seems kinda gross and whatnot, but it's tactical. Y'all came to this weird-ass place on purpose. But most of us never imagined leaving Earth, much less having to fight aliens with superpowers."

"We're the aliens, man," Jay says.

Hart shrugs. "You know what I mean. We're pretty much scared as hell all the time, and the LT is just trying to lighten the mood. That's all."

Tarn's face flashes before my eyes, bone and muscle painted by the furious glow of the blood pumping under his transparent skin as he loomed over Shelby and me.

Glow worm.

Would thinking of him that way stop the nightmares?

I don't think I could, even if it helped. I know who he is inside the transparent skin.

"They're just like us," I say.

"Hell," Jay says. "Probably just as scared as us, too."

"Of us fearsome aliens from outer space?" Hart quips.

Jay makes a face. "Are you saying I'm not fearsome?"

"Yes," Hart fires back jovially. "Yes, I am."

Jay grins. "Fair." He checks his flex. "We'd better get back to it, man. Gonna miss our check-in."

"Oh. Right," I say. "Sorry."

Jay hugs me. "I'm never sorry to see you."

I blush.

Hart makes melodramatic gagging noises.

Jay ignores him. "I'll see you tonight, Hotshot. Fly good." He starts up the perimeter again. Hart follows a few steps, but then stops and turns back.

"Hope I didn't offend you, Jo," he calls. "I really didn't mean to be an asshole."

"I know," I say. "It's okay. I get it."

He grins. "Good. Wouldn't wanna land Lim in the dog-house."

"But you're fine with making me late for the LT?" Jay calls back to him.

Hart throws me an exaggerated eye roll and calls back, "Coming, Mother."

With a little salute, he jogs after Jay.

I stand there at the edge of the shield for a long time after they're gone, watching the moons set. Hart is wrong about at least one thing. The *Prairie* squad and the survivors aren't the only ones who are scared. We all are.

Tarn's face floods my mind again, but not the furious Tarn who haunts my dreams. Tarn, staring up at the landing. At the second shuttle. The end of all hope his world would return to normal. The aching familiarity of his despair crashes through me.

Mom's voice trails through my mind.

I don't see a way forward that isn't hideous.

I didn't understand what she meant then. Not really. I never imagined this.

But I see it now. And I can't live with it.

I won't.

Glow worm.

I have to do something. Change something.

And I think I know where to start.

EIGHT

Two hours later, I'm lying on the port wing of delta flyer, installing a new conductor in the rotor control system. We have enough flyers now that they need names, but nobody has the energy to do better than their boring official designations.

I have to twist at a weird angle solder the contact wires, so I'm sweating even though the sun is still just a promise of light on the eastern horizon.

Beth's voice intrudes on the early-morning quiet.

"What are you doing?"

"There was a short in the solar-collection system," I say as I double-check my weld and snap the panel closed.

I can almost hear her eyes roll. "You're being deliberately obtuse."

"Fine," I say, pulling up the diagnostic app on my flex.

"I traded assignments with Leela."

That came out almost as casually as I wanted it to.

"Joanna—"

A long line of green lights pops up on my screen. "We're good to go," I say, cutting her off before she can finish her thought.

I can feel Beth studying me as I slide down to hang by my hands from the end of the wing and drop to the ground, but I ignore her not-subtle unspoken questions and duck into the flyer.

Beth follows me in.

"Why would you give up an orbital trip for survey duty?" she demands as I tether into the pilot's chair.

"Flying is flying," I say, trying to keep my voice light.

"That's not even factually correct," Beth says, "much less believable in the context of your personality and history."

In other words, she knows me too well to believe me. Which is fair, but that doesn't mean I'm going to answer her question. There's no way to say *I need to fall in love with this planet again* that isn't just going to sound sentimental and ridiculous. Especially to Beth.

I plant my hands on the nav app. They're shaking. My heart is thudding in my chest.

This is ridiculous. I've flown into the Diamond Range dozens of times. I could do this trip in my sleep. Except all I do in my sleep these days is scream.

That's when it hits me that I've barely left the shield perimeter since the *Prairie* appeared over Tau's orbital horizon, three weeks ago. I've been to space multiple times. But not out there. I haven't even walked through the orchid forest to River Bend. Not once.

I'm not afraid of Tau.

I'm not afraid of Tau.

I'm not afraid of Tau.

But my hands are still shaking, and I haven't even closed the rear doors yet.

"We going or what?"

Lieutenant Shelby's voice snaps me back into the moment. I twist to look back as she climbs through the rear hatch and collapses into a chair in the back row.

"We're about to take off, Lieutenant Shelby," I say, letting irritation burn away my nerves.

"Be weird of you two to hang out in here, otherwise," she replies, tethering in.

"The lieutenant insists on accompanying me on surveying trips," Beth tells me, like Shelby isn't sitting right behind us. "You would think she has better things to do, but apparently not."

Shelby smirks. "Do you really want to tiptoe through the plant monsters without a security detail?"

"Yes," Beth says.

Shelby barks a laugh. "Well, we can't always get what we want, Einstein."

Beth huffs out a sigh. "I'm a botanist. Mendel is a more apt comparison."

"I'm not known for my historical accuracy," Shelby says. "Hit it, Junior. We've got places to be and attack-flora to stare at."

I shoot a look at Beth. She shrugs.

I guess we're taking Shelby with us.

My brain churns as I request clearance from Ground Control. Why is Shelby really here? Beth is right. Even if we needed a security detail, Shelby has better things to do. Especially since Leela was meant to be flying this mission, not me. Leela has combat training. And there's no way Shelby could have known I swapped assignments with her.

So what is the lieutenant actually doing here?

Mom's voice on the comm line interrupts my thoughts. "You're a go, Delta Flyer."

I press my hands to the nav app and lift. A little rush of pleasure pouring through my fingertips as the flyer leaps into the air at my command. I can still feel the jittery fear underneath, but I try to focus on the joy. I've missed this. Flying space shuttles might be more challenging, but it isn't as much fun.

"Three-sixty mode, please," I ask the computer.

"Certainly, Joanna," it replies, and the steel-gray Tau morning floods in around us. The Diamond Range looks icy in this light, the prismatic effect of its crystal cliffs dulled by the cloud cover. There's real snow draped over the higher peaks, and the veins of green that twist through the crystal spires and cliffs are darker and browner.

"Footage in the report doesn't do it justice, does it?" Shelby says as we soar over the rolling foothills and up among the jagged crags.

At her question, I risk a quick look back to Shelby. She's still sprawled in her chair, but her eyes are alive with what seems to be genuine awe.

"No," Beth says quietly. "It doesn't."

According to the flight plan, we're headed for the first raptor nest my friends and I stumbled on, months ago. Beth spends a lot of time there. The raptors who learned sign language from our scouts are part of this group. They've been teaching the others. Their nest is our best hope for understanding the species.

The Maze Plateau rears up ahead of us. I push my hands up on the controls, gaining altitude so that we soar over it. It's huge, and so high that you can see the sky bleeding into space from here. The plateau below is laced with narrow box canyons, many of which aren't much bigger than crevasses. It's hard to believe Jay flew us right through the middle of that thing and we survived.

Shelby leans forward in her seat as we shoot out over Angel Valley, drinking in the view. The expanse of green grass is unbroken now that the wreckage of our first shuttle, the *Wagon*, has been recycled. In the gray predawn, it looks like an inland sea crashing against the cliffs.

I'm surprised Shelby is so affected. I didn't think she cared about stuff like natural beauty. But I guess I don't know her very well, after all.

We swing wide over the valley and climb through the steep, intertwined ravines and cliffs that cut through the gray-green canopy of solace trees. We're high enough to see the ocean beyond, still dark despite the fading dawn sky.

I accelerate, pushing the flyer to full speed as we shoot down the western side of the softening mountain range. Bob's nest is in a deep ravine that's hidden in a long stretch of solace tree forest, a few kilometers from the place where the mountains melt into the turquoise ocean beyond.

The sun is just cresting the mountains as we settle onto a clear, flat patch at the edge of the ravine. As I power down the flyer, the nest explodes with light.

Phytoraptor nests are designed to trap and refract sunlight so that the raptors can absorb it. Meter-high pillars built out of crystal shards and now salvaged human scrap metal and solar panel pieces are strategically placed around the ravine. These intricately balanced structures splinter the light of the rising sun, breaking it apart and weaving it together again in a delicate fractal web that arches over the nest. It doesn't matter how many times I see these cathedrals of light. They don't get less astounding. Especially considering that the beings who designed this are not, so far as we can tell, even tool using.

But maybe it's wrong to judge them on the spectrum of our own evolution. Maybe tool using isn't a goal the phytoraptors ever need to aspire to. Our tools destroyed our whole planet. Not like I'd want to give up my flex or live without the chance to ever fly or go to space or anything. But it's something to think about.

"Perfect timing," I say.

"Actually, we're early," Beth says, without looking up from the flex she's working on. "I calculated our travel time under the assumption that Leela would be my pilot. Your tendency to use manual control shaved almost twenty minutes off that estimate. But I can use the extra time to check my spectrometers."

"Extra time?" I say, my brain catching up with what she's saying. "You mean you're planning to interact with them? Awake?"

"Nope," Shelby says. "She isn't. I did not bring enough guns for playtime in the carnivorous alien vegetable patch."

"Asleep or awake, phytoraptors aren't interested in humans unless we threaten them," Beth says. "We will be perfectly safe."

Shelby bursts out laughing. "Girlie, it's only mostly safe to step out of your damn cabin in the morning on this planet."

"I wouldn't think safety was such a high priority for someone in your line of work," Beth says, untethering from her chair and starting toward the rear hatch.

"Clearly, you don't know much about my line of work," Shelby fires back, bouncing to her feet. "And at the moment, my job is to keep you and little sis here from being eaten by those beasties. And the only way I can do that without risking my own hide is for you to stay put."

Beth expresses a wealth of irritation in a single sigh. "They are classified as *Chorulux phytoraptor*, but we commonly refer to these *sentient* beings as raptors. Not 'beasties.' And, assuming you can contain your anxiety, I should be able accomplish my current goal without interacting with them at all."

"It takes a lot more than some hyperactive houseplants to make me anxious, *Mendel*," Shelby grumbles.

"That's probably for the best," Beth says. Then she reaches past Shelby and smacks the door controls. The hatch swings open and the ramp unfolds.

"If you'll excuse me," Beth says, raising a pointed eyebrow at Shelby.

Shelby rolls her eyes but steps aside. "Be my guest. But if you get eaten, I'm not gonna be the one to tell your grandfather."

I untether and follow Beth out into the blue-green dawn. She strides down the ramp and crosses to the nearest prismatic spire, but I don't make it past the top of the ramp.

You can hardly even see the raptors in the nest from here. Just the dome of light and the thick solace forest around the ravine. It's so quiet. Quiet enough that I can hear my heart thundering frantically in my ears. Every muscle in my body is locked tight.

I take a deliberate breath, pulling in air and letting it go, trying to exhale the irrational fear. And it is irrational. The raptors are asleep. They could care less about us. And there's no way the Sorrow can know we're up here.

Unless they're watching the Landing. Unless they followed us.

Stop it, Joanna.

The Sorrow do have flyers—Dr. Brown gave them the 3D printers from the *Vulcan* and taught them to build vehicles and equipment. Including guns. But we'd have noticed a strange flyer following us. It's just us and the raptors up here.

Shelby elbows past me and strides to the bottom of the ramp. She stops there and scans the area, her fingers restlessly toying with the safety catch on her rifle. She's anxious, no matter what she says. She's also heavily armed—she's got a pistol and a stun gun holstered on her belt. Whatever her reason for being here, this mission has her on edge.

Maybe that means I should stay in the flyer.

Or maybe it just means Emily Shelby doesn't belong here. She doesn't even try to hide her xenophobic tendencies. She would never have been selected for an E&P if it hadn't been the end of the world. But I was raised for exploration and pioneering. I don't fear things I don't understand.

At least, I never used to. I've done way more dangerous things on Tau than this. I've walked through this nest before, more than once.

For a second, I can almost see Miguel standing at the edge of the cliffs. Grinning. Triumphant. Oblivious to Sunflower charging toward him, their ruff of yellow blossoms glowing in the rising sun. I don't want to see this again, but my memory doesn't care. Closing my eyes doesn't help. I can still see Miguel dying.

I might have trained for life here, but that doesn't make me safe. It doesn't make anyone safe.

Since when do I care?

I half run down the ramp.

"Guess I'm not the only one who needs to contain my anxiety," Shelby says dryly, without turning to look back at me.

An answering quip goes dry and sticky in the back of my throat as my eyes catch on a vivid burst of yellow, only just visible in the ravine below. Sunflower is down there.

Miguel's last smile pops into my head again. He opens his mouth to call out to me in victory, but the vicious *crunch* of his body hitting the rocks comes out instead.

I gasp, taking an inadvertent step backward.

"Seen some nasty shit up here, haven't you?" Shelby says, quietly interrupting the rising tide of my silent panic.

"Yeah," I say, sloshing through the memories to string words together. "You read about it in the reports?"

She shakes her head. "Nah. But I know that face you're making."

She looks up, her gaze drifting through the knotty solace tree branches that tangle around the flyer, their big round leaves occasionally licking insects out of the air.

"Pretty trees. Remind me of the big ol' oaks, back home." She makes a face at the word. "Habit is a funny thing. That place hasn't been home for twenty years."

"You grew up somewhere in North America, right?" I guess, from her accent.

"Mississippi," she says. "Of course, you probably don't even know where that is."

"It's part of the depopulated zone now," I say. "Isn't it?"

"It was plenty populated when we were kids." A little smile crests her lips. It's startlingly gentle. I almost wouldn't recognize her. "Joined the IntGov marines because they saved our butts, back in the day."

"You survived the flu?" I say, more pieces sliding into the puzzle that is Lieutenant Emily Shelby. The flu epidemics that hit after the Storm Wars were devastating. I thought everyone in depopulated zones had died.

She nods.

"*We* survived. They separated us for a while. Couple of the real little ones like Hart even got adopted. But we swore we'd join up, as soon as we could. Be a family again."

"'We'? You mean, your whole squadron . . ."

She nods. "We've been to hell and back. And now we're

on a goddamn alien planet. But we survived. And we'll survive this, too. And so will you." She raises her voice. "Unless your sister turns us into a morning snack for the phytoraptors when they wake up."

"If you're scared, you can always wait in the flyer," Beth calls back without looking up from the notes she's taking on her flex.

"Your sister is kind of a bitch, you know that?" Shelby says. "I like it."

With that, she strolls over to Beth's spot on the cliff. I watch her go.

Shelby looks . . . I don't know, different somehow. Like she's been out of focus this whole time and now I can see the flecks of gray in her blond braid and the nanofilament tape patching the heels of her boots. But it's more than just noticing details. It's like my brain recognizes her now, in a way it didn't before.

"You might wanna stick to your inside voice," Shelby says as she reaches Beth's vantage point. "Avoid waking up the murder grove down there."

"We landed a flyer five meters from their nest without attracting their attention," Beth points out coolly. "Our rep-artee is hardly a concern."

"Shucks," Shelby says. "I didn't know we were having a repartee."

"Well, it hardly qualifies as a conversation," Beth says, noting something in her flex. "But if you're so concerned about waking the nest, perhaps you should keep your thoughts to yourself."

But Shelby isn't listening anymore. Something down in the ravine has caught her attention.

"Are those juveniles?" she says, pointing into the nest.

"Yes," Beth says.

I hurry to join them and peer down into the ravine.

"Oh." Joy claws through me, splintering into longing and regret as it rakes through my fear. There are a dozen almost identical little phytoraptors crouching in the shallow river. They're tiny. The huge white flowers that bloom from their spines look sort of like the folding solar sails on Grandpa's boat back on Earth. Which is exactly what they are, I realize. Big petals to suck in as much light as possible for their growing bodies.

"They're . . . cute," I say, surprised. Not so much that baby raptors are cute, but that I feel so fuzzy about it.

"And someday they'll be killers," Shelby says. "Just like Mommy and Daddy."

Bob is planted at one end of the tiny garden of baby raptors. Sunflower is perched at the other. Will the deadly raptor let Bob teach their babies sign language, so that they can talk to us? Or will Sunflower teach them to hunt humans, just like the raptors hunt the Sorrow?

Maybe they'll do both.

"Oh come on," I say, shoving the thought away. "They're babies."

Shelby rolls her eyes. "I'll never understand why people are so impressed with procreation."

"The propagation of life is a biological imperative," Beth says, a gentle awe lingering under the clinical words.

"I must be wired backward," Shelby snarks, patting her pistol. "I've always been more interested in ending life than multiplying it."

But Shelby is studying the swaying patch of tiny raptors just as intently as Beth and I are. No. I take it back. Beth isn't watching the raptors at all. She's watching Shelby. She has a weird look on her face. Calculating.

Without looking down, Beth folds the flex she's been working on and tucks it into the pocket of her parka. Then she unwraps a second flex from her wrist, casually letting it unfold into tablet mode. If I hadn't seen her do it, I would never have known it isn't her original tablet.

My brain churns, trying to come up with a good reason for my sister to be doing sleight-of-hand tricks with her flex. I can only think of one: Beth is hiding her data.

"Learn something new every day, don'tcha?" Shelby says, cutting through my speculation. She nods to Beth's flex. "You get footage of those things?"

"Obviously," Beth says. "Given that they are my mission objective."

"Well, sync your 'mission objective' with the shared drives, hmm?" Shelby says.

"That is standard procedure," Beth says, making a show

of swiping at the new flex like she's closing an app before folding it around her wrist. The tiny hairs on the back of my neck prickle. Beth didn't have any apps open.

My sister is meant to be collecting vital data on these dangerous predators so we can protect the survivors. Instead, she's hiding it. Sabotaging our team. Our species. And Shelby knows it. That's why she's really here. It has nothing to do with protecting Beth.

Shelby's trying to catch her in the act.

NINE

"Don't we have other spectrometers to check?" I ask, grabbing Beth's hand. I tow her away without waiting for an answer, dragging her around the edge of the ravine.

When we get out of Shelby's earshot, Beth hisses, "Can you at least attempt to be subtle? Lieutenant Shelby is suspicious enough as it is."

"Why are you hiding your data?" I demand, trying to drop my pace back to something that will pass as casual.

"I would have thought it was obvious," Beth fires back.

"No," I say. "It isn't obvious. It's sabotage. And Shelby knows."

"She's not subtle, either," Beth snaps, crouching beside another light-catching pillar and adjusting the tiny spectrometer planted at its base. "But she is observant. Protecting even a fraction of my results has been tediously difficult since she arrived."

"Since she . . . you mean you've been hiding data since before the survivors got here?" I gasp, startled.

"Of course I have!" Beth jumps to her feet and turns on me, glaring. "I was nearly responsible for a genocide, because the ISA lied to us about this planet and our mission on it. Why would I ever trust them again?"

With that, she strides toward the next light catcher.

"You're talking about Grandpa," I protest, chasing after her. "And Mom. They *are* the ISA now.'"

Beth stops and turns to stare at me, wide-eyed. "Joanna. Mom lied to us. For years."

"She was ordered to—"

"Being under orders is no excuse," Beth says. "Even Mom acknowledges that. If not for you, those lies would have made me responsible for a genocide, if not a complete ecological collapse."

"Okay. Fine. But Grandpa is in charge now."

"And I don't trust him either." Beth's response is so rushed, it sounds like a single word.

We stare at each other. She looks as surprised that she said that as I am to hear it.

"Why don't you trust Grandpa?" I ask quietly.

She throws a look to Shelby. "You really want to get into this now?"

I want to say *yes*. Badly. And for some reason that makes

me angry. "You know what? No. I don't. I don't care. We've got thousands of untrained civilians coming down soon. We need your data to protect—"

"Do we really?" Beth snaps, cutting me off. "What do you think Lieutenant Shelby is going to do with the data on phytoraptor babies that will protect the survivors?"

I don't want to answer that question. It's too horrible to contemplate.

I look from Beth to Sunflower, swaying in the sunlight beside the little crop of baby raptors. The sound of Miguel's body hitting the ravine floor thuds wetly through my brain again.

He died because the ISA kept vital information from us. Now Beth is doing the same thing to the team. What if she's protecting the raptors at the expense of the survivors? What other horrors might come of this?

"You ladies decide to take a tandem crap or something?" Shelby calls across the ravine.

To all of our surprise, Sunflower's head snaps up, as though roused by the sound of Shelby's voice.

Fear catapults through me, its momentum shoving me back toward the flyer before I have a chance to think.

"Don't be ridiculous," Beth says, catching my arm. "Just stand still. The raptor will settle again if not provoked."

But Sunflower doesn't settle. Their ruff of yellow petals stands out around their head in a stiff halo as they rear up on their hind legs. Claws slide out of their huge fingers and they yawn wide, showing their fangs.

"Unusual," Beth says calmly, like Sunflower isn't totally capable of scaling that cliff and killing us all before we can make it back to the flyer.

But then logic pokes a hole in the gauzy fear swaddling my brain. Sunflower isn't looking at us. Or at Shelby. Their eyes are on the other side of the narrow ravine, where a thick tangle of solace trees is growing halfway down the sharp slope. At first, I don't see what they're glaring at. Then I catch a flare of light in the shadows between the trees.

Two Sorrow Takers in hooded black robes are leaning out over the sloping cliff face. Each has a heavy staff in one hand and something small in the other that catches at the newly risen sun, throwing rainbow sparks.

As I watch, they toss whatever it is out over the river and onto the crop of little raptors below.

Sunflower screams, throwing themselves between their babies and the glittering dust. The big raptor's outrage explodes into pain as the prismatic stuff hits them and opalescent white blood wells all over their broad back. Whatever that stuff is, it's sharp enough to do serious damage just floating on the breeze. It would have shredded the babies' petals.

Bob is waking up now, too, as are other raptors around them. Groaning and shrieking in protest as they drag their sleep-logged limbs from the dirt to try to help Sunflower.

Sunflower doesn't wait for them. They rip themselves from the soil, streaks of white blood spraying out behind them as they hurl themselves up the cliff toward the Takers.

The two Sorrow bolt, disappearing into the thick trees. Sunflower is right behind them, leaving Bob to care for the babies down below.

"Get back to the flyer!" Shelby bellows, tearing after Sunflower and the Takers.

"What are you—"

I don't get all the way through the mostly rhetorical question before Beth bolts after Shelby. I don't know what Shelby thinks this is going to accomplish, but there's no way I'm letting my sister run into a mess of angry raptors and Sorrow on her own.

My boots slip-slide over the rocky soil, my feet almost shooting out from under me every few steps as I follow Beth up a steep wash between a pair of gently rounded hills. Shelby is out of sight, but I can hear her ahead of us, crashing through the underbrush. We crest the wash and half slide down the other side.

The rocky ground gets softer the farther downhill we get. The trees are thinning out and getting scraggly, too.

The ground climbs again, so steeply we have to scramble on our hands and feet for a few meters. Then we explode over a ridge, and bright turquoise water fills the horizon.

This is the beach where we found the Ranger team's abandoned hot spot. The sugary white dunes are framed by crumbling gray-white cliffs. Shelby's dark silhouette, clambering across the white expanse, wavers as light refracts off the sand around her.

There are no Takers or raptors anywhere to be seen.

"Where—"

"Shhhh!"

Beth widens her eyes pointedly, then looks up and to the left.

I follow her gaze to one of the scrubby trees huddled where the dirt fades into the sand. Its branches are moving restlessly, shifting under the weight of what has to be a camouflaged raptor.

"Sunflower won't follow us onto the beach," Beth says, quietly, "as long as we don't run or display fear."

"Oh sure," I say, digging my nails into my palms. "Why would we do that?"

But the huge raptor makes no move to follow as we trudge across the sand to Shelby. The fine white dunes suck at my boots with every step, their heat burning through my soles despite the biting chill of the air.

"You two are distinctly lacking in survival skills," Shelby snaps as we catch up with her.

"We're not the ones who decided to chase a phytoraptor and two armed Sorrow," I point out.

"Yeah, well, takes one to know one," Shelby growls, hitching her rifle over her shoulder and shaking out her flex.

"I don't see any evidence of your quarry," Beth points out.

Shelby snorts. "If you're using that ten-dollar word to

describe the black-robed dudes, they disappeared into those cliffs with a buncha gray-robed assholes who were makin' off with our equipment."

"Equipment? What . . . oh. The hot spot?" My eyes dart to a rock formation just offshore that used to have an antenna jutting from its highest point. "What would the Sorrow want with the old Ranger hot spot?"

"They're trying to cripple us," Shelby says, pulling up her camera app and increasing magnification to 100 percent so that she can see the cliff face in detail. "Keep us out of network up here."

"Doubtful," Beth says as Shelby pans the cliffs. "Tarn has a satellite phone—he knows that hot spots are simply conveniences."

"Guess they're just being jerks, then," Shelby snarls, her eyes still on her flex.

"No. The Sorrow don't leave their caves unless it's absolutely necessary," I say, information sliding in and out of focus in my head. "And they don't just have sat phones. They have recyclers and 3D printers. They could definitely build their own hot spots if they wanted to."

"Jee-zus wept," Shelby breathes, leaping over my train of thought to a new one. "Those things are recycling our gear to print guns."

"You don't have any reason to assume that," I protest.

She arches an eyebrow at me. "Oh yeah? So what exactly do you think they're doing with that equipment?"

Possibilities yawn out like an airless vacuum around me, crushing the last of the hope from my bones. Every single one leads to the same conclusion.

War.

"Beings," Beth says, breaking the tense quiet.

"Excuse me?" Shelby tosses the words over her shoulder as she paces up the beach, still panning her zoomed-in camera over the cliffs.

"The Sorrow aren't *things*," Beth says, "even less so than the phytoraptors are *beasties*. They're a highly sophisticated culture of sentient *beings*."

"Who are stealing our shit so they can recycle it into weapons and kill us all," Shelby retorts.

"All the more reason not to underestimate—"

"Gotcha!"

Shelby bolts for the cliffs. By the time we catch up, she's already hauling herself up the soft cliff face toward a narrow tunnel entrance five or six meters overhead.

"That tunnel appears to be artificial," Beth says.

"It'd have to be," Shelby huffs, deliberately sending a shower of dirt clumps down on us as she kicks out a new toehold in the cliff. "No natural cave system is going to last for long in ground like this. Too soft."

"And yet you're planning to go inside?" Beth calls after her.

"Yup," she says. "I'd tell y'all to stay down there, but I know how you feel about following instructions."

Beth throws me a questioning look.

"Yeah," I say, responding to the unspoken query. "But I want to see."

"Me too," she says.

I'm a stronger climber, so I go first. I can feel the cliff crumbling under my boots as I scramble upward, but I keep going, ignoring the sparks of fear and adrenaline dancing up my spine.

I drag myself over the lip of the tunnel. The white bubble of Shelby's flex light is already a few meters ahead of us in the darkness.

"There's Danger Twin one," Shelby says, impatience dancing in her voice. "And . . . Danger Twin two."

Ignoring Shelby, I grab my sister's hand as she scrambles over the lip of the tunnel and haul her the rest of the way up.

"They must be printing laser drills," Shelby says as we activate the flashlight settings on our flexes and catch up with her. "Walls are smooth."

"Not necessarily," Beth says. "They may be able to tunnel like this without any technology at all. Remember, the Sorrow have biological abilities that far exceed our own."

"Yeah, well, I have a bigger gun," Shelby drawls. But the bravado doesn't quite hide the fear in her voice.

She points into the darkness ahead. "What the hell is that?"

I peer past her to see a distant glimmer of bright pink and burnt orange.

"Solace tree roots," I say. "I think."

"Looks more like Vegas," she mutters, continuing up the tunnel.

"The Ranger team classified them as *Chorulux neon*," Beth says. "Presumably because they shared your sentiment."

We emerge into a high-ceilinged cavern filled with tangled root clusters that drip color and light from the darkness above.

"Just when you think you've seen weird," Shelby mutters, craning so hard to look at them that she turns a lopsided circle through the clusters. "What good does it do a tree to have glowing roots?"

"They're predators," I say. "They feed on invertebrates that live in these caves."

Shelby snorts. "So they're giant bug zappers?"

"You have an interesting way with words," Beth observes.

"Thanks, Mendel."

"Not a compliment," Beth says.

Shelby barks a belly laugh. "I like you too, kid." Then she turns to me. "But you called them something else, right? Solace?"

"Yeah," I say. "That's what the Sorrow call these trees."

"Same as their city, huh?" Shelby says, twisting to look up at the root clusters again. "Because it gets light from a grove like this, right?"

"Right," I say.

"Do we know what that grove looks like? Up top?" she asks, her eyes still on the tangles of light overhead.

A horrible certainty creeps up my spine, carrying Shelby's words with it: *I've always been more interested in ending life than multiplying it.*

Shelby isn't curious about Sorrow culture. She's looking for weaknesses. She's trying to figure out how to attack the Solace.

My hand goes to the ensign pips on my collar. When Grandpa gave them to me, I thought I was going to be helping him understand the Sorrow so he could negotiate peace. But he and Shelby need to understand them just as badly if we're going to war. Maybe even more so. How can I refuse to help them? To help us?

"It's a yes-or-no question, Junior," Shelby snarks. "Shouldn't require deliberation."

I wish that was true.

"No," I say, finally. "No one's seen it, but the grove is supposed to be ancient. The root clusters in the Solace are way bigger than these. The trees must be enormous. Much bigger than the ones we saw at the raptor nest. The ones you said reminded you of Mississippi."

"Is that so?"

I can't really see her face in the neon-painted dark, but there's something weird about her tone. She sounds satisfied. And kind of smug. What is she planning? How can knowing what the grove that lights Sorrow's Solace *might* look like help her attack the city below?

Abruptly, Shelby pushes ahead, darting through the root clusters so quickly that she disappears between the glowing tangles. When we catch up, she's standing at the farthest edge of the grove's light, where the rich darkness of the cavern takes hold.

Shelby doesn't acknowledge us as we approach. Her eyes, and her mind, are drilling out into the dark as though she could see Sorrow's Solace, if only she looked hard enough.

Then she turns and starts back the way we came without another word.

TEN

The sun is setting as I shift our rotors into upright position for landing. Shelby insisted on collapsing the Sorrow tunnel before we left. Then she spent hours in the Solace grove on the cliffs above it, taking pictures of the trees and gathering fallen branches. She's sprawled in the back row now. Beth is sitting next to me, quietly looking out at Tau.

She's calm.

I feel like I want to climb out of my skin.

My stomach is churning, like I'm really nervous about something. Or I've made a horrible mistake. Logically, I know that's not true. If the Sorrow are arming themselves to attack us, then helping Shelby understand them is more than my job. It's the best thing I can do to protect the human species.

So why do I feel like a traitor?

Shelby's flex buzzes. She checks it and then kicks the seat in front of her. "Goddamn it."

I throw a look at Beth. She ignores me, but I can tell she's listening to Shelby's muttered curses as the lieutenant texts her reply, fingers flying at an irritated clip.

"Idiot," Shelby growls under her breath, flopping back in her chair.

"What's wrong?" I ask cautiously.

Shelby hurls a glare at me across the flyer's cabin. "What isn't?" She looks to Beth. "I need access to that footage, Mendel. Yesterday."

With that Shelby untethers, staggering to the rear doors before the flyer has even touched down. The second we're on the ground, she smacks the door controls and storms down the ramp while it's still unfolding.

"What are you going to tell her?" I ask Beth once Shelby is gone.

"Equipment failure," Beth says. "I don't expect she'll believe me, but she can't prove otherwise."

"I won't tell anyone."

Beth untethers and gathers up her sample bag. "I didn't think you would."

"Really?"

"I know you, Jo," Beth says. "Apparently better than you do."

She leaves.

I take my time shutting the flyer down.

I'm so incredibly confused. Helping Beth hide her data,

lying to everyone, maybe endangering our whole species, feels right. And helping Shelby understand the solace trees, doing my job, feels so wrong. Logically, it should be the other way around. But that's not what my gut is telling me.

I've always trusted my instincts. But my instincts told me to let Tarn through the shield and he almost killed me. If Shelby hadn't come along . . .

What would have happened if Shelby hadn't come along?

Glow worms.

The anxious tapping of Shelby's long fingers on the butt of her rifle this afternoon accompanies the ugly words through my brain. Shelby might be a battle-tested marine who survived the flu, but she's also a xenophobe who never dreamed of ending up on another planet. She said Tarn was about to snap my neck when she saw us. But looking back on it now, Tarn had his hand locked around my throat for what felt like a long time before Shelby showed up. If he was trying to kill me, why spend all that time singing to me first?

Glow worms.

That was the first time Shelby had ever seen an extraterrestrial. How much did fear influence what she saw? How much did my own fear influence how I reacted? How much did it influence my memory of what had happened after it was over?

How much did my memory of what happened influence everything that's happened since?

Glow worms.

I half run to Ground Control.

Grandpa's office door is closed. I can hear voices inside. Shelby. Grandpa. And another, so quiet I can't make it out. Probably whoever was responsible for the text that made Shelby so furious. I can hear the outrage in her voice through the door. Whatever is going on, I can't just burst in there. I have to wait.

It's physically impossible to stand still, so I pace. Up the hall. Down the hall.

That's when I notice that Mom's office door is open.

Mom is in there. Of course. She always is these days.

Her new office is the smallest room in the building. Basically everyone offered to let her take their rooms after Grandpa took over the command office, but she didn't want to displace anyone. Grandpa insisted that she cram a desk and chair into the tiny space, even though Mom has never liked sitting while she works. She's sitting now, with her back to the mountain of flexes on her desk, watching the live feed from the central square that's playing on her wall screens.

I hesitate in the open doorway. I want to go inside. I want to tell her . . . what do I want to tell her? What do I really want to say to Grandpa? That Shelby is a xenophobe? They both know that. That war with the Sorrow is a bad idea? They know that too. We all do.

"What's up, kiddo?" Mom asks, without turning to look at me.

"The Sorrow are salvaging old Ranger gear," I blurt out. "Lieutenant Shelby thinks they're printing guns."

Mom sighs, slumping in her chair. "I suppose it was only a matter of time."

"No!" The word bursts out of my mouth of its own accord.

"No, what?" Mom snarls, her voice rising in volume with every word. "No, the Sorrow can't attack us for settling on their planet against their wishes? No, we can't just decide this world is ours, even though it belongs to another species? No, Earth can't be dead because of a ridiculous coding error? What exactly are you objecting to, Joanna?"

I feel a tear slip down my cheek.

"There must be something we can do," I whisper. "Something *you* can do."

Mom yanks a satellite phone from her harness and hurls it across the desk at me.

"Check the call list," she snaps.

I do.

Fifteen outgoing calls. All to Tarn.

"I tried," she says. "I tried, and tried. And your Grandfather won't risk lives sending a delegation to the Solace. Not after Tarn tried to kill you. It's out of my hands."

I stare down at the list of uncompleted calls. My heart is pounding and I feel like I can't get enough oxygen. It's like I'm standing in front of a phytoraptor, not in my mom's cramped, uncomfortable office.

I look up at Mom.

"It can't be out of your hands."

"That isn't fair, Joanna." She chews each word out individually. "What do you expect me to do?"

"I don't know!" The words tumble out so fast I couldn't stop them if I wanted to. "I don't know what to do. I don't know what I want you to do. Everything is so . . . wrong. And we can't just sit here and be wrong with it. There has to be a better way."

Mom meets my eyes. "I don't know what it is. If I did, I'd . . ." She trails off, slumping down in the chair again. Her eyes drift to the stacks of flexes on the desk I know she must hate.

My stomach hurts.

I want to leave. I want to hug her. I want to scream at her. I want her to be, I don't know, not this. No. That's wrong. I know exactly who I want her to be.

The commander.

Without warning, she smacks the flexes off her desk, sending them crashing into the wall screen.

When her eyes meet mine again, there's anger in them along with the misery.

"There has to be another way, doesn't there?"

It isn't a question. It's an answer. It's why Mom has been hiding in here, bathing in a misery of paperwork. It's why I've been bolting for space every chance I get. We're both so afraid that there *isn't* another way that we're literally hiding from the world.

From each other.

Before I can figure out how to say that out loud, voices burst in from the hall.

"I'm sorry, Private." Grandpa's voice is grim.

"So am I, sir." That's Jay's voice. And he sounds like he's about to cry.

I dart into the hallway and almost run into Jay, who is hurrying toward the exit. He sucks in a sharp breath when he sees me, then quickly looks away.

"Jay—"

But he just steps around me and keeps going.

I spin back to Grandpa. "What's going on? Jay isn't a private."

"He is now," Shelby growls, stomping out of Grandpa's office. "If I didn't need every warm body I can get, he wouldn't even be that."

"He was demoted?" I gasp. "Why? What happened?"

"Go ask your boyfriend," Shelby snaps. "The Admiral and I have more important things to discuss."

My eyes dart to Grandpa. He nods.

"Go, Little Moth," Grandpa says. "I'm sure he can use the consolation."

"But—"

Grandpa waves away my protest. "Don't worry. I'll text you when the lieutenant and I are finished."

Then he follows Shelby into his office.

A sharp pain in my jaw makes me realize my teeth are clenched so hard, they're grinding. My jaw crackles as I force them apart.

Don't worry.

I can't think of a single moment when the words *don't worry* ever made me do anything but.

Jay is halfway to the barracks before I catch up.

"What happened?" I ask.

"I don't want to talk about it." He cracks each word off with effort, like they're frozen together.

I grab his hand, pulling him around to look at me.

"Jay."

"Don't, Jo," he says. "Just, don't, okay?" He sounds tired. And sad.

I can't stand how sad he sounds.

"I can talk to Grandpa," I say.

"No!" he yells. "No special treatment because my girl-friend is the admiral's granddaughter."

"Then tell me what happened," I demand. "Because I can't imagine you doing something to deserve a demotion."

"None of us deserve this," Jay says, so quietly I can hardly hear him.

"Please, Jay. I want to help."

It comes out more like a request than an offer. No. That makes it sound too dignified. It isn't a request. It's a plea.

Jay turns away from me.

"You can't help, Jo. This is on me. I failed." He sags a little further. For a moment, I think he's going to sit down, right there in the middle of the path. "The admiral was nice about it, but it's my job to protect our people. That means doing whatever it takes. Even if . . ." He shudders convulsively, as though he can't even think the words, much less say them. "But someone has to do it."

"Do what?"

He walks away so abruptly, it takes me a moment to process what's happening.

"Jay!" I call, racing after him.

He stops again, turning to grab my shoulders as I nearly barrel into him. His eyes are burning.

"Just leave me alone, okay?"

I don't want to do that. I want to throw my arms around him. I want to force him to tell me what's going on. But everything I can think to do or say sounds like another demand. Like I'm asking something of him instead of giving him what he needs. So instead I just nod.

"Okay."

He leaves so fast, he's almost running.

What happened to him? Today was supposed to be his first day on Shelby's special phytoraptor team. How did Jay "fail," exactly? What did he do?

What didn't he do?

A horrifying thought runs its fingers up my spine.

Grandpa demoted Jay. Personally. Whatever it is Shelby's special team is doing, Grandpa thinks it's necessary. And if Grandpa thinks it's necessary . . .

What are we going to have to become, in order to survive here?

ELEVEN

"Joey?"

Chris's voice jumps out of the darkness.

Startled, I spin to find him standing a few meters behind me, his tool belt slung over his shoulder.

"Hi," I say, trying to sound normal.

He makes a face. "What are you doing standing out here in the cold without your jacket?"

At his words I realize just how cold I am. I didn't bother to grab my parka when I stormed off the flyer, and now it's full night. My fingers are numb and I can feel gooseflesh prickling all over my arms and back, under my thermal and flight suit. How long have I been standing here, lost in my raging thoughts?

I shove my hands into my pockets and toss the question back at Chris. "What are you doing out?"

"Heading to River Bend," he says. "Didn't get to finish what I was working on yesterday."

"The *Vulcan*?" I guess.

"Yeah," he says. "I've got a double shift tomorrow, and she's so close to done. Chief G said I could take a jeep."

"Oh," I say.

"Wanna come?"

I shouldn't. I should go back and talk to Mom, now that she's finally talking.

There has to be a better way.

But what if there isn't?

Grandpa fought in the Storm Wars, but he's also one of the architects of the peace accords that united Earth for the first time in human history. If he doesn't think it's possible to make peace with the Sorrow, then it probably isn't.

There are almost ten thousand people sleeping in orbit. All that's left of us. Grandpa and Shelby are just doing what they think is necessary to protect them. To protect us. How can I question that? How can I not?

"Yeah," I say. "I'll come."

I follow Chris to the airfield. He uses Chief G's code to activate one of the jeeps parked beside the flyers, but he lets me drive. It's not as much fun as flying, but there's something satisfying about accelerating through the dark trees. I can almost imagine I'm digging my own feet into the dirt, pushing the jeep forward by sheer force of frustration.

"You wanna talk about it?" Chris asks.

"No," I say, swinging the wheel a little too hard around a big orchid tree. I swear under my breath as I wrestle the vehicle back into line.

"Okay." Chris leans back against his seat to look up at the stars. The moons are slim crescents tonight, and the unnatural glimmer of the *Prairie* stands out like a beacon. She's hovering just over the treetops ahead of us.

I wish she weren't.

I wish they'd never come.

The thought is followed by a wave of nausea. I just wished ten thousand people dead. My friends' families. My own grandfather. I can't wish for that. But I do.

I wish that ship would just disappear.

I didn't know it was possible to be this selfish.

"We have to do whatever it takes to keep the survivors safe," I say. "Right?"

Chris shrugs. "Depends on what it takes, doesn't it?"

I want to agree with him, but I'm not sure I do. What wouldn't I do to assure the survival of the species *Homo sapiens*?

What wouldn't Jay do?

The question surfs back into my brain on a wave of dread.

"Joey!"

I slam on the brakes just in time to avoid ramming the jeep into River Bend's shield. I sit there, trying to catch my breath, as Chris pulls up the shield app and carves a portal for us. My heart is still pounding as I drive the jeep through the square opening in the force field and into the fast-growing settlement.

The five ruined cabins Dr. Brown's team left behind have been replaced by three dozen new ones. The *Prairie*'s marine squadron and their families have taken over the little settlement. It won't be little for long. There are two jeeps with huge bulldozing attachments and ripper claws parked beside the orchid trees, ready to clear them in the morning.

The thought of those claws ripping into the forest makes my stomach hurt. Beth would say I'm being sentimental. The orchid trees aren't sentient. They aren't even hybrids like the fidos. I still hate the thought of plowing them under, especially if this settlement turns out to be temporary.

There has to be a better way.

I turn my gaze from the construction equipment to the *Vulcan*. The scout ship is perched right in the bend of the river so she isn't in the way. Work lights trace her high, curved wings and graceful body in the darkness.

She looks so different than she did the first time I saw her, listing over the rotting, abandoned camp. Now she's straight and sure. Beautiful.

"Guess we aren't the only ones looking for some distraction," I say, gesturing to the work lights.

"Nope," Chris says. Then he raises his voice and calls out, "Sorry I'm late, Lee-lu."

"Leela's here?" I ask, surprised.

"Obviously," Leela says, sticking her head out of the hatch. "Come on. It's freezing out there."

I try to ignore the twist of childish hurt in my gut as I follow Chris up the ramp. "If you guys had plans, I can just head back."

"Don't be a drama queen," Leela says as we step through the hatch into the ship. "We're testing our new system. That's not 'plans.'"

"A new system?" I say. "You guys added something to the *Vulcan*?"

Leela grins. "Yup. Chris designed it. It's awesome. We've been working on this for weeks."

For weeks? Where was I?

Running away, I remind myself.

"It was your idea," Chris tells Leela, pulling the hatch closed behind us against the cold. "I just figured out the mechanics."

"'Just'?" Leela fires back, arching an *oh really?* brow at him.

Chris has grown, I realize. He's gotta be almost as tall as Jay now. His shoulders are broader too.

Chris grins, flushing in pleased embarrassment. "It *was* kind of a challenge."

"What was?" I ask.

"C'mon," Leela says. "I'll show you."

We follow her into the *Vulcan*'s bridge. The dome-shaped

room is just like the *Pioneer*'s bridge but smaller. The wall screens are set to three-sixty mode, showing the camp around us so vividly, it's like we stepped outside again, minus the cold.

"Computer, run simulation twelve," Leela requests.

The bridge plunges into absolute darkness. Reflexive anxiety splashes through me. But before I can even switch my flex to flashlight, red light zips around the seams where the wall screens meet the floors.

It swells, filling the room. A sentence fades up on each wedge of wall screen.

Emergency power cells activated.

"It works!" Chris crows, grabbing Leela and swinging her around in a joyful victory dance.

"You gave the *Vulcan* emergency power cells?" I ask, pivoting to take in the stark message on the screens. "Doesn't it already have backup systems?"

"This is a backup to the backup," Leela says, "It has just enough power to save our butts if something happens to the computer."

"ISA ships depend on their central computer to activate their backup systems," Chris explains. "Which is all well and good, usually. The mainframes have independent power. But if your computer dies, you're screwed. That isn't supposed to happen—"

"But we all know *supposed to* doesn't mean crap out here," Leela says, her voice gruff with emotion. "Hindsight sucks, but it's useful."

"Oh," I say, abruptly understanding where all this came from. "If you'd had this when the *Wagon*'s computers failed last year . . ."

She nods. "Yeah. Exactly."

If there had been a system like this on the *Wagon*, Leela would have been able to land our old shuttle safely on the airfield, instead of crash-landing in the mountains. Thirteen people might still be alive if she'd had this system. Including Chris's mom and Miguel.

I can't help but imagine that alternate history. It's like prodding a sore tooth. It hurts, but I can't stop. Chief Penny, alive. Miguel, alive. Mom making first contact with the Sorrow like she planned, instead of us stumbling into it. Mom and Penny working together to repair the *Prairie*, instead of this headlong rush to bring down the survivors.

Everything would be so different.

But it isn't.

"Of course," Leela says, breaking my list of might-have-beens, "accidentally triggering the nanoscrubbers would have sucked harder."

"Nanoscrubbers?" I ask, startled. "The *Vulcan* has an atmospheric filtration system?"

"Yeah," Chris says. "I mean, not exactly. It's the same system, but the programming is completely different from the ones that—"

"Destroyed Earth?" Leela supplies, her dry tone not quite hiding her grief at the thought.

Chris shakes his head. "Still have trouble getting my

head around that one." He hunches his shoulders a little, like he's trying to make room for the apocalypse under his skin. "But yeah, the *Vulcan*'s scrubbers are the same basic idea as the Earth system, except they're programmed to search and destroy organic waste on the surface instead of carbon in the upper atmosphere. The Rangers adopted it to clear Earth DNA off planets they'd finished exploring."

"Are you serious?" I say, a whole other set of fears churning into my guts. "And we just left it sitting here, in a rusting old ship?"

The atmospheric filtration system's nanobots are designed to chew through unwanted molecules and break them down to their component atoms. If these scrubbers do that to Earth DNA, that means they'd chew through *us* if they were activated.

"It wasn't dangerous until Dr. Brown died," Chris says. "The scrubber system has a fail-safe linked to the *Vulcan* crew's RFID identification implants. As long as a Ranger was alive on planet, the scrubbers stayed dormant."

"But after that, yeah, a couple more centimeters of rust, and we could have all been reduced to our component molecules," Leela snarks.

Chris rolls his eyes. "Oh come on. It's not just instant death if those things get out. It takes hours for them to saturate the atmosphere enough to initialize the system. We'd have shut them down long before that happened."

"Assuming we knew the killer nanobots had gotten

loose, which we wouldn't have known, because we didn't know they existed." Leela shakes her head, disgusted.

"Mom has most secret clearance," I say. "She must have known about this."

Chris shakes his head. "Nope. It was above even her clearance level. I'm not sure the admiral would have told anyone, if we hadn't asked for access to the *Vulcan*'s mainframe. The commander and Chief G are still the only other people who know. The admiral said that he and Dr. Brown kept their modification to the scrubber system secret because they were afraid of them getting into the wrong hands."

"Which would have been ours, if we'd started messing around with the power systems before the admiral segregated the planet scrubbers on their own hard drive and locked it under his command codes," Leela says. "Secrets are stupid. I'm over them." She pulls off her flex and presses it to the wall screen, syncing with the *Vulcan* to bring the computer back online. "But the ship's basically done now," she says as she works, "so we can get the *Vulcan* into orbit to dispose of those things in space, where they can't hurt anyone."

"And then it's back to cabins and cargo runs for us," Chris says, as the ISA logo appears on each wedge of the wall screen.

Leela sighs. "Who knew the post-apocalypse would be so dull?"

The three-sixty view from the exterior cameras flows back over the dome, surrounding us with the cold dark outside once more. But it isn't as dark as it looks. Pale light is flickering through the tidy rows of cabins. Weird.

"What is that?" Leela says, peering at the light.

Something bright flashes through the sky and lands in the cluster of cabins.

"What the—"

"Oh my god!" Leela gasps as a ball of fire balloons out of the settlement, scattering flame across the cabin roofs.

Two more flashes of light burst through the air. Firebombs.

It's finally happening. We're under attack.

Chris and Leela and I drag the hatch open and race down the ramp toward the burning cabins.

"Get your breathers!" Leela shouts.

I don't slow down, fumbling blindly in my utility harness pockets until I find the slick membrane. I smear it over my nose and mouth and cough on the abruptly clean oxygen. I didn't even realize how smoky it was.

The *Prairie* squad members who were off duty are already pounding on doors and hustling squad families away from the flames. Sergeant Preakness is checking people off on his flex and shouting out names to the others as he gets them.

Something hard thuds into my solar plexus and a little voice rasps, "Move! Move! Get out of my way!"

I snag the kid before he can push past me. He looks

five, maybe six. His face is sooty and his eyes are red and furious.

"Let me go!" he shrieks. "I have to get back to my house!"

"Is someone stuck in there?" Chris asks, darting back to us and crouching next to the kid.

"My bear!" he wails. "I need my bear! He'll burn!"

Chris looks up at me, aching regret in his eyes.

"We can't," I say to him.

"I know," Chris responds.

Neither of us means it.

Then someone swoops the little boy out of my arms. It's Shelby, though I hardly recognize her under the thick layer of gray ash that coats her face.

"Come on, little punk," she growls, shoving a bedraggled stuffed bear into the child's arms. "Your daddy's having a conniption."

Did Emily Shelby actually just risk her life for a stuffed animal?

"Don't just stand there," Shelby snarls at us. "Go do something useful." With that, she strides away, carrying the child out of the smoke.

Sergeant Preakness assigns us to a fire-suppression team.

For what feels like a long time, it's just the *Prairie* squadron and us, fighting the flames. The heat and smoke make it hard to think, much less keep track of time. I keep expecting more firebombs, or attacking Takers, but they never come.

Eventually more people show up from the Landing to

fight the fires. I catch glimpses of Mom and Grandpa darting between groups, coordinating fire suppression. And I see Beth and Dad down by the river, helping to haul water up to the settlement in a long cooperative chain. But I haven't seen Jay at all. I hope he's okay.

Leela and Chris and I are all caked with soot by the time Mom hurries up to us.

"What's happening, Mom?" I demand. "Is everyone—"

"Lots of smoke inhalation." Mom anticipates my question. "But no fatalities."

"What about the construction?" I ask.

She shakes her head. "Unclear what we'll be able to salvage." She turns to Leela. "Is the *Vulcan* flyable?"

"Yes, ma'am," Leela says. "She's finished."

"Okay then," Mom says. "I need you kids to get her out of here."

"Oh crap," I say, the realization snapping through me. "The planet scrubbers."

Mom nods.

"But they're locked down," Chris says. "Command access only. And only a few of us even know they exist. How could the Sorrow?"

"Dr. Brown followed Ord," Leela says.

"And she was a colonel," Mom says. "Did you remove her codes from *Vulcan*'s computers?"

Chris shakes his head, wide-eyed. "You really think she told the Sorrow about the scrubbers?"

"I hope not," Mom says. "But we can't take that chance."

Fear hammers into my heart. "Where do we go?"

"Just get her off the ground," Mom says. "And stay there until this is over."

She squeezes my hand quickly, and then she's gone.

My heart pounds all the way across the smoldering camp. The *Vulcan* is just sitting there. Ramp down. Powered up and ready to go. We left her that way, even though we knew the Sorrow were firebombing the camp and Takers could be all around us. It didn't even cross my mind that they might steal the *Vulcan*.

How could I be so stupid?

Chris and Leela are still tethering in as I shove my hands up the nav app and the little ship jumps off the ground.

"Maybe they don't know. Maybe the firebombs *were* the attack," Chris says, staring down at the burning settlement below us in the three-sixty. "They certainly did plenty of damage."

"Not enough," Leela insists. "Why would they attack *just* River Bend? And *just* with firebombs? There's more to this. Tarn's up to something."

The answer flashes into my brain half a second before a blast of light bleaches out the night. A flat *boom* follows on its heels.

"What was that?" Leela gasps.

"Tarn isn't coming for the *Vulcan*," I say, pointing down to where the Landing now sits bare and vulnerable in the darkness. Its particle shield is gone. The fire at River Bend was just a diversion to draw away the marines and everyone else old enough to defend themselves.

"The Sorrow are attacking the Landing."

TWELVE

Leela reaches over and grabs the nav app, pulling it across the wall screen to take control of the ship.

"What are you doing?" I demand.

"Putting us down," she says, initiating a spiraling descent toward the Landing's airfield. "Aai and the kids are down there all alone. We can't just watch the Sorrow—"

"Tarn's not going to kill a bunch of little kids," I say.

"We're not talking about Tarn," she counters. "We're talking about angry Takers who look at us and just see alien. Everyone old enough or strong enough to fight is at River Bend."

I look down at the airfield below us on the floor screens. A pair of black flyers perch beside the 3D shop. Blackout-robed Takers are pouring out of them, visible in the darkness only because of the light from the shop's touchscreen walls.

"There are too many of them," I say. "We won't be able to hold them off, and if they get their hands on the *Vulcan*—"

"So just drop me off!" Leela shouts, hurling a glare at me. "I'm not going to let my mom die down there while I sit up here and watch."

"Oh sure," I snap back. "So I'm supposed to sit up here and watch *you* die?"

"No!" she growls back. She sucks in a desperate sob. "Yes. I don't know. I don't know what to do, Jo!"

Neither do I. But we can't just sit here, too close but not close enough. We have to do *something*.

A shockingly loud burst of gunfire cuts through my desperate confusion and muzzle flashes light up the night below us as marines storm out of the 3D shop and charge the Takers.

"Shelby knew." Leela exhales the words, relief flowing through them. "Shelby knew the fires were a diversion."

A flare of blue-green light wipes out the starboard wall screens a heartbeat before a roaring explosion crashes over us. I spin to see a third black flyer fall out of the sky and slam into one of our parked flyers with a tearing shriek of metal.

Flames leap from the wreckage.

"Holy— Shields up!" Leela shrieks at the computer. Red impact marks popcorn over the *Vulcan*'s force field even as it shimmers into place. Friendly fire.

"Can't they see it's us?" Chris demands.

"Apparently not." Leela gasps, swiping up an open comms feed. "Friendly! Friendly! Watch where you're—"

Bullets spray over our shield again.

"Get on the ground, *Vulcan*," Shelby growls over the open comm. "Or we'll put you down."

"Yes ma'am," Leela says. Her hands are shaking as she taps and swipes at the nav app.

More impacts slam into the shield all around us, shaking the ship with repressed kinetic energy.

"Jo!" Leela pleads.

"I'm on it," I say, my hands already skimming over the shield app, which popped up on the wall screen when Leela activated it. I shift power flow, keeping the force field steady as Leela swings the *Vulcan* away from the fighting and sets her down at the far end of the field, between the *Trailblazer* and *3212*.

"What do we do now?" Chris demands.

"You two are staying here," Leela says, untethering and shoving to her feet. "If they get too close, take off again. Go . . . somewhere." With that, she starts up the corridor to the main hatch.

"Where are you going?" I call, fumbling with my own tether.

"I spent four years training to be a marine," Leela growls. "I'm going to help."

"Leela!" I protest, but she's already opening the hatch. I follow her out onto the ramp. "You're unarmed and—"

"Shh!" She yanks me back against the ship. "Did you see that?" Her whisper is so thin, I can hardly hear it.

I look out into the darkness around us. I don't see—

"Takers!" I gasp as the silhouette of a robed figure slips across *3212*'s standby lights. "What are they doing?"

She ducks back through the hatch and I follow her, whispering, "Computer, screens off!"

The corridor plunges into darkness.

Chris gasps, startled. "What are you—"

"Shhhh!" I whisper. "There are Takers out there. They must have seen us land."

"I don't think so," Leela says, peering through the hatch. "They're headed for the *Trailblazer*."

"The raw!" Chris whispers.

"Yeah," she says grimly.

"You mean it didn't get offloaded?" I breathe.

"We were going to hop over to River Bend in the morning." Leela grinds the words out as she texts on her flex. "Crap. Jay says the squad is pinned down by the 3D shop. They'll get out here as fast as they can, but it's gonna be a minute."

"A full sixth of our raw supply is on that ship," Chris says. "Losing it will cripple us."

"It's worse than that," Leela says, pointing through the wall screen to where white light is spilling through the *Trailblazer*'s unfolding rear doors. "If they got those doors open, then they have access codes."

Crap. She's right.

"Dr. Brown must have given them hers," Chris says.

"Yeah," Leela agrees. "That means they don't have to steal the raw. They can just steal *Trailblazer.* Then all they have to do is take her into orbit and ram the *Prairie's* solar sails . . ."

And our whole species is dead.

"If they have Dr. Brown's command codes, they could just as easily take the *Vulcan,*" Chris points out.

"If they wanted the *Vulcan,* they'd be coming for her," I say. "They aren't. I don't think they know about the scrubbers."

"So we leave *Vulcan* and try to stop them from taking *Trailblazer?*" Leela says.

"Yeah," I say. "I think we have to. Somehow."

"I might be able to take one of them hand to hand," Leela says, dubious. "But I counted at least four of them, and they're armed."

"So are we," Chris says, pulling a laser welder from his belt. "It worked before. With the raptors."

"Only sort of," I remind him.

Leela pulls out her own laser welder. "Better than nothing."

"Title of my autobiography," I say, amazed at how steady my voice sounds. Is this how Mom feels when she slaps on her commander face and convinces us all that she knows what she's doing and everything is going to be fine?

We slip out of the *Vulcan* and double-time through the grass toward the *Trailblazer*.

The shuttle's open ramp glows gently in the darkness. It's only a dozen meters long, but knowing there are armed Takers waiting inside makes the narrow gauntlet look like a light-year. We're never going to get close enough to use our welders. One of them will see us coming before we're halfway up.

"The emergency hatch!" I realize abruptly. "We can get in through the cargo pod."

"Yeah," Leela says. "The element of surprise sounds good right about now."

She taps her flex a few times, and I hear the slither of her tether extending into the darkness overhead, snicking into the contact point on the emergency hatch. I'm opening my tether app to do the same when I feel a quick stab of itchiness at the back of my neck. I think it's an insect at first, but then I feel it again. Stronger.

That's Sorrow sonar.

"Get down!" I hiss, pulling Chris and Leela back against the *Trailblazer*'s hull as a huge Taker emerges from the flame-lit darkness of the airfield, tugging a Sorrow in a faintly glowing gray robe along with them. That's weird. I've seen Sorrow wear gray like that before, in the Solace, but we've only ever seen Takers and Givers outside the caves.

That itchy feeling comes again, louder and stronger,

164

followed by a sharp, chilly declaration. The two Sorrow are arguing.

The gray-robed Sorrow stops and holds both of their hands up to cover their face, palms in. That's the Sorrow gesture for *no*. Green biolight oozes between their tri-jointed fingers.

The Taker spins on the gray-robed Sorrow, hefting a massive battle hammer made of Diamond Range crystal. They growl something that makes me feel terribly embarrassed, like I'm ten and Mrs. Divekar just caught me stealing jelly beans from the guess-the-number jar in the back of the classroom all over again.

The gray-robed Sorrow doesn't move.

The Taker hefts their hammer a little higher and grumbles something low that hits my body squarely in the fight-or-flight response. That Taker is going to kill this Sorrow if they don't play along. The gray-robed Sorrow gets the message. They spin back toward the *Trailblazer* in a whirl of dully glowing robes and stride toward the shuttle. Their hulking escort follows.

Leela swears. "That's eight of them, and the last one had a battle hammer. We can't go in there."

"We can't let them take the ship, either," I say.

"Thank you, Cadet Obvious," she snaps. "But how are we supposed to stop them?"

"We don't have to stop *them*," Chris says. "We stop the ship."

"Cuz that's easier?" Leela snaps.

"No," he fires back. "But it's possible. We can cut the power regulator. Engine won't fire without it."

"No way!" I gasp at the same moment that Leela snaps, "Absolutely not."

"I know, it sucks," Chris whispers. "But if they ram the *Prairie* . . ."

"To get to the regulator, we'll have to crawl up the fuselage," I say. "They're powering up now. If they fire the engines while we're in there, we're toast. Literally."

"You got a better idea?" Chris says.

I don't. Neither does Leela. I can see it in the grim look on her face.

"I'll go," Chris says. "I can do this."

"No, you can't," Leela says. "You're too tall." She looks to me. "It has to be us."

My skin knows what it is to burn. Sixty percent of my body had full-thickness radiation burns after the accident. I shudder, trying to drive the sensation back into my memory, but it clings. I can hardly convince my head to move on my neck, much less climb up a fuselage. The flashback is holding me prisoner. Again. And I'm going to let the people I love down. Again.

Then Leela grabs my hand.

She's shaking. Clammy.

She's just as terrified as I am.

"This might be the stupidest thing we've ever done,"

she says. "And that's a pretty damn high bar."

Impossibly, her fear seems to dull mine.

"It's getting stupider, the longer we stand here," I say.

She nods.

I surprise myself by taking a step toward the *Trail-blazer*'s fuselage. And another. Then I'm running. Tugging Leela along with me. I can hear Chris behind us.

I drop Leela's hand as we reach the huge black cones and tap into the tether app on my flex.

"Searching," the computer announces. "Searching. Searching. Searching."

"Damn," I say. "There aren't any tether points up there."

"Our stupidity is literally inconceivable to others," Leela growls. "You're gonna have to boost us up, Chris."

"I'm not sure that's gonna get you high enough," Chris says.

"You get me up there," I say. "Then I can brace Leela and—"

"I can stuff myself into the live space engine exhaust port," she says, finishing the ridiculous thought.

"Yeah."

"Let's get this over with," she says.

Chris weaves his fingers together into a sling and I plant my boot in his hand, clinging to his shoulders as he hefts me up to the edge of the fuselage.

I grab the rim of the tube and plant my boots against the *Trailblazer*. Then I pull, my arms burning as I force them to bend and drag my body into the hot, grainy funnel.

With my boots and shoulders planted, I snatch a climbing spike from my harness. I stab it into the carbon skin of the fuselage, mentally apologizing to the engineers who are going to have to repair the damage.

"Hit your autoconnect," I whisper-shout down to Leela.

Her tether slithers past me and thuds into the spike. Seconds later her retracting line hauls her up into the fuselage.

I grab her arms and heave. Leela isn't a big person, but she's solid muscle. The world narrows to my straining muscles and grinding joints as we work together to get her past me into the narrowing tube.

Then she's up.

I help her plant her boots on my shoulders and lean against the searing wall of the fuselage to hold her steady. I can't see what she's doing—just the pale glow of her flex in flashlight mode and flares of light from the laser welder.

For about seven seconds, I think we're going to make it through this.

Then the ship comes to life against my back.

The rising thrum of the engines is so familiar, I can almost see the preflight sequence, like the app is running on the inside of my skull.

"Leela—"

"Nagging isn't helpful," she snaps.

"They're powering up," I say.

"Gee, thanks for the update." She pounds on something

above me with what sounds like her fist, then shouts in pain.

"Leela!"

"Shut up. I have one more wire to cut."

The engines are singing in harmony now.

"Lee-la!"

"No! No, no, no, I can't reach it!" she sobs. "Please! Come on!"

But it's too late.

We've done everything we can.

"Brace yourself, Chris!" I shout. Then I let us fall, grabbing the edge of the fuselage so that only Leela drops into Chris's arms.

"I wasn't done!" she shrieks.

"Too late!" I cry as I drop to the grass beside them, already fumbling for the autoconnect button on my harness.

Heat blooms over my skin as my tether flies out. I don't know what it's connecting to. It might be my climbing spike inside the fuselage, but we'll be just as dead if we stay here long enough to find out.

I wrap my arms around Leela and Chris as I shout, "Retract!"

The tether snaps tight, whipping us into the air. The weight of my friends feels like it's going to rip my arms out of my sockets, but I hang on. I just hope I'm strong enough to—

WHAM!

I feel my ribs cracking as we slam into something

smooth and warm. Sparks spin through my vision and my stomach heaves. I try to hold on to Leela and Chris, but my arms are going numb. They fall away from me.

I pass out. I don't know for how long.

The next thing I know, the *Trailblazer*'s engine is on fire.

I twist on my harness, my brain struggling to figure out why I'm looking down at the flames. I'm hanging from the side of the *Trailblazer*. Apparently, my harness autoconnected to the emergency hatch at the top of the shuttle. Five meters below me, Chris is dragging Leela's limp form across the icy grass.

I smack my autoconnect button again and my tether retracts with a slither and a *thud*. Gravity claims me and I half slide to the tiny frozen spikes of grass. Pain claws at my rib cage but I ignore it, rolling to my feet and staggering toward my friends.

"Is she—"

"She's breathing," Chris sobs. "She's breathing."

I hook my arm under Leela's limp shoulders, relieving Chris of half her weight. My ribs scream with pain, but I don't care. We have to get back into the *Vulcan* before . . .

Light cracks through the *Trailblazer*'s main airlock, stabbing through the orange flicker of the flames as the ramp unfolds behind us.

Chris screams, dropping to his knees and taking both of us with him.

"Chris!"

He gasps. "I'm hit!"

A flash of rainbow light catches the edge of my vision. I throw myself sideways across Leela as a crystal shard the size of my palm slams into the frozen mud where I was lying seconds before. From here, I can see that another shard is buried in Chris's shoulder.

Beneath me, Leela moans. "What the—"

Snick. Snick. Snick.

"Run!" I scream to Chris, throwing my arms around Leela and rolling as shards smack into the grass all around us. He grabs Leela's arm and hauls her into his arms instead.

I roll to my feet and lurch between my friends and the Takers who are storming out of the Trailblazer.

The tall one spins their battle hammer as they stride toward me. I know I must be afraid, but I'm not feeling it now. I'm not feeling the pain I know is burning through my chest, either. All that matters is staying between that hammer and Leela and Chris.

The Taker winds up, two hands gripping the glittering hammer.

Time slows to a crawl, and I can see individual colors refracting through the crystal as it catches the dancing light of the burning shuttle.

When that thing connects with my torso, I'm going to die.

At least it'll be quick.

A flat *crack* echoes from behind me, so loud it makes my ears ring. The hammer drops from the Taker's suddenly limp hands. Their body follows, bioluminescent hot-pink blood spurting from a bullet wound in their chest.

The other Takers charge.

More gunshots roar behind me in quick succession.

Neon blood spatters over black robes.

The Takers fall. One. Two. Three. Four. Five.

A white-hot roar of Sorrow sonar slams into me as the last Taker throws themselves off the ramp. They hit the ground, but not before they are shredded by bullets.

Then there's nothing but my heart hammering in my ringing ears.

I crawl back to Leela and Chris. She's sitting up now and shaking her head repeatedly, like she can get her ears to work right again if she just jiggles them around some more.

"Are you okay?" I shout over the screaming of my own eardrums.

"Define 'okay,'" she shouts back.

Then Jay and Hart are there, slip-sliding over the icy grass to crouch beside us.

"Good shooting, bro," Hart says. "I think you got 'em all."

"Lim, cover us," Sergeant Nolan calls, striding past with a pair of marines I can't identify under their helmets. "Hart, scramble a fire-suppression team. Get them back here ASAP."

"Yes sir!" Hart calls, racing toward the 3D shop as Sarge turns to me.

"Watson, how many Takers are still on that ship?"

"I think there's one more Sorrow on board," I say. "But I don't think they're a Taker, so they might not be armed."

"Copy that," Sarge says, waving to two other marines to follow him up *Trailblazer*'s ramp.

"The kids—" I start to ask Jay, but he waves the question off.

"They're safe," he says, swinging his rifle to his shoulder as he pivots to scan the airfield. "Shhh."

Leela, Chris, and I huddle next to him as a handful of minutes stumble past. Slowly the ringing in my ears begins to fade, only to be replaced by screaming pain in the rest of my body. I shift my weight, trying to find a position where my ribs don't feel like they're going to tear out of my chest. That's when I hear a jagged moan. My head snaps up just in time to see the gray-robed Sorrow scrambling down from the *Trailblazer*'s emergency hatch.

"Jay!" I hiss, as the Sorrow races for the burned-out shield perimeter.

Jay pivots, training his rifle on the dulled glow of the fleeing Sorrow. I can feel his body go tense against mine

I brace for the crack of the shot.

It never comes.

Jay tracks the slightly glowing form until they disappear, then swears and drops to his haunches.

"Damn it," he mutters.

"That Sorrow was running away," I say. "And I don't think they're armed. It wouldn't have been right to shoot them."

A piercing Sorrow scream rips through the night.

Pain explodes through my head. I clutch my temples and twist, searching for the source of that terrible sound.

"No!" Jay shouts. I follow his gaze up the airfield, where the gray-robed Sorrow Jay didn't shoot is running straight at a marine. The Sorrow screams again and the sound pounds into my ears like nails. The marine collapses and the Sorrow bolts away into the night.

Jay races toward the fallen soldier. I limp after him, texting Doc as I go. Whoever that is, they clearly need a medic.

But when I get there, I can see it's already too late.

Jay is cradling Hart's head in his lap. The private's eyes stare wide into the starry sky, empty and red with burst blood vessels. More blood runs from his ears.

Hart is dead.

THIRTEEN

For a while, things happen faster than my brain can process them. Everything is a mash-up of sounds and sensations and images. Cold. Angry voices. Dr. Kao's hands on Jay's shoulders. Leela and Chris being loaded onto a hover carts. Pain radiating through my ribs. Familiar hands on my chest and shoulders. A pain patch on the back of my neck. The stiff, metallic sound of the zipper on a body bag, closing over Hart's empty eyes.

"Joanna." Doc's gentle voice slips through the fog in my brain. "We need to move him now, dear."

I look up and see Doc and Dad standing over me.

Jay is gone.

I look past them, scanning the airfield for him. *Battlefield*, a little voice whispers in the back of my head. That's what this is now.

The fires are out and someone has set up work lights to illuminate the wreckage. There's a lot of wreckage. The crashed Sorrow flyer is twisted in a deadly embrace with the flyer it fell on. Across the field, engineers are swarming over the *Trailblazer*. Her fuselage is a charred mess, and it looks like there might be hull damage. Leela must have cut just enough of the power regulator to make the inexperienced Sorrow pilot overload the engines.

The *Vulcan* is crouched beside her. The little ship looks undamaged. So does *3212*.

I step back, giving Dad and Doc room to pull the hover cart close. Then I help them heft Hart's body onto it. The pain in my ribs is dulled by the patch, but it's there. So is the biting wind, which cuts effortlessly through my thermal. My arms ache, too, in the dull way of overstrained muscles. I'm sure my whole body will hurt by morning, but pain is better than the formless unreality of shock.

"How many people did we lose, Dad?"

Dad sighs. "Six. But they took a lot of Sorrow with them . . . we've found a dozen Taker corpses so far."

Eighteen beings. Dead. For some raw.

For a moment, I think I'm going to throw up.

"I think you should come back to medical with me, young woman," Doc says. "Chris and Leela are already there."

"No!" I blurt the word out louder than I mean to. "No, please, I want to help. I need to . . . please."

"If Doc wants you in medical, you're gonna go, kiddo," Dad says.

But Doc shakes his head.

"Sometimes, the needs of the mind outweigh the needs of the body," he says. "Do what you feel you must, Joanna."

"And after that, you hit medical," Dad insists. "You read me?" Then he gently pulls me close. I wrap my arms around him and squeeze. Hard. I don't care if it hurts. "You terrify me, kid," he mutters into my hair. "You and Leela are lucky you didn't fry yourselves alive with that stunt."

With that, he helps Doc push the hover cart with Hart's body on it back to the 3D shop, where a line of other carts bearing black-shrouded bodies is waiting.

I didn't see the dead after Ord attacked us using the raptors. I was in medical, being treated for the concussion and dislocated shoulder he left me with. By the time I got out, the dead were just gone. A list of names on the memorial stone.

I don't even know who else is in those body bags. Marines, I'm sure. But which ones? Are they from the *Pioneer* squadron? Familiar faces twist through my mind. Or are they *Prairie* squadron? Is that little boy going to lose more than his bear tonight?

"You should get out of here."

I turn toward Jay's voice to find him trudging across the field carrying a half dozen empty fire suppressors in each hand. His face and hair are caked with soot.

"Are you okay?" I ask, hurrying to take some of the canisters from him.

"That isn't even relevant," he says. "I'm doing my job. Too late. But I'm doing it."

"What are you talking about?" I say. "You saved my life tonight. And Leela and Chris."

"And I got Hart killed."

"What?" I nearly choke on the word. "Jay. You didn't—"

"Exactly. I could have shot that Sorrow. Easily. Hart would still be alive if I had."

"You don't know that," I say.

He laughs, harsh and bitter.

"Yeah. You're right. I could have missed. Then I'd just be a bad shot instead of a coward."

"That Sorrow was running away. You couldn't have known—"

"EXACTLY!" Jay roars, dropping the suppressors and spinning on me. "I didn't know where that thing was going or whether they were armed or how many ways they might be able to kill us without a weapon. But I knew the Sorrow were attacking us. Killing us. I knew our people were counting on me. And I failed."

"Damn straight, *Private*." Shelby sneers, striding up the field toward us. "But that's a big-ass club today. You want to start making up for it? Fall in."

Jay follows orders without another word, marching stiffly up the field behind her. Other marines join them as they go, falling into two straight lines behind Shelby. They march to the six float carts bearing human bodies. Each pair takes the handles of one cart.

Shelby calls out, "Honor guard, at-ten-TION!"

The whole airfield goes quiet as the marines snap to attention. Shelby lets the moment hang for a few seconds. Then she calls out, "Honor guard, MARCH!"

The silence lingers as the marines slowly walk their dead comrades up the street toward the medical center, and for several minutes after. Their grief is almost as palpable as the lingering smoke.

"Hello, Little Moth."

I turn to find Grandpa standing a few meters behind me. He's streaked in soot and blood and grease. The skin of his face is red, like he got too close to the fire at some point.

"Are you okay?" I ask.

"I think that's my line," he says, a spare smile touching his lips. "Dr. Divekar's last report said you had broken ribs and possibly whiplash. Shouldn't you be in the medical center?"

"Probably," I say. "I wanted to help. But . . ."

"It's easy to feel helpless in the face of such violence," he says, understanding what I'm trying to say more clearly than I do.

"I don't like it," I say.

"Neither do I," he says.

We stand there, quietly taking in the smoking wreckage

around us. Then he asks me, "After the Sorrow brought down the Landing's shield, you took the *Vulcan*, and your friends, straight here. You didn't know our marines were waiting, did you?"

"No," I say, the word dry and crumbling in my mouth. "Leela was worried . . . we thought Mrs. Divekar and the kids were here alone."

"So you three decided to risk your lives, and a ship with technology on it that could kill us all, to try to help them," he says. His voice sounds strange. Tense. Almost tearful.

"I'm sorry, Grandpa," I say, startled. "I know it was a risk—"

"A risk I wouldn't have taken," he says, cutting me off. "And my caution would have cost us dearly. If you hadn't been here, we wouldn't have known they were after the *Trailblazer*. Not until it was too late. We'd never have recovered from the loss of that much raw. Much less what they might have done, had they been able to reach orbit." He drags his hands through his white hair, just like Mom does when she's upset. "Everything I did could have been for nothing, Little Moth."

He drops to his knees in the fire-scarred grass, like he suddenly lacks the strength to stand.

I don't know what to do. Mom's meltdown was awful, but this is worse.

This is Grandpa.

He's lived through every kind of trouble. He never loses

his cool. But right now his eyes are wide-open windows to the raging storm of pain inside his head.

A faint memory surfaces at the thought.

Grandpa, in his cabin, sitting in a deck chair looking out on the lake. I must have been little. The chair looks huge in my memory. I could hear the murmur of Mom's and Dad's voices in the background but didn't know what they were saying. I was totally focused on Grandpa. On the burning coals of his eyes as he stared out at the water.

It's just a fragment. I don't remember anything happening when I was little that could have put that look on Grandpa's face. I don't remember anything really bad happening at all in my life, until Teddy died. But clearly, there are things about Grandpa's life I don't know.

"It's okay, Grandpa," I say, quietly. "We stopped the Sorrow. They didn't get the raw or the shuttle. The fires are a setback, but we still have nine weeks before the survivors have to come down. We'll find a way." I take one of his hands in mine and tug. I need him to get up. I need him to keep going. "Just gotta catch one little fish at a time, right?"

He looks at me and his face creases into a smile so sad, it makes me want to weep.

"Have I ever told you how much you remind me of your grandmother, Little Moth?" he says.

"Um, no," I say, confusion twining around my sadness and fear and exhaustion. I've seen footage of my grandmother Cleo. She was petite and blond and elegant. I'm none of those things.

"She never let me give up," he says. "I wouldn't be here if not for her." Longing washes over his face. "Some days I wonder . . ."

He trails off, his gaze slipping away from mine again.

"What do you wonder, Grandpa?"

He looks surprised at the question, like he didn't mean to say that out loud. "Nothing, Little Moth," he says, taking my offered hand and using it to lever himself to his feet. "Just an old man's wandering mind."

He shakes his whole body like he's flinging the stress and sadness away. Then he grins. The expression is so out of place that it isn't at all comforting. "I told you that you'd earn that promotion."

"I, ah, yeah. I guess you did," I say, trying to not sound freaked out by the sudden turn in mood and conversation.

"You're a bright, passionate girl," he says. "A credit to humanity." He gazes back at what's left of our shuttle and the charred remains of the new construction beyond it. "But this is not your burden, Little Moth. It's mine. And I will make it right, without any more bodies being carried through these streets."

"Admiral." Grandpa and I both turn to find Shelby standing behind us. "We need to talk."

"I know," he says. There's so much pain in his voice. It makes me ache. "Joanna, if you'll excuse us."

"Sir—"

"Don't make the admiral ask you twice, Junior," Shelby snaps. "Get moving."

Grandpa doesn't contradict her, so I leave, the ruins of everything I wanted this world to be sprawling out behind me.

FOURTEEN

I thought my ribs hurt before, but now that my body has had time to stiffen up, I can hardly put one foot in front of the other. I need pain patches. So, so many pain patches.

When I get to medical, Leela is curled on a scanner bed with a nebulizer over her nose and mouth. She aspirated some fuel while cutting the power regulator. Chris is sitting on the scanner bed next to hers, tapping his foot impatiently as Dr. Kruppa fits a sling over his wounded arm.

"It feels fine," he complains. "I don't need this."

"Maybe not," Kruppa fires back. "But the dermaglue does. If you rip that wound open again, the nanobots will leak out and it'll take weeks to heal. Do you want that?"

"No," I supply, sliding onto the bed next to his. "He doesn't."

"What I want is some food," Chris grumbles.

Kruppa rolls her eyes. "Then what are you still doing here?"

She doesn't have to ask Chris twice.

"Catch you later," he calls out as he flees.

I try not to doze as Dr. Kruppa checks me over. It turns out I don't have whiplash, but I do have four cracked ribs. Kruppa draws some blood and then disappears into Doc's lab to program a nanobot injection that will help them heal faster.

I haven't had nanobots in my system in months, not since the Sorrow healed my cardiovascular system. I am unreasonably squigged out by the thought of having a couple of million robots smaller than my blood cells running around my body again. When Kruppa comes back with a syringe full of gently sparkling liquid, I almost say no. My ribs will heal on their own, after all. It'll just take a lot longer. But then I look at Leela, trying to sleep through her treatment, and the dozen injured marines and civilians in the beds all around us.

There's no time for me to sideline myself being squeamish.

Kruppa makes me stay for another hour, so she can make sure the nanobots are working. By the time she releases me, it's so late, it's early. The Landing feels too quiet without the gentle hum of the shield. I can't believe the force field is still down. It's been hours. The damage must have been extensive.

It isn't just the shield. The streets are empty, except for

one grim, soot-caked marine standing guard in front of Ground Control. Even when no one's around, the Landing is never this still. You can always hear the murmur of voices or footsteps from somewhere. But not tonight. Tonight, the camp feels like a wounded thing, trying to disappear into stillness.

The silence is broken by Chris's voice.

"Joey!"

I drag myself out of the bleak maze of my thoughts and turn to see him hurrying across the square toward me.

"What's wrong?" I say.

"It's Jay. He's . . ." Chris shakes his head. "Come on."

I follow Chris to the supply depot. We wind around racks of equipment and stacks of extra clothes and boots to a door in the back wall. Chris pushes it open and ushers me into a walk-in supply closet, like the one Beth and I have coopted in the greenhouse.

The shelves that line the walls are mostly empty. A low table in the center of the square room holds a tangle of beakers and metal tubing suspended above a pair of Bunsen burners. Clear liquid drips out of one of the tubes into a bag.

I knew the engineers had a still somewhere, but I didn't know where they kept it. I'm the commander's daughter and the admiral's granddaughter. Nobody's going to tell me where they keep the contraband.

"I told you to leave me alone." Jay's voice is sticky and slurred.

I look past the still, into the shadows at the back of the little room. He's sitting on the floor, clutching a mostly empty bag of alcohol. A second bag is empty at his feet.

"You're drinking," I say, shocked. Jay never drinks. Alcohol messes with the nanobots in his nervous system that let him control his braces.

"I'm drunk," he corrects, sucking the bag dry and dropping it on the floor.

I throw a look back at Chris. He shrugs. "That's why I went to get you. I didn't want to risk someone else finding him and reporting him."

"Relax, squirt," Jay says. "I can take care of myself."

Chris's eyes narrow. He hates it when people talk to him like he's a little kid. Jay knows that. He's being a jerk on purpose.

"You did the right thing, Chris," I say. "Can you get him some coffee?"

"*That* is going to be counterproductive," Jay grumbles. "To my goal. Of being drunk."

"I think you're mission accomplished on that one," Chris mutters sourly. Then he shoves his way out of the storage room, leaving us alone.

I sit next to Jay and slip my hand into his. I almost expect him to push me away, but he doesn't.

We sit there for a while. Finally, he says, "I killed seven Takers today, and it wasn't enough."

"You saved my life today," I say. "And Leela's. And

maybe the lives of all the survivors on the *Prairie*, if the Sorrow had gotten away with the *Trailblazer*. Your mom. Your sister."

"Don't you think I know that?" he whispers. "I had to do it. I didn't have a choice. But neither did they."

"They attacked us, Jay," I protest, but he cuts me off.

"They're just trying to defend their home," he says. "And I had to kill them for it. Seven beings. And it should have been eight. But I couldn't . . ." He slams his head back against the shelves behind us. "Why couldn't I pull the trigger?"

"The gray Sorrow was running away," I point out again.

"And they didn't hesitate to kill Hart, when he got in their way." Tears start to roll down Jay's cheeks. "Pulling the trigger was so easy, the first time. That Taker was swinging his hammer at you and I . . . it was like my hands just did it. All on their own. But once we were out of the heat of the moment, it was different. I knew I needed to shoot that gray Sorrow. I knew it. But I went to pull the trigger and . . ." He scrubs at his face. "Damn it. What's wrong with me?"

"You couldn't have known what would happen," I insist.

"No. And I can't know what will happen if I hesitate again. I need to be . . ." He trails off. Swallows hard. "I don't know if I can be what I need to be."

"You mean the kind of person who'd shoot another being in the back?"

"Hart had three younger brothers," Jay whispers. "His adopted parents died last year, so he was raising them. Those kids are sleeping in the mess hall right now, with the *Prairie* families. One of them is only ten. And now they're going to be orphaned all over again on an alien planet because I am not the kind of person who can shoot another being in the back."

I want to tell him he's wrong, but he isn't.

I want to tell him that doesn't matter, but it does.

I want to tell him that we need him to be exactly the kind of person he is. I want to tell him that *I* need him to be himself. But I don't know if that will help him. I don't know if this world is going to let him be the sweet, thoughtful man he is.

"What does it matter how I shoot a Sorrow, anyway?" Jay cries. "It's not like anything about this is *ever* going to be fair. This is the Sorrow's planet and we have to take it from them. Our people need it. My mom, my sister, they need this place. And it's my job to make sure that they're safe here. I want to do that. I really do. But doing that means that I'm going to have to kill more beings who are just trying to protect their home. Their families. Their way of life. How do I live with that?"

How can any of us live with that?

I have no idea.

I wrap my arms around Jay's waist and pull him against me, like I can put myself between him and all the horrible thoughts. His arms close around me, hard enough to shoot fresh pain through my ribs. I ignore it and burrow closer.

We stay that way until Chris comes back with Beth instead of coffee.

"I thought Dr. Kao would ask a lot of questions if I took a thermos at this hour," Chris says. "So I went to the greenhouse to use the coffee maker, and . . ."

"And I had a better idea," my sister says, pulling a patch out of her pocket and holding it out to Jay. "This will help metabolize the alcohol. Much more effective than caffeine."

"Thanks, B," Jay mutters. But he doesn't take the patch from her. I grab it and activate the adhesive, then press it against his neck. He doesn't try to stop me.

It takes all three of us to get Jay to the greenhouse. Whatever the engineers are brewing in that still is strong. Even with the patch, he has a hard time staying awake on the walk. We help him onto my bed, and he's snoring before I manage to get his braces all the way off.

When I come back into the greenhouse proper, Leela is there. She's pale and her breath is ragged.

"Why aren't you in medical, sucking nanobots?" I demand.

Leela shrugs. "Ask Beth. She texted. Said you needed me."

"Overreaction," I say. "Jay's okay."

"He's not going to die of alcohol poisoning," Beth says. "But that's not the same as 'okay.'"

"Don't you think I know that?" I collapse at the lab table, fighting to hold back tears. "He's not okay at all. And now . . . it's just going to get worse."

"You think the admiral's going to go on the offensive?" Leela asks.

"Don't you?"

She nods. "I'm going to enlist in the morning."

"No!" The word jumps out of my mouth before I can stop it.

"Why not?" she demands. "Why should Jay and everyone else in the squads have to fight for us while I waste years of combat training sitting on the sidelines?"

"Lee-lu—" I start to say, but she cuts me off with a wheezing gasp.

"No, tell me, Jo. I'm begging you. Give me a reason not to pick up a gun."

"If you'd seen Jay tonight—"

"Not good enough!" Leela cries. "I had three semesters of trauma-informed cognitive behavioral training at the Academy. Jay didn't. I can take it."

"No," I say, more sure than I've been of anything in a long time. "You can't. It's not the violence. It's . . . this isn't self-defense. It's survival. But that doesn't change the fact that we're taking their planet." Jay's words echo in my ears. "Killing beings who are protecting their home."

Leela sucks in a ragged breath. "I can do that. I can do that to save our species. No. Screw that. To save our families. My cousins are up there. Ruti and Som and Bella and Harsh and . . ." She sucks in a shaky breath and swipes at the tears gathering in her eyes. "I can't let them die because I don't want to do what it takes to save them."

I know that. But the pain in Jay's eyes is painted over everything I see now. Every thought I have. I don't want to see that look in Leela's eyes. But I will. There's no way to stop her. And I shouldn't. We're going to need her on the front lines, right next to Jay.

And what will I be doing? Delivering their bodies back to the Landing?

There has to be a better way.

I turn to Beth.

"This morning, up at the nest, you told me that you don't trust Grandpa."

She nods.

"I need you to tell me why."

Beth stares at me. I meet her gaze and wait, trying hard not to hold my breath.

"Okay." She shoves both hands through the ruff of hair that's grown out from her usual buzz cut. "Okay."

She takes a deep breath. My stomach clenches.

"You've always idolized Grandpa. And he has never given you reason to doubt him. But I know the lengths he's willing to go to, in order to get what he wants. And I know . . ." She shakes her head. "No. I don't know. I *hypothesize* that he often prioritizes his own needs over those of others. I don't believe we can assume he has the best interests of our species at heart."

"Nope." Leela turns on her heel and marches to the exit. "Nope. I'm not doing this. If we start questioning each other. Fighting amongst ourselves—"

"We might find a better way to survive," I say, cutting her off.

She stops, her hand on the door.

"You really think so?"

"There has to be a better way," I say, trying to convince myself as much as Leela. I turn to my sister. "Tell me."

"I was supposed to go to Stanford, remember?" Beth says. "I applied with a research proposal that the Earth Restoration Project had already committed to fund. I wanted to tailor bacteria to terraform soil on Earth to help repair the planet. Fix new nitrogen in the blight zones. Grow crops that would utilize the excess carbon in our atmosphere and stabilize the food supply. In success, it would have allowed the planet to find a new equilibrium. We would have been able to phase out artificial efforts that required maintenance."

"Like nanofilters that might malfunction when you push an OS update, causing a cascade failure that eventually destroys the planet?" I say dully, realizing where she's going with this.

Beth nods.

"My work would have made the filtration system obsolete, and the admiral killed it. He got the ERP to pull my funding and informed Stanford that he considered the research dangerously reckless." She shrugs. "Given our experiences with my terraforming bacteria on Tau, he may have been right."

"That was the ISA's fault," I protest. "If you'd known about the phytoraptors, things would have been different."

Beth looks up at me, and just for a moment I see the grief burning in her eyes. The guilt. The longing. It's easy to forget how deeply Beth feels things.

"Perhaps," she says finally, "perhaps not. But it was a valid idea that might have saved Earth. It should have been explored."

"But it would have made nanofilters a thing of the past. Which would have wiped out a big piece of the admiral's legacy," Leela says, realization wicking up the words.

Beth nods again.

"Mom tried to convince me that the atmospheric scrubbers had nothing to do with Grandpa's decision," she says. "Dad didn't. He and Dr. Howard had to pull a lot of strings to get me into MIT and undo the damage Grandpa's letter to Stanford did."

I take the thought a step further. "The atmospheric scrubber system, his legacy, which destroyed Earth," I say. "It killed most of humanity. That's his legacy now. . . ."

"Unless he is the one who gives the human species a 'new beginning,'" Beth says, quoting the words that Grandpa spoke that first night, minutes after he first stepped onto Tau soil. "Since he took command, we haven't even stopped to debate his strategy. His way may be the right way. But it might not be."

"I have to go to the Solace," I say. "I have to go back and try to talk to Tarn."

"What!" Leela cries. "Jo, the last time you saw him, he tried to kill you."

"And Shelby tried to kill him," I say. "Nobody did the right thing that night. Including me. And we never gave ourselves a chance to do better."

Leela shakes her head. "Best-case scenario here is that we all get court-martialed."

"No," Chris says. He's been quiet up till now. "Best-case scenario is we stop a war that should never have started in the first place. If I get court-martialed for that, I'm cool with it."

"Agreed," Beth says.

My hand drifts to the pips on my collar. These two little pins are literally the only thing about my life that turned out the way I expected it to. Better than I expected, really. Grandpa gave them to me himself. And he did it because he believes in me.

I don't want to give that up.

I don't want to let Grandpa down.

A wheezing snore sounds from the open door to Beth's and my room, like a punch thrown wild against a harsh world.

Jay.

All I can see of him from here is one of his still-booted feet, hanging off the end of my cot. Even if he doesn't die, he won't survive a war with the Sorrow. Not as the boy I know. Not as the boy I love.

I love him, I realize, so abruptly and completely that my brain can't even bother to be surprised. With that realization comes a certainty. The first one I've felt in a long time. Maybe since before we woke up in the Solace, almost a year ago.

It doesn't matter if Tarn is my friend. It doesn't matter if I can trust him. It doesn't even really matter if he kills me. I have to go to the Solace, and I have to try to stop this war now, while I still can. Not just for the Sorrow's sake, but for ours. For Leela and Jay and Mom and even Grandpa. He was just as crushed by the attack as the rest of us. And he said it himself. His caution might have cost us everything tonight. And if I don't do this, it might still.

"I have to go to the Solace," I repeat.

Leela huffs a sigh. "Don't be stupid. *We* have to go to the Solace."

"No," I say. "Leela, I don't want to risk—"

"Neither do I," she snaps. "But I want to kill people who are just defending their home even less. Chris is right. At least this way, we die trying."

"It probably won't work," I say quietly.

"So let's be improbable," Beth says. "Please."

The words rebound through my brain, summoning another moment. Another certainty.

I knew for sure that I could save the *Pioneer*, even though Mom and everyone else thought the solar flare had doomed the ship. I was right, but Teddy died because of it.

I look from Beth to Leela to Chris, to the open door into the room where the boy I love lies heartbroken. Will one of them die for this? Can I live with that?

Does it matter?

If there is a better way, we're it. Our people need us. This planet needs us.

We have to go back to the Solace.

FIFTEEN

The others are sleeping.

We agreed we won't leave for the Solace until dawn, so resting is the smart thing to do. I can't, so I'm packing. We're not just going to run off with nothing but whatever happens to be stashed in our utility harnesses this time.

About 47 percent of me wants to go to Grandpa's cabin and tell him what we're planning. He'd stop us. Then my friends would be safe. I would be safe.

My stupid ensign tabs would be safe.

And everything and everyone I care about will be ruined.

But what if Grandpa is right? What if it is too late?

What if the Sorrow kill us all?

I shy away from the question and try to focus on my

list. I've already packed beta flyer with dried rations, fresh water, three satellite phones, two tents, and a portable particle shield. It took some work to fit it all in. I thought about removing the flyer's emergency water-landing kit, which is bulky because it contains a self-inflating Zodiac and inflatable life jackets. If this goes according to plan, we won't need them. We won't be going anywhere near water. But nothing ever goes according to plan on Tau, so I found a way to fit it all in.

The next thing on my list is a fresh medical kit. The flyer's kit is gone—someone must have grabbed it last night. I'll have to sneak into the medical center for a new one. If I get caught, it's going to be tough to explain why I'm restocking flyers in the middle of the night. We might not be able to get away.

I kind of hope I get caught.

I close the flyer's ramp behind me and walk through the empty streets of the Landing to the medical center.

When I get there, the lights are turned low, so that the wounded can try to sleep. Doc has taken over for Dr. Kruppa, but they're short staffed, so it's just him and a medic. I wait until they're both focused on a patient and then slip into Doc's lab, where he keeps extra supplies.

The lab is the size of a single-family cabin. More than half of it is taken up by floor-to-ceiling shelves crammed with diagnostic equipment and pharmaceutical supplies. There's also a lab table, benches, and a small 3D printer used to print medical nanobots.

I grab a new medical kit from storage, then turn to leave and nearly collide with my mother.

"Mom!" I blurt out, startled.

"Joanna." Her voice sounds calm, but it isn't. There's something tight inside it. Not anxious, exactly. There's more anger in it than that.

She doesn't ask me what I'm doing in Doc's lab in the middle of the night. She doesn't even slow down as she crosses to the morgue door and goes inside.

That room was supposed to be storage. We've been using it as a morgue since Ord called down a raptor attack on the Landing. We didn't include one in the original plans for the medical center because it didn't occur to anyone that we'd have a surplus of dead bodies anytime soon.

I follow her.

A big medical composter crouches at the back of the square room. Six insulated sleep crates are lined up on the floor in front of it. Inso crates are designed for deep sleep, but they work just as well to seal and preserve dead bodies so that their families can have a chance to say goodbye.

Mom walks from crate to crate, studying each face intently.

I should get out of here before she bothers to wonder what I'm doing. I watch her instead.

I'm starting to think she forgot I'm here when she straightens and looks me right in the eye. "Your grandfather tried to stop me from marrying your father."

The non sequitur is surprisingly urgent. Like she's try-ing to tell me something. Or maybe like she's trying to tell herself something.

"Why?" I ask cautiously.

Mom looks down at the inso crates holding our dead marines again. "He thought your father was frivolous. Ideal-istic. Ridiculous. Dreaming of other worlds while ours was collapsing."

She quirks a tiny smile. The kind that isn't meant for anyone else to see. "But that's why I married Nick. He had . . . ideas. Hope. He thought that humanity needed to do more than just survive. He thought we needed to strive for something bigger."

"'Unrealistic goals are what makes us human'?" I say, quoting one of Dad's favorite self-made clichés.

She nods. "Without his unrealistic goals, we wouldn't have discovered Tau. And without Tau . . ."

"We'd already be gone."

She shoves a hand through her hair and straightens her shoulders, pulling her body upright and square. "But we're not gone," she says. "We're here." Her eyes drift back to the dead marines. "And we can do better than this."

Her voice is different. But familiar, for the first time in weeks. She sounds like herself again. She sounds like the commander.

"What are you going to do, Mom?"

"I don't know yet," she says. Then she throws a pointed look at the medical kit slung across my shoulder. "Whatever it is *you're* going to do, bring a second kit. You might not need it, but if you do . . ."

"Mom—"

"Yes?"

I want to tell her everything. I want her to help. Or at least tell me I'm doing the right thing. But if she could do that, we wouldn't be in this situation. This is a choice I have to make for myself.

"I love you," I say instead.

"I love you, too," she says. Then she leaves the morgue.

I take her advice and grab a second medical kit.

First light is just staining the edges of the sky as I walk back to the greenhouse. I feel strange, after that conversation with Mom. Better, sort of. Worse, too.

She told me that she needed me, two months ago, when we still thought we had a home to go back to. She needs me still. Not as a cadet, following her orders, but as . . . I don't know what I am now.

I push the greenhouse door open and walk into a tangle of angry voices.

Chris is saying something about how we'll get caught before we even leave, if everyone doesn't shut up, but I can hardly hear him over Leela and Jay yelling at each other.

"Oh, so you just decided to get wasted for kicks, then?"

Leela demands, talking over Jay as he bellows, "This isn't about *me*!"

"Yes, it is," I say, raising my voice to cut into the argument.

Jay pivots to glare at me. "Well, save it, then, because I don't need your pity. And I won't let you put the whole species in danger just because I felt sorry for myself for a minute."

"It isn't pity, Jay," I say. "It's love. I love you. And I can't just stand here and watch them break you when there might be a better way."

Color blasts into his face. He stares at me. I grit my teeth against the qualifiers and retractions in my head. I'm about to put my life on the line. Why not put my heart out there, while I'm at it?

"Nobody's asking anything of me that isn't being asked of everyone else," he says, very quietly this time.

"This shouldn't be asked of anyone," Beth says.

Jay shakes his head. "*Shouldn't* has nothing to do with this. The IntGov *shouldn't* have wrecked Earth with an operating system update, either. But they did. So here we are. And I have to get over myself and deal. Not ignore my orders and run away to try to . . . what the hell do you all think you're going to accomplish, anyway? Talk Tarn into being nice to us?"

It sounds so stupid when he puts it that way. Ridiculous. Dangerous. Naive.

Panic tugs at my throat, clinging to the words I'm trying to slap together into an argument. But the fear doesn't make me want to run away. Not anymore. It makes me angry.

"No," I snap. "I'm going to *ask* Tarn to give us asylum on his planet. He might say no. He might kill me just for asking. But if last night is the other alternative, then I have to try."

"Jo." Jay is almost whispering now. "I can't let you do this for me."

"You aren't *letting* me do anything," I say. "I don't need your permission. I need your help."

He shakes his head, turning away from me to look out through the glass wall.

It gets painfully quiet. I don't know what else to say.

"Which flyer are we taking?" Beth asks.

"Beta," I say. My eyes still on Jay's back.

"Fine," she says, striding to the door. "Don't waste too much time talking him into it."

Chris and Leela follow her.

Now it's just Jay and me. I know Beth is right. We need to go. I don't know how to convince him. Maybe I can't. But I can't just walk away either. If I do that, I have the worst feeling I'll never see him again.

"Come with us," I say. "Don't do this for yourself. Do it for me. Do it for all of us. You won't be the only one who gets ruined by this."

All of a sudden, I know why Mom told me that story about how Grandpa didn't want her marrying Dad. I know what she was trying to tell me.

"War might be our best hope for survival," I say, the words coming together faster now. "But surviving isn't enough. To be human, we have to be more than that. So I'm going to try to convince Tarn to help us. I have no idea how, but . . . I know I need your help."

I walk out of the greenhouse without waiting for him to reply. My heart is pounding. I don't realize that I'm holding my breath until I hear the wheezing whisper of his braces behind me as he jogs to catch up.

SIXTEEN

By the time I reach the flyer, Leela has finished preflight. She's sitting in the copilot seat, leaving the pilot seat for me. The others are already tethered in. Fear prickles over my skin as I make my way to the front. But it feels different from the negative emotions that have been choking me for the last three weeks. Cleaner. I'd be delusional if I weren't afraid right now. This mission is unauthorized and wildly dangerous. It probably won't work.

But it's the right thing to do.

I know that, on a level that's more physical than intellectual. It's like that feeling I get when I'm lining a shuttle up for docking. I'm in the right place at the right time.

I hear the rear hatch sealing behind me as I attach my stiffened flex to the arm of my chair and bring up the navigation app.

"All present and accounted for," Jay says. The mundane words tense with emotion.

I pivot my chair to look back at him as he tethers into the back row.

"Last chance for regrets."

"Been there," Jay says. "Bought the T-shirt. And the postcards."

"I didn't know you were such a souvenir guy," Chris says, relief in his light tone.

Beth rolls her eyes. "Must we engage in witty banter at this hour of the morning?"

"Yes," Leela and Chris say, simultaneously.

Jay chokes on a tight laugh.

I feel lighter as I twist my chair back to face the wall screens and press my hands gently up the nav app.

The flyer leaps into the air.

I breathe out. It feels good. Like I've been holding my breath for weeks and didn't notice until just now. I drag air into my lungs again, letting my body soak in the oxygen. I don't know what's going to happen when we get to the Solace. We might not live to see another sunrise. But at least I can breathe now.

Walk in the present, Joey. That's the only way we get to see the future.

Miguel's voice runs through my brain, his laughter ghosting under the words. He was dead less than an hour after he said them. But, impossibly, that doesn't seem to sour the memory. The ghost of his laughter twists into a different remembered scene. Different words, spoken in the minutes before another untimely death.

This new world is going to be ours. Not a hand-me-down that's held together with solar paneling and wishful thinking.

Teddy never got to see Tau. And it isn't ours, not by a long shot. But we still have a responsibility to it. And to our species. There has to be a way to protect them both.

The prismatic crystal peaks of the Diamond Range spike out of the softer hills up ahead. Tendrils of morning light twist between the crystal crags, and their fragmented rainbows catch in the exterior camera lenses, splashing color across our 360-degree view.

"I forgot," Chris says, quietly. "I've been locked in the 3D lab for so long, so . . ."

"Scared," Beth says.

He nods. "Yeah. That, too. I was busy and scared and I just . . . forgot."

Walk in the present, Joey.

I feel a little smile spreading over my lips as I raise my fingers, giving us the lift we need to rear up over the Maze Plateau. Then I pour on the speed, letting myself enjoy the rush as we hurtle through the thin air, just at the edge of the sky.

"We've got company," Leela says, swiping quickly at her flex as we wheel out over Angel Valley. "Flyer, twelve klicks out."

"They already sent someone after us?" I say, disbelieving.

"No," Leela says. "Can't be. They're ahead of us on a northeast trajectory. Looks like they're headed back to base."

"What were they doing out there?" Chris asks.

Jay makes a little noise, somewhere between a gasp and a groan. I'm not sure anyone else notices, but it fills in the last gaps between several things I already know.

"Take over, okay?" I ask Leela.

She nods.

I pivot my chair again to look back at Jay.

"You know, don't you?"

The misery in his eyes is so intense, it makes me want to take the question back. Tell him he doesn't have to talk about it. Ever.

But he does.

"No point in following orders now, is there?" he says, almost choking on the words. "Shelby's been sending a handful of her squaddies on a special duty they weren't supposed to talk about. Since their second week here. I didn't know why, until—"

Black smoke abruptly chokes the three-sixty view around us.

"What the hell?" Leela mutters as she shoves her hands upward on her nav app, pulling us up and forward above the blinding smoke.

"Ten o'clock," Chris says, pointing ahead of us on the clearing screens. "Forest fire, maybe?"

"Wood smoke wouldn't be so black," Beth says. "The crystal in the rocks is burning."

"That's impossible," Chris says. "The temperatures required—"

"Can be easily attained with a simple flamethrower," Beth says.

"That flyer . . ." Leela can't force herself to finish the thought.

"Yeah," Jay says. "I was getting to that."

"What?" I say, nausea rolling over me with every heart-beat. "What are they doing?"

"Just . . . take us to the source of the smoke, okay?" he says. "You'll see."

I take control back from Leela and swing our flyer wide, heading for the column of smoke, which I can now see is pouring from a familiar deep ravine that would be almost invisible below the tree canopy if it weren't on fire.

"They burned Bob's nest," Chris says, his voice thick with horror.

"Why?" Leela demands. "Why would they go after the raptors? They're not the ones who attacked us."

"No, but they are one of the Sorrow's most danger-ous weapons," Jay says. "The last time the Givers called raptors down on us, we lost half the E&P team. When he demoted me, the admiral said we had to know how to take the raptors out of the equation if that became necessary. I guess, after yesterday, he thinks it's necessary."

There are no words left, after that. Silence fills the flyer as I flip the rotors horizontal and maneuver us between the cliffs, into the billowing black haze.

"Put on your breathers, everyone," Beth says grimly. "We don't know what's in that smoke."

"What's a few unknown toxic chemicals at this point?" Leela rasps, pulling the membrane from her utility harness and spreading it over her nose and mouth.

"Little help?" Chris asks her, fumbling to get his on one handed. As she reaches over to help him, Jay snaps out of his chair and marches to the rear doors, without bothering to put on a breather.

"Jay!" I call to him, but he's already opening the hatch. "Jay, you need a—"

The ramp unfolds and he's gone, storming out into the smoke.

I smack awkwardly at my autoconnect button while trying to fold my flex and get my breather out at the same time. I end up dropping everything instead.

Beth crouches to pick my flex up as I slap my breather over my face.

"You can't help him unless he wants to be helped," she says, her voice pitched low so only I can hear her.

I grab my flex from her. She squeezes my hand. I squeeze it back. Then I slap my flex over my wrist and hurry out of the flyer after Jay.

Beth was right. The crystal burned. The ravine walls are clouded and dark, their jagged edges melted away. Charred forms stagger across the ravine, sprawling and twisting

211

together like cooling lava flow. I can just see the outlines of arms and big-clawed hands in the nearly unrecognizable ash. Phytoraptors. Dozens. The whole nest, burned while they slept.

"How hot do you have to make it to melt that crystal?" Leela says, looking up at the cliffs.

"Seven hundred Celsius," Chris says. "But a nitrogen flamethrower can do that, easy. And Shelby ordered two dozen of them. First priority."

"When?" My mouth feels so dry, the word crumbles on my lips.

"Two weeks ago," Chris says. "Chief Ganeshalingam said they were going to be used to clear land."

"That's one way of putting it," Leela says, bitter humor in her voice.

Jay is standing knee deep in the river, staring down at the charred remains of the juvenile phytoraptors. Bob's babies. They're all dead.

I can feel tears running down my cheeks as I wade into the water to stand beside him. I can't tell if they're tears of grief or outrage. I guess the two aren't mutually exclusive.

Jay doesn't look up as I approach.

"This . . . this is why you think you're weak?" My voice rises of its own accord. "Because you wouldn't burn phytoraptors alive in their nests?"

"They hadn't actually tried it. Yet," he says. "They were still experimenting." He sucks in a shaky breath. "They had captured a couple of raptors. Small ones. They had them in an empty canyon, somewhere south of here. They'd already tried fire, I guess, and it hadn't worked. But Shelby wanted to see if it would work better while they were . . ." He chokes on the word.

"Sleeping," I supply, faintly.

He nods.

"I didn't stop them, the first time they flamed the raptors. Or the second. The raptors didn't even seem to notice the fire. But Preakness just kept telling Hernandez to turn the heat up, and when they finally got to the highest setting and the raptors started screaming, I just . . . couldn't."

"Of course, you couldn't let them keep tormenting captive—"

"Hernandez got mauled because I stopped them," he says. "The raptor charged and . . . she lost so much blood. I really thought she was going to die. Because of me."

He crouches in the water, trailing his fingers over the blackened remains of one of the baby raptors.

"Preakness hustled me straight to Shelby when we got back," he continues. "I don't think I heard a word she said while she was chewing me out. I just kept demanding to see the admiral."

"But my grandfather knew exactly what Shelby was doing," I say, my heart sinking. I already knew that, but standing in the carnage of my grandfather's decisions . . . it's different from just knowing.

I can see my heartbreak reflected in Jay's eyes.

"It isn't . . ." He trails off, then tries again. "The admiral knows this is . . . terrible. He said when you're young, you think that sacrifices mean stuff like going hungry or dying to protect people. He said surviving and being able to live with yourself aren't always the same thing. That it's our job, as leaders and soldiers, to take on that burden for the rest of our people."

I can hear Grandpa's voice in the words.

"Do you think he's right?" Jay asks.

I turn and look at the devastation behind me, then down at the crumbling remains of Bob's children. For just a moment my brain replaces the ruined nest with the deep-sleep center on the *Prairie*. Thousands of humans, helpless. Maybe dying soon, if we can't make this world safe for them.

I blink, and it's gone. I'm surrounded by destruction again.

What if this is what it takes for them to survive?

"Uh-oh."

My whole body goes light at the dread in Chris's voice. I turn to look back at him. He's staring up at the cliffs. I follow his gaze and see phytoraptors silently dropping down the melted ravine walls all around us. They're only visible because of the soot streaking their skin, breaking the effect of their chameleon-like camouflage.

"Everybody back to the flyer," Leela shouts, but it's

too late. Sunflower leaps onto the ramp, blocking our path to safety. Their mane of yellow petals is a charred, stubby mess oozing thick white blood, but there's no mistaking the deadly being.

Sunflower hisses, and claws flash out of their huge hands.

"Get behind me!" Jay shouts as we slosh through the stream and race back to the others.

"Noble, but not helpful," Beth says. She's right. Raptors are circling us now. Claws and fangs flashing in absolute silence.

Even when they were stalking us around the wreckage of our first shuttle, the phytoraptors were loud. Vicious and terrifying, but in an exuberantly gleeful way. Like hunting was a kind of game for them.

But this isn't hunting. This is rage.

I frantically scan the tightening knot of furious beings, searching for Bob's smooth, round head. I don't know if he'll help us, but at least I can talk to him.

He isn't here. He's probably dead.

We're not going to make it out of here.

Thunk.

A long, flexible shaft buries itself in Sunflower's eye.

The huge raptor topples off the ramp, exposing the jagged crystal tip of a spear jutting from the back of their head.

That's a Sorrow weapon.

That's the last thought I manage before crystal shards

215

and raptor screams fill the air around us. Everything is bright and loud and fast. Except me. My body feels slow and heavy, like I'm moving through water.

Leela's hand clutching at my pant leg is enough to snatch me back into the moment. I drop to the ground beside her.

"We can make it to the ramp!" she shouts, dragging Beth along as she crab walks forward on her elbows. I throw a look back at Jay, who is crouched behind a cluster of melted parrot palms with his body wrapped around Chris like a shield. A chaos of dying phytoraptors and flying crystal boils around them.

We might make it to the flyer, but they won't.

We're going to have to leave them behind.

As though he can hear the awful thought, Jay looks up and meets my eyes. His gaze is like a living thing. A burning cord tethering him into my soul and my mind and my memory.

My heart thuds, echoing against my eardrums. Once. Twice.

Then it's quiet.

Broken phytoraptor bodies litter the ground around us, their sticky white blood sprayed over the flyer and the charred dirt. It smells sweet, almost sugary. Blue Jell-O. Just like the solace trees. Half a dozen heavily armed Sorrow are standing in tight formation a few meters away.

I think I'm going to scream.

I press my lips together until the fear thins into something I can stuff back into my chest. Then I say, "Thank you."

One of the Sorrow strides forward, holding a massive war hammer at the ready.

Okay, so maybe I jumped the gun on the *thank-you* thing.

I shove the thought out of my head. We can't expect them to welcome us. Not after everything that's happened. Actually, it's kind of a miracle they haven't killed us yet.

I guess that's what we're looking for, really. A miracle.

This one will have to do.

I raise my hands slowly. "We're unarmed," I say. "We come in hope of peace. Please. Bring us to the Followed."

SEVENTEEN

The Solace feels sour. Anxious. It's as though the dense hum of Sorrow voices that flows through the cavern city is out of tune.

"What is that?" Jay asks, rubbing his head.

"A city full of beings hating us," Chris says morosely.

"Not hate," I say, feeling the mass of sonar pressing against my skin. "Fear. They're afraid."

"Just one of many things our species have in common," Beth says grimly.

"Goodie," Leela says.

The city reminds me of a toy Teddy had when we were kids—a building kit made of magnetic sticks you could use to build three-dimensional geometric shapes. The asymmetric scaffolding structures are crowded together in a way that seems haphazard but isn't. If you look from the right angle, the city is a huge shadow box that paints moving images of Sorrow fighting phytoraptors on the walls of the cavern.

The mural of light and darkness stands ten or twelve stories tall, and the ceiling is at least twice that here at the outer edges of the cavern. It slopes downward to the city's center—low enough that the massive bioluminescent root clusters that light this hidden world almost brush the cavern floor there.

The discordant ambient melody seems to be putting the Takers who brought us here on edge, too. None of them speak English, but until we got into the Solace, they had seemed pretty low-key about having just captured a bunch of space aliens.

The whole flight back, they were tossing spurts of conversation back and forth between themselves that sparked and bubbled like the air was carbonated. I didn't understand any of it, of course, but the conversation felt familiar. I could have been listening to my friends trading barbs and stupid jokes to keep from being scared.

But now our captors are quiet. They're keeping to the outer edges of the grand boulevard that wraps around the city, probably trying to avoid attracting too much attention. This close to the walls, the shadow figures cast by the city's intricate buildings are warped and lopsided. I know I'm just looking at them from the wrong perspective, but it's unsettling.

A sharp sound pops against my skin, exploding into a

froth of anxiety-barbed chatter from our escorts. They fall into two lines. At attention, I realize, as a glowing figure strides toward us.

Ord! my brain shrieks reflexively. But the flowing robes radiate soft yellow, not Ord's icy violet. Ord is dead. Tarn is the Followed now.

Tarn doesn't even slow down as he slings me over his shoulders like a sack of beans and carries me away into the shadows of the Sorrow city.

"Tarn," I say. "Please. Listen. We came to—"

"Quiet!" he bellows. Then he leaps straight up, catching the cross bar of a skeletal building and swinging a long, triple-jointed leg past my head to grasp the scaffolding above us with the wide-spread digits of his foot. He crouches deeply against the beam, then pushes us up again with another great leap that leaves my guts feeling like they're somewhere around my ears.

The cave floor recedes with terrifying speed as he hurtles through the city, using his free arm and his legs with equal dexterity. I've never seen a Sorrow move like this, but only, I realize, because I wasn't looking. Flecks of light swarm over the buildings around us. Each one is a Sorrow, their biolights gleaming as they catapult through the dark.

The flickering swarm of biolights thins out as we climb higher and higher. Where is he taking me? How am I going to get down? Will I live long enough to try? If I do, how will I ever find my friends again? Will they be safe down there in the angry, fearful city, full of beings we've made our enemies?

We're almost as high as we can go now. The root glow is brighter here, and I can see a single building that stretches above the others. Its dull white frame is draped in stiff, opaque fabric, but multicolored light slips through the scams.

Tarn leaps up to the highest level of the building and throws me at a long stretch of cloth. I have just enough time to scream before I hit the draped wall and roll straight through it, cracking my knees and then my chin on a hard, warm floor inside.

Stars swim through my vision, from both the impact and the light, which seems incredibly bright in contrast to the cave outside. My cracked ribs scream as I struggle to my hands and knees.

"Get up," Tarn growls, grabbing me by the shoulder and yanking me to my feet.

I blink furiously. As my eyes adjust to the light, I can see that the fabric walls and the tiled floor and ceiling are spattered with glowing sprays of every color I've ever imagined.

Blood.

The realization burns through my brain. This room is soaked in layer upon layer of Sorrow blood. Generations' worth, it looks like. And it's all still glowing. That's where the intense light is coming from.

Half a dozen naked Sorrow are moving around us. The

layers of brilliance blur my vision, blending the living light of their bodies into the blood-soaked walls almost like the chameleon camouflage of the phytoraptors.

Rows of dead bodies fill the room, resting on low slabs made of the same off-white material as the floor and ceiling. There are least thirty in here. They aren't all Sorrow—there's a handful of phytoraptor bodies as well. Some have been skinned. Some have been gutted and eviscerated. Some have been stripped down to the bone. The naked Sorrow are dissecting them, I realize, fascinated and horrified at the same time.

"Look!" Tarn snarls, dragging me to one of the skeletons. It's missing the long bones of its legs, but the knotted joints are still lined up on the slab like it's a puzzle with missing pieces. One of the naked Sorrow is sitting at the partially dismantled skeleton's feet, carefully whittling at a creamy white crescent of what must be bone.

The naked Sorrow doesn't even look up as Tarn grabs me by the back of the neck and forces me to look closer at the carving. "Look!" he repeats. "Look!"

My body wants to fight. Or run. I squash the instinct. If I want any hope of Tarn listening to me, I need to listen to him.

My eyes focus on the delicate pattern the naked Sorrow is carving into the bone. It's so familiar. It takes me a moment to realize I've seen it before. On the root cathedral in the heart of the Solace. At the time, I thought those pillars were made of stone, but they aren't. Neither are the tiles of the floor under our feet, I realize, acid welling in the back of my throat. Or the scaffolding holding up this building.

The whole city is made of bone.

"This is how we end," Tarn growls, releasing me so abruptly I nearly fall into the skeleton. "Our bones become the bones of this city. We live as long as it lives. That is the only comfort I can find in knowing I will soon join my pouch mate in this room."

"Your . . . Ord? That's Ord?" I whisper, staring down at the bones.

Tarn hisses something cold and horrible in Sorrow. I don't need him to translate. This is all that's left of the brother he killed to save my life. Ord's death saved the phytoraptors, too, and probably Tau itself, but I bet Tarn still blames me for it.

"Together our bones will make something beautiful out of all the ugliness and death we've left behind," he says, his voice suddenly quiet. Almost a whisper. "All of the lies."

"We were going to leave," I say, my own voice also a shadow of itself. "My mom was ready to take us all back to Earth when the *Prairie* arrived. She was trying to do the right thing. And she kept trying. I've seen her call log, Tarn. She's called you every single day—"

"Since your soldier attacked and nearly killed me!" he snarls, cutting me off.

He's outraged. What right does he have to be outraged?

"She shot at you because you were strangling me, Tarn," I say, fighting to keep the anger from my voice. "You attacked first. She was just protecting me."

He stares at me for a long beat. Then he raises his hands to cover his face, his palms in, in the Sorrow gesture for *no*, and then turns them outward so I can see the glowing yellow veins that run up his wrists and disappear into the thicker skin of his palms. That's the gesture for *yes*. I've never seen them used together that way.

"We will never understand each other," Tarn says. "This is impossible."

"I don't care," I cry, letting my own anger pour out. There's plenty to go around. I'm mad at him. At my parents. At my grandfather. At myself. "If we don't find a way to understand each other, we're going to keep fighting until we destroy ourselves. There has to be a better way."

"My brother didn't think so," Tarn says, looking down at the skeleton between us. "He always planned to kill your team, once he had taken as much of your technology as he could."

"And Ord isn't Followed anymore," I say. "You are. And I think you and I . . . we can find a better way. Maybe we can't understand each other. But we can respect each other."

"Respect?" His mouth flexes, pulling back to reveal his blunt teeth as silent sonar pops over my skin like sparks off a fire.

He's laughing at me.

"Remember where my Takers found you, before you speak of respect." Tarn hums the words in a tone that makes my skin crawl.

"The nest." Just saying the word brings the remembered smell of burned phytoraptors to my nostrils.

"Yes, the nest," Tarn says. "Just one of a dozen my Takers found as the sun rose. Your marines are remarkably effective at destroying the Beasts."

A dozen nests burned. I want to scream. Everything I thought I knew about who we are and why we came here is gone. Rotting in the graveyard that is our home world.

I have no words left. Tarn doesn't seem to, either. We sit there, tied in a silent knot of anger and guilt and desperation over the body of a being we both admired and feared. And hated. The naked Sorrow silently continue to butcher and reshape the dead all around us as though we are not here at all.

"What do you want from me, Joanna?" Tarn says finally.

It's a real question, and I thought I knew the answer. I thought I knew a dozen answers to that question. But they're all gone. What can I possibly ask of him, knowing the things humanity is willing to do to survive on this planet?

No. Not humanity.

Grandpa.

Grandpa did this.

Bob's babies fill my mind, their little bodies swaying as their wide white flowers stretch up to greet the sun.

I'm going to be sick.

I run for the cloth-draped entryway and hurl myself out of the glowing room. I just barely manage to grab onto a railing around the narrow walkway outside, stopping myself before I plunge over the edge.

I collapse to my knees, leaning against the bone railing. Gasping for air. I stay there until the acid in the back of my throat settles, twisting into a thick knot of something that might be tears and might be rage.

I rip the flat silver disks of my rank insignia off my collar and stare at them. I've worked my whole life for these, but if wearing them means being a part of this horror . . .

My first instinct is to hurl them off the edge, but littering a dozen stories up doesn't seem like the best way to rebuild our relationship with the Sorrow. I can't put them back on, either. I don't know if I ever will.

Tears run down my cheeks as I look out over the labyrinthine city below. It all looks so small from up here. We're practically eye level with the cavern ceiling. Higher than some of the solace tree root clusters that give the city life. The clusters are thick and wild up here, unlike the artistically shaped clusters in the garden at the center of the city.

A root cluster at the farthest edge of the cavern starts to dim.

Did I imagine that?

No.

Another fades. Another.

What's happening? What could make solace root clusters go dark?

It hits me like pulling three G's from standing still. The roots aren't going out.

They're dying.

EIGHTEEN

"Tarn!" I scream, my heart hammering against my ribs. "Tarn!"

He emerges from the death room. "What's wrong?"

I point to the darkening roots, just as another cluster flickers and fades.

Tarn throws his head back and lets out a deafening roar.

My ears are ringing as he swings me to his back. *"Hold on!"* I feel the words snap through his elongated body more than I hear them.

He leaps, shooting up the roots above us so fast I don't have time to scream before we're moving *through* what looked like solid cave ceiling. It's a chimney in the rock, so dark and narrow I didn't see it before.

The narrow passage is choked with glowing root tendrils. Tarn uses them as a ladder, scuttling upward so fast I can't think about anything but clinging to his back.

Then I smell the smoke.

I can hear the roar of flamethrowers as we explode out of the rock chimney into the most amazing forest I've ever seen.

I knew the solace trees that lit Sorrow's Solace had to be big, but these are indescribable. Ancient giants that soar over the marines in shiny black fire gear who are trying to burn them down.

I roll off Tarn's back as he catapults upward into the canopy; then I scramble to my feet and run toward the marines. Branches and leaves tear at my hair and clothes as I race through them, but I hardly feel them. I have to stop this.

A horrifying *CREAK* fills the air, followed by a rustling through the branches overhead. I stumble back as a tree as wide as a cabin crashes to the ground, flames chewing at its smooth, peeling bark.

"Yee-haw!" a rough voice cries.

Shelby.

I scramble over the fallen tree to see Shelby sitting in the driver's seat of a bulldozer jeep whose massive blade is still buried in the trunk below me.

"Are you insane, Junior?" she shouts, reversing to pull the blade free, then spinning the jeep toward the next tree, which a black-clad and hooded marine is already spraying with blue-white flame.

"Stop!" I scream at her, throwing myself in front of the

bulldozer. I spin, shouting at the marine with the flame-thrower. "Stop! You don't have to do this!"

"Get out of my way!" Shelby growls.

"No," I shout back. "Never!"

"Joanna, what the hell are you doing here?" Sarge's voice hurtles through the smoke behind me. I turn to find him jogging toward us, fire hood pushed down and a flame-thrower slung over his back.

His familiar face feels like a stake in my heart. It's not just Shelby and her people trying to destroy Sorrow's Solace. It's all of us.

"I'm here to stop you!" I shout at him, at every one of the anonymous black helmets around me. "Please! We can't do this. You're destroying their home."

"They attacked us!" Shelby roars back at me.

"It's not the same!" I shout back, pointing to the exposed taproot of the tree Shelby just killed. Its dark orange glow is fading as the tree dies. "Look! That light is what makes the Sorrow's whole ecosystem possible. Kill the trees, and you don't just destroy their home. You destroy the Sorrow's world. Just like ours. Just like Earth. Do you really want to do that to another species?"

I don't realize how quiet it's become until I pause to take a breath.

The marines are still spread out through the trees, but most of their flamethrowers are switched off and they're all looking this way. The featureless black fire masks they have on make it impossible to tell who is watching me and who is watching Shelby.

"There has to be a better way," I shout, fighting for volume in the smoke-clogged air. "No. There *is* a better way. I know there is. Just give me some time to find it. Please."

"They burned us out!" Shelby bellows, jumping up to stand on the seat of the bulldozer jeep. "Now we burn *them* out. What could be better than that!" She throws her arms wide to indicate the smoke and flames. "This is justice. Plain and simple. So GET BACK TO WORK."

My stomach drops as I hear flamethrowers roar back to life around me. But then I hear voices. Shouts. Sharp. Angry. Pleading. The squad members are arguing among themselves.

"Sarge?" one of the marines calls. Her fire hood is still in place, but I recognize the voice. It's Greta Horgan. She used to babysit for us, sometimes, when we were little and she was a teenager. There's hope in her voice. She's looking for a reason not to do this.

"No! Not 'Sarge?'" Shelby whimpers the word in a mocking tone as she jumps down from the jeep and puts herself between Greta and Sarge. "There are no questions here. You have your orders. You follow 'em." She pivots, including the others in her glare. "You don't look at him. You. Look. At. Me."

But Greta doesn't look at Shelby. She doesn't take her eyes off Sarge.

"Goddamn it! This is mutiny!" Shelby shouts, turning on me. "You. This is *your* mutiny. You're gonna pay for it, too. I'm gonna line you up against a wall and—"

I catch a spark of light just at the edge of my vision. Without thinking, I reach forward and yank Shelby to the ground as a throwing shard punches through the air where she was standing.

Before either of us can react, there's a stiff *whoosh*ing sound and a Sorrow war hammer slams into Greta's head, spraying fiberglass and blood in all directions as it crushes through her helmet and her skull.

The Sorrow are fighting back.

Sarge hits the deck, screaming orders I can't hear through the smoke, which is suddenly sparkling with crystal shards and muzzle flashes. Takers are leaping through the trees overhead, dodging bullets at unbelievable speeds as they rain death down on us.

Shelby shoves me away and rolls to her feet, bolting through the trees. I crawl into the roots of the dying tree and press myself into the sticky, wilting mass as the battle rages around me.

Flames. Bullets. Shards. The horrifying crunch of war hammers sinking into flesh.

It's hard to tell the difference between the oil-slick black of human fire gear and the shadowy folds of Taker robes. Even if I could pick out who was who, I'm not sure which direction to move. Who to trust.

Whose side am I on?

Out of nowhere, Jay's voice is in my ear.

"Crawl to the next tree when I say go!"

My first, insane impulse is to throw my arms around him, but there's no time for panic hugging. I twist and see Leela racing through the trees up ahead. Beth and Chris are crouched behind Jay.

"You followed the Takers up?" I guess.

"Seemed like a better idea at the time," Jay says, his eyes scanning the turmoil that surrounds us, looking for an opening. "Go!"

I scuttle forward, staying low and close behind Jay as he darts from tree to tree. I don't know where he's leading us. It's hard to imagine right now that there's anything left of the universe that isn't fire and smoke and death.

Rich yellow light gleams through the smoke to my right. Tarn. He strides through the trees with his light-amplifying cloak swirling around him like sunlight burning through fog.

I veer toward him. Maybe, together, we can put a stop to this.

Then I see the dark smear on the end of his staff.

Blood.

Human blood.

I stop, watching him as he disappears again into the morass.

I thought I knew what despair was. I didn't. Now I do.

"Friend!" Beth's voice rings out behind me, sharp with fear. "I'm a friend!"

I spin to see a Taker yank my sister to her feet and swing a hooked, black-bladed knife at her belly. Beth goes limp, throwing her weight backward to avoid the flashing blade. Then Jay is there. He tackles the Taker, grabbing their knife hand and twisting it at an angle that would have broken a human arm. But the Taker's arm just keeps bending, their lower joint folding back along the middle segment of their arm to plunge the knife into Jay's hip.

The blade skitters off the hard carbon of Jay's braces and sticks into the softer bands that strap them to his legs. The Taker yanks, but the knife is stuck fast. Jay takes advantage of the Taker's surprise to shift his weight and swing his other leg around, driving it into the Taker's torso.

The Sorrow warrior slumps.

Jay spins and bolts after Beth, who has already joined Chris and me in the shelter of two enormous trees growing from the same trunk.

"Go! Go! Go!" he shouts, waving us forward. He clearly has a plan. I don't ask what it is, I just run.

Seconds later, the silver and blue of three *Prairie*-printed flyers loom out of the smoke. The rotors of the first are already spinning. Leela pokes her head through the open rear doors as we approach. "Hurry!" she shouts. "We have to get out of here."

"We can't just leave!" I cry.

"You have to." Sarge's smoke-harsh voice hurries ahead of him as he limps toward us through the trees. Bloody and panting. "You kids get out of here. Go tell the commander what's happening. She needs to know." He meets my eyes hard. "The commander, you hear me, Ensign?"

Mom. Not Grandpa.

"I hear you."

"We *all* need to leave," Beth says. "Immediately." She points ahead of us through the trees.

"I wish, B," Sarge says, as I stare past Beth's pointing finger. Did I just see—

Yeah. I did. Movement. Like someone is carrying a huge mirror through the trees.

"Raptors!" I shout as a human scream punches through the air, followed by the higher, purer shriek of a phyto-raptor.

Sarge swears as answering screams of pain and terror and raptor outrage ping-pong around us through the trees.

"Divekar, you go north. Lim, you go south. Get as many people as will follow you back here." As Jay and Leela race off, Sarge turns to me. "Watson, keep this bird ready to fly." He pulls out his sidearm and hands it to Beth. "Cover us as well as you can, okay?"

"Sarge!" I protest, but he's already gone, disappeared into the soup of violence and smoke.

"We aren't combat trained," Chris says. I can hear my

frustration echoed in his sensible words. "We'd just be a liability."

"Still," I say.

"Focus!" Beth says, raising Sarge's pistol and firing at an unnatural rustle in the branches overhead. A camouflaged raptor shrieks in response, leaping away as Watkins and Munda stagger through the smoke toward us, carrying Horowitz between them. She's hurt. Bad. Chris and I run to help them get her up the ramp.

More marines follow, staggering into the flyers. Another flyer's rotors chop to life. Then the third. Thank goodness. I'd hate to be the only hope these people have of getting out of here alive.

Then I hear a familiar voice, shouting curses through the trees.

I run to the bottom of the ramp and peer through the smoke. Shelby is dragging Sergeant Preakness toward the flyer, firing wildly behind her as they lurch along.

Preakness is mostly unconscious and almost twice Shelby's size. She'll never make it to the flyer with him. Not alone.

A wiry raptor with huge flapping membranes fanned out around their body charges at Shelby. She shoots them. They don't stop coming. She shoots again and again, but the raptor is almost on top of her when they finally collapse, their suddenly dead weight sending her sprawling on top of Preakness's limp form.

I can't just stand here and watch.

I throw myself down the ramp and race to Shelby and Preakness. I shove the dead raptor off them and hook one of Preakness's arms over my shoulders. Together, we can almost run with him, despite the blood streaming from Shelby's knee. She doesn't say a word to me as we haul her sergeant's limp form through the trees.

Chris is waiting at the bottom of the ramp. He helps us get Preakness inside, where Leela is now in the pilot's seat and Beth is helping Jay tie a pressure bandage on Sarge's shoulder. Below it, his arm looks badly mangled.

I help Shelby lower Preakness into a seat in the back row, triggering his harness to tether in.

"Do we have everyone?" I ask.

"Close," Chris says. "One of the other flyers is already gone."

"Take off," Shelby snarls. Then she grabs the back of my harness and hurls me into a chair beside Preakness.

"Harness, restrain wearer!" she hisses. "Authorization Alpha Zeta 221."

My tether slithers out around me, binding my arms and legs to the seat.

"What the hell—"

"I told you you'd pay," Shelby growls, rubbing her hands over the huge smear of blood Preakness has left all down her side.

"Run!" I shout to my friends. "Get off! Now!"

"Nah," Shelby snarls. "Sit. Stay for the court-martial." She leans in close and wipes her bloodstained hands down my cheeks. "This is yours. And you'll pay for every drop. You hear me?"

The flyer's engines are whining. The chair I'm bound to is pivoted backward. I can't see who's flying. It can't be Leela. She wouldn't follow Shelby's orders. Not now. I just hope my friends made it off.

"Sir?"

My heart sinks at the sound of Jay's voice.

"Jay!" I shout. "No! Run!"

Shelby bursts out laughing.

"Harness," she snarls, turning to face Jay. "Restrain wearer. Authorization—"

Jay interrupts by punching her in the face.

Shelby stumbles backward, tripping over Sarge's outstretched boot. He lurches forward out of his chair, pinning Shelby to the deck.

"Go!" he shouts.

Jay lunges at me, brandishing the knife he took from the Taker who attacked Beth. The hooked black blade shears through my harness as if the nanoteflon cord were a blade of grass.

"Hurry!" I shout, fighting the clinging vines of the tether. I can feel the rotors biting into the air. We're taking off even though the rear doors are still open and the ramp is only half folded.

I throw myself forward as the last bond snaps, pulling Jay with me toward the quickly closing doors.

"Stop them!" Shelby cries, shoving Sarge away. But

she's too late. Jay wraps his arms around me and we leap into open air.

Terror steals the scream from my throat as we plummet. Then Jay's tether hurtles out behind us to bond with the rising flyer. It snaps taut, breaking our fall, but we're still few meters from the ground. And rising.

"Hold on!" Jay shouts. Then he swings the black blade again.

The tether snaps.

We hit the ground hard, my weight driving the air from Jay's lungs in a vicious *whoosh* that leaves him gasping.

I scramble to my feet and reach down to help him up.

Somewhere in the trees ahead, Leela screams, "Joanna!"

The gunshots crack out even as the word blasts through the air.

I throw myself forward again, putting my body between Jay and the bullet. It's all I have time to do. But the fleshy *thud* that follows doesn't come with a rush of pain or a sudden loss of consciousness.

The shot didn't hit me.

I roll over and look up to see Shelby retreating into the rising flyer, gun in hand. She just tried to kill me.

Tarn is standing between us. Gleaming yellow blood is spreading across his translucent robes.

"Joanna," he whispers.

Then he folds in on himself and collapses at my feet.

NINETEEN

The thudding of my own pulse fills my ears as I scramble to Tarn's side and press my hands against his wound to stanch the blood.

"Why did you do that?" I gasp.

"I don't know," he rasps. His voice is strange. Thin. Blood bubbles through the gaping hole in his chest with every word. "I couldn't . . . I couldn't . . ." He trails off into another sticky gasp.

"Tarn!"

Suddenly Jay's hands are on my shoulders, pulling me away from Tarn.

"Jo. Come on. Step back."

I look up and find myself blinded by a blurry rainbow of neon light. I blink furiously. Again. The blinding glow sharpens, resolving itself into a ring of Givers in biolight-amplifying robes standing around us.

Of course. They need to try to heal him. I have to get out of the way.

I stumble to my feet and allow Jay to pull me out of the glowing circle. I'm relieved to see that Beth, Chris, and Leela are tightly bunched beside the ring of healers. A second circle of black-robed Sorrow fans out around us. Putting themselves between us and the phytoraptors who have clustered around the protective circle, perching in the trees and on the ground.

"Why aren't the phytoraptors attacking?" Leela mutters under her breath.

"They haven't made an aggressive move since the flyers left," Beth says.

"Shhh!" Chris hisses. The Givers are starting to sing.

It begins as a sensation, not a sound. A buzz, like touching a low-voltage electrical circuit. It brushes over my skin with staticky fingers.

The Givers raise their arms in a single shared gesture, the voluminous folds of their robes unfurling to make a continuous circle of light around Tarn. The song swells with the motion, exploding into a huge sound so deep, it seems impossible that it could be coming from a group of living beings. The moaning chant booms, so powerful that I can almost *see* it thrumming through the air. A pillar of pure sound stretching through the forest's soaring canopy.

Then a second layer of sound soars over their impossibly dense tonal chant. A gentle keening.

What is that? It sounds almost more human than Sorrow, but it definitely isn't.

The weirdly beautiful hum fills my mind with memories. Physical sensations more than pictures. Teddy's sandy hands, reaching down to pull me from cold waves the first time he and Miguel took me surfing. Mom's hand against the small of my back as I climbed up the hot dunes of Death Valley when I was nine. Tarn's hand, wrapped around his knife in Ord's back.

"It's the raptors," Leela breathes, almost silently.

I look around and realize that the predators are sitting on their haunches, their fanged mouths open in almost comically identical oblongs.

They're singing.

The contrast between the delicate song and the burly, terrifying beings is so strange and beautiful that I don't know what to feel. Is "elated" the thing that happens when you're so terrified, it's kind of breathtakingly amazing?

"Did the Sorrow know this would happen?" Jay whispers.

"I don't think so," Chris says. "Look at the Takers. They're as surprised as we are."

I think he's right. The Sorrow soldiers are still on high alert, looking around at the raptors and at each other like they can't figure out what to do next.

Finally, they start to lower their weapons, slinging guns and hammers across their backs and sheathing knives. The phytoraptors ignore them completely and keep singing, their attention utterly focused on the glowing Givers as their healing crescendos build. The Sorrow and raptor songs twine together into a strange harmony that feels like a living thing wandering through the air. Then it evaporates, notes and breath drifting apart like morning mist in sunlight.

Silence fills in the space it leaves behind.

No one moves. Sorrow. Raptor. Human. Even the flames have died out. It's like the whole forest is holding its breath. Then the cocoon of shimmering fabric opens, robes whirling back around the Givers' bodies as they kneel in a single motion.

Tarn stands.

His blood-spattered robe hangs open, but he's glowing like a beacon all on his own.

Our eyes meet.

He rumbles something in Sorrow that blows through the clearing like cold ocean spray flying off the wake of a speeding boat. His Takers and Givers echo it.

The raptors listen. Still intent. Fascinated.

Movement darts through my peripheral vision. Before any of us can react, Bob drops out of the trees and lands in front of Tarn, inside the circle of Givers. My relief to see him alive is quickly followed by a flash of anxiety, as he rears up on his hind legs.

The Takers yank their weapons out again, but Tarn booms a single word, bright as a bugle blast, and they sheathe them once more.

Bob growls. Then he looks past Tarn to me and raises his hands to sign.

Tell.

I sign back with shaking hands, *I will.*

He turns back to Tarn and begins to sign. My heart breaks as he draws the words from the air with his gnarled hands. I speak them anyway: "We will protect your trees. No. Humans. Here."

With that, Bob springs straight up, into the canopy.

A rustle of motion sizzles through the trees and the raptors all disappear, melting back into the green.

TWENTY

We're back in the cabin Ord's Takers brought us to after the *Wagon* crashed, what feels like several different universes ago. Dr. Brown built this cabin in the massive caverns around the Solace while she was living with the Sorrow. The sparsely furnished space looks the same, except for the fine layer of glittering dust that's gathered on the cot, storage locker, and portable recycler/3D printer in her absence.

Leela is sitting on the storage locker, her back tense with pain. Her leg got clawed pretty badly while she was helping Sarge sound the retreat. But this time it's Beth painting her with dermaglue instead of Miguel. I'm sitting on the floor next to the camp bed and Jay is stretched out on it. His braces are charging and he's got three pain patches on his bruised back.

I try to call Mom again on the satellite phone Beth had stached in her utility harness.

The satellite rejects my uplink. Again. I can't tell if we're too far underground or if Grandpa has blocked me.

I try Dad, with the same result. I know it's just a waste of battery charge, but I'm desperate to connect to someone, anyone who might be able to tell me what to do next.

Chris slipped out a while ago. Maybe I should be worried, but I'm sure there are Takers out there watching us. They won't let him get lost, if only because they'd never allow a human to wander their dark unsupervised. Besides, Chris is a lot older now than he was six Tau months ago, the last time we were here.

I guess they're just months now. Not Tau months. There's no point in keeping track of Earth time anymore. The thought makes me dizzy. The whole universe has shifted on its axis.

No. That's not true.

The universe is exactly as it was. The only thing that's changed is my point of view. Nothing will ever look the way it did, from where I'm standing now.

Strangely, I don't think that has anything to do with Earth dying.

Another human being shot at me.

Another human being tried to kill me.

I know. I know. Human beings have been killing each other for as long as there have been human beings. But not in my world. Not the human beings I know.

Knew.

My parents were born just after the Storm Wars. Mom was three when the newly formed International Space Agency gave Grandpa a medal for his work negotiating the peace accords. I've seen pictures of the ceremony. Mom's generation was too busy fighting to survive the famines and flu epidemics that followed the wars to fight with each other. By the time I was born, we were flourishing again. Working together, possibly for the first time in history. That's the world I grew up in. That's the humanity I know. But an IntGov marine just tried to kill me. Has losing Earth broken all the bonds we formed trying to save it?

We will protect your trees. No. Humans. Here.

The phytoraptors and the Sorrow are forming those bonds now. Pulling together to survive. To save their world. From us.

We will protect your trees. No. Humans. Here.

I'm human. I should resent those words. Shouldn't I? But I'm relieved. Does that make me a traitor, like Shelby says? Do I owe it to my species to work with Grandpa? To compromise my beliefs for the sake of humanity's survival?

I can't.

The answer comes without my having to search for it. I don't know if it's the right one, but it's the only one I have.

No. Humans. Here.

I wonder what the Sorrow think of their unexpected new allies.

Once the raptors left, the Givers ushered Tarn away,

247

and four Takers brought us back down into the caves, to a place that was too dark for any of us to see. They kept us there for what turned out to be hours. Then they brought us here.

They hardly said a word to us the whole time in English, but I could feel them talking to each other in Sorrow. The sonar in their voices made my stomach flip like I was on a roller coaster. My brain's way of interpreting fear and excitement in their sonar, I think. Both emotions make sense. As far as most Sorrow knew before today, the raptors were mindless predators. But they just watched a phytoraptor speak to their Followed and promise to protect the Solace. Their world must feel as upside down and inside out as mine does.

Jay's hand slides through my hair to squeeze my shoulder. "I can hear you thinking from here."

I twist up to my knees to lay my head on the pillow beside his. "How's your back?"

"It sucks," he says. "But I'll live."

I don't know what to say next, so I just lie there looking into his eyes. His irises are only a shade lighter than his pupils. A subtle brown so deep you'd think it was black unless you got this close. They're so sad, I want to crack a joke or kiss him or something. Anything to paper over the shadows.

Before I can give in to the impulse, he says, "Thank you."

"For what?" I snort. "Dragging you along on this AWOL suicide mission? Getting you court-martialed? Using you as a parachute?"

He almost smiles. "It was more like an airbag."

"Good point," I say. "But you're welcome, if you're into that sort of thing."

"If not for your AWOL suicide mission, Shelby would have put a flamethrower in my hands this morning," he says. The words are so quiet that I can hardly hear him, even with our noses almost touching. The next words are even softer. "I don't know what I would have done with it."

I hadn't thought of that.

Every marine from both squadrons was out there today. Jay would have been with them if we hadn't snuck out. If Jay had refused to burn the Solace grove, what would Shelby have done?

The tormented look on his face as we crouched over Hart's body last night slides into my head. Would Jay really have refused that flamethrower? Or would he have felt duty bound to use it, to make sure his mom and his sister and his squad mates survived?

That thought tugs another worry along behind it.

What's happening to Sarge and the others right now? Sarge ordered the retreat. Not Shelby. And he tackled her in the flyer to give Jay and me the opportunity to escape. Will she punish him for that? What will Grandpa do when he hears what happened at the solace grove?

What will Mom do?

Jay fingers the torn edge of my flight suit collar. "What happened to your pips?"

"I don't know," I say. "I had just torn them off when I saw the roots going dark. I guess I dropped them somewhere."

"I know what they meant to you," he says.

"Not as much as I thought they did," I say, realizing the words are true even as I say them.

We slip into silence, just lying there, studying each other at close range. After a while, his eyes drift closed. His hand settles on the pillow between us. His breathing slows.

He's asleep.

I ease back to sit against the cot again. Beth is quietly going through the med kit, taking inventory. Leela is sitting against the wall on the other side of the cabin. Our eyes meet. She offers me a bittersweet smile.

She's missing Teddy.

I know it as surely as if she'd said it out loud. If he were alive, he'd be sitting next to her right now. Or maybe we wouldn't be stuck out here, AWOL and alone in the middle of an impending war. Maybe he would have had a better idea. Maybe everything would be different.

The cabin door opens and Chris skids in. "You guys—" He sees Jay sleeping and lowers his voice. "You gotta see this."

"Is it going to explode?" Leela groans quietly. "Immediately?"

"No, but—"

"Then I'm out," she says, before Chris can argue with her. "Had enough excitement for the day."

"I need to monitor Leela," Beth says.

"No, you don't," Leela snips. "I can watch the glue dry just fine on my own."

"You know, there's a relevant Shakespeare quote about excessive protestation," Beth replies, shooting Leela an arched brow, "but it's overused and I try to avoid clichés."

Leela rolls her eyes. Beth goes back to her inventory.

I follow Chris into the dark.

"What did you find?" I ask him as the lights of the cabin dwindle behind us.

"You'll see," he says. He sounds excited. Not excited and terrified or excited and stressed. Just pure, bouncing-off-the-walls excited. It makes him sound younger. Like the kid I used to know, before his mother died in our arms.

When the graceful curve of a matte-black wing emerges from the darkness ahead of us, I understand why.

"Is that . . ."

"Hell yes, it is," Chris crows.

Tarn is building a spaceship.

"It's a Ranger scout ship," Chris says, the words he's been holding back tumbling over each other. "Like the *Vulcan*. It's only half done, but the construction is solid. It's—"

"Beautiful," I breathe.

"Yeah," he says. "It is, isn't it?"

I circle the fledgling ship. It's just as unimaginable as Shelby shooting at me, but in a totally different way. This is . . . new life. A new future. Not just another tile ripped free from the one I always thought was waiting for us.

Teddy would love this.

The thought doesn't ache the way I expect it to. It's just there. A simple truth. Teddy loved spaceships. I can just picture the look on his face, looking up at this beautiful, impossible ship.

"I want to help them build it," Chris says abruptly. "I want to make her fly."

Me too.

But it isn't that simple.

"We don't know what they're planning to use it for."

"I don't care," Chris says. "Is that . . . I know that's bad. I know it could hurt us, probably, somehow, but I want to be part of this. Part of their future. Not . . ."

"Not their enemy," I say, finishing his thought with my own.

"We'll find a way," Chris says.

"You think so?"

"Yeah," he says. "I really do."

I reach out and grab his hand. He squeezes my fingers and hangs on. We stand there in the dark, at the foot of a spaceship that shouldn't exist, and just believe. Just for a moment.

"Joanna Watson." A voice like a chorus flows out of the

dark behind us. I turn toward it. I can just barely see the Sorrow past the light of my flex, which is surprising. They are wearing a gray robe, not the nearly invisible black of a Taker.

"Can I help you?" I ask. I'm surprised how calm my voice sounds.

"That is unlikely," the Sorrow hums. They drop their hood, revealing a blindfolded face traced with delicate whirls of bright spring green. "But the Followed wishes to see you anyway. Come with me."

The messenger turns and walks away without giving me a chance to object.

I throw a look to Chris.

"I'll be okay," he says firmly.

He will. He isn't a little kid anymore.

I wish Teddy could see that, too.

As I hurry after the retreating green glow of the Sorrow's biolight, I look back at Chris, standing tall and unafraid in the cool white glow of his flex, the beautiful black ship perched behind him in the dark. The image cuts straight through all the uncertainty I've been wrestling with.

That's what we are. That's what we need to be.

That's what I can fight for.

I don't even know what it means, not in a practical way. But I know that somehow, some way, I want to live in a world where Chris can help the Sorrow finish that ship.

We just have to figure out how to get there.

The grass-green Sorrow doesn't say a word as they lead me across the expansive cavern to the tunnels into Sorrow's Solace. I catch up with them as we enter the city. There's something familiar about this Sorrow. The delicacy of the veins that branch below their eyes and up over their forehead, maybe? They look almost like they're wearing a mask of glow-in-the-dark lace. And their biolight is such a distinct color, like new grass in spring back on Earth.

The memory slaps me in the face.

Hands outlined in pale green light, raised in front of a hidden face under a faintly glowing gray hood.

This is the Sorrow Jay didn't shoot.

This is the Sorrow who killed Ryan Hart.

I stop walking.

I don't really mean to—it just happens. I stand there gasping, like the rage in my chest has sucked all the oxygen out of the tunnel.

This is the Sorrow who killed Ryan Hart.

I want to turn and run. To get as far away as I can from this being who killed a kind, funny man not that much older than me. Jay's friend.

Jay . . .

Abruptly, I wonder if any of the Takers Jay killed last night are friends of this Sorrow.

The thought reshuffles reality. Again.

How can I hate them for killing Hart if I expect them to not hate Jay? Jay killed seven Takers last night. And I came here to make sure he doesn't have to do it again.

"Is there a problem?" the green Sorrow hums back at me. Their voice a rich minor harmony.

Yes.

"No," I say, scrambling to catch up with them. "No problem."

The grass-green Sorrow stares at me for another endless moment. They don't believe me, I think. But they turn and walk forward again without another word.

We avoid the spiraling boulevard around the Solace this time, slipping instead through the narrow alleys that run through the edges of the city. We stop at a single-story structure huddled below a soaring scaffolding structure of bone and translucent fabric. In contrast, this building is small and dark, with coarse opaque fabric draped over its bone framework.

The green Sorrow reaches for a seam in the wall hanging, but then they hesitate and turn back to me.

"He's risked a lot for you. Make it worthwhile."

The inner harmony of their voice is melancholy, and I can feel the depth of emotion there. Whoever this being is, Tarn matters to them.

"I will," I say.

My escort raises their hands to cover their face, palms out. Then they pull open the seam-door and usher me into a spacious room with high ceilings. Cascades of something soft and fuzzy drip blue light from spherical pots suspended at different heights around the room. It's some kind of bioluminescent plant.

A bigger clay sphere, the size of one of Dr. Kao's cooking vats, rests on a simple bone frame at the center of the room. The lattice of bone that supports the fabric walls is simple and unadorned by carvings. Tangles of opalescent cloth fill each corner. Their graceful folds catch and amplify the light of the fuzzy plants.

Tarn slips in through an opening I didn't notice in the far wall. His hood is pushed back and his robe hangs open, revealing the dark gleam of the phytoraptor-skin armor that covers his narrow torso and hugs his legs to their first joint.

He hums something in a soothing harmony to the green Sorrow. Their reply pops back at him like water on a hot pan; then they turn and march out of the room.

"They don't like humans much, do they?" I ask.

Tarn raises his hands in front of his face, palms in. "It's more complicated than that. And Nor is very loyal. She's anxious about my well-being."

"She has good reason," I point out as he crosses to the clay sphere at the center of the room. "You were shot today."

"But I have been healed," he says, reaching into it and pulling out two smaller orbs.

He holds one of them out to me. I take it. It's filled with thick, dark liquid.

Tarn crosses to one of the tangles of glowing fabric and settles into it in a splayfooted crouch, his trijointed legs folded like paper fans on either side of his body.

"Sit."

It's physically impossible for me to imitate him, but I manage not to fall or spill whatever is in this orb as I work my way into another length of hanging fabric.

Tarn takes a sip from his orb, his round eyes on me. Waiting for me to match him.

Ingesting unknown substances is high on the list of stuff pioneers aren't supposed to do. I'm sure Tarn knows that. He's testing me. He wants to see if I trust him. I don't know if I should. I put the orb, which is obviously a Sorrow cup, to my lips and drink anyway.

The liquid is warm and thick and sweet, with a sharp coppery flavor.

"Lucille called this tea," Tarn says. "It is made from the flowering trees your people find so attractive."

I take another sip. It's good. And I feel like the heavy exhaustion is lifting from my shoulders. Fido flower tea must be a stimulant. Sorrow coffee.

"You've made some unexpected choices today," Tarn says.

Like siding with him against my own people? *Unexpected* is one word for it. I bet Shelby has a few others. But she seems to prefer bullets to words.

"You've made some pretty unexpected choices yourself," I say.

He nods. "And perhaps a few foolish ones, as well." He drinks again. "It has been a very strange day. I have seen things I never dreamed possible. Including a few so terrible,

I cannot imagine them to be real, even after seeing them with my own eyes."

The acrid smell of burning solace trees floods my memory.

"I'm . . . I . . ." I swear under my breath. "I want to say I'm sorry, but that isn't enough to express how much I regret what my people did today."

Tarn raises one hand to cover his face, palm in, and then lets it drop to his chest. Running his fingers over the armor that hugs his body.

"I am wearing the skin of a being whose descendants saved my home," he says. "Thinking, feeling beings whose bodies my people have stolen and used to build our city and craft the very weapons we use to kill them. Humanity is not alone in its horrors."

"You didn't know," I say.

He covers his face with an out-turned hand this time. "I should have. My people have used the Beasts for more than their skin and bones. Fear is a powerful tool."

Jay's voice grates through my brain.

He said surviving and being able to live with yourself aren't always the same thing.

Grandpa made Jay fear what would happen to his family and his friends if he wasn't willing to kill innocent, sleeping beings in order to protect the people he loves. Grandpa and Shelby have been using that same fear to control all of us since they arrived.

"A weapon we've been aiming at ourselves, this whole time." The words are bitter in my mouth.

"And at each other. Your grandfather's attack on the Solace today was a retaliation for our raid on your settlement. Wasn't it?" Tarn says.

"That doesn't make it right," I say.

"No," Tarn agrees. "That makes it war. My Takers are already planning a counterstrike. I don't have any reason to stop them."

"I wish I could give you one."

"You could," Tarn says. "You could challenge your grandfather."

"It isn't that simple," I say. "Our society doesn't work that way."

What would I do, if it did? Could I kill Grandpa to end this? To save us all, and the Sorrow? Tarn did it. He killed his own brother to stop him from committing genocide and destroying their ecosystem. I'm glad I don't have to make that choice. I just wish I could think of another choice to make. A choice that would change all of this.

"It seems that nothing is simple anymore," Tarn says. "The Beasts protected us today. They sang with our Givers as they healed my body. A song sung by enemies . . . and now those notes are sewn into my flesh."

A song sung by enemies.

For some reason, the words conjure up the yearning I heard in Chris's voice as his flex light caressed the high-arched black wings of Tarn's ship.

"Why are you building a spaceship?" I ask.

Tarn rumbles a sound that pops over my skin like a million tiny bubbles.

"So you found it," he says, without answering the question. "What do you think?"

"I think it's beautiful," I say. "Chris wants to help you build it."

"Imagine," Tarn says, slowly, like he's savoring the word and the thought that goes with it. "A craft built by Sorrow and humans that can travel beyond the ceiling of this world. What a song that would be."

Before I can respond, my satellite phone blurbs an alert.

Relief splashes through me. Mom. It has to be Mom. She finally got through. My legs tangle in the soft web of fabric as I struggle to my feet and pull the sat phone from the pocket of my utility harness.

"I'm sorry . . . I need to . . . I have to . . ." I trail off as I see that it isn't a call from Mom. Or Dad.

It's a text from Grandpa.

Joanna. We need to talk. Come alone. You can reach me.

The last sentence is linked to a set of coordinates, far at the northern tip of the Diamond Range. Why does he want to meet me up there? And why does he want me to come alone?

My mind spirals around his invitation.

You could challenge your grandfather.

I can't do that. No matter what he's done, he's still Grandpa. I can't kill him.

But what if I don't have to?

Another voice slices through my memory. Grandpa on the first day, after the survivors came.

I need to see this world through your eyes.

After everything that's happened, can I still do the job he promoted me to do? Can I make him see what I see? If I try, will he listen? Will I know what to say if he does?

"Sometimes, it is easier to carry the weight of those who follow your path if you maintain your momentum," Tarn says, gently pulling me out of my spiral of indecision.

"No one follows me," I say.

He covers his face, palms in. A Sorrow *no*. "For your sake, Joanna, I wish that were true." He's glowing a fiercer, deeper yellow than usual. I can see the waves of brightness pumping through him with every beat of his heart. Is he excited? Or terrified? His choral voice is higher than usual, less complex, like many voices singing the same note. "It is a difficult thing, walking with no footsteps to guide you. But willful blindness will not change your place in the melody."

Willful blindness.

Grandpa is reaching out to me. Offering me another chance to show him Tau as I see it.

I have to take it.

TWENTY-ONE

Like Jay said, there's no point in following orders any-more.

I am going to meet Grandpa, but I brought my friends with me. We're in beta flyer—Tarn must have sent one of his Takers to retrieve it, sometime after we were brought to the Solace. The coordinates Grandpa sent me are almost an hour's flight away. Every ten minutes or so, I try to get through to Mom and Dad. The calls never connect. Chris says Grandpa must be controlling our access to the satellites—that's why he can reach me, but I can't reach any-one else.

I hope Chris is right. Any other alternative is too terrible to consider.

As we go farther north, the mountains crumble into high desert—long expanses of glittering opalescent sand punctuated by clusters of parrot palms and massive crystal formations that jut over the soft, sandy hills. A sculpture garden built by the patiently brutal hands of sun and wind and time.

We reach the coordinates Grandpa sent me and I set the flyer down on a broad mesa. Huge chunks of crystal are scattered through the sand at its feet, casting broken rainbows through the blinding sparkle of the desert.

With the sun high overhead, I have to turn the brightness down on the screens before I can pick out the *Vulcan*, crouching below a towering lopsided arch of crystal less than half a klick from the mesa. Grandpa is sitting on top of the arch, his silhouette like a black hole in the bright.

You can reach me.

"What the hell?" Leela says.

"It's a test," I say, dread coiling in my guts. This is just like the lake. He wants to see if I'm strong enough and clever enough to get to him. But why do this now? What's the point?

I leave the exterior cameras running and recording, zoomed in on his hunched form sitting in zazen on the arch.

"Stay in here. Unless . . ."

"He's not going to hurt you," Beth says quietly.

"I hope you're right. I just—" I shake my head. "I don't know. I don't know him. At all."

"You know him better than you did a week ago," my sister points out. "And no matter what he's done, he loves you very much."

My whole body clenches involuntarily around the thought. I don't know if it's rejecting the idea or clinging to it.

"Whatever," Leela says. "Keep a feed open on your flex, too, so we can hear. We can be in the air in less than a minute, if you need us."

I walk down the ramp. My eyes water as I emerge into the radiant brilliance of the desert. I wish I hadn't had to abandon my utility harness with all my gear in it when Shelby tried to capture us. I thought to bring extra harnesses during my middle-of-the-night packing session, but spare sunglasses weren't on the list of gear I thought we'd need in the Sorrow caves.

It takes almost a full minute before I can see clearly. I walk to the edge of the mesa and look out at the arch. Grandpa hasn't moved. If I didn't know better, I'd think he didn't notice us landing. But he knows I'm here. He's just waiting for me to get to him.

How the hell does he expect me to do that? Climb the arch? That will take ages.

You can reach me.

No way. It can't be that easy.

I clamber out on the farthest tip of the mesa, as close as I can get to the arch. I tap the autoconnect button on my harness. My tether zips out across the open space and thuds into what must be a climbing spike anchored on the top of the arch. I can't see it from where I'm standing, but my harness buzzes gently, letting me know the tether has connected with an anchor point and the contact is secure.

That wasn't much of a test.

I jump, letting my momentum swing me down like a pendulum toward the glowing desert sand for a few seconds before I hit the button again and the tether begins to retract, pulling me up and onto the arch.

By the time I reach the top, I'm tingling with effort and exhilaration. It's almost enough to overcome the pain singing in my ribs and the dread churning in my stomach. Then I look down, and a sick thought bursts through the glow of achievement—I had no idea where or how that anchor point was set. I just tethered in and jumped.

After everything he's done, I still trust him.

That was the test.

Anger jabs at me as I scramble up the rocks to the top of the arch.

"Are Mom and Dad okay?" I demand as I retract my tether.

Instead of answering the question, Grandpa eases to his feet and crosses the arch to take me in his arms. My ribs ache at the strength of his embrace. He encloses me completely, blocking out the world. Once, his arms felt like the safest place in the universe. Now they feel like prison. The emotional double vision makes me want to scream in his face.

I restrain myself and push him away.

"Answer the question, Grandpa."

He sighs a wealth of mixed emotions. "The last time I saw your parents, they were alive. But there was a great deal of confusion after your mother's rebellion."

"Rebellion?" I gasp. But relief chases the dread through my veins as I hear the truth behind the word. "Oh. Mom found you unfit for command."

"She asked me to retire." His face twists into a bitter mockery of a smile. "Apparently, your parents disapproved of my decision to attack our enemy's resources."

Every breath I take feels a little easier.

"So Mom is in command of the Landing now?"

He hunches his shoulders against the words. "When the situation became violent, I chose to fall back to River Bend with Lieutenant Shelby and the others who remain loyal. The only reason I let them engage at all was to secure *3212* and *Vulcan*." He draws in a shaky breath. "It's been a long time since I've seen human beings fight each other. Kill each other. Brings up a lot of bad old memories."

"They . . . *we* didn't have a choice, Grandpa," I say, as gently as I can. "You were asking us to participate in atrocities."

Rage snatches his bowed body upright. He glares at me.

"You're a child," he snarls. "You don't know the meaning of the word *atrocity*. I do. God help me. But you . . . You. Know. Nothing."

I don't flinch away from his anger.

"I know we can do better than this."

"*We* didn't start this!" he roars. "You told Tarn that our species was on the brink of extinction and he tried to strangle you with his bare hands. Then *he* ordered his soldiers to set our homes on fire so they could steal our technology and our raw. And yet you accuse *me* of atrocities."

"Yes," I cry. "I do. You tried to destroy their primary ecosystem. The fact that they attacked us first doesn't make that any less wrong."

"Every step we take on this world is wrong!" he shouts back. "You know that. You told me so while we were watching my very first Tau sunrise."

I take a deep breath, trying to steady myself.

"When I told you that, you said you needed to see this world the way I do, so you could find a way to make things better." I fight to keep my voice low and steady. "After what happened with Tarn, I was too frightened to see much of anything. But I'm not afraid anymore. I can show you what you need to see, if you're willing to look."

Grandpa sags again, folding in on himself as though the righteous anger was all that had been holding him upright.

"Cleo was right," he whispers, almost like he's talking to himself. "She was right."

"What does Grandma have to do with this?" I ask, confused.

His face twists into a sad smile. "Everything. She is everything, to me. She's everywhere. In every face I see.

Every sunrise. Even here, in the midst of all this beauty she never had the chance to see. I carry her with me, always. That's how I found the strength to do what had to be done."

"What had to be done?" I ask, fresh confusion surging. "What did you do, Grandpa?"

"What?" His eyes snap into focus, like the question is a light in the fog. He looks at me. His lips twitch. He opens his mouth as though to speak, but then he squeezes his eyes closed and swallows hard, like he's physically restraining the words.

"I did what had to be done," he says finally. "What she would have done, if the opportunity had presented itself. Cleo was a ferociously brave woman. You get that from her."

"I get that from Mom," I say.

He sucks in a loud, shaky breath that could be a sob or a bark of laughter.

"Maybe you're right," he says. "Maybe you're right." He shakes his head. Hard. "But now is not the time for you to be brave. I know how to end this conflict, but I can't do it unless you're safe. You're going to come with me back to the *Prairie*."

"No," I say. "This is my planet now. I'm a part of this, whether you like it or not."

"You mean that, don't you?" he says, studying me.

"I do," I say without hesitation.

"Oh, Little Moth." He closes his eyes, pained. "This

isn't . . . it wasn't supposed to be this way. I want you to know that. When I realized the *Vulcan* was still on Tau, I knew she would be the solution, but this . . . this wasn't at all what I imagined."

He runs both hands through his white hair, making it stick up all over his head. For a heartbreaking moment, he looks so much like Teddy. Like Beth. Like Mom.

"I tried to reprogram the *Vulcan*'s scrubbers," he continues. "For weeks, I tried. Starting that night when Tarn nearly killed you. But the Sorrow share over ninety-seven percent of their DNA with other species on this planet. There's no way to be sure the nanobots could seek them out without endangering the greater ecosystem."

"You tried to program the scrubbers to attack the Sorrow?" I gasp. "To just . . . wipe a whole species away?"

"Without a single human casualty," Grandpa says wistfully. "But the algorithm just isn't sophisticated enough. So we're going to have to fight this war with the Sorrow. It's going to be ugly. And we're going to lose, if we remain divided against ourselves. People will die. There are so few of us now. We can't afford to sacrifice lives for the sake of Nicholas Watson's fine ethical principles. So I'm going to wipe the slate clean and we're going to start again. United. Humanity deserves that."

"Wipe the slate clean?"

My eyes jump to the *Vulcan*, perched in the sand below us. No. I must be wrong. He would never do such a thing. Not to his own people. His own family.

"Grandpa," I say, my pulse thudding so hard I can hardly hear myself speak over its frantic tattoo. "What do you mean by 'wipe the slate clean'?"

He hears the understanding in my voice.

"I know it's awful, Little Moth," he says. "But it's necessary."

I'm not wrong. He's going to turn the planet scrubbers against us. He's going to kill everyone who won't follow him.

I have to stop him.

I look up to the mesa, where my friends are waiting in the flyer. My flex is transmitting this conversation to them, but the moment I try to alert them, he'll run. I can't use his tether to restrain him the way Shelby did to me—I don't have command authorization. And I definitely can't fight him. I'm not armed, and he's bigger and has decades of combat experience. I don't know what would happen if I tried. Especially up here. We'd probably end up going over the side.

That gives me an awful idea.

I look down again. Rainbows blaze off the crystal sand, a dozen meters below us. Vertigo spins through my guts, hurling waves of remembered pain over my skin. But the sensory flashback is different this time. Incomplete. I can still feel my boots planted on the rocks. I can still feel the ineffectual sunlight on the back of my neck.

I'm still here.

I charge Grandpa.

The top of the arch is just wide enough to give him time to react. He throws himself forward, using his greater weight to send us both sprawling back onto the rock instead of over the edge.

My head cracks against the arch.

The world swims around me as I scramble away from him and stagger to my feet.

He holds his hands out to me. Pleading. "I know this is hard, Joanna. But you're brave. You'll see how necessary this is, if you're just willing to—"

The roar of beta flyer's rotors spinning to life drowns him out.

I raise my wrist and shout directly into my flex, "Leela, you have to get the *Vulcan* out of here. He's going to—"

That's as far as I get before Grandpa slaps me across the face, hard enough that I stumble-step backward. He grabs my wrist just before I fall and pries off my flex.

"Power down, Cadet Divekar," he snaps into the flex, glaring past me to the flyer. "The *Vulcan* will only respond to my command codes. She's not going anywhere without me."

"Please," I sob, twisting against his iron grip. "Please, Grandpa, you can't deploy the scrubbers. That will kill every human being on Tau."

"I designed them," he snarls. "I know what they do."

His eyes jump back to the flyer, which is lifting off the mesa despite his orders. "Goddamn it. This is what happens when you tell children that everyone can be a hero."

"How could you . . . You *just* finished telling me how precious every human life is now," I sputter.

"Exactly!" He flings my wrist away and paces up the length of the arch, still clutching my flex. "People died today, thanks to your mother's little insurrection. And so many more were wounded. If I allow this conflict to continue, how many more will die? We only have five qualified space pilots. What if all of us are hurt or so badly injured we can't fly? What if the *Vulcan* and *3212* had been damaged in the fighting? We could have lost all means to get into space. If we can't wake the survivors and shut down the deep-sleep system, *Prairie*'s orbit will decay and she'll crash into the planet and destroy us all. I *have* to end this."

"So you're going to reduce everyone who won't follow you to their component molecules?" I gasp. I feel like my lungs can't get a full breath.

"Do you think I *want* to do that?" Grandpa cries.

"So let Mom take command!" I cry. "Give her a chance to find a better way."

"No!" he shouts. "No! I can't."

"WHY NOT?" I scream back at him.

He doesn't answer. He just stands there, staring at me, a weird expression creeping over his face. Then, to my shock, tears start running down his cheeks.

His hand goes to his flex. He swipes and taps a few times. His tether rears up over his shoulders, swirling around him like someone is scratching him out of the world in black pen. Then it snaps down to bond with the anchor point at our feet.

"I'm just not brave enough, Little Moth," he says. "I thought I was. But I'm not."

Then he runs off the edge of the arch, disappearing into the blinding light of the desert below.

TWENTY-TWO

I feel like the sun is trapped under my skin.

I tried to follow Grandpa down, but his climbing anchor wouldn't let me connect. He must have locked me out. All I could do was watch and hope Leela and the others would get to him in time.

They didn't.

Grandpa had the *Vulcan's* hatch sealed by the time Leela got beta flyer down to the desert floor. She jumped out of the flyer and ran at the scout ship anyway. Jay had to drag her away before Grandpa fried her with backwash from the *Vulcan's* engines. I couldn't help her. I couldn't stop him. All I could do was stand up here and bake. My exposed skin feels hot to the touch, even though I'm shivering.

The wind from beta flyer's rotors whips around me,

spinning my hair into a blinding confection of tangles. The arch is too narrow for Leela to land on, so she hovers beside it and Beth and Jay open the rear doors. I tether into the flyer and leap across.

Beth throws her arms around me the second I'm safely inside.

"You would have died," she snarls, furious, even though she's clinging to me like she'll never let go. "If he hadn't stopped you from pushing him off, you'd have fallen with him."

"I had to, Beth," I whisper into hair. "I had to try to stop him before it was too late."

"How much time will it take him to activate the scrubbers?" Jay asks.

"He probably already has," I say. "It'll take a few hours for the nanobots to saturate the atmosphere, but once they do . . ."

"That's not going to happen," Leela says firmly. "Because we're going to use every second we have to stop him."

"How?" I ask, truly hoping she's got an answer. "You know he's headed straight back into orbit. They have *3212*, and the *Trailblazer* is still out of commission. We can't follow him. We can't even evacuate the Landing."

"So we'll think of something else," Leela says, her voice cracking with tears.

"Leela," I whisper. She shakes her head, biting her lip in a vain attempt not to cry.

"Damn it!" Chris shouts, crumpling his flex up and hurling it across the flyer. "Goddamn it! I'm so close." It's almost a sob.

"So close to what?" I ask.

"Saving everyone!" he cries. "But I can't get into the *Vulcan*'s computer. He has us completely locked out of the network. I tried everything, including Mom's old codes for the *Pioneer*. But I can't even get access to one of the satellites to call the Landing, much less hack the *Vulcan* from here."

"Even if you could, you'd need Grandpa's command codes to shut down the planet scrubbers," Beth points out.

"I don't need to shut down the scrubbers!" Chris says. "All I have to do is run simulation twelve."

"Oh shit," Leela breathes. "You're right."

"What's simulation twelve?" Jay demands.

"Leela and I installed a new backup power system on the *Vulcan*," Chris says. "To keep her going even if there was a computer failure. To test it, we had to kill the power to the computers, which is a pain. I was sick of having to run a bunch of overrides every time, so I wrote a program to do it all at once. *Simulation twelve*. I never had the chance to strip it out. It's still there."

"And if we can just run it, then *Vulcan*'s computers will lose power," Leela says. "The planet scrubbers would do a hard restart along with everything else, which would set them back to default. Harmless."

"But I can't access the *Vulcan* from here," Chris says. "And we can't get to her in orbit. So it's all useless. We're dead."

Grandpa has turned Tau into our tomb.

For a moment, I can almost feel his hand on my back. Comforting me in our first moments together on the *Prairie*.

Hello, Little Moth. How are your wings? I see them there. Still beating.

The memory rakes through me like a sob. The man who taught me to fly has stripped my wings away and left me stranded. Helpless. Hopeless.

Then another voice slips through my head, carrying with it a single image painted in deep shades of gray and darkness.

I want to make her fly.

Tarn's beautiful, half-built ship gleams in my memory. It's such a shame Chris won't have time to help the Sorrow finish it.

And then, without warning, a spark of hope floats up my spine.

"Chris," I say, "when you told me about the scrubbers, you said there was a fail-safe, right?"

"Huh?" he says. "Yeah. Attached to the Rangers' ID implants. The system won't activate if one of the crew is still on the surface. But the Rangers are all dead now. Why does that matter?"

The tiny spark flares brighter, filling in all the empty space despair left behind. I throw myself into the copilot seat and tether in.

"Let me fly," I say to Leela. "I'm faster."

"Oh no." Leela moans, relief making it impossible for her to sell her fake annoyance. "Jo has a plan."

"About time," Beth snips, her voice still shaky.

"Don't get your hopes up," I say. But the stubborn little spark in my chest flares brighter as I press my hands harder into the nav app, goosing the flyer past full speed. We have a chance.

Thirty-seven minutes later, I'm standing in front of Tarn in the enormous cavern the Sorrow use as a hanger for their aircraft. My friends are gathered behind me on beta flyer's ramp. Takers drift restlessly through the darkness around us, just visible enough to make the little hairs on the back of my neck stand straight up.

"Please, Tarn," I say, finishing up my hastily explained request. "We need your help."

Tarn doesn't respond. He just stands there, invisible beneath the heavy drape of his glowing robes. The grass-green Sorrow he called Nor hovers beside him. Nor's biolight is so dimmed by her robes that she looks like a shadow, in comparison to Tarn's brilliance.

"What makes you think Lucille Brown is alive?" Tarn asks finally.

I swallow hard. Am I wrong? Please, don't let me be wrong.

"You're building a spaceship," I say. "Having a 3D printer and plans doesn't mean you can build a ship that'll actually survive in space. Much less fly one. You'd need an experienced engineer and pilot to do that."

"The only probable candidate to fill that role is Dr. Brown," Beth says. "Which makes it likely that she is, in fact, still alive."

"If she is, then we have to keep her safe," I say. "The planet scrubbers on the *Vulcan* won't work as long as she's on the planet. That means she's the only thing stopping our grandfather from massacring us all and starting over with a new group of survivors from the *Prairie*."

"If she's alive, the admiral will know it," Chris says. "The moment he activates the scrubbers, the *Vulcan* will alert him that she's still on the surface. And if we're right, and he's already tried, then I'm sure he's using our satellite system to search for her right now."

"We have to find her before he does," I say. "And I think you can help us do that."

"Why should I?" Tarn asks.

It's a valid question. I knew it was coming. I've been trying to think of a good answer since I realized Dr. Brown was probably still alive, but I haven't found one yet.

Logically, Grandpa is right. Conflict between our species is inevitable. The safest thing for the Sorrow would be to let Grandpa wipe us out and then attack his new team before they have time to get oriented.

But letting us die isn't the best thing Tarn can do for his people. I'm sure of it.

I just don't know why.

"You don't have to help *us*," Jay says from behind me. "The admiral will kill her if he finds her. It would be wrong to just let her die."

Tarn pushes his hood back. As usual, his eyes are unbound. Their black orbs shine in his yellow biolight as he paces to where Jay is leaning against the flyer.

"That might be so," Tarn says. "But wearing this mantle means I must do what is right for my people. That isn't always the same as what is right."

Abruptly, I know the answer to Tarn's question.

"My grandfather agrees with you," I say. "But you're not going to help us because it's right. You're going to help us because it's better."

Tarn turns back to me. "Because you are, to borrow a human phrase, *the devil I know*?"

"No," I say. "Because it's *better*. We tried fighting each other. We lost six marines, four weeks of work, and a space shuttle we could *really* use right now. You lost twelve Takers. And how much raw did you actually get from the 3D shop? A few dozen kilos?"

Tarn doesn't answer.

"It can't possibly have been enough," I say. "Which

means death and destruction is all any of us got by acting in what's supposed to be our own self-interest. But when we don't, it's—"

I stop myself before I repeat *it's better* again.

"You could have killed us, after your Takers found us at that burned-out nest," I say. "You could have killed me before that. At the Landing. But you didn't. Which meant I was there to see the solace roots dying and warn you. I stopped my people from burning any more trees. I think I could have stopped it altogether, without anyone else dying, but then your Takers showed up. Then we were fighting again and everything got so—" I cut myself off. I don't want to sound like I'm blaming his Takers for defending their home.

"After everything, you saved my life," I say, trying a different tack. "Why did you do that?"

Nor hisses something in Sorrow that feels like sticking my hand in boiling water.

"I acted on impulse," Tarn says. His voice pops with heat. Anger. Or fear, I can't tell.

"You acted on instinct," I say. "Because it's better. Helping each other is better."

"I almost died helping you," he points out. "It wasn't better for me."

"But it was!" I cry. "While the Givers were healing you, the Sorrow made their first meaningful connection with the phytoraptors." A strangled laugh squeezes my lungs.

"The raptors figured it out before we did. They helped you, even though you've been their enemy for as long as anyone can remember. But they promised to protect the solace grove. Your home. A city built of their ancestors' bones. Because it's better. Working together is better."

"Perhaps it was," Tarn says. "But if your grandfather is truly prepared to destroy his own people, then I don't need to work with you. All I have to do is wait."

"Maybe," I say, hoping I don't sound as desperate as I'm starting to feel. "But he'll bring more survivors down from the colony ship. There will still be a war. Sorrow will die, fighting it. And they'll attack the solace grove again. You know that. How many more trees will you lose?"

"Cooperation does not guarantee peace," Tarn says.

"You told me once that the Followed decides who your people are. My grandfather thinks we have to destroy you if we want to survive. I came here to help you stop him, because I don't want that to be who we are. I think there's a better way. I don't know what it is, but I came anyway. I placed my bet. Now it's your turn. You can let us die and then fight Grandpa and Shelby and whoever else they bring down with them from the *Prairie*. Or you can help us protect Dr. Brown and we can work together to stop Grandpa and Shelby. Which do you choose?"

I hold my breath as Tarn studies me. Impassive. I wish I knew how to read Sorrow facial expressions. I don't know if he understands what I'm trying to say. I don't know if he cares.

Tarn turns to Nor and says something in their language. Nor snaps a reply that makes me feel like the floor just got ripped out from under my feet. Then the pale green Sorrow covers her face with her hands, palms out.

Yes.

"Nor will fly," Tarn says in English. Then he walks up the ramp into our flyer.

TWENTY-THREE

I sleep.

I don't mean to, but my body insists. When I wake up, we're over open water. There's no land visible in any direction.

Nor is in the pilot seat. Tarn is sitting beside her. Hood up. Staring out at the waves ahead of us. Leela and Chris are sleeping and Beth is working on her flex.

Jay is hunched in his chair, watching Nor fly. He's digging his fingers into the armrests like he's afraid he'll float away. Or lunge across the flyer at Nor.

He's figured out that she killed Hart.

I catch his eye. He looks away.

That hurts, which is silly. Jay isn't obligated to share his feelings with me.

Or maybe he is.

I don't know how this works. I've never been in a relationship this serious. I don't even know how serious this relationship is. I told Jay that I love him and he hasn't acknowledged it. Of course, we've been a little busy since then. But we might not live past tomorrow. If there was ever a moment to talk about our feelings, it's now.

Maybe he doesn't love me.

Maybe I need to stop worrying about my love life and focus.

The problem is, with Nor in the pilot's seat, I have nothing to focus on. She seems to know what she's doing. And I can't even back-seat fly, because she's crouched in her chair, navigating on a flex that's nearly hidden in the folds of her dark gray robe.

Nor's eyes jump to Tarn's brooding form every few minutes. She's worried about him. I wonder if she loves him. I wonder if he knows.

The water below us looks like shattered green glass scattered over shiny black solar tile. This ocean is deep and rough. And enormous. Crossing it will take six hours at top speed. If Grandpa gets to Dr. Brown before we do, we won't make it back in time to say goodbye to our families.

Of course, getting to Dr. Brown isn't going to be easy for any of us. The Rangers didn't do a full survey of the southern continent. They thought it might be uninhabitable, or at least so dangerous that it wasn't worth going too far inland without an established infrastructure on planet to back them up.

When the Planetary Survey Report first came in, that didn't seem like a big deal. We didn't need the *whole* planet to be safe, after all. Earth isn't.

Wasn't.

I don't think I'll ever get used to that.

My eyes drift back to Tarn.

Why is he here?

I had expected Tarn to just tell us where Dr. Brown is. Well, actually, I had *expected* Dr. Brown to be somewhere in the Solace. But there was no reason for Tarn to come with us. Less than no reason. A sense memory of the unsettling, out-of-tune hum of the city jangles my skin. His people are in turmoil. They need him. He should have just given us coordinates. Or asked Nor to take us to Dr. Brown on her own.

But I guess his motives for coming along don't matter. All that matters is that we get to Dr. Brown before Grandpa finds her and kills her so that he can trigger the scrubbers and kill us all.

Grandpa is trying to kill us.

The thought is so ridiculous that I want to laugh. Or scream.

Why is he doing this?

I'm just not brave enough, Little Moth.

That's what he said. But it doesn't make any sense. None of this makes any sense.

It's like a whole other person I've never met has crawled into my grandfather's skin. The man who taught me to swim, to hike, to drive, to fly . . . that man couldn't do this. He wouldn't. That man would have died on Earth, fighting to save it with his last breath. So how did he become . . . this?

Tears drip down my face. My chest heaves with sobs I refuse to release. I don't want the comfort they'll draw from my friends. Or the release they'll bring.

I don't want to feel better.

I swipe at my burning eyes and yank the band out of my hair. It's sticky with dried sweat and ash. I lean forward, letting my hair fall straight down from my head so I can gather it into a knot. When I straighten up again, Tarn is crouched in the empty chair beside mine.

I just barely manage not to shriek in surprise.

"Hello, Joanna," Tarn half sings, painting the tactile sensations of his own language over the English words. The sonar draws a memory from the depths of my brain—surfing with Miguel in Australia, back on Earth. Paddling hard, my heart racing and Miguel encouraging me to paddle even harder as a wave roars up behind us.

What does that mean? What is Tarn feeling? Exhilaration? No, that doesn't make any sense. Fear does. Anticipation. But his sonic undertones carry something more than that. Something I don't really understand.

"Thank you," I say, finally. "For . . ." I don't know how to put it. *Thank you for not just letting us die* seems like a weird thing to say.

"It is I who should thank you," he says. The same tense terror/joy supercharging the words.

That was not what I was expecting. At all.

"The timing of your request for help was . . . fortuitous," he adds.

"It was?"

He raises his hands to cover his face, palms out. "Shortly after you left the Solace, one of the Takers came to Nor and asked her to back a challenge against me. It was not a surprising development. When I first became Followed, this Taker argued that we should finish what Ord started and wipe you all out."

"But you gave us time to rebuild our shuttle and go home instead," I say, putting it together. "So we were still here when the *Prairie* arrived."

"And now we will never be rid of you," Tarn said. "My people may have followed me to their doom."

I shake my head. "No, Tarn, you saved your whole planet when you saved us."

"I do not see how that could be true," he says.

"But it is," I insist. "Before we left Earth, Mom spent months doing a test mission on the *Prairie*. The big ship that followed us here. She's a prototype. A lot of her systems weren't really ready for a long space flight, but there was no time to perfect her. When the *Prairie* got to Tau, her solar power system failed. Her orbit was decaying. She didn't have enough power to fight the planet's gravity.

288

Everyone who knew how to fix her was dead, except Mom. If you had let those Takers kill us, kill her, then the *Prairie* would have fallen out of orbit, crashed into Tau, and caused a catastrophic impact event that could have destroyed the *Sorrow*."

Tarn pushes his hood back and stares at me.

"Is this true?" he demands.

"It is," I say.

His eyes go to Nor.

"I was ready to surrender today. I thought my intended challenger was right. I thought I had been a fool."

"But Nor wouldn't let you give up?" I guess.

He raises his hands, palms out again. *Yes.*

"But . . ." How do I ask this question without offending him? "Tarn, you're here. Can't your challenger just . . . take over?"

Tarn flips his hands palms in.

"No," he says, a sonic charge I've never felt before snapping through the harmony of his voice. It feels like docking without autopilot. "A Followed can only be replaced by a challenge."

"So if you're not there . . ."

"He cannot challenge me."

Suddenly a lot of things make sense. Tarn might be helping us, but we're also helping him.

"Why did you hesitate, then?" I ask. "Why did you make me give you a whole speech to convince you to do something that was going to save your life?"

"I am Followed," Tarn says. "I cannot make decisions based solely on my own needs."

"So you would have stayed and faced the challenge, if you'd thought helping us was the wrong thing for the Sorrow?"

"Of course," he says. "And if your grandfather is still Followed when I return, I will face my challenger anyway. I'm certain of it. And I will deserve it. Because I will have failed."

The stark, minor harmony of his voice makes me feel heavy with an exhaustion that isn't mine. It's his.

"I wish we'd never come here," I say.

Tarn raises his hands in front of his face, palms out, then flips them in.

We sit quietly, watching the water and the sky roll past below and above us.

"The spaceship was Nor's idea," Tarn says after a while.

"Oh?" I say, following his gaze to the Sorrow pilot. "I hope . . . The people on the *Prairie* . . . none of this is their fault. I know this isn't the Sorrow's fault, either, but please don't—"

"The *True Dark* wasn't built to reach your colony ship," Tarn says, cutting me off.

"It wasn't?" I say, startled. "But . . . the raid. They were stealing raw. I thought . . . What else would you need that much raw for?"

Tarn draws his mouth up in an O, and a tingling pop of silent Sorrow laughter dances over my skin. "Did you really imagine I'd ask my Takers to risk their lives for such a daydream?"

"Lieutenant Shelby thought you were using it to print guns," I say.

"My brother was very impressed with your firearms," Tarn says. "I am not. But raw is useful to us, and vital to your way of life. Taking it seemed like the best way to contain your people."

The simple arrogance of that rings true. Tarn has never sought out human techonology. Not like his brother did.

"Nor and I started building *True Dark* long before the *Prairie* arrived," he says, returning to the original subject. "Shortly after I became Followed."

"Oh," I say. Then, because I think he wants to tell me, I ask, "Why?"

I feel Tarn laugh again, like silent sonic bubbles popping all around us.

"I asked the same question," he says. "But Nor is . . . ambitious. She does not fear what she does not know," Tarn hums. The words are warm and sweet.

Love. He loves her.

"Some of my other advisers called the endeavor foolish and wasteful," he continues. "Even before the *Prairie* came."

"No," I say, thinking of the look on Chris's face as he

stared up at the beautiful black ship, perched in the darkness. "It's not a waste. What happened yesterday . . . what my grandfather is doing. That's wasteful. Your ship is—"

My flex buzzes with a text, cutting me off.

I check it with shaking hands. Is it Grandpa? Mom?

It's neither. The text is from Lieutenant Shelby. It's just one word.

Gotcha.

"Pull up!" I shout, but it's too late.

BOOM!

A sonic boom slaps the flyer hard to starboard.

Pain implodes through my healing ribs as I slam against my harness. Chris moans in pain too, feeling gingerly at his injured shoulder as Leela, still disoriented from sleep, fumbles for her flex and the nav app.

I can see Nor struggling to pull the flyer up away from the choppy water below us.

"Careful!" I call. "Don't—" It's too late. She pushes the engines too hard, overcompensating. The flyer spins out, nearly flipping end over end.

The rotors sputter and the engines scream, drowning out my friends' startled swearing and shouting.

"Nor!" I scream. "Let me—"

But before I can finish my offer, the flyer levels out.

Nor snaps out a few Sorrow phrases that feel like panic. Tarn rumbles something back that is both sharp and soothing. I can almost hear Mom's voice in the harmony of his.

Take a deep breath, Joanna.

He's telling Nor to stay calm.

"What's going on?" Chris demands over Tarn's reply.

"It's Shelby," I say as Leela presses her hands to the wall screen in front of her and zooms in on something moving over the water up ahead. "They've figured out where Dr. Brown is."

The blur of motion comes into focus abruptly. It's *3212*. The sharp tactical shuttle is making a wide loop to shoot back toward us.

"She's going to ram us," Leela yells at the same time I shout, "Dive!"

Nor shoves her hands down on the nav app. The flyer drops hard, its rotors nearly skimming the waves.

3212 hurtles overhead, its wake slapping us backward and down. A screaming whine explodes through the flyer as the port rotors stall.

Tarn bellows something in Sorrow and Nor spins, hurling her flex into my lap.

"Fly!" Tarn thrums.

My hands start moving before my brain has the chance to catch up, slapping down on the app controls and twisting to drag our nose up, out of the waves.

"Chris!" I yell.

"On it," he calls back. He already has the rotor calibration app up on the wall screen in front of him. Leela has the nav app up on the wall screen too; her hands dart over it. Helping me.

I snap my eyes back to Nor's flex, fighting to keep our

remaining rotor clear of the water.

"Come on, come on," Chris mutters as the flyer begins to tilt, leaning toward the waves.

Beth calls out, "Evacuation procedures—"

"No," Chris shouts, cutting her off by slamming his hand against the wall screen. As if on command, the dead rotor roars to life and the flyer rights itself.

I shove my hands out and up, throwing the flyer back to top speed without bothering to climb up out of the waves.

"Jo, shouldn't we—"

"Another haircut like that from *3212* and this thing is going to come apart," I say, weaving the flyer through the chop. "Whoever's flying that thing isn't that great a pilot. Otherwise they'd have come in at a lower speed so they could loop back around and hit us again while we were down. I don't think they'll come this close to the water."

Leela swears again as a massive wave licks the belly of the flyer.

"You sure we should risk it?" Chris says.

"Yeah," I say, without hesitating. "I'm sure."

My brain has been crowded with doubts for so long, I didn't remember what *sure* felt like until just now. But this is just flying. And I know how to fly.

I take a deep breath and edit out the nervous chatter of my friends and the pounding spatter of the waves. The only thing I want to hear is the high, rhythmic song of the rotors and the rumbling hum of the engines. The groan and shriek of the hull and the gutter of the wings. I let my fingers move with the flyer's melody, surfing the ship through the spinning air currents and lashing waves.

"There's land ahead," Tarn says, his layered voice ringing with urgency.

I see it. Green-tinged brown slipping up over the horizon.

Snick. BOOM!

3212 shoots overhead again, snapping through the sound barrier for no reason at all.

"You're right about that pilot, Joey," Leela says, watching the shuttle hurtle over the landmass ahead. "Whoever it is, they're showing off, but they don't have much control."

"They're going to overshoot Lucille's camp at that speed," Nor says. "By a great distance."

"But they'll still beat us there," Chris points out.

The thought pulls my focus for less than five seconds. It's enough.

The ocean rears up ahead of us, a huge wave crashing through the rotors and sending the flyer into a spinning dive.

"No!" I scream, twisting my hands to compensate and pulling upward as . . .

SNAP!

Smoke starts pouring from the starboard wing.

"What was that?"

"Lost a strut," Leela hisses between clenched teeth as she struggles to help me compensate.

"It's still there," Chris shouts. He's got the engineering app open on the wall beside his seat. "But it's cracked."

I swear. That strut could take out the rest of the rotor if it snaps at the wrong angle. Worse, it could cut straight through the hull and destroy the whole flyer. We need to shut that rotor down as quickly as possible. That means we need to land.

"We're still twenty klicks out," Jay says.

"She'll get us there," I say, punching the engines. "Please, get us there," I beg the flyer as we shoot over the churning waves.

"That strut is pulling away," Chris cries.

"We're seconds away!" I shout.

"We're losing it!" he shouts back.

My fingers move on the nav app. I let them, not trying to let my brain get in the way as I cut thrust completely.

"Jo—"

"Trust me," I breathe, using both hands to hold the nose of the flyer high. I need to maintain our lift for as long as I can. The flyer arches into a long, shallow dive toward the sliver of brown and green on the horizon. It's growing. Spreading.

We're almost there. Gravity and momentum hurling us toward a wide, dark beach studded with spindly trees.

When I can see their twisting branches, I smack the

thrusters back to life. In reverse. The engines scream and a huge sound rips through the flyer as the busted strut tears free.

The whole flyer tilts violently to port, its broken wing trailing down into the water and . . .

WHAM!

The impact of the flyer skidding into a stand of trees snaps me hard against my seat, and pain explodes from my abused rib cage, blowing stars through my vision.

"Not your smoothest landing, Hotshot." Jay groans as the flyer shrieks to a stop.

"You wanna go back and swim in, be my guest," Leela fires back. She heaves out a breath. "I can't believe that worked."

"I'm not sure it did," Beth says.

That's when I realize the flyer is sinking.

TWENTY-FOUR

I knew we'd need the damn boat. That's all I can think as we pile into the inflatable Zodiac I nearly didn't pack.

What I thought was solid ground when I was trying to land the flyer turned out to be a huge swath of wetlands that stretches inland for kilometers. The water is only a meter or so deep, but that was more than enough to flood the flyer's engines. It's not going anywhere soon.

Silty green water sloshes against the hull of the raft as I weave it between the clusters of whip-thin trees that stretch out of the dark water.

The trees don't react to us as we pass, so I don't think they're carnivores. I see the occasional flash of movement in the water, but not much else. No animals calling to each other or movement through the trees. That's for the best.

Judging from the Rangers' report, there's nothing here we want to meet.

Nor programmed the coordinates for Dr. Brown's camp into my nav app. It's just at the edge of the swamp. Tarn says that Dr. Brown has a flyer there. I hope he's right, because otherwise we're going to become permanent residents.

3212 made one more sweep overhead, about ten minutes ago. We were already in the trees, so they may not have seen us. Either that, or they don't think we can make it to Dr. Brown in time to stop them from killing her.

They may be right.

The trees are a little farther apart here, so I push the Zodiac faster, taking advantage of the open water. Even if we get to Dr. Brown in time, I'm not sure we can stop Shelby and her team. They'll be armed to the teeth. Leela and Jay both took stun guns with them when we left the Landing, but that's it. And Nor and Tarn only have staffs and knives. And their voices, I realize. Sorrow screams are just as deadly as gunfire.

The engine dies.

"Seriously?" Leela breathes. She starts to reach her hand into the water to check the outboard motor, but Beth snaps, "Leela! Unscouted swamp, remember?"

Leela swears and switches her flex to flashlight. She shines it down into the murky water. Then she swears again.

"What is it?" I say, leaning out to see. Where the light

from her flex penetrates the cloudy water, I can see pale green globes that look like fleshy bubbles suctioned all over the engine.

"That's . . . gross," she says, as Tarn comes to peer over the edge beside us.

"An apt description," he agrees, sticking the end of his staff down into the water. "Though perhaps an understatement."

The water fills with tiny bubbles as the creatures hurl themselves at his staff.

"Stand back," Tarn says, carefully pulling the laden staff out of the water. The round bodies shrivel as the air hits them, losing their grip and splatting back into the swamp, where they immediately swell up again like sponges.

"Do you know what those things are?" Chris says.

Nor makes a noise that feels slimy. "Our name for them would best be translated as . . ." She has to think for a moment before she settles on "bubble of death."

"Excellent," Jay says grimly. "Killer bubbles. Just what we need."

Tarn passes his hand in front of his face. Palm out, then palm in. *Yes* and *no*. "These may be something similar, but different. The bubbles of death glow, as we do." He looks back down into the water, where the gray-green bubble creatures have clustered around the engine again. "These will be harder to avoid."

Beth plunges her hand into the water.

"Beth!" I cry, pulling her back as the fleshy green orbs swarm her fingers.

"Joanna!" she snaps, pushing me away so that the death bubble she has trapped in the sample bag I didn't see was wrapped over her hand and arm doesn't latch onto me instead.

"Oh," I say, my heart still hammering as she flips the bag over the shriveling creature to trap it before it tumbles back into the water.

"Ignorance is a far greater danger than a calculated risk," she says, watching the death bubble gnash a spiral of spiny teeth at its plastic prison. "I don't think they can penetrate the hull of the Zodiac."

"We don't have time to worry about it," Chris says. "*3212* has already set down, which means those marines are going to catch up with Dr. Brown any time now. If they haven't already."

"We aren't going anywhere with those things attached to the engine," Leela points out.

"I will deal with the—" Tarn flutes a word in Sorrow that turns my stomach. It must mean *death bubble*.

He sticks his staff back into the water, bracing it against the side of the boat and resting the other end at the center of his chest. Then he begins to sing. The sound stings, like antiseptic in a wound.

Beth leans out next to him, shining her flex light into the water.

"Amazing," she whispers.

I peer over the side, too. The death bubbles are withering, sucking into themselves and bursting into slimy streams of oil-slick fluid.

In seconds, the engine is clear.

I press the ignition switch, and the Zodiac roars to life.

I gun the engine and we shoot forward through the skinny trees. They get taller as we go, their clumps wider and woven with sea grass that transforms the clusters of trees into tiny islands. Their tangled branches stretch high to brush leaves with their neighbors, making the waterways feel like arched tunnels of brown and green.

In the lull, I become aware of fresh aches spreading over my back. I probably did more damage to my ribs getting knocked around like that. I wonder if the nanobots in there will be able to heal it. I wonder if I'll live long enough for them to try. Next to me, I notice Leela scratching at the dermaglue on her leg. The claw wound beneath it is swollen and bright red.

"That looks infected," I say.

She shrugs. "It doesn't hurt. Just itches."

"We should pull the glue," I say. "Those are Tau germs. Your immune system—"

"You really think we're going to live long enough that I'll have to worry about dying of some crazy Tau bacteria?" she asks.

"Gee, I hope so," I reply.

She tries to laugh. It doesn't work.

"I don't know what I'm going to do, if we do survive," Leela says, keeping her voice low so the others can't hear her over the engine. I know she's not talking about her infection.

"You could still enlist," I say. "I'm sure Mom will put Sarge in command of the marines again. She probably already has. He would take you back in a heartbeat."

"Yeah," Leela says. "But . . . I don't know. I don't know if I can do that."

That surprises me. It must show.

"I know, I know," she says. "And it's not . . . I thought I was willing to do anything it took to protect my family. But if I'm a part of the squadron, I won't have a say in what that means. I'll just be following orders. And after the last thirty hours . . ."

"Yeah," I agree, as I start to understand what she's saying.

"Your mom. Sarge. I trust them," Leela says. "But they both let the admiral and Shelby take command. They had to. And I don't know about the commander, but Sarge knew Shelby was bad news. But what could he do? Quit? Leave the squad at her mercy?" She shakes her head.

"Mom could have said no," I say. "We'd have backed her up, if she refused to give up command." The words are like a key unlocking a well of self-loathing I didn't want to know was there. "I should have—"

"You shouldn't have had to," Leela says sharply. "I shouldn't have had to, either. To choose between following orders from someone so full of hate and mutiny . . . I won't do that again."

I don't argue with her this time. The rules matter to Leela. And knowing the rules are wrong . . . that must feel intolerable.

"So what will you do?" I say.

"I don't know," she says. "All I ever wanted was to be a marine. Protect people. And now—"

"What is that?" Chris interrupts us, pointing straight ahead.

I look out into the water. At first, I don't see anything. Just dappled light gleaming over the murky water.

Then I realize one of the shimmering patches is moving.

As the wavering glow approaches, I can see that what I thought was light is actually a writhing mass of opalescent creatures rolling over each other as they surge across the surface of the water. They're small. No bigger than my thumb. Their segmented bodies bristle with long stick-like legs and . . .

"Do they actually have feathers?" Jay asks. "Or am I losing it?"

"Both, probably," Leela says.

"Do you recognize them?" I ask Tarn and Nor.

"No," Nor says. She rumbles something in Sorrow to Tarn.

He waves his free hand in front of his face, palm in to indicate the negative. Then he raises his voice, intensifying the stinging song so much that it makes me wince.

It doesn't affect the insect bird things at all.

A flash of dark blue between the writhing creatures snatches my attention. There it is again. Too bright to be water. Or anything that grows on Tau.

"Is that a *Prairie* uniform?" Chris asks.

It is.

Without thinking, I reach for the floating marine.

"Joanna!" Beth's sharp voice freezes the insane impulse. "You can't help whoever that is. We should avoid disturbing the swarm."

She's right. I know she's right. But it's still physically painful to pull our boat away from the floating body and leave them behind.

"Shit," Leela breathes as I accelerate away. I throw a look back to see what she's looking at. The shimmering ant-bird things are streaming off the body, splashing and tumbling over each other to follow our boat.

"Go faster," Beth says.

"Yeah," I say. "I think you're right."

I pour on the speed, but it doesn't help. A glassy clacking sound bites through the air seconds before half a dozen little opal-feathered ant things skitter over the rails of our raft.

I smack at the side of the boat, shouting, hoping to scare

them off. Instead, an ant-bird leaps straight up in the air and lands on my hand.

The creature's legs drive through my skin and into the back of my hand. Blood wells around its barbed feet and wicks up its opalescent legs, staining its pearly white body a deep pink.

I stare at it, frozen in shock until pain rings through the haze of horror and I scream, flailing to get it off.

"Stop!" Beth shouts, grabbing my arm. "Leela, take the throttle! Jay, hold Joanna still."

Jay folds his arms around me as Leela grabs the controls and Chris, Nor, and Tarn scramble to smash the other ant-birds with their boots.

"Beth!" I shriek. "Get it off! Get it off! Please . . ."

"I don't want to leave any barbs behind," she says, still outrageously calm as she watches the creature, which is slowly turning red as it drinks my blood. "I don't know what sorts of toxins it might release if we kill it."

At the moment, I don't care. I've never felt pain like this, and I've been boiled alive in the vacuum of space.

"Do something," I moan, beyond stoicism. "Please."

Beth pulls a pair of pruning shears from her harness and runs the edge over her forearm. Blood wells from the cut and Beth flings it at the creature's feathered back.

It flips, pulling its barbed legs free of my skin in its lust for fresh blood. I hurl the creature away from me, off the boat. It spins, unfolding its arms, and skitters away over the surface of the water.

"We're clear," Chris shouts.

"No," Nor hums, pointing behind us. The ant-birds are converging into a writhing mass of white feathers and legs. In seconds, they're rolling across the water toward us like a floating beach ball of death, building up mass and momentum as they go.

"Should have kept one of those flamethrowers," Leela mutters, pushing the throttle to the max. But the extra speed just makes the pursuing ant-birds faster—they're riding our wake.

"I wonder if they leave the water," Tarn says, thoughtfully watching the closing horde.

"Let's hope not," Chris says.

Nor gasps, then hums something urgent in Sorrow that conjures up the first time Mom ever let me sit in the pilot's chair. Excitement/awe/fear.

I follow her gaze and see massive trees with stiff, dark green leaves looming over the swamp ahead of us. They look like solace trees, except they're more root than tree. Their stout trunks rest on massive glowing root cones that climb meters above the water line.

As we zag through the neon-tinted shadows, the ball of ant-birds thins out into a stream behind us, slowing way down as they give the swamp solace roots a wide berth.

"They fear the trees!" Nor calls out.

Relief charges through me. "Leela—"

"Yeah," she says. "I think so too."

She's already twisting the yoke to weave us closer to

the huge glowing cones. Close enough that I can see the fine tendrils sprouting from the bioluminescent roots like clumps of hair.

The ant-birds don't stop coming, but they're definitely slowing down. It's working.

"Over there!" I say, pointing ahead of us to a dome of blue roots that looms almost four meters above the water. There's a gap in the roots big enough to fit the Zodiac through.

Leela twists the yoke, turning so hard that one of the pontoons dips down into the water as we hurtle toward the enormous, blue-rooted tree.

We slide into the hollow space under the shining cluster.

The ball of ant-birds turns around and rolls away without even a hint of hesitation.

That was easy.

That was too easy.

Chris huffs a relieved sigh. "Thanks, super solace trees."

"Don't get too excited," I say, my stomach twisting into knots as I look up at the icy blue tangle of roots that surrounds us, thanks to my brilliant idea.

"Yeah . . . ," Jay says, following my gaze. "If those ant-birds are scared of this thing, we shouldn't get too cozy with it."

A flash of movement catches at the edge of my vision. I twist, looking around us. There's nothing there. No sign of the ant-birds.

There it is again.

Something moving, just out of sight. What's going on?

"Not like we have time to camp out anyway," Leela says, swerving the Zodiac back toward the Y-shaped opening we came in through.

That's when I realize what I've been seeing.

"Wait!" I shout. But it's too late.

Wham!

The edges of the Zodiac slam against the roots. The opening is smaller than it was seconds ago. The flashes of movement I kept seeing were the roots themselves, closing in around us.

We're trapped.

TWENTY-FIVE

"Keep the motor revving!" Chris calls, reaching for one of the knotty loops of glowing blue root that have us pinned.

"Don't!" Nor cries, but Chris's fingers are already closing around the gnarled blue twist.

His arm drops to his side, instantly limp.

He gasps, yanking his other arm from its sling to clutch at it.

"It's numb!" he cries. "I can't feel anything all the way up to my elbow."

"Our solace trees use their sap to stun their prey," Nor hums as Jay yanks open the med kit and fumbles for the sanitizer spray.

"And these exposed roots are likely designed to attract much larger prey," Beth says grimly. "Ergo, the paralytic substance they use to stun and then dissolve their prey is stronger."

"Dissolve?" Chris shrieks.

"Just hold still!" Jay says, dousing Chris's hand.

Nor lays her staff down in the bottom of the Zodiac and pulls a narrow black knife from under her robes. "Stay back," she says, carefully pushing the tip of her blade into one of the thick twists that are blocking our path.

She pulls, expecting the knife to cut through the root.

It doesn't.

"That knife cuts through Beast skin," Nor gasps, her voice humming with something that makes the hair stand up on the back of my neck.

A strange, sweet smell fills my nostrils. Sharp and tangy. Like the solace trees back in the Diamond Range, but thicker. Sickly sweet. I sniff, my eyes following the scent up to see a long gob of liquid oozing down from the tree's core, which isn't as far over our heads as it used to be.

Tarn grabs me, pulling me out of the way as the gob of sap falls. It hits the Zodiac and begins to sizzle.

That stuff is melting our boat!

"Get rid of it!" Leela shouts.

Chris is already yanking his parka off with his good arm. Jay grabs it from him and uses it to sweep the acidic goo overboard.

"There's another one building up there," Beth says, pointing.

"I am *not* going to get eaten by a tree today," Jay growls, yanking his stun gun from its holster. He presses it to the nearest root and fires. The blue glow sparks brighter for a moment, and an ugly crackling shriek tears through the air. The strand of root withers.

"I'll second that," Leela says, yanking her stun gun from her harness. She plants it against another twist of root and fires. Then another. And another. There's a sound so high, I'm not sure I really hear it so much as feel it. The hypersonic shriek is followed by a *snap* as a whole tangle of roots gives way.

"Careful!" Beth shouts, pointing to the other side of the cluster. "The root cone is tightening faster every time you damage it."

"Got a better idea?" Leela says, frying another root.

"Yeah," I shout over the tree's nerve-wrenching cries of pain.

I grab Leela's stun gun, aim it straight down at the water on the other side of the pontoon, and fire a sustained burst.

Blue light flares and the tree screams. The cage of roots around us convulses, pressing in on the sides of the Zodiac even as its roots start to wither.

"So this is what you call a better idea?" Leela shouts.

"Do it again!" Tarn cries.

"What?" I stammer, staring up at the disaster I just literally brought down on our heads.

"Do it!" Nor shouts, dropping into a crouch in the bottom of the boat and pulling Chris and Beth with her.

I fire into the water again, holding my finger down on the trigger as long as I can. I can see the roots around us going dark, dying, but the tree doesn't collapse.

I look up and see Tarn standing above me, holding his staff over his head with both hands to keep the withering roots off us. He groans with effort. The urgency of the sound has me moving before I have the chance to think. I reach up and grab the other end of the staff, gasping at the incredible amount of weight Tarn is withstanding.

"Help!" I try to shout, but it comes out in a whisper. Thankfully, Jay and Nor are already bracing Tarn's legs. Then Chris is there, leaning his back against mine, his feet pushing into the side of the Zodiac to brace me.

Leela scrambles for the helm.

"Punch it," I shout. "As hard as you can."

"I was gonna take my time," she snarks, "but if you insist . . ."

She throws the yoke forward, hard.

The tree screams again, its cry fading into a booming groan as Leela slams the Zodiac forward against the dying roots. Once. Twice. Again.

Tingling numbness sweeps over my fingers, which are still clutching Tarn's staff, as we burst through the shrieking, fading roots and shoot into open water.

"Woo-hoo!" Leela shouts.

Then her victorious cry is consumed by a massive *BOOM* as the towering tree crashes into the water, tossing huge waves after us as we tear away through the lurking glow of the solace swamp. The silence that follows is so complete, I can hear each of my friends breathing even as we roar away through the trees.

I check the time on my flex. We were in the tree for less than four minutes. There's still a chance we can make it to Dr. Brown.

"Uh-oh," Chris says.

"No," Leela snaps. "No more 'uh-oh.'"

"Tell that to the boat," Chris fires back.

I look down. Water is welling up through the melted spot in the middle of the Zodiac.

We've sprung a leak.

"We can make it," Jay says, checking the nav app. "We're less than a klick from Dr. Brown's coordinates."

"That's gotta be on solid ground, right?" Leela says, already pushing the engine to its limit as she dodges the deadly glowing webs of tree root.

"Help!" Chris calls from behind me. I turn around just as he dumps the med kit, emptying the rectangular, reinforced case of its contents.

"What are you—" I cut my own question off as he sweeps water into the now empty kit and dumps it out over the side. He's bailing.

Beth rips off her jacket and plunges it into the rising

314

water. She grabs the corners, pulling them together to transform the waterproof fabric into a pouch to scoop up water and hurl it overboard. I yank my own jacket off to do the same, but Nor shouts, "There!"

The boggy black mud rising out of the water ahead of us is the most beautiful thing I've ever seen.

Leela turns the yoke and aims the boat at the squishy shoreline. I grab Beth and Chris, steadying them as the abrupt turn tosses the boat sideways.

WHAM!

The impact hurls me almost over the side. I throw my hands out, desperately grasping for something, anything to check my momentum, but my fingers slide over wet neoprene. I'm going over. Then Jay's arms close around my waist, yanking me against his chest, inches away from the deadly water.

Our eyes meet. I can feel his heart racing, matching pace with my own.

All around us, our friends are talking at the same time.

"What was that?"

"We hit something."

"Damn it. I can't get the engine started."

"There's more water coming in!"

The look on Jay's face is strangely calm. Like all the things that have been tearing him up inside over the last few days are suddenly gone.

"Jay—"

"It's okay, Hotshot," he says, quietly.

Then he vaults into the water.

"JAY!" I scream, but he's already dragging the Zodiac away from the rock that smashed the outboard. In seconds, we're free and Jay is pulling us toward the shore.

Nor shrieks something in Sorrow. I tear my eyes away from Jay to see Tarn leap into the water beside him and grab the boat, lending his strength to haul us forward.

My heart hammers in my ears once. Twice. Three times.

Then there's a *thunk*, and a shrieking rasp as the bottom of the Zodiac scrapes over solid ground.

I throw myself out to help them drag the boat out of the water.

"I got it!" Leela shouts, pulling the handle from my fingers. "Go! Help Jay!"

I scramble to Jay's side. He's sagged to his knees in the swampy grass. I can hear Nor behind me, humming anxiety at Tarn.

"I'm good, Hotshot," Jay pants, trying to wave me off.

"You just waded through a death bubble–infested swamp," I say. "Humor me."

I run my hands down his legs. There are huge rents in his cargo pants left behind by the fleshy predators, but no death bubbles. I'm starting to get relieved when I find it. A huge swollen lump on his left hip, just below the arc of his braces. And another. And another.

"Jay." I gasp, my hands flying to my utility harness for my knife. "Don't move, okay?"

He looks down. Swears.

"I can't feel them," he whispers, his face going unnaturally pale. He must be losing so much blood. "I can't . . . I can't feel them."

"I'll get them," I chant, digging my knife under one and trying to pry the gnawing teeth away. "I'll get them. I'll—"

Then Nor shoves past me to crouch over Jay, her doubled knees protruding above her as she lunges down at him and screams something far beyond the range of human hearing. My whole body clenches; then the water and ration bars I've eaten in the past day hurl themselves from my stomach. I dry heave. Again. Again. My body feels like it's turning itself inside out.

Is this what Hart felt, right before she killed him?

The awful sound drops away.

I lie in the mud, weeping in relief at the quiet.

"Thank you," Jay whispers.

Startled, I struggle to my knees and see that Nor is crouched beside him in the beaten-down swamp grass. Her blindfold has fallen down around her neck, and her glowing blood is pumping furiously through her veins, flushing dark green as she catches her breath.

Four death bubbles lie dead on the grass between them.

Nor just saved Jay's life.

We sit for a moment. Staring at each other. Maybe seeing each other for the first time. Then I hear something above the liquid music of the swamp.

A human voice. Quiet. Desperate.

"Help! Help!"

TWENTY-SIX

"Did you hear that?" I whisper, twisting to look back to the others.

The faint plea comes again.

"Help me! Please!"

"Holy crap," Jay breathes.

Leela runs toward the pleading voice, her stun gun clutched in her hand. Beth and Chris follow her.

"Can you walk?" I ask Jay.

"Your guess is as good as mine," he says, groaning as he pushes himself up onto his knees. "So far, so good."

But it hurts. I can see it in his face.

I want to tell him to stop. To stay here and rest.

"Keep going." Nor hums the words with a thick, almost electric undercurrent of Sorrow sonar. "You are capable."

She holds her hand out to him. Jay looks up at her for a long beat. Then he grabs her hand, her trijointed fingers wrapping around his and pulling him to his feet.

"Thank you," he says again.

She follows Leela and the others without a backward glance.

Jay limps after her. I slide my arm around his waist to take some of his weight. He squeezes my shoulders, but doesn't comment as we cut through the trees. Tarn takes up the rear, his staff gripped across his body, at the ready.

The gray sunlight barely penetrates the murky shadows of the swamp solace canopy. The trees aren't nearly as big as the ones back in the Diamond Range, but they're big enough. Their stiff branches tangle a half dozen meters over my head.

We don't have to go far before cloying smoke creeps through the jungle shadows. The trees ahead of us are sagging. Charred. My stomach twists as we emerge into an open hollow that has been melted out of the swamp by the backwash of *3212*'s engines. The sharp-nosed shuttle crouches at the center of the blackened clearing.

Its ramp is down, and its airlock doors are standing open. There's no movement inside. There's nothing human moving around outside the ship, either, except us.

"Can anyone still hear that voice?" Beth asks.

I shake my head. "Dead?"

"Probably," she says, as Tarn and Leela circle the shuttle

and then duck up the ramp, Leela clutching her stunner and Tarn his knife and staff.

I hold my breath until Tarn emerges, Leela on his heels.

"Empty," she says as Tarn leaps off the ramp and strides back to Nor.

"So what makes a team of marines abandon their only ride off a planet that's going to turn them all to soup in less than ten hours?" Leela says.

"Nothing good," Chris says.

That's when I hear it. A wordless wheeze, like someone trying to call out who can't get enough air to scream.

I bolt toward the sound.

"Jo!" Leela calls as she chases after me.

"Shhh!" I hiss, stopping to listen. Leela skitters to a stop beside me.

We're quiet.

Just when I start to think I imagined it, a faint choking sound rasps through the trees.

"We're close," Leela breathes. I just nod and keep going. We pass a swamp solace with a dark green root cone and another with a crooked dome of roots so pale they almost look like a fibrous soap bubble.

There's another helpless wheeze.

I spin and see Preakness is hanging from a tight fist of silver-gray roots. Blood drips down the translucent gnarls, mingling with the tree sap that's running all over his body, slowly burning away uniform and skin alike.

321

"Oh my god," Leela says from behind me. "He's alive."

Preakness groans at the sound of our voices. Eyelids fluttering.

He's not just alive. He's conscious.

"Stay alert, you two," Jay calls as the others hurry through the rainbow-stained murk to catch up with us. "They wouldn't have left him behind like that if they didn't have a damn good reason."

"Look," Chris says, pointing into the marine's shredded abdomen. I come to stand beside Chris. From that angle I can see that a prong-tipped Sorrow knife is buried in the mess of blood and gore and bioluminescent root. Someone sliced open his belly and ripped up his intestines. Now the tree is dissolving him from the inside out.

"Did Dr. Brown have a knife like that, Tarn?" I ask, numb.

He comes to study the gruesome wound. "Several."

"This is promising," Beth says. At my look of horror, she makes a face. "Don't be ridiculous, Joanna. These people came to kill Dr. Brown. Clearly, she fought back."

"Which means there's a chance she's still alive." Leela grimly stares up at Preakness.

I guess they're right. This is a good sign. Still . . . gutting a man and feeding him to a carnivorous tree seems . . . excessive.

A Sorrow throwing shard buries itself in Preakness's throat.

322

He sags, dead. I spin to glare at Tarn.

"How can you—"

"Even an enemy cannot be left to suffer," he says. "Come. We must find Lucille."

He strides forward into the dim light of the jungle, his robes gleaming in the green shadows.

We follow.

The quiet is rich with rustling branches and our squishy footsteps. The gentle clicking sound blends right in, at first. Then it gets louder.

"Tell me that isn't what I think it is," I say.

"What are you—" Jay cuts himself off when he catches the noise. "Oh. Crap. So much for those things staying in the water."

Leela gasps. I spin, following her horrified gaze past a bright purple cone of roots.

Apparently, the ant-birds can fly.

A shimmering cloud of them swarms a few meters beyond the tree. They're all shades of red, from pale pink at the top of the swarm to a deep, almost black scarlet at the bottom.

Below them, another human body lies in what's left of a pool of blood. Her head is lying several meters up the path. It has its own, smaller cluster of ant-birds hovering over it like a slow-motion geyser plume.

"Shit. That's Cardwell," Leela whispers. "Shit. I can't deal with this. I can't."

I grab her hand. "Yes," I say. "You can. *We* can."

"How do you know?"

"Because we have to."

"Stay where you are." Tarn's multitoned voice is sharp as he slips past us, holding a lit flex out in front of himself. The cold white light catches on something I couldn't see before, stretched between two trees. A wire.

It glitters in the light as Tarn cautiously slices one knotted end with his knife, then winds the gleaming line carefully around the handle of the blade.

"We soak these threads in pulverized crystal," he says. "They are used to protect our Growers during the warm season, when the Beasts are hungry. They're quite dangerous."

That's a ludicrous understatement.

"I think Lieutenant Shelby might have underestimated Dr. Brown," Jay says, coming to stand beside me.

Tarn tucks the shining flex into the raptor-skin armor he's wearing under his robes. The light catches in their amplifying folds and multiplies, eating up the shadows for meters all around him. It's so bright, it hurts my eyes. It must be horrible for Tarn' sensitive eyes.

"Stay behind me," he hums. Then he starts off through the trees.

As we follow him, I struggle to reconcile the brave, selfless being I'm trusting with my life right now with the being I've been having nightmares about for the last three weeks.

Fear is a powerful weapon.

Fear. And anger. I don't know if Tarn was trying to kill me that night, but I know he was angry. I know he was hurting me. I wasn't wrong to be afraid. But it was wrong to let that fear hold me back.

I can almost feel Mom's hand on the small of my back, pushing me forward to confront my fears even as Grandpa lunges out to stop her. To protect me.

To hold me back.

His fear became my fear. It almost made me sit back and watch while he ripped my world apart in the name of keeping me safe.

I should hate him.

I can't.

I think I miss him. Or I miss the person I thought he was. My head is full of things he's given me—memories, skills, knowledge. Little pieces of who he is that have become part of me. And now they all feel tainted and strange. Suspect. I'm going to have to rebuild my own self-image from the ground up. Assuming I don't die in the next couple of hours.

We pass two more glittering trip wires, and one rigged at ankle height that Tarn almost walks right into before Nor calls out to stop him. We don't see any more dead marines. Or Dr. Brown. Or Shelby.

Are any of them still alive?

The shining black and red of a *Vulcan*-marked flyer slips through the palette of brown and green ahead of us.

Dr. Brown's flyer is parked at the foot of a swamp solace. Its shields are up. Two portable projector pylons stretch the shimmering force field around a tent and a fire pit. A long tangle of gray fabric is strung through the lower branches of the tree. It's a Sorrow hanging chair like the ones in Tarn's house.

The shield extends about halfway through the swamp solace's bright orange root cone, which doesn't look particularly cone-like at the moment. It's tangled into a tight fist below its rotund trunk. The tree caught something. Recently.

"Dr. Brown?" I call, dread engulfing the words. "Are you here?"

There's no response.

"Why would she build her camp in one of those things?" Chris says. "Imagine getting up in the middle of the night to pee, tripping on something . . ."

And falling into the paralyzing tangle of roots. Yeah. I can imagine it. But I can also imagine what ant-birds must sound like, swarming a particle shield. And who knows what else is out there that this tree scares away?

"Dr. Brown?" I call again, louder this time.

"Do you smell burning?" Jay asks, making a face.

"Yeah," Chris says. "But I don't see a fire. Could it be the shield pylons?"

"No," Beth says. "It doesn't smell like an electrical fire."

She's right. But what is it? I don't see any flames or smoke.

A ragged sliver of sound catches at my ears. Then another. It's familiar, but also not. The bursts are so short that I can almost believe I'm imagining them. Or having some kind of a flashback. But of what? What is that sound?

A longer, sustained shriek rips through the air. Then I know.

"It's the tree!" I shout as a sharp burst of light crackles through the knotted roots. Thick white smoke follows, pouring through the ropy orange tangles from the heart of the cluster.

"Get back," Chris shouts, dragging me with him as he stumbles behind the flyer. The tree screams again as one side of the orange root cluster abruptly withers. Then a hollow sound rips through the clearing and the tree keels backward, howling, withered roots flailing up to the sky.

A pair of human bodies tumbles free. At least, I think it's two people. They're twisted together into a single knot of raw flesh.

Beth turns away, hand clamped over her mouth. I can't even find the energy to be sick again.

There isn't much left of the first body but bones and half-melted *Prairie* blue fatigues. The person sprawled below the dead marine is wearing phytoraptor-skin armor, but they're clearly human. It has to be Dr. Brown.

She's dead.

That means we're all dead.

A deep guttural moan ripples up from the ball of flesh. The marine's corpse shifts, vertebrae poking through its melting flesh as it slides into a heap beside Dr. Brown. Her head and torso are shrouded in a metallic black solar-collection tarp. The tarp writhes, then flies back. A painful groan heaves from its depths.

She's alive.

"Lucille!" Tarn bellows. "Lower your shields!"

Dr. Brown lurches up out of the bloody mess. She stares at us; then she collapses again. Limp.

She's unconscious. Or dead.

"Chris!" Jay shouts.

"She's got the shield locked to her command codes." Chris is already crouched over the pylon, his flex bonded with its cracked, muddy skin. "It'll take me a couple of minutes."

"I don't think she has a couple of minutes," Leela says.

A high, piercing hum grates through the air around us. I spin to see Tarn pressing his trijointed fingers deep into the force field.

He drops the tone of his hum lower. Then higher. Like he's tuning himself. Which he is, I realize. He's searching for the right frequency.

Tarn starts to sing.

The sound is thin and hot, like an invisible needle digging into my brain. I press my hands over my ears. but that's useless. The sound is everywhere.

The shield crackles, warping around Tarn's wide-splayed hands. His voice cuts through the humid air like a blade. I can't hear his song anymore—it's way above human hearing range. But I can feel it. We all can.

"Tarn!" Jay shouts, clutching his head.

Then the shield disintegrates.

Leela hurls herself through, collapsing on her knees beside Dr. Brown. Beth hurries to help her peel back the solar canvas. Underneath, Dr. Brown's face and arms are red, like she's been in really hot water for too long, but otherwise her upper body looks okay. Her legs are another story. Where her armor ends, the flesh bubbles with chemical burns from the tree sap. I see a few puncture wounds too, where the vines burrowed into the flesh.

"She's breathing!" Beth calls. "But I think she's in shock."

"We need to stop the bleeding," Leela says. "Is there a med kit in the tent?"

"Out of my way," Tarn hums, pushing past them to sweep Dr. Brown up in his arms.

He carries her to the flyer, up its open ramp, and slams the airlock closed behind them.

TWENTY-SEVEN

Nor is sitting on the ramp of Dr. Brown's flyer, her back to the tightly closed doors. I don't know if she's guarding Tarn while he tries to heal Dr. Brown or sticking close to him because she isn't comfortable being alone with us.

Not that we're particularly threatening, at the moment. All five of us are a mass of cuts and bruises coated in mud and something green and sticky that the drying water left behind. I really hope none of it is toxic, or infectious, since everyone has at least one open wound.

Tarn has been working on Dr. Brown for a long time. Long enough that Beth and I have already helped Chris find new battery packs for the shields, to replace the ones Tarn blew out.

The force field is online again, but Leela is perched on

the flyer's wing keeping watch anyway. She has a rifle we found on the ground by the fallen swamp solace. It must have belonged to the marine Dr. Brown dragged into the tree with her.

We covered what's left of the body in a tarp, but I can still smell the blood. I wish we could put it outside the shield, but who knows what else would smell it.

No. Not it. Them. The pile of flesh under that tarp used to be Corporal Isis Green. At least that's who Jay thinks. He recognized the gold ring that's half melted into the body's illegible dog tags. He says they have a wife and kids back at River Bend, though I'm guessing Corporal Green's family is probably in space now. Shelby would never have agreed to help Grandpa activate the planet scrubbers unless the squad's families were safe.

I wonder if Shelby's still alive out there.

I hope not.

I wish that were hyperbole. It's a weird feeling to fervently, unquestioningly wish another person dead. I don't like it, but that changes nothing. If Shelby's out there, she's a threat to all of us. She's a threat to our whole species.

But there's nothing I can do about Shelby right now, so I focus on getting my friends patched up instead. Beth found some medical supplies in Dr. Brown's gear while we were looking for the battery packs. It isn't much, but antiseptic, pain patches, and dermaglue are better than nothing.

While Beth and Chris keep searching for food and other

supplies we can use, I make Leela peel off the glue on her leg so we can wash the wound out again. Then she helps me wash out the puncture wound the ant-bird left on my hand and covers it with a layer of dermaglue. We've both got brewing infections, but we'll live. Assuming Tarn can keep Dr. Brown alive.

I turn my attention to Jay's legs. Whatever Nor did to get the death bubbles off seems to have stopped the bleeding, but the bites are gooey rings of gore that look like they've cut into the muscle in places. He's going to have some nasty new scars.

I rip open a cleansing pad and gently press it to the first bite. The antiseptic bubbles and hisses through the torn flesh. Jay hardly seems to notice. He's staring at Nor. His jaw is clenched tight, like he's trying to carry something that's too heavy. I can't tell if it's anger or guilt. Maybe both.

I want to help, but I'm scared he'll push me away again if I try, so I stay quiet as I finish cleaning his wounds and cover them with dermaglue.

I paint over the last of his bites, sealing the fizzing antiseptic in to do its work.

"There you go," I say. "Not even close to good as new, but I don't think you'll bleed to death."

Jay drags his eyes away from Nor and offers me a hollow smile. "Gee. Such an encouraging bedside manner you have, Dr. Hotshot."

"You know me," I say. "Always upbeat."

His unconvincing smile gets a little bigger, like he's trying to laugh, but the unbearable tightness sucks the humor away again.

His eyes go back to Nor.

My stomach clenches. I can't just sit here and watch him quietly tear himself apart. And I don't want to watch him snap and tear Nor apart, either.

"She saved your life," I say, as gently as I can.

He huffs a bitter laugh.

"I know." The resentment in his voice is so palpable that the words almost feel like Sorrow. "And I'm really, really glad that I didn't shoot her." He sucks in a shaky breath. "Which means I'm glad Hart is dead."

"No," Nor says from across the camp. "It doesn't."

Surprise snatches my gaze to her gray-shrouded form. Jay's voice was hardly more than a whisper, but I guess the hum of the force field wasn't enough to hide it from Sorrow hearing.

"I never wished to take a life," Nor continues, her harmonic voice simmering in a minor chord that feels like sitting by the memorial stone on a sunny day. "That is why I wear the gray. I chose to build instead of fight. So I'm not glad I took your friend's life. But I am glad that I didn't give mine. The two thoughts are not mutually exclusive."

Jay doesn't respond. Or even move. He just keeps staring at Nor with an awful closed-up look on his face. Nor returns his gaze steadily. I almost feel like I'm intruding.

Jay shudders all over, like he's suddenly cold despite the moist, warm air. Then he sighs and the tension in his face and body fall away all at once.

"Nothing is ever simple, is it?" he says.

Nor raises her hands, palms out, in a Sorrow *yes* of agreement. Then she drops them back to her sides.

"Soup's on!" Chris calls, breaking the moment as he and Beth emerge from Dr. Brown's tent with their arms full of supplies. He tosses me a couple of ration bars. I pass one to Jay and rip mine open as Chris tosses another to Nor. "They're gross, but it's calories."

"How . . . simple. Simple enough," Nor says, her choral voice simmering with something that feels like sunlight. I feel Jay's rib cage buzz with a quiet chuckle at the comment, and something unknots itself in my gut. I don't know if that conversation actually solved anything, but laughter is . . . well, it's better than whatever was going on inside his head before.

"While Jay's observation on the complexity of life here does border on cliché," Beth says, "it is certainly apropos. Which makes one wonder how our grandfather has managed to forget such an obvious truism."

"I don't know," Leela growls, catching the ration bar Chris tosses up to her. "Convincing himself that multiple genocides was a reasonable plan of action must have been pretty damn complicated."

"No," Chris says around a bite of bar. "Beth is right.

It's a lot simpler to decide you can do whatever you think is necessary to survive than worry about right and wrong with the future of your species on the line."

"Simple, perhaps," Beth says, handing thin silver emergency blankets to me and Jay. "But not particularly effective."

"If Dr. Brown dies, he's going to be able to kill everyone who disagrees with him with the push of a button, Beth," I say. "That's pretty effective."

"Not if his goal is survival of *Homo sapiens*," Beth says. "If he wipes us out, he'll have killed every human who knows anything significant about this planet. Then he and his followers will still have to contend with two powerful enemies they don't understand, whom his actions have united for the first time in their history. All without making meaningful progress on our goal of waking ten thousand survivors before the *Prairie*'s power drain begins to destabilize the ship."

"When you put it that way, it does sound like a pretty stupid plan," Leela says.

"Yeah," Chris says. "And here I thought it was just really, really mean."

"It's both," Beth says, "which is inexplicable. Our grandfather is a veteran of multiple ethically complex conflicts. He helped orchestrate the peace accords that ended the Storm Wars and united humanity for the first time in our history. He may be self-centered and egotistical, but he's neither stupid nor mean. So why is he resorting to such ineffective brutality now?"

"Some emotions are so bright, they blind us," Nor says quietly.

"What do you mean?" Chris asks.

"It is literal for my people," Nor says, folding her hood back to reveal the grass-green light of her blood pumping under her transparent skin. "Strong emotions make us brighter, and in the dark, very bright light can be blinding. Love. Anger. Guilt. Fear. My mother's fear of humanity was so great that it led her to challenge a Followed."

Abruptly, I realize why Nor looked familiar the first time I saw her face. It wasn't just the glimpse of her biolight I caught during the attack.

She looks like her mother.

"You're Pel's daughter?" I say, my mind already layering the scarred Sorrow warrior's face over Nor's. It isn't hard. Pel's face is burned into my brain. She almost killed me a couple of times. And the delicate, almost lacy pattern of veins that flared over her forehead and across her cheeks was identical to Nor's.

Nor covers her face with her palms facing out. *Yes*.

"My father begged her to wait. He had a fresh litter. So small that he was still unable to work or feed them on his own. I tried to help him after the challenge, but we were shunned. They all died.

"He became a Giver soon after. I have not seen him since. He may be dead."

Her voice maintains a neutral harmony as she speaks, but pulses of brightness wash through her veins with the words. Strong emotions. And no wonder. She's talking about the destruction of her family.

I never once stopped to wonder if Pel had a family.

Nor jerks her hood up again, like she just realized we know how emotions affect her light now. Something about the nervous gesture makes me like her a little more.

The thought of Pel being afraid of humans is startling, but it's even more startling to realize that she was right to fear us. Less than a year after Pel's failed coup, Shelby and her people tried to burn the solace grove.

Our people. I remind myself. Fear has blinded us all.

But I'm not convinced that fear is what's driving Grandpa. I know he likes to be in control, but what could possibly frighten him so much that he'd rather kill his own family than turn over command?

Something he said the night of the Sorrow attack on the Landing creeps into my head:

Everything I did could have been for nothing.

The remembered words sound different, as I think back on them now. He wasn't afraid. Or despairing, like Mom. He was angry.

He was guilty.

Everything I did could have been for nothing.

What was he talking about? At the time, I assumed he meant the struggle to get the survivors onto the *Prairie* and get the colony ship here in one piece. But now I don't think so. He would have no reason to feel guilty about that. And he hadn't yet ordered Shelby to massacre the phytoraptors or attack Sorrow's Solace. Whatever it was, it had to have happened on Earth. Not here.

So what did my grandfather do that he's willing to kill everyone he loves to justify?

Before I can even begin to get my head around that question, the flyer doors slide open and Dr. Brown stumbles out.

"No! I don't want to hear any more," she sobs, tripping over Nor and falling off the ramp onto the soggy ground.

"Dr. Brown," I say, scrambling to reach for her, but she curls in on herself, moaning.

"No! No! It isn't true. It can't be . . . a whole planet? Earth. Oh my god. Earth."

Shock punches through me. Dr. Brown is freaking out because Tarn *just* told her about Earth. But he's known for weeks. How could he keep something like this from her?

"Stand aside, Joanna," Tarn says, emerging from the flyer and striding down the ramp toward Dr. Brown and me.

I don't move. His hood is up and his blindfold is on against the soupy sunlight. The amplifying properties of his robe just make it easier to see that his biolight is visibly pulsing. His heart must be pounding.

"She didn't know?" I ask, glaring into his blindfolded face.

Tarn doesn't say anything, but his light flares, blinding bright.

"If she'd known . . ." My words stumble over each other as I try to process all the possibilities. "She's a colonel. *She* could have challenged Grandpa. Or at least kept him in check. Tarn . . ."

Dr. Brown gasps a sob, drowning out my argument.

"Stand aside, Joanna," Tarn repeats, the harmony of his voice sinking into urgent bass tones. "She needs me."

My heart is still hammering with confusion and anger and might-have-beens, but I step aside. He hurries down the ramp and crouches in front of Dr. Brown.

"I'm sorry, Lucille," Tarn hums in a gently minor harmony. "But we don't have time for you to hide from this loss. Your species needs you."

He pulls off his blindfold and takes her by the shoulders, lifting her face to his. He presses his broad forehead against hers and wraps one trijointed hand around her throat, his fingers pressing vividly into her larynx.

She gags on another sob. Behind me, I hear the wheeze of Jay's braces as he shoves to his feet.

"Let her—"

"Do not interrupt," Nor says, stepping into Jay's path as Tarn begins sing.

"He's hurting her!" Jay snaps, ducking around Nor.

"No," I say, grabbing his arm, my eyes still glued to Tarn and Dr. Brown. "I don't think he is."

339

I recognize this. The strange, uncomfortable song. The iron grip on her throat. Whatever Tarn is doing, he did it to me the night of the memorial for Earth.

"He is grieving with her," Nor hisses, her pale green light flaring bright with anxiety and irritation. "And you are distracting them!"

Tarn's song swells, not louder, but thicker. Stronger. Then the tactile melody settles into a profoundly unsettling hum. A thick, wet sound that seems to pluck at every nerve in my body.

I remember now why I thought this was an attack. It wasn't painful, just . . . awful. "Nor—" I start to say, but she twists to place her long fingers against my lips.

"This song is meant to help the body release its light," she thrums quietly, "and the painful emotions that come with it."

The sound becomes even thicker and more oppressive as it moves beyond the range of human hearing. Tears run down my cheeks as the silent crescendo racks my body. I hear sobbing behind me. I tear my eyes away from Tarn and Dr. Brown and look back to my friends. Beth is weeping unabashedly. Jay is trying hard not to. Chris's face is buried in his hands. His shoulders are shaking. I look up and see Leela scrubbing at her eyes as well.

It's impossible not to cry, in the boiling wake of that song. The sound feels like it's digging through my emotions and tossing them all to the surface. Fury. Terror. Sadness. Guilt.

So much guilt.

I should have known Tarn wasn't trying to kill me. Then again, he should have explained the grieving ritual before he started. He should have realized I had no way of knowing what he was doing. We both should have known better. We were both blinded by our emotions.

Nothing is ever simple, is it?

My relationship with Tarn certainly isn't. We both knew we weren't simply allies. Or even simply friends. But there was never any reason to assume the arrival of the survivors would make him *just* an enemy. At least, not until Shelby's fear made him seem that way. And my fear, too, I remind myself. She wasn't the only one who jumped to the conclusion that Tarn was trying to hurt me. I did too. Beings died because of those assumptions—human, Sorrow, and phytoraptor. And the trees. Those beautiful, ancient trees. How many of them did Shelby destroy before we stopped her?

I can't take it anymore. It's too much. I think I might scream. I don't know if I can help it.

Then it's over.

A profoundly empty silence follows the song. The oppressive tactile sensation is gone, and so is the over-whelming soup of emotions it dragged out of me. I feel hollow. I feel . . . better.

I swipe at my streaming eyes and look around the camp at my friends. Each one of them looks devastated in their own way, but I can see the lightness unfolding in my chest reflected in their eyes. Wonder and awe, blossoming in the empty space left behind by their purged emotions.

"Thank you, old friend," Dr. Brown says, looking up at Tarn in something close to adoration. "That you would come so far to . . ."

She trails off then, her eyes going wide as she looks past Tarn and sees me. "Joanna Watson? What are you doing here?" She twists, taking in my friends. "All of you. You're all here. Why? Why were those marines trying to kill me? What happened?"

To my surprise, my voice stays calm as I tell her that my grandfather ordered our marines to destroy the Solace and massacre the phytoraptors and that he's planning to massacre us all with the *Vulcan*'s planet scrubbers. I sound dry and clinical, just like Mom in disaster mode. You'd never know that every word is making me want to panic vomit.

Grandpa wasn't kidding about how much a poker face costs.

"I should never have let them convince me to use that old fool's ridiculous nanobots," Dr. Brown snarls when I'm through. "I told them the system was too powerful. Too easily weaponized. If I'd known Alice let him take command . . ."

My eyes jump to Tarn. He raises his hands with the palms turned out in a Sorrow *yes*.

"Keeping the truth from you was a mistake, Lucille," he murmurs. "An error made in anger. And fear."

"Yes," she says, twisting to look into his unbound eyes again, "it was. But I've made plenty of those."

"We all have," I say, meeting Tarn's wide black eyes across the camp.

"And I think we can all agree it's time to shake the habit," Dr. Brown says in a too-brisk-to-be-believable tone as she pushes herself to her feet. "We have better things to do." She looks down at her stained, shredded robes. "Starting with finding me some pants. If you'll excuse me."

She walks quickly to her tent and ducks inside. Jay and I are the only ones close enough to hear her gasp a jagged, hiccupping sob the second she's out of sight.

"She's still a mess," he says, quietly.

"She just found out Earth is gone *and* that all life on this planet is resting on our ability to stop my grandfather from murdering her," I whisper back. "That's freak-out-worthy."

"You think she can pull it together?"

"I think I'm gonna stop thinking about what happens next for a while," I say.

I start gathering up the medical supplies that are still scattered around us. Who knows what we'll need later. Jay puts a hand on my shoulder. I stop and look up at him.

"What?"

Instead of answering the question, Jay pulls me into his arms. Neither of us says anything, but I can feel all the things he's trying to tell me anyway.

"Given the circumstances, I will grant you the public

display of affection," Beth says from behind me. "But keep it brief, please."

"In other words, get a room," Leela snips from her perch on the flyer wing.

"But maybe after we avert the apocalypse," Chris tosses in.

"You guys!" My protest comes out as a squeak, which they all find very amusing.

"There is, however, something to be said for comic relief in stressful circumstances," Beth says.

"You're welcome," I mutter, burying my face in Jay's shoulder again to hide my blush.

Jay chuckles, pulling me tighter for just a second and pressing his lips against my hair. "After."

A whole other sort of heat flares over my body as he crouches to gather up the rest of the medical supplies. He looks up and shoots me a wicked grin. "Come on, Hotshot. Apocalypse isn't over yet."

TWENTY-EIGHT

Grandpa and I are standing on the crystal arch in a blinding sunlit vacuum. I can't see the mesa. I can't see the desert floor. I can't see the flyer where my friends are waiting. Grandpa and the rocks are all that's left of the universe.

He's staring straight forward, but he's not seeing me. His eyes are wide-open windows to the raging storm inside his head.

"She's everywhere."

I can hear Grandpa's voice clearly, but his mouth isn't moving.

"I carry her with me, always," the disembodied memory continues. "That's how I found the strength to do what had to be done."

"What are you talking about?" I plead. "Just tell me!"

The world skips a frame and suddenly Grandpa is in motion. He backs away from me to the very edge of the arch. "I'm just not brave enough, Little Moth," he says. "I thought I was. But I'm not."

Then he jumps. Instead of falling, he dissolves into the blinding light around us, his body breaking apart into billions of individual molecules.

"Joanna."

Beth's quiet voice snaps me out of the nightmare.

It takes me a moment to convince myself I'm in Dr. Brown's camp on the southern continent with my friends, not on that arch, watching Grandpa fall apart.

Beth is sitting next to me with a flex on her lap and one earbud in.

"Thanks," I whisper to her.

"You're welcome," she whispers back. Then she slides her other earbud back into place and hunches over her flex again.

I sit up and look around.

The sun is hanging low over the trees. Shadows are congealing around us. Chris and Leela are still asleep. Jay has taken her place on the flyer's wing, keeping watch. Tarn and Nor are crouched back to back by the ramp, leaning against each other with their heads bowed under their hoods. I assume they're sleeping, too.

It feels strange to be taking a nap with the threat of the scrubbers hanging over us, but even with *3212*, we can't evacuate the Landing. The tactical shuttle is way too small. And as long as Dr. Brown is alive, it's pointless to rush into orbit and confront Grandpa. There's no way he'll just let us board the *Vulcan*, and forcing your way onto an orbiting spacecraft is almost impossible. Right now, the best way to protect our friends and families is to protect Dr. Brown, and there's no better place for us to do that. The camp shields will keep us safe from the swamp, and the swamp will keep us safe from anyone else Grandpa sends.

I should try to get some more sleep while I can. But I don't want to.

I can feel the nightmares waiting.

I put a hand on Beth's knee to get her attention.

She pulls her earbud out again.

"What, Joanna?"

"What are you listening to?" I ask, hoping it's something soothing.

Instead of answering, she hands me the earbud.

I slide it into my ear.

"Please," my recorded voice sobs. "Please, Grandpa, you can't deploy the scrubbers. That will—"

I yank the earbud out. I don't need to relive this moment again in real life any more than I need to have nightmares about it.

"You pulled the recording from the flyer?" I guess.

Beth gestures to the flex in her lap.

"I synced up as much of the audio with the footage

from the flyer's exterior cameras as I could during the flight here."

"Why?" I ask.

She shrugs a big, shaky breath. "I'm just trying to understand."

I hug her. She hugs me back, burying her head in my shoulder.

I don't know how long we sit that way before the gentle growl of velcro draws my attention to the tent.

Dr. Brown steps out. She's wearing a faded ISA uniform that hangs loose on her thin body. Something about her posture is different. Or maybe it's the sharpness of her gaze. She looks more like the woman I expected her to be, back when I was obsessively reading her books on interstellar exploration in the Academy.

"Can you come in here, Beth?" she says quietly. "I need your help."

I'm not invited, but I follow them inside anyway. I'm tired of secrets.

Neither of them objects.

Dr. Brown has all four of the touchscreen canvas walls of her tent in notebook mode. The whole interior is covered in handwritten notes, diagrams, and equations. It's overwhelming, like stepping into a whirlwind of information.

"What is all of this?" I ask.

"Earth's atmospheric filtration system," Beth says, her eyes skipping through the equations.

"Hubris is what it is." Dr. Brown sighs. "I should have put a stop to it when Eric first proposed the idea. But the others were so convinced, and we built in so many fail-safes . . ."

"Not enough, apparently," Beth says.

"No!" Dr. Brown insists. "They were enough. More than enough. The sequence of events Tarn described to me should have been impossible. But he only has secondhand information. That's why I need your help, Beth. I need to know exactly what the failure point was."

Unease prickles up the back of my neck.

"Why are you doing this, Dr. Brown?" I ask.

"She's trying to understand," Beth says, pulling a tightly folded flex from her pocket. "Just like me." She hands the flex to Dr. Brown. "That contains everything I could find in the *Prairie*'s databases about the cascading failure in the Earth's atmospheric filtration system."

Dr. Brown shakes out the flex, and what has to be a hundred files fade up on its screen.

"You just happen to have all the available data on the apocalypse in your pocket?" I ask Beth as Dr. Brown scrolls through them.

She shrugs. "I was in the middle of reviewing it for the eighth time when we left camp, so it was in my harness."

"You read all that eight times?" I gasp.

"More like seven and a half," she says. "Compulsive behavior, I'll admit. I keep meaning to recycle that flex, but then . . ." She shrugs again and looks to Dr. Brown. "The algorithmic error is easy to find. It's a simple miscalculation based on a faulty date. So simple that it was overlooked until it was too late. By the time they fixed it, the system was suffering from a series of cascading failures that couldn't be contained. It all makes sense. But I can't shake the feeling that I'm missing something."

"Because you are," Dr. Brown says, looking up from Beth's flex. "There's no way an error like this could have been simply overlooked. The atmospheric filtration system was too dangerous to just—"

"Wakey, wakey, cutie-pies!"

Lieutenant Emily Shelby's voice slices through the tent walls like a crystal shard, cutting Dr. Brown off. Then a crackling *boom* slaps through the air, shaking the tent around us.

"Oh shit." I gasp, diving for the tent flap.

Outside, the shield projector pylons are on fire. The force field is gone. My friends are still scrambling to their feet. Except Leela. She's already up, with her stun gun pointed at Shelby.

Shelby has a gun the size of a Sorrow war hammer pointed back at her.

"Hiya, Junior!" the Lieutenant chirps, madly. She's in even worse shape than we are. Filthy, beat up, and spattered with burns. What's left of her blond hair tangles across patches of red, blistered scalp. "The look on y'all's faces. Priceless. I'd take a picture but I lost my flex somewhere."

Jay jumps off the wing of the flyer behind Shelby and points Corporal Green's rifle at her back. "Put the gun down, Lieutenant," he says.

Shelby tsks. "I thought it wasn't fair to shoot folks in the back, Lim."

"Shoot her, Jay," Leela demands.

Shelby barks a savage laugh. "As if he could get one off before I kill you."

"So?" Leela hisses.

Shelby swipes at her face, smearing a streak of bright blood through the drying mud that coats her skin. "I like you, Divekar. Did I ever tell you that? You're not that bright, but I like you." She looks past Leela to Dr. Brown, who has just emerged from the tent behind me. "You should consider coming quietly, Lucille. I don't know how well you know these kids, but they're stubborn little assholes. I'm pretty sure I'll have to kill them all to get to you, and that would be a real shame."

"You're not going to hurt them," Dr. Brown says, stepping past me.

"No, Dr. Brown!" I grab her arm, trying to pull her behind me again. "Don't! We can't risk you."

"See?" Shelby says. "Stubborn. But don't you worry. I *am* going to finish this mission. Whether Junior likes it or not."

"This is between you and me, Lieutenant," Dr. Brown says, shaking me off. She walks slowly toward Shelby, hands out placatingly at her sides. Her voice is level and cool, but

I can see her trembling. "These juveniles aren't responsible for the deaths of your team."

"Spare me!" Shelby snarls. "These little traitors started this, running off to help their glow worm buddies."

"Joanna did not start this war," Tarn says, stepping to Dr. Brown's side. "I did."

"True, ya creepy mo-fo," Shelby snarls. "But if Junior had just stayed in her lane, then Dr. Brown here would be having lonely s'mores with her pet carnivorous tree and my squad would be back in River Bend with their kids now." She hurls a glare past them to me. "But your precious bleeding hearts couldn't handle a little harsh reality, so here we are. Now, if you'll excuse me, I'm going to follow *my* orders and kill this bitch. Then I have to go tell Isis Green's wife some crazy woman fed them to a tree." She coughs violently and spits up a gob of bloody phlegm. "I really, really hate this planet. You know that?"

I barely hear her words. "The squadron is still at River Bend?" I ask, realization ping-ponging through my head. "And your families. They're all still on the planet, aren't they?"

"Only planet we've got, at the moment," Shelby says. She sneers at Tarn. "Sorry 'bout that, bro."

"She doesn't know about the scrubbers," Beth says slowly. "The squadron isn't a part of this. He's just using them."

"Of course the admiral is using us, Mendel," Shelby snarls. "That's what commanding officers do."

"No, you don't under—" I cut myself off midword and backtrack. "The *Vulcan* has a nanobot system programmed to search and destroy Earth-based organics. The Rangers used it to make sure they weren't accidentally contaminating planets they explored. Grandpa is planning to use it against us. All of us. That's why he needs to kill Dr. Brown. The system won't activate if her ID implant reports that she's alive and on the planet. Once she's dead, he's going to kill us all. Including you and your squadron and their families."

I always thought *jaw dropped* was just a figure of speech, but that's exactly what happens as Shelby processes the implications of what I just said.

Then she bursts out laughing.

"Junior, you have a wild imagination, you know that? Killer nanobots. That's hysterical."

"Hysterical right up until they break you into your component molecules," Chris snaps.

"You're telling me the admiral is going to compost us all?" Shelby snorts. "Including his own family? You kids really need a more believable story."

"Lieutenant."

The discordant harmony in Nor's voice is like a thrown brick. It makes Shelby stagger back a step. She twists to glare at Nor, and the green Sorrow flings a fistful of something glittery into Shelby's face.

Shelby throws her gun arm up to protect her eyes. The cloud of razor dust shreds the sleeve of her uniform instead, and tiny points of blood well all over the skin underneath. Shelby howls in pain and fires blindly toward Nor, who ducks, evading the wild shots.

"Please." I'm startled to hear my own begging voice cut through the gunfire. "Please, Grandpa, you can't deploy the scrubbers. That will kill every human being on Tau."

I spin to see Beth holding up her flex. It's playing the recording of Grandpa and me on the arch.

"I designed them," Grandpa says on the screen. "I know what they do."

Beth pauses the recording.

"I can play the rest for you," she says, "if you want to watch my grandfather lose his mind in real time."

I can see the truth assembling in Shelby's shocked eyes. Dr. Brown can see it, too.

"There you have it, Lieutenant," she says. "Straight from the source. The question is what you're going to do about it."

"Jesus," Shelby says, still staring at the frozen image of Grandpa on Beth's flex. "Jesus Christ."

"You can keep your people safe," I say. "But only if you let Dr. Brown live. Please, Lieutenant Shelby. Help us. Help your people. Don't do this."

She just stares at me. Wide-eyed. Overwhelmed.

"My team was killed," Dr. Brown says very quietly. "Years ago. Phytoraptors ripped them apart right in front of my eyes."

She takes a step toward Shelby.

Shelby doesn't move.

"I know what you're feeling right now," Dr. Brown continues. "I know the anguish. The grief. The guilt of survival."

She takes another step. When Shelby doesn't react, Dr. Brown reaches out to grip the barrel of Shelby's gun. They're eye to eye now. Shelby starts to shake, but she doesn't remove her finger from the trigger.

"I am also intimately familiar with the unquenchable greed of vengeance," Dr. Brown says without changing her tone at all. "I let vengeance make my choices for years. People have suffered because of it. Everything that's happening now . . ." She shakes her head. "But it's useless to consider what might have been. Suffice it to say, you have what I didn't have, all those years. You have a reason to do better. The living need you now, more than the dead."

Shelby drops her gun.

My knees almost buckle with the sudden release of tension as Dr. Brown lets the huge weapon fall to the mud and kicks it away from them.

"You're a strong woman, Lieutenant," Dr. Brown says. "Hardly a surprise, given the formidable team you led here to capture me. I am deeply sorry that the admiral wasted their lives this way."

"Yeah," Shelby says. "Me too."

With that, she turns and walks away into the jungle.

We all just stand there and watch her go for a long beat. "That's it?" Chris says. "She's just walking away?"

"I doubt it," Dr. Brown says. "I pity the admiral, if she gets her hands on him." She bends to pick up Shelby's rifle. "We're going to recycle this. We're going to recycle every single one of these on the whole—"

The gun and Dr. Brown's hand disappear in a spray of blood and screaming.

"No!" I scream as a huge blur of creature drops on Dr. Brown again. This time it stays, driving the tip of one of its many clusters of razor-thin legs into her belly and wicking blood up its opalescent carapace.

It's an ant-bird the size of a jeep.

It's eating Dr. Brown.

Before I can move, or think, Shelby is there. She bolts past me, sending me stumbling into Tarn as she hurls herself at the massive bird and punches it in the head.

With a hard flutter, the creature shoots up again, disappearing into the canopy.

Dr. Brown curls into a ball, screaming in agony.

"Where is my gun?" Shelby shouts.

"The bird ate it!" I yell back.

Shelby swears copiously as I scramble to Dr. Brown. Blood is pouring from the stump of her arm and the hole in her abdomen. "Keep breathing. Please, keep breathing."

I don't know if I'm chanting the words out loud or just in my head as I rip at my thermal and try to tie a tourniquet around Dr. Brown's stump. Yellow light tints the world as

Tarn crouches beside me, pressing his trijointed hands to the wound in Dr. Brown's belly in an effort to stanch the blood.

"Can you heal her?" I beg him.

Dr. Brown grabs at my hands, digging jagged nails into my skin. "Stupid," she coughs, blood bubbling at her lips. "Took armor off. Fresh start."

She gasps for air.

"Hate. Irony."

That's when I hear the clattering of wings.

I dive forward, throwing my body over Dr. Brown. But before the creature's needle feet connect with my back . . .

WHAM!

I look up as the giant bird slams into the nearest swamp solace. Nor stands above us holding her staff like she's just hit a home run. She just saved my life.

The ant-bird screams.

Shelby screams back in wordless defiance, and tackles it head on, fighting the enormous bloodsucking creature with her bare hands.

"Go!" Tarn shouts, scooping Dr. Brown up in his arms and bolting, with Nor hard on his heels.

"We gotta get to *3212*," Jay shouts as we race after him through the glowing trees. "It's our only shot."

He's right, but we'll never make it. It's too far. There's no way Shelby can hold that thing off long enough.

Without warning, Shelby's enormous gun drops out of the trees in front of us. Dr. Brown's hand is still shriveled around the grip, like a piece of dried fruit.

"Crap!" Jay swears, hurling himself sideways to avoid stepping on it.

I'm almost as surprised as Jay when I snatch up the gun and run back to where we left Shelby.

I find her lying at the foot of a swamp solace, covered in blood.

"Don't be stupid, Junior!" she rasps. "Get out of—"

Shelby's voice is drowned out by the clatter of wings as the ant-bird dive-bombs her again.

I get closer. I'm a terrible shot and I'm only going to get one chance. I have to be right on top of that thing.

Shelby screams in pain.

I raise the huge gun and spray the bird with bullets.

Rainbow-sheened blood explodes from the creature as it collapses beside Shelby. I throw myself backward, but it's too late—the blood spatters over me and immediately starts eating through my flight suit. I roll, shrieking, as I rip at the fasteners and tear myself free of the quickly melting fabric.

I hurl the dissolving suit away and sprawl in my thermal and shorts, heaving for breath.

Shelby rolls on her back, choking on what sounds remarkably like laughter. "Jesus. I hate this planet."

TWENTY-NINE

Dr. Brown is dead.

Tarn tried to save her when they got her back to *3212*, but it was too late. By the time Shelby and I limped into the burned-out clearing around the shuttle, she was gone.

But we're not giving up.

We have a plan. It's not a good plan, but it's the only one we've got.

Assuming the scrubbers went live the moment the *Vulcan* registered Dr. Brown's death, Beth calculates that we have five hours and twenty-three minutes before the nanobots saturate the atmosphere and initiate their programming. After that, everything and everyone with Earth-based DNA will be disintegrated.

The only way to stop that from happening is to cut power to the *Vulcan's* computers with simulation twelve.

Grandpa is still jamming our satellite communications, so we're going to have to go into orbit and intercept the *Vulcan*.

Trying to dock with another ship in orbit is complicated even when both pilots are working together, and Grandpa definitely isn't going to cooperate. I'm going to have to out-fly him, which is just ridiculous. I might be younger, but he's got decades more experience than I do. He's actually seen space combat before. And won.

I've never even beat him at chess.

I want to get this over with. If I could run from here into orbit, I would. I'd rather do that than sit here, waiting for our launch window. But space doesn't hurry. If we take off now, it'll actually take us longer to get to the *Vulcan* than it will if we let Tau bring us to her. So I'm sitting on *3212*'s bridge trying to be patient and watching Leela run the pre-flight checks.

"All systems are green," Leela says, swiping at the flex that's mounted on the arm of the copilot's seat. "Do you really think we can pull this off?"

"What choice do we have?" I say.

We sit there for a while, side by side, staring at the three-sixty view of the jungle around us on the wall screens.

"Jo," she says.

"Yeah?" I say.

"I love you, you know," she says.

"Yeah," I say. "I know. I love you, too."

The words don't change anything. But they matter.

"I've done what I can." Tarn's voice breaks through the moment as he, Jay, and Nor duck into the little bridge. "The lieutenant will live."

Nor makes an acidic comment in Sorrow that carries the tingling satisfaction of really excellent sarcasm. She didn't want Tarn to heal Shelby, and I don't blame her. Shelby is a xenophobic murderer who tried to destroy the Sorrow's city and kill us all. She hasn't even stopped referring to Tarn and Nor as "glow worms." But if we let her die slowly from wounds she got trying to help us save Dr. Brown, then how are we any better than Grandpa?

"She's tethered into one of the bunks," Jay says.

"By which you mean hog-tied, I hope," Leela says.

"Beast-skin rope," Tarn hums. "Unlike your tethers, it will not respond to the lieutenant's command codes."

"Kind of overkill," Jay says. "She's in bad shape. Tarn healed her stomach wound, but her left arm is still pretty much useless. I think she might lose it."

"Dr. Brown's remains have also been secured," Beth says, as she and Chris enter the tiny dome of a room. The two of them volunteered to get the body into 3212's cargo hold. It's too dangerous to go back into the swamp looking for the others. We don't know how much is left of them to find, anyway.

"Are you sure you don't want to take Dr. Brown's flyer back to the Solace?" I ask Tarn.

"I told you, Joanna. If your grandfather is still the human Followed when I return, I will be challenged," he says. "I'm going to see this through, wherever it leads." Then he switches to Sorrow, rumbling something to Nor that makes my stomach clench.

She shoots him a look I can tell is a glare even through her blindfold. "I Follow," she snips back at him in a buzzing minor key, "even if your path takes us beyond the sky."

"Well, nobody's going beyond the sky just yet," Leela says. "We don't have a clean launch window for another forty-three minutes."

Beth checks her flex. "That leaves us with less than five hours to get into orbit, intercept the *Vulcan*, and run simulation twelve."

"If you can make the planet rotate faster, I'm happy to take off sooner," Leela fires back.

"Hey, hey," Jay says. "This is no time to lose our chill."

Leela rolls her eyes. "Since when have any of us had any chill?"

"You know what I mean."

"Yeah, yeah." She waves his point off like a gnat. "Beth, check my trajectory, will you?"

"I could—" I start to say, but she cuts me off.

"No. You are going to go take a shower. Right now."

"Seriously, Joey," Chris says. "You stink."

"Go, Hotshot," Jay says. "You'll feel better clean. And dressed in something that hasn't been . . ."

"Ant-birded," I supply, suddenly acutely aware that the thermal undershirt and shorts I'm wearing are sticking to my skin and the seat under me.

"That's one way of putting it." Leela makes a face. "Go. Now."

"Okay, okay," I say. "You only have to tell me I'm disgusting once."

"It was three times," Beth responds.

"Do you have to count everything?" I grumble, heading for the door.

Thankfully, tactical shuttles are designed to be temporary base camp for a squadron, if necessary. A narrow ladder leads me down into the galley, which is flanked by two doors. The one on the right has a toilet icon on it, the other a bed. That's where they have Shelby tied up.

The bathroom is tiny. The toilet is in the single shower stall, so you have to fold it up to have room to bathe. The rest—a stool, a recycler, and a storage cabinet that holds towels and extra clothes—is crammed into less than a square meter.

Forty-three minutes before our last-ditch effort to save our loved ones is a stupid time to take a shower, but when the hot water starts flowing over my tormented skin, I'm glad my friends shooed me down here.

It takes a long time to get clean. There are long streaks of red on my legs and chest and belly from the few seconds the ant-bird's blood had to seep through my flight suit. Chunks of my hair come free as I struggle to get the sticky, acidic stuff out of it, but there's still enough to pull the uneven, wet mass back into a tight ponytail. If I don't accidentally crash *3212* into the *Vulcan* and kill us all, I'll have to cut most of it off.

If I can't outmaneuver Grandpa and get us on board the *Vulcan*, I might have to ram the ship on purpose. There's no guarantee we could do enough damage to stop the scrubbers, but if it's our only chance to save our families . . .

I push the thought out of my head and towel off. There's no point in dwelling on all the ways this could go spectacularly wrong.

I put on a clean bra and shorts. I have to dig through the cabinets a bit to find pants and a thermal that will fit. Most of the marines are taller and bigger than I am, so it takes a while to find something that will work. I'm still in my underwear when Jay walks in with a bag of drinking water and a first-aid kit.

"Oh, sorry! I . . ." He spins, ready to bolt out again.

But I say, "Don't go."

He stops. I am pretty sure every inch of me is blushing.

"I just didn't want to—"

"It's okay," I say. "I don't, I mean, you don't have to . . ."

"Oh," he says.

"Yeah."

The look on Jay's face is somewhere between amusement and awe and anxiety. It's more awkward than sexy, but that's . . . perfect.

It makes me want to kiss him. A lot.

I want to feel his hands on my aching, burned skin.

I also want to tell him to turn around so I can yank my clothes on.

I don't do either. I just stand there. Staring.

He stares back.

This goes on for a long time.

Then he hands me the water and fishes in the first-aid kit for a tube of burn cream.

"Your burns," he says. "I, I mean, they, ah, need ointment."

"Yeah," I say. "Probably."

"Just . . . sit down, okay?" he says. Is he blushing? Yeah. He's definitely blushing.

I sit on the stool.

Jay kneels in front of me and squeezes out a pool of the yellowish stuff into his palm. He starts with the burns at my ankles. His fingers are so gentle, I can hardly feel them brushing the thick ointment over my skin. I'm surprised how much it helps. Or maybe I'm just distracted from the pain by the sparkling electricity of his touch.

That's gentle, too, and overwhelming. Not in a bad way. The glowing static washes over the pain and the grief and the anger, drowning them out with the simple heat of his hands. Of his breath on my belly as he massages ointment into the curve of my hip.

He sits back.

I start to protest, but I don't get the chance because his

lips are on mine. The kiss is deep and hungry and singular. He doesn't touch me anywhere else.

I pull the tube of ointment from his hand and toss it to the floor. I want to forget everything else. Just for a little while. But he catches my hands before I can touch him, pulling back so he can bring them to his lips.

"What if there is no better time?" I demand.

He squeezes my fingers. "I need . . . a future. Whether this works or not, we're going to have to deal with your grandfather. The things he did. The things he convinced the rest of us to do. . . ." Jay shakes his head. "I need something on the other side of that."

Our faces are still centimeters apart. I could lean forward and kiss him again. It would be so easy. It would be easy for him to pull away, too.

He doesn't.

Before I can do anything about it, both of our flexes buzz an alert and T – 15:00 fades up on the wall screens around us.

Jay quirks a wry smile. "Guess that's our cue."

"If we die, I'm going to be really pissed off," I say, trying to make it come out like a joke.

He laughs, so it must have worked.

"Guess we'd better not die, then," he says.

I start for the door.

"Um, Hotshot," Jay says, still laughing.

"What?"

"I think you might want some pants. And shirt."

I blush all over. Again.

I grab the thermal and drag it over my head. "Go!" I tell him. "I'm right behind you."

"But will you be wearing pants?"

I throw the water bag at his head as he flees.

I yank on the pants and reach for my boots, but they're sticky with ant-bird gore. I can't stand the thought of putting them on, so I don't. I don't need them to pilot *3212*.

My stomach grumbles loudly as I step out of the bathroom into the galley, reminding me that I haven't eaten more than a few bites of ration bar in the last twenty-two hours. I open a cabinet and find it stocked with bags of freeze-dried chickpeas. I snag a bag and pour a handful of peas into my mouth. The salt-crusted nuttiness is almost enough to make me cry. Real food. Earth food. How long until this stash is gone and it's just one more thing I might never taste again?

A thread of sound winds through my self-pity. A human voice, humming. The melody is familiar, but I can't place it until the humming drops into a raspy whisper of lyrics.

I once was lost . . . but now I'm found. Was blind . . . but now . . . I see.

Goose bumps prickle all over my body. "Amazing Grace." When I was really tiny, Grandpa used to sing that song to me while he walked me around the house at night when I couldn't sleep.

Now Shelby is singing it to herself, in the bunks. Grieving. I can hear the sadness there, underneath the cracked and broken words.

I should leave her alone.

Instead, I push the narrow door open and slide in between the two racks of cramped bunk beds.

"Howdy, Junior," Shelby says, dropping seamlessly from the whispered prayer of a song into sarcasm. "Come to mock your prisoner?"

"No," I say.

I'm not sure why I'm here, so I don't elaborate. She doesn't ask.

Shelby is stretched out on a lower bunk with her harness tethered to the wall. Her ruined shoulder is swathed in a pressure bandage and a sling. Her good arm is lashed against her side with black-green cord. Her ankles are bound the same way.

"Guess I should take it as a compliment that your glow-in-the-dark buddy thinks I'm dangerous enough to tie up." She sneers.

"His name is Tarn," I say.

"Yeah." She sighs. "I know it."

Then she kicks at the bunk a little with her bound feet, like she's trying to get comfortable and can't.

On impulse, I reach out and pick the knot at her ankles loose. The green-black cord falls away in my hands. It's smooth and cool, almost like a braid of rubber, though I know it's raptor hide.

"Why did you do that?" Shelby demands.

"I don't know," I snap, sudden embarrassment crackling in my belly. "I don't know why I'm here, talking to someone who hates everything I have ever believed in."

I reach for the door to leave, but Shelby calls after me, "That's not true at all."

I really don't want to care, but I stop and look back at her anyway.

"My parents were both born in Mississippi, just like me," she says. "Even before the flu, it was a mess down there, but they got out. They were missionaries when I was young. And doctors. We traveled all over the world with a group of like-minded medical types, helping folks and praying with them. Us kids were tight. We all wanted to be doctors just like our parents, when we grew up."

Recognition flares.

She could be describing the Galactic Frontier Project. My childhood. My friends.

She sucks in a little breath. "Then the flu came to Mississippi. My parents went back. Moved into my grand-parents' house. The tire swing was still there, in a big ol' tree with these thick low branches. Looked like some kind of giant, just about ready to give you a hug. Or smack you upside the head. That tree would have fit right in on this planet."

"How long before the quarantine was that?"

The corners of her mouth lift in wry grin. "Not long enough." The expression fades immediately, leaving behind naked grief. She flops back on the bed and looks up at the ceiling. "People got sick fast. Dropped like flies. My parents stayed to treat the infected. They shouldn't have. They should have locked them in a room to die. That's what the IntGov Marines did in the end." She swears. "Either you're gonna have to untie my arm, too, or I'm gonna have to wipe my nose on this sling, and I don't think that's gonna turn out well."

I untie her arm. She sits up, fishes a handkerchief from a pocket in her utility harness, and blows her nose. She studies the contents and shudders. "Rainbow snot. This planet just has no end of gross."

She stuffs the handkerchief back in her harness pocket and looks up at me. "I wouldn't have cut you loose, if our positions were reversed."

Fear shoots through me. Even with only one hand, I'm sure she can hurt me faster than I can get out of here.

But she doesn't.

"You learn a lotta stuff when your parents lock you in the school cafeteria with twenty other kids while they're all busy dying outside," she says. "You figure out how to take care of you and yours, and not give a damn about anything or anyone else. So if I were in your shoes, I wouldn't care if some crazy asshole who just tried to kill me had rainbow boogers dripping down her throat. Or that her feet were falling asleep. And for sure I'd never have made an alliance with an alien freak who attacked my own people." She runs her good hand over her her ruined shoulder. "Which means, if it'd been up to me, I'd have bled out a couple of minutes ago."

"Oh." I'm slowly understanding what she's saying. She's right. She'd be dead if not for Tarn.

"Yeah," Shelby says. "It's damn disconcerting, realizing you may have been playing the game by the wrong set of rules your whole life."

"I'm not sure there are any rules left," I say.

"Speaking of," Shelby says, pointing to the countdown clock on the wall screens, "I assume the fact that we're launching means you have some kind of heroic plan to stop Grandpa Dearest from scrubbing us off the face of the universe?"

"Not so much heroic as desperate," I say.

"Same difference," Shelby says, settling back against the pillow again. "Wake me when it's over. Unless we're all dead."

I pull the sliding door open, but then I turn back to Shelby.

"We're going to intercept the *Vulcan* and board her."

Shelby bursts out laughing. "You really do think highly of yourself, Junior, if you think you have a chance in hell of boarding a ship piloted by Eric Crane. Or anyone else, for that matter. You don't have any combat experience at all, much less space combat experience. Hell, *I* don't even have space combat experience."

I know she's right. It just doesn't matter.

"I have to try," I say.

"Why?" she demands. "If you somehow manage to pull off the impossible and board her, you really think he'll just *let* you shut down the system?"

"No," I say. "I don't. But we aren't going to try to access the computers. We're just going to turn them off. Chris and Leela programmed a testing protocol into the *Vulcan*'s mainframe while they were rebuilding her. Simulation twelve. It kills power to the whole computer system. Including the planet scrubbers."

Shelby sits up and stares at me.

"You sure it works?" she says, her voice suddenly intense.

"Yeah," I say. "I've seen Chris do it."

A predatory grin spreads over her face. "I can't wait to see the old man's face when we kill his ship right out from under him."

"'We'?" I say. She can barely stand.

"That's right," Shelby says, holding her good hand out to me. "Help me up, Junior. Unless you'd rather hold a grudge than save the world."

THIRTY

The wall screens read **T – 03:53** as I help Shelby limp onto the bridge.

"What is *she* doing here?" Nor hisses.

"We can't trust her, Jo," Jay agrees.

"Probably not, Slow Hands," Shelby says, easing herself into the nearest chair. "But you're still gonna be happy Junior dragged my sorry butt up here, in a minute."

"You have space combat experience?" Leela asks, dubious.

"No," Shelby says. "And I don't plan to. Two of my folks are on the *Vulcan* with the admiral, which means all you gotta do is get me within radio range. If I tell them to initiate this simulation twelve thing, they will. No questions asked."

"Are you sure?" Beth says. "Our grandfather was alone when he met Joanna in the desert."

"He came to River Bend last night, ordered two of my people to come with him, and told me to find Dr. Brown and kill her. Told us she was a traitor. Giving technology and weapons to the enemy." Her eyes dart to Tarn and Nor. "Of course, *enemy* seems to be a fluid term on this planet."

"She could be lying," Nor hums. Her hood is down. The artificial light from the wall screens is bright enough to wash out her internal glow. The muscles and bones and ligaments under her transparent skin are painted in vivid shades without the usual tint of her pale green light. It makes me kind of uncomfortable, for some reason. Like she's naked and doesn't know it. Vulnerable, I guess.

"Hate me all you want," Shelby says. "But don't let it make you stupid. A lot of people I love already died on this planet. I don't want to lose the ones I've got left."

None of us do, but the others are still dubious. I don't blame them. The prospect of pinning our last hope on Emily Shelby's word seems crazy.

"Working together is better," Tarn says. The gentle harmony of the words is quietly inexorable. Undeniable.

"We're T minus thirty-four seconds," Leela says. "This is not one of those occasions where we want to be fashionably late."

I drop into the pilot seat, shaking out my flex as I tether in. It snaps stiff into tablet mode. I press it against the arm of my chair, transforming it into a console for the nav app.

I take a deep breath. I put my fingers on the velvety screen.

"Engage thrusters in three . . . two . . . one."

The engines fire below us, their vibration flooding upward through the floor and my chair, into my bones.

"Liftoff," I breathe, pressing up on the nav app.

The charred and twisted swamp solace trees on either side of us burst into flames again as our engine backwash roars over them. Guilt twists up the back of my neck. Every move we make leaves a fresh scar on this world.

As we ascend into the darkening gray sky, gasps and whispers of Sorrow language brush over my skin. Tarn and Nor are talking quietly behind me. Some of the exclamations are sharp edged. Is that fear? Or pain? Abruptly I realize how bright it is, with the last light of the setting sun pouring through the three-sixty.

"Lower the brightness on the screens, please," I tell the computer. "Twenty percent."

"Certainly, Joanna," the computer says.

The screens dim. The palpable atmosphere formed by Tarn's and Nor's voices shifts, warming. Easing.

"Thank you, Joanna," Tarn hums. "I did not anticipate that."

"I think we're past the stuff we can anticipate," I say.

"Max Q," Leela says, as the slipstream whistles past the exterior cameras. "Exit velocity in three . . . two . . . one." I can feel the acceleration pushing me back, grinding me into the seat a little harder with each count. Worry tangles with the familiar exhilaration pumping through my body. Are Tarn and Nor okay? I can't look back at them to see, but nobody's screaming or anything.

Pink flames lick up the three-sixty.

"Killing thrust . . . now," I say, tapping the command into the nav app. Just like that, the grinding pressure evaporates. My body floats gently upward against my tethered harness.

We're in space.

I twist to look back at Tarn and Nor. Nor is looking around like a little kid, trying to take in everything at once. Tarn is sitting very still, staring down at Tau below us.

This is the first time he's ever seen his home from space. The thought is breathtaking.

Mom took me up for the first time when I was four. All I remember about the experience was the lollipop I got in the launch center gift shop and how much the pressure hurt as we crossed the atmosphere. I guess candy was more striking to me than the idea of spaceflight, at the time.

I wasn't that impressed with the view the last time I saw Earth from space, either. I was just impatient, eager to get to Tau. Now I'd give anything to go back and see Earth buzzing with life again.

Nor says something to Tarn in Sorrow. Her voice bright and fizzy. Excited. Amazed. Invigorated. Tarn thrums something low and thick in response.

"There she is," Chris breathes.

I turn back to see the elegant form of the *Vulcan* spiraling through orbit up ahead like a diving bird.

"That's my cue," Shelby says, toggling the radio pack she's white-knuckling. "Shelby to Batten. Please respond."

The only response is static.

Shelby's eyes dart up to meet mine. She swallows hard, clinging to her cool as she toggles the radio again.

"Shelby to Hendrick. Please respond."

The gentle hiss of an empty radio frequency fills the cabin.

Shelby toggles her handset again.

"Batten! Hendrick! Goddamn you, get on this radio and ANSWER ME," Shelby shouts.

There's no reply.

Shelby swipes at her face, dashing the tears that are crowding her cheeks.

"He might have taken their radios," I say quietly.

"Nice try, Junior," she whispers. "But optimism isn't really my thing. That bastard killed them."

"LT!" A crackling voice blasts over her radio. "LT! Thank god! Please tell me you copy!" the frantic voice cries.

Shelby snatches up her handset. "About time, Batten. You need to shut *Vulcan* down *now*."

"Can't, sir," the voice replies. "We're not on *Vulcan*."

"What?" Shelby demands.

"They're on the *Prairie*," Beth says, pointing beyond the

Vulcan to where a sliver of gold is just visible past the orbital horizon. "She just crested the planet."

"He left us with a list of people to pull out of inso," another voice I assume belongs to Hendrick chimes in. "But we don't have a doc here, and these people have been under a long time. I tried to point that out, but he said limited casualties were acceptable. Then he took off alone in *Vulcan*. Something's up, LT. Something bad."

"You ain't wrong, Henny," Shelby says. "Sit tight, you two. Don't wake anybody up. I'm gonna take care of this—then we'll come for you."

"Yes sir!" Batten says, her voice thick with relief.

Shelby toggles off the radio and wilts in her chair. "We're screwed."

"No," Beth says coolly. "We're just back to plan A."

"And you're a cocky asshole, Mendel," Shelby hurls back at her.

"That's probably true," Beth says, turning to me. "But I know my sister. She can do this."

She sounds so sure of that. But then again, she doesn't know that the last time I did orbital docking maneuvers, I hit the wrong button and nearly destroyed both ships. It's totally insane to even try this, but the only other option is giving up.

We aren't giving up.

I swipe at the nav app, and pale red ellipses of light flow out from the *Vulcan* and the *Prairie*, revealing their trajectories around the planet. I swipe again and our own trajectory line shifts, twisting to cross the *Vulcan's*.

"Okay," I say. "Five-second burn. On my mark."

I take a deep breath and let it out, listening to the ship around me. Feeling it move. Trying to imagine the *Vulcan* out there. To feel it. I can't. It's so far away. I feel numb. Disconnected.

"Take a deep breath, Hotshot," Jay says quietly from behind me. "You got this."

His voice is like oxygen. I breathe in and out.

I close my eyes.

The low hum of Sorrow sonar skates over my skin.

Of course.

"Tarn," I say. "You guys mind being quiet a second?"

The conversation drops to silence immediately, as though their mingled voices are one.

The sudden quiet is eerie. Oddly empty. Like I just stepped out of glaring sun into the shadows.

Then the quiet starts to fade. The grumble of the engines swells in my ears, a steady descant to the hum and crackle of gravity and radiation pressing in on the hull. A smile darts over my lips, unbidden. I can't help it. I may not know this ship, but I know the song.

I let my hands rest lightly on the controls and wait, listening to *3212* move through space for a few more heartbeats.

"Mark."

The engines roar. We accelerate over the green arc of the world.

I breathe in. I breathe out. I breathe in.

The engines die. Too soon. That was too soon. The *Vulcan* looms large on the wall screens, but not nearly large enough.

"We're going to miss her," Chris calls, zooming the exterior cameras in on his portion of the wall screens. "Our trajectory is totally wrong."

"No kidding," Leela says as we both frantically swipe-tap at the nav app. "This isn't—" She cuts herself off, swearing copiously. "Maneuvering thrusters are dead."

"What?" Jay exclaims. "Why?"

"How am I supposed to know?" she shouts back. "I'm just telling you they're gone."

"So is the main engine," I say. "I'm not getting any thrust at all. From anything."

Chris hurls himself out of the bridge and up the hallway. Beth follows him.

"I swear, we were green on all checks," Leela says, her hands skimming frantically over the diagnostic apps. "We were green."

"I believe you, Lee-lu," I say.

"What does this mean for us?" Nor hums, behind me.

"It means we're dead in the water, sister," Shelby says. "Cuz this day just keeps getting better."

"Goddamn it!" Chris shouts so loudly, we can hear him from the engine room.

380

"That's not encouraging," Jay mutters, untethering himself to start after them. But before he makes it to the door, Chris hurls himself back onto the bridge.

"Swamp goo," he snarls.

"What?"

"Solace tree sap," Beth says, pulling herself through the door behind him. "Likely from the trees destroyed by *3212*'s landing. It seems to have been slowly eroding the engine casement this whole time."

"Then we did a hard burn," Leela says, putting it together, "the casing blew and . . ."

"Yeah," Chris says. "We're dead."

But it's not just us. Everyone. Mom. Dad. Dr. Howard. Doc. Mrs. Divekar. I have to cut the mental tally off before I burst into tears. Everything we've gone through, and stupid tree sap is going to kill us all.

"What's happening to your grandfather's ship?" Nor demands, pointing at the wall screen. I look up and see that the *Vulcan* is spreading her arched wings.

"He's stopping," I say as the sleek ship's maneuvering thrusters fire. "Why is he stopping?"

"*Vulcan* to *3212*," Grandpa's voice swells over the comms. "What the hell do you think you're doing, Lieutenant?"

"This isn't my rodeo anymore, Admiral," Shelby drawls.

"Hi, Grandpa," I say.

"Joanna?" His voice cracks as he says my name. I can't tell if that's shock or horror or relief. It might be all three.

The video chat window unfolds on the wall screen in

front of me, layering my grandfather's narrow, crinkled face over the exterior three-sixty. He's alone on the bridge of the *Vulcan*. He looks so much older than he did when I saw him last, less than a day ago.

"What's wrong with your ship, Joanna?" he demands.

"How the f—"

"You're drifting, Cadet Divekar," he snaps, cutting Leela off. "Any fool could see that. What happened?"

"You sent Lieutenant Shelby and her team into a swamp full of trees with corrosive sap that destroyed the engine casing," I say. "That's what happened." Suddenly, I'm too exhausted and achy to worry about what I should and shouldn't tell him. "We just didn't realize it until now. So yeah. Maybe you win. Maybe we're all going to die and you get your fresh start. Does that make you happy?"

He closes his eyes for a moment, like he's in physical pain. "Of course that doesn't make me happy, Little Moth."

"Then don't do this!" I plead. "Turn off the scrubbers."

"I. Can't." He grinds the words out between his teeth. "I wish . . . but this situation is—"

He keeps talking, but the sound is suddenly gone.

"Don't turn around," Shelby says. "I muted the maniac. He hasn't noticed yet, so just keep on staring at him like he grew a second head."

"What—Why, I—"

"I don't need him to mansplain his egomaniacal plans," Shelby says. "Neither do you. We need to get on board that

382

ship, and he's at a full stop less than ten klicks off to star-board. We're not going to get a better chance than this."

"Oh," Beth breathes. "The emergency docking tube."

"Danger Twin Two's got it—what about you, DT One?" she snaps. "You with me?"

Our emergency docking tube will automatically syn-chronize the two ships' computers and put them in search-and-rescue mode. Once it's attached to the *Vulcan*, Grandpa won't be able to shake us off. But someone's going to have to go out there and guide the tube between the ships manu-ally, and EVA prep takes time. You can't just throw on a spacesuit and take a stroll. Or I guess you can, but it's a truly terrible idea. But then again, so is this whole mission.

"I'll try to keep him talking," I say.

"Do better than try, Junior," Shelby snaps. "Divekar, Lim, with me. Subtle like."

Then the sound is back.

"—do you understand, Joanna?" Grandpa says.

Leaving me in charge of lying to Grandpa is also a truly terrible idea. It takes everything I have to keep from look-ing at Leela as she slips after Shelby. Forming full sentences at the same time feels impossible.

"Joanna may understand, but I do not." Tarn's harmonic voice is like a hive of angry bees. "How can wiping out your own team be helpful to your cause?"

"I could ask you a related question," Grandpa snaps. "If you want us off your planet so badly, why are you risking your life to help my granddaughter stop me?"

"Letting you murder your followers won't stop you, Admiral," Tarn replies. "But Joanna may. Given the chance."

"She's a child," Grandpa snaps. "A very bright one, but a child nonetheless. And this alliance of yours is unsustainable. There will be war eventually."

"I already tried war," Tarn says calmly. "Both sides lost. But my alliance with Joanna, as you call it, has already had moderate success."

"Short-term thinking." Grandpa shakes his head in disgust. "Just like the others." Then, more to himself than us, he mutters, "Cleo was right. Cleo was right. They'll never change."

His mouth is twisted into a disdainful smirk, but he looks like he might burst into tears at the same time. It's so far from the calm, kind face I thought I knew that it makes me dizzy.

My flex vibrates, but I don't dare look down to read the text. I can't break eye contact with him. Beth hears the vibration.

"Do you really think Grandma would approve of this?" Beth says, sliding over into Leela's seat so we split the screen.

"Don't be obtuse, Beth," he snaps, pivoting to glare at her. "Of course she wouldn't approve."

"Curious, then, that you persist in invoking her name," Beth says, holding his gaze as my eyes dart to the flex spread out in front of me.

It's a text from Shelby.

Do it.

"Tell me about her, Grandpa," I blurt the words out, snapping my eyes back up to the wall screens just as he looks my way. I hold his gaze, sliding my hands over my flex and hoping against hope that I've got the right app open. "Tell me about Cleo."

For a moment I think he's going to hang up. Then he slumps against his harness, scrubbing his hands over his face. "She . . . she would be so disappointed in me. In all of us."

I take the opportunity to look down at my flex. I tap the emergency docking symbol, hit the green launch button, then yank my eyes back to the chat window just as he looks up at me again.

"Maybe it would have been better if I'd gone with her. I wanted to. It took three weeks for her to die. Cleo fought. I wanted to fight, too. I've been fighting my whole life. But I couldn't fight the flu for her. All I could do was sit there and . . ." He sucks in a shaky breath. "The night she died, we knew it was over. I was so tired. I didn't want to fight anymore, without her. She knew it. That's why she made me promise her that I'd finish her research. Actually, her words were 'Save humanity from itself.'" He snorts a watery laugh. "Cleo always did have a flair for the dramatic. She said I needed a challenge. A reason to keep going, once she was gone. She was right."

Grief washes over his face and his eyes go distant for a moment.

I throw a look at the exterior camera feed playing out behind the chat window. Jay and Leela are guiding our emergency docking tunnel as it unfolds between the two ships like a huge, fabric-covered Slinky. Their suits glitter like cut gemstones as unfiltered sunlight catches on their camera lenses and sensors. I can only tell the difference between them because Leela is smaller.

"Mom was only nine when Grandma died," Beth says, snagging my attention back to Grandpa just as Jay pushes off the unfurling tube and glides through empty space to the *Vulcan's* docking port. "Wasn't she enough of a reason to live?"

"No," he says, without even a beat of hesitation. "And Cleo knew it. She never suffered any illusions about me. She knew I needed . . . more. I loved Alice, but that was never—"

Reet. Reet. Reet.

The alert pulses red up from his screen, transforming the tragic folds of his sadness into vicious shadows. His eyes snap wide and his face twists into a mask of rage as he looks down at his flex console. Then he glowers up at me. "You used your grandmother? As a diversion?"

The chat window disappears. He's hung up.

On the wall screen, I can see that Jay and Leela have fully extended our docking tube. They're both perched on

Vulcan's hull now, with the tube pressed against the airlock between them. I look down at my console flex, hoping for green lights. But the emergency docking app displays three green lights and three red ones. It's only half sealed. Leela still has to clamp her side into place.

I open a comm line to Leela and Jay with shaking fingers. "Hurry! Grandpa knows what we're doing!"

Leela swears. Then Leela screams.

A perfectly round sphere of blue fire explodes silently around the emergency docking tube, like the *Vulcan* is blowing a bubble. Then the tube shoots into full extension, sending Leela spinning into open space.

"My tether," she screams over the comms. "My tether is gone. I'm drifting!"

"Magnetize your boots!" Jay bellows.

"Too late," Beth says, her eyes glued to Leela's tumbling form on the wall screen. "She's out of range. You have to stay as still as you can, Leela. Minimize your momentum."

"Beth!" Leela cries.

"Stay calm," Beth says. "Just stay calm."

I am not calm.

Leela's only twenty meters from where Jay is still clinging to the *Vulcan's* hull. Maybe less. But it might as well be light-years. I can see Jay's snapped tether streaming out behind him, outlined against the dull gray of the docking tube. Without a tether, Jay can't get to her.

In a few minutes, she'll be lost in the black.

Meanwhile, the half-collapsed emergency docking tube is twisting slowly in on itself. It'll tear soon, or tear *3212* apart. Grandpa is trying to rip the *Vulcan* free, and he doesn't care if it kills us. Why would he? This is what he wants. *A clean slate.* And he's going to get it, unless someone finishes sealing that docking tunnel.

No one else on *3212* is trained for EVA, except possibly Shelby. And she's hurt. But the last time I tried it, I couldn't even step out of the airlock.

No, I realize, my brain racing. I didn't get a chance to step out of that airlock, because Grandpa did it for me. But can I do it now?

I guess we're about to find out.

"Lieutenant Shelby!" I shout over the open comm line as I untether and hurl myself out of the pilot seat. "I'm going to need a spacesuit!"

THIRTY-ONE

I rip my clothes off as I race through the ship to the airlock where Shelby is already hauling a fresh suit from the lockers for me. She fumbles it with her limp, useless arm, but I snatch the gear before it hits the floor.

"You couldn't keep him busy ten more seconds?" she demands, reaching for a helmet as I stuff my legs into the suit. Terror makes my fingers clumsy.

"I'm still earning the poker face." I gasp, shaking my hands out before I shove the suit seals into place.

"Well, let's hope you live long enough to be a better liar," she mutters. Then she calls out over the comm, "You holding it together out there, Divekar?"

"Oh sure," Leela replies, her voice trembling. "Got a view of Tau and everything."

That's bad. If Leela can see the planet, she's beyond the *Vulcan*'s shadow. EVA tethers are longer than the ones in our regular harnesses, but they aren't infinite. Once she's out of reach, we'll never get her back.

I don't realize that Beth's behind me until I feel a second pair of hands pulling the O_2 tank onto my back as I seal the suit and it slithers tight over my body.

"You'll have to complete the docking tube seal first," she says as I jam my feet into EVA boots and grab the helmet from Shelby.

"I know," I say, sliding the helmet over my head and initiating the exterior cameras and comms.

"You can do both." Beth's voice is muffled as I wait for the cameras to come online. "You can save Leela and the ship."

"Maybe," I say as the three-sixty inside the helmet goes live, revealing my sister standing in front of me. "But if I can't—"

"It's improbable," Beth says. "But that's never stopped you before."

"In other words," Shelby says, "get it done, Junior."

With that she pulls Beth out of the airlock and seals it behind them.

"Decompression in ten . . . nine . . . eight . . ." I can't listen. I can't think. I just watch the red light running around the hatch.

I hit the autoconnect button on my harness. My hands

are shaking. It takes three tries before my tether slithers out to bond with the airlock tether point.

What you're afraid of isn't out there, Jo, Mom's voice whispers in my brain. *It's in here.*

Okay, Mom. Okay.

The hatch turns green.

I swipe the door release.

The exterior hatch pops open, letting in the silence of space.

There's no time for hesitation.

I jump.

Then I panic.

I'm spinning, falling in every direction at once as infinity opens around me. I'm screaming. In my head. Out loud. I can't tell. It doesn't matter. I'm alone. In the dark. Just like Teddy.

My tether snaps taut.

"Hotshot!"

"Joey!"

"Joanna!"

The voices of my friends layer over each other through the comm line. Concern. Fear. Love. The snarling panic fights back, but the pull of their voices is stronger than the fear.

"Snap out of it!" Leela's voice roars over the others.

I breathe. Again.

I'm not falling. I'm tethered. I'm suited up. I'm breathing.

I'm okay.

"Copy," I whisper.

An avalanche of concerned questions fills the open comm line. Instead of responding, I grab a handhold on the twisting docking tube and pull myself forward, toward the *Vulcan*.

My panic attack stole fifteen seconds. I need to get them back.

I plant my boots on the next handhold and push off, shooting past the next one to snatch the one beyond it.

This is still too slow.

I curl my body into a crouch and tuck my boots against the twisting tube.

"What are you doing?" Beth demands over the comms as I push off and shoot up the tube, bypassing the next three handholds.

"Being improbable." I gasp, grabbing the final handle and pulling myself onto the hull of the *Vulcan*. Jay is clinging to the other side of the docking ring, his snapped tether floating out behind him like streamers on a little kid's bike handles.

In my head, I can see him losing his grip. I can see him disappearing into the dark. I blink, hard, driving the fear away.

I grab the free edge of the warping docking tunnel and pull, dragging it toward the hull. But I'm moving too fast. The Teflon-Kevlar weave twists in on itself instead, snapping me out into the stars beyond the linked ships.

Memory shrieks through me. My fear is like a club pounding on the inside of my skull. I ignore it this time, dragging myself back along the tether line.

I check my chrono. That just cost me eight more seconds.

"How do I keep this thing from bucking me off again?" I demand over the comms as I hurl myself back toward the tube.

"You need to straighten out the kink before you connect it," Shelby replies.

"How?"

"Your tether," Chris chimes in. "If you can create a second contact point at the center of the tube, you should be able to straighten it gradually as you move toward the *Vulcan*."

"Right," I snap, reaching out to grab a handhold at the midpoint of the twisted tunnel. I don't have any anchor points, so I loop my tether into a mooring hitch knot.

Grandpa's hands fold over mine in my head, shaping my fingers around a different, rougher rope. The memory is so vivid, I can almost smell the sea around us. I snap the knot tight, dispelling the ghosts it carries as I do. Then I leap straight for the *Vulcan*'s hull. I don't have time to be cautious now.

"It's working!" Chris crows over the comms. I don't look back. I don't look at anything but the EVA handle I'm aiming for on the *Vulcan*. Moving between two handholds this far apart is incredibly stupid, even tethered in. If I miss, I'm dead. But I can't care about that right now.

I need eighteen more seconds.

My glove connects with the *Vulcan*'s hull.

I wrap the fingers of my left hand through the EVA handle and lean back to grab the still dangerously torqued emergency tube with my right. I can see the contact points—three glowing red disks on the tube's docking ring. I pluck them free and smack them against the *Vulcan*'s skin.

Then I reach for the warped edge of the docking tube once more.

I hook my fingers under the rim.

I pull.

The tube twists, straightening behind me. Pulling tighter and tighter until . . .

The contact points snap together, turning green silently under my fingers.

"Sealed!" Chris shouts over the comms.

My eyes leap to the chrono in my helmet. I still need twelve seconds I don't have, but I think I know how to get them.

I release my tether and try not to watch the fine black cord eat itself up, unraveling the quick-release knot I tied on the docking tube as it races backward into the fabric of my harness.

My fingers are all that's between me and the black.

My harness vibrates gently as the tether settles.

I plant my boots against the EVA handle and reach up, stretching my body over the hull.

I kick off.

My untethered, frictionless momentum carries me forward over the skin of the ship, the tips of my gloved fingers stretched out in front of me.

The *Vulcan*'s folded wing rises ahead of me. I cup my hands, sliding up and . . .

"Magnetize!" I shout at my suit.

My boots magnetize. The force of their sudden attraction to the *Vulcan*'s hull yanks me backward so fast that whiplash snaps through my neck.

"You're insane," Leela breathes over the comms.

I don't reply. I don't stop moving. Ignoring the pain in my head, I crouch, my knees almost to the hull.

I can see Leela now. A glowing speck in the darkness.

I lean forward, stretching over the inner dip of the wing.

"Mag off."

Then I jump.

I shoot down the wing and up, off the edge like a snowboarder on a half pipe.

Eternity explodes all around me.

It's so beautiful that, for a single heartbeat, there is nothing else.

"Joanna!" Leela's voice yanks me back into the moment.

She's floating ahead of me, arms and legs carefully tucked to try to create as little momentum as possible.

My hand shoots to the autoconnect button on my harness.

My tether hurtles out behind me. I don't look back to see if it connects with the *Vulcan*'s hull. I can't risk breaking my momentum. I can't take my eyes off Leela.

I reach my hands out to her, fingers stretching. Straining.

She shifts her body, risking the momentum gain to reach out for me. Then her hand is in mine. I close my fingers. They catch, hooking into hers as our combined momentum throws us into a dead spin.

I hang on, reaching up to grab her wrist with my free hand as her other hand closes over mine.

I can't see her face, just the many faceted lenses that line her helmet.

"You caught me." Leela gasps. "You jumped off the stupid ship and caught me."

"Couldn't let you have all the fun," I heave back, trying to focus on Leela, not the stars and planet and ships blurring around us.

Any second now, my tether is going to reach its full extension. It will snap tight. Then we'll stop spinning.

Except we don't.

My harness vibrates gently.

"Contact failed," the computer informs me. "Out of range."

My tether didn't connect.

"It's okay, Jo, it's okay," Leela chants. "You tried. Which was a stupid, ridiculous thing to do. But I love you and we came so close and I thought . . . It's okay, Jo. It's okay."

Teddy's voice slips over hers in my head.

Tell me you can do this, Jo. Tell me you're going to be okay.

We aren't okay.

Soon, we're going to be dead.

This can't be how it ends.

Then the blunt silver nose of *3212* flashes in the corner of my eye. We're spinning so fast and so aimlessly that it's impossible to tell which direction our momentum is taking us. Could we be headed back toward the shuttle?

I smack the autoconnect button on my harness.

My tether starts to retract.

I breathe in.

I breathe out.

My harness vibrates.

I hit the autoconnect button again.

The tether flies out.

Searching.

Searching.

Searching.

All the air slams out of my lungs as my tether snaps tight.

"Oh my god." Leela gasps. "We're tethered. We're . . . Holy crap, Jo, you did it."

I can hear Jay and Chris and Beth shrieking over the comms, their joyful voices tangling with each other. But in my head, there's just one voice. A distant one, echoing across time and space.

Tell me you're going to be okay.

We aren't okay yet.

THIRTY-TWO

Tarn and Nor are waiting for us just inside *3212*'s aft airlock.

"Did it work?" I demand. "Did simulation twelve work?"

"Hurry," Tarn thrums in a broken harmony that makes me want to weep. "They need you."

It didn't work.

Leela is already sliding down the ladder at the other end of the corridor that leads to the cargo bay and the emergency docking tube. I fling myself after her, across the bay, and through the airlock into the tube. It has contracted, pulling the two ships together. Its flexible canvas gives under my feet like a trampoline, turning every step into a leap.

We charge onto the *Vulcan*, but a few meters from the bridge, she skids to a stop so fast I nearly slam into her.

"Leela," I start to say, but then I see why she stopped.

Chris is sitting in the corridor in front of her with his back against the wall, staring at the opposite wall screen, which is covered in apps and diagnostics.

"What happened?" Leela cries, dropping to her knees beside him. "Are you okay? Simulation twelve—"

"I can't access it," he says. His voice is grim but calm. Adult. All the little boy squeakiness is gone. "The ship is on autopilot and the whole system is completely locked out."

"Where's Grandpa?" I say.

He points up the hallway toward the bridge.

"Shelby said she was going to shoot him. I couldn't . . ." He shakes his head. "I left. I just left."

I bolt past them and hurl myself onto the bridge.

The *Vulcan*'s dome of wall screen isn't as big as the *Pioneer*'s bridge, but it's big enough to make it look like we're standing in space. Tau is stretched out below us, shrouded in flecks of green light. A countdown clock is superimposed over the planet. **T – 00:12:32:57.**

Those green dots are scrubbers, I realize. The *Vulcan*'s computer is tracking their progress.

Jay and Beth are just inside the door. Grandpa is standing in the center of the bridge, outlined against the cloud of death he's gathering around our world.

Shelby is standing in front of him with a pistol pointed at his head.

"Don't!" I cry.

"Why not?" Shelby snarls. "We may have lost, but that doesn't mean he's going to win."

"We haven't lost yet!" I say, pointing down at the countdown clock. "We have time. Let me talk to him. Let me try."

"I know you've got great faith in your own charm, Junior," Shelby snaps. "But he's about to vaporize two hundred fifty-odd people, including a bunch of kids, for no good reason. I think I'm just gonna shoot him."

"Go back into the corridor, Little Moth," Grandpa says. "You don't have to see this."

"You're a piece of work, old man." Shelby snorts. "Acting like I'm the one traumatizing your precious granddaughter when you're about to vaporize her mama."

"Alice didn't give me a choice!" Grandpa howls at her. He seems just as devastated by the idea as we are.

"What did she do, Grandpa?" I ask. "Why don't you have a choice? Why are you really doing this?"

"I told you—"

"No," I say, cutting him off. "You didn't. You said a bunch of stuff about unity and protecting the survivors that makes no sense. You're about to kill everyone who knows anything about this planet, along with some of the most skilled human beings left in the universe. Engineers. Scientists. Doctors. Teachers. They're our best hope. You must know that. And as for unity, you crafted the Storm War Accords. You really expect me to believe you can't find a way to compromise with your own daughter?"

Grandpa opens his mouth to respond but closes it again. He shakes his head. "No amount of compromise

401

will change what's already done. What had to be done." He sucks in a breath that's close to a sob. "I did what was necessary. I know that. But Alice will never, ever understand."

"And surviving and living with yourself are two different things?" Jay says, from where the others are gathered in the doorway behind me. All the stuff I knew but didn't yet understand slides together into a single, horrifying truth. I know why my grandfather turned on his own people. On his own family. And it has nothing to do with a fresh start for humanity.

"Grandma told you to save humanity from itself," I say, each word shattering my heart into smaller pieces. "But you couldn't, could you? It was too late. There were just too many people."

"Until the atmo scrubbers melted down and killed most of them," Jay says. He's put the pieces together, too.

"No," Shelby says, shaking her head hard, like she can somehow hurl the truth away. "No way. Not even this asshole would kill billions of people on purpose."

"I did what needed to be done," Grandpa says. His voice is quavering. Teary. "I knew there would be consequences. I thought I was prepared to face them. But . . . I am a surprisingly selfish man. I should have realized that. I should have known I wasn't strong enough. I never have been. Not alone. Not without Cleo. The day after she died, I was lying in our bed, staring at the ceiling. I couldn't sleep. I couldn't move. I felt like I was pulling G's just lying still. Then your mother came in." He moans, like the memory is physically painful.

"She just stood there. Looking at me with this expression . . . She was disappointed in me. She was only a little girl, but even she knew I wasn't what she needed. I knew it too. So did her mother. That's why Cleo forced me to make that ridiculous promise. She knew I was too selfish to be a good father on my own."

"You were a good grandfather," I say. "To me, at least."

His smile makes me want to weep. "That was selfish, too. By the time you came along, I thought I'd fulfilled my promise. The atmospheric filtration system. A monumental feat of human engineering that *should* have saved us all. And for a while, it looked as though it was working. But a few years after you were born, it became clear that we were wrong. All the atmosphere scrubbers did was buy us time. And not nearly enough of it."

The memory of his ashen face, staring out at the lake from his chair, surfaces in my mind. I must have been two or three at the time. And he'd just figured out he couldn't save Earth.

"I wanted to give up completely," he continues. "To give in and follow Cleo into the dark. But there you were. So tiny and ferocious and so determined to make me smile. You gave me a reason to go on. Maybe, if I'd been able to see your mother that way, things would be different."

His jaw quivers, like he's biting down on a sob. Then

his whole body shudders. "No!" He hurls the word at us. "I refuse to toil under regret. If I had made different choices, Earth would still be choking to death on human greed."

"Perhaps," Beth says, stepping past our friends and coming to stand beside me. "Or perhaps someone else might have found a better way."

"Someone like you?" he snaps, anger swallowing what's left of the remorse I had seen in his eyes.

"Perhaps," she says.

He snorts a hard little laugh. "I suppose you come by your arrogance honestly, little girl."

"Was there even really an operating system error?" I'm surprised I can get the words out.

"Oh yes," he says, his face shifting back to intense sadness as his focus shifts from Beth to me. "I wouldn't have thought of such a thing if there hadn't been. It was pure luck. An opportunity to reduce the population and give the planet a chance. No matter what I did, billions of humans were always going to die. And soon. But Earth didn't have to die with them."

"It's already dead!" Leela cries. "Your nanobots killed it when they chewed up the atmosphere!"

"No!" Grandpa insists. "No. I was careful. I thought of everything. The filtration system's fail-safe systems *will* kick in. It will reset itself before it reaches a threshold that the plant life wouldn't be able to recover from. The survivors—and there will be survivors, living in the domes, in shelters—they'll be able to start again with a manageable population." He meets my eyes. "I thought through the moral implications of this decision, too, Little Moth. Please believe that. I planned to die with the others. To pay the same price I asked of all of them. But then the ISA offered me command of the *Prairie*. A new planet. A new beginning. With you. I was too weak to say no."

He turns to look out at the planet below, slowly disappearing in the cloud of green dots that mark the scrubbers. "I thought I could build a life for myself here. For my family. I thought I could finally be the father Alice deserved. But all my good intentions just slipped through my fingers."

"Something you said while you two were arguing about that fiasco in the solace grove tipped the commander off, didn't it?" Shelby says, putting the pieces together. "I wondered why she freaked out that way. Bolted out of the room like you'd just set her on fire."

Grandpa sighs. "I was angry. It made me careless. And then it was too late. The look on Alice's face when she and Nick confronted me . . . it was like I was lying in that bed again. I thought the guilt would crush my bones. I couldn't live with it. I can't. And I won't."

"You don't have a choice anymore," Beth says. "We know. You can't kill us all. In fact, given Lieutenant Shelby's proficiency with her weapon, I doubt you'll survive more than a few seconds after the scrubbers initialize."

"Aw." Shelby coughs. She's out of breath, just from

holding her gun on Grandpa. "I think that might be the nicest thing you've ever said about me, Mendel."

"I'm not afraid of a bullet." Grandpa laughs morosely. "Actually, it will be a relief."

"No!" I plead. "You can still make a different choice. Turn off the scrubbers, Grandpa. Live with what you did. Do it for Mom. Do it for me."

"Joanna," he starts to say, but I keep going.

"You said you wanted to see Tau through my eyes, but that's not what you need. You need to see *yourself* through my eyes. I know you're strong enough to face what you've done. All you need to do is believe me."

He stares down at the planet, his cocked shoulder blades jutting against the fabric of his uniform like clipped wings.

"I believe you," Grandpa says. He turns to look back at me then, his eyes aching with something that looks like real regret. "I believe you, Joanna. But it's too late. There's no way to stop it now."

"What?" I stammer. "What do you mean, there's no way to stop it?"

"Exactly that, Little Moth," he says. "I knew I would second-guess myself, in the end. Especially after you refused to come with me to safety. So I removed the temptation." He smiles wryly. "I told you once that I was building this future for you. That's still true. More than ever, now. Make wise choices."

"Screw that," Leela snarls, pointing to the countdown clock. "We've got seven minutes until the scrubbers go live. We can still stop them. We're going to find a way. Aren't we, Jo?"

I turn to look at Beth. Then Chris. Then Jay. Then Shelby. Her arm is shaking, but she's still got her pistol pointed at Grandpa's chest. I pivot away from her awful certainty, searching the three-sixty of space around us for answers I know aren't there. The *Pioneer* is cresting the planet beyond the *Prairie*, her elegant fins spread behind her like she's swimming through the stars.

For a moment, I'm in another place and time. *Pioneer*'s cargo bay. My friends around me. Teddy's arm around Leela. Miguel grinning. Excited.

This is going to be our world. Not some hand-me-down held together with duct tape and good intentions.

Tau might not be our world, but it's our home now. I don't want our history here to start like this. But it's going to. There's no way to change that now.

The wall screen flickers and my parents' bruised and filthy faces replace the view of space around us.

"Mom!" I cry, longing and fear and relief that she's still alive splashing through me. "How did you—"

"I turned off the jamming," Beth says, looking up from the comms panel she has open on the wall screen in front of her. "I wanted to see Mom and Dad one last time."

"No! No! Not one last time." The words shatter the acceptance in my head. "We're going to fix this. We can find a way—"

"Chris," Beth says. "Is there any hope that we can hack into the *Vulcan*'s computer in time to stop the scrubbers?"

"I already tried," he says, "But there's nothing to hack." The despair in his voice is crushing.

"So we destroy it, then," Leela cries. "Ram it into *3212*—"

"*Vulcan* is on autopilot," Grandpa says, quietly. "You can't take manual control. I did not want to be able to stop this. There is no way you can, Little Moth. Don't blame yourself."

"Never." I hurl the word at him. "I will blame you forever."

"Listen to me now, Joanna," Mom says, pulling my attention away from him. "We're going to have to ask more of you five than I ever dreamed. And I'm sorry for it. But you can do this. I trust you."

"No, Mom," I beg. "Don't say that. I don't . . . We're not ready to take responsibility for the survival of the human species.'"

"You think we were?" Dad says with a bleak chuckle. "No one is ready for something like this."

"Wake your aunt when you go to the *Prairie*, Lee-lu," Doc says, stepping up beside Mom. There's a fresh red scar running over his bald head. "She's a neurosurgeon, but she should be able to serve all your medical needs and help you wake the others."

"Okay, Baba," Leela says. She's crying, but her shoulders are square and firm.

"I'm putting field promotions in all of your files," Mom says. "No one currently on the *Prairie* will be able to give you an order."

"What? What does that mean? How do we—"

Mom cuts me off gently. "You'll figure it out, love. But right now, Trey and Kirti are here." She gestures for Dr. Howard and Mrs. Divekar to step into the three-sixty. "We need to give them time to say goodbye."

Chris bolts.

Dr. Howard closes his eyes. Pained. His brown skin has gone gray. "He's so young."

"We'd never have gotten so far without him," I whisper. "He's not a little kid anymore."

Dr. Howard offers me a sad smile. "Yes, he is. But I know you'll take care of him."

"They'll take care of each other," Mrs. D says.

"Ninety seconds to activation," the computer informs us.

My whole body clenches.

"We love you," Leela says. Her voice still clear and calm, despite the tears running down her cheeks.

"We love you, too," Mrs. D says. "All of you. But now it's time to hang up."

I shake my head.

"Turn it off now, Joey," Mom says. "You don't need to see this."

I want to turn it off. I want to run away to wherever Chris is hiding. But then Leela grabs my hand. Jay's arm goes around my waist.

I can face this. We can face this.

"No, Mom," I say, holding my other hand out to Beth. "We're not going to leave you."

"Thirty seconds to activation," the computer says in its bland voice.

Doc grabs Mrs. D's hand and starts speaking in Hindi, something soft and repetitive. He's praying. Beside me, Leela mouths the words along with him.

Mom looks past me to where I've completely forgotten Grandpa is standing behind us.

"Don't get in their way, Dad," she says. Her voice isn't even angry. The words are clear and empty. Less of a request or a demand than a warning.

"I've done what I can," he says. "This is not the new beginning I planned, but it is a new beginning."

"We'll be okay," I say. I don't believe it for a second, but to my surprise, my voice isn't even shaking. It's even. Confident. I recognize it, but not as my own.

That's the commander.

"Activation in ten . . . nine . . . eight . . ."

Mom turns into Dad's arms, clinging to him. He buries his face in her hair.

"Four . . . three . . . two . . ."

Doc reaches a hand out to the screen. "Lee-lu!"

"Baba! Aai!" Leela cries, weeping for her parents.

Sound slams into me on all sides. It feels like someone jammed my whole body in one of the ship's superconductors.

The screens sizzle to black.

The sound dies away.

It's quiet. Quieter than a spaceship should ever be. The background hum of the wall screens, the environmental controls, the computers, it's all gone.

"Was that the scrubbers?" Jay says. His voice sounds loud in the unnatural quiet.

"No," Grandpa says sharply. "That was our ship. Dying."

Red light zips around the seams where the wall screens meet the floors. It swells, filling the room with orange light. A sentence fades up on each wedge of wall screen.

Emergency power cells activated.

"Did it work?" Chris demands, charging back onto the bridge. Nor and Tarn follow him. I hadn't even noticed they were gone.

Nor and Tarn.

"You destroyed the computer." I gasp. "You . . . Tarn. And Nor. And—"

"If they can take down a shield pylon, why not a mainframe?" Chris says. "I can't believe I didn't think of it before. Did. It. Work?"

"I don't know," I say. "The feed cut, and—"

My flex buzzes on my wrist, cutting me off.

It's an incoming call.

Tears are already running down my face as I slap my flex to accept the call.

"Mom?" I whisper, not daring to believe it's possible.

"We're still here," she says, her voice filled with marvel.

"It worked!" Chris cries, grabbing Nor and spinning her into a combination hug and jig. "We did it!"

I shake out my flex with hands so numb, I'm afraid I'll drop it. The video feed flickers up on its screen. There's a lot of hugging and shouting going on there, too, a jubilant backdrop to Mom's incredulous smile.

"We're safe," Dad says, leaning in to add his bursting grin to hers. He looks past me to Grandpa, his goofy grin going ferocious. "See, Eric? I told you including families in the E&P team was a necessity."

Grandpa doesn't try for a retort. He's staring at my flex. At Mom, I think. There's so much emotion in his face. Anger. Relief. Resentment. Love. Fear. Not that long ago, I'd have wondered how all those conflicting emotions could fit together. But not anymore.

There's only one thing left to do.

I look back to Mom.

"Permission to come home, Commander?"

"Granted."

THIRTY-THREE

The *Prairie* is fully visible above Tau as I swing the *Vulcan* into the long elliptical arc that will take us back through the atmosphere.

It took us a couple of hours to pull enough power couplings from *3212* to replace the ones that Tarn blew out on the *Vulcan*. Some of the systems are still fried, but navigation is online and that's all I need to get us home. Beth says the scrubbers are designed to break apart when they run out of power. Their remains will become part of Tau.

So will we.

Even if Grandpa is right and Earth isn't dead, we can't just go home. The survivors have been in deep sleep for too long. We have to wake them up and bring them down to the planet. Then we'll have to figure out how to repair the *Prairie*. It's going to take time. Maybe years. By then we'll be a part of this world, no matter what happens to ours.

The *Prairie's* enormous golden disk soaks in the light of our new sun. Ten thousand people. All depending on us, on the choices we've made. I look back at Tarn and Nor, who are studying the planet as we drop toward it. Make that ten thousand people and I don't know how many other beings on this planet who are all depending on us to work together. To be better than we have ever been. Will this work? Will we take the Sorrow and the phytoraptors down with us?

I have no idea.

But I know how to land this spaceship. Right now, that's all I have to know.

I'm okay.

I kept my promise to Teddy, after all.

The realization washes over me in a wave of emotions that aren't entirely happy or sad. I don't force myself to dissect them, I just feel them.

I look up at the wall screen ahead of me, and for just a moment, the great green belly of Tau is gone and my soot-streaked, singed big brother is standing there, hand pressed against the screen.

I reach out to place my hand against his ghostly fingers. Everything we thought our lives would be shimmers between us.

"I'm okay," I whisper. To myself. To the universe. To him.

"What are you muttering about?" Leela asks, throwing me a curious look.

"Just talking to myself."

She shoots me a dubious look as pink flame licks at the shields, painting the black glow of space in a thousand shades of fire. Then the brilliant turquoise skies of Tau burst onto the wall screens and dense green and glittering crystal spread below us.

A soft sound brushes at the back of my neck, like the leaves of a fido tree nuzzling me. Tarn is singing. Nor joins in as we drop through the morning, her delicate voice weaving through his swelling melody. They aren't singing to us, I realize. They're singing to their planet, spread out below them.

The song fades as I twist the *Vulcan* belly down so she can settle on her haunches in the shorn grass of the Landing's airfield, where a pair of Sorrow flyers is waiting beside our own. A dozen humans and Sorrow are already running across the airfield toward us.

Mom and Dad are first to the ramp. They look like they might smother Beth, both trying to hug her at once.

I should go out there.

What am I waiting for?

"Joanna?"

I turn to look at Grandpa, who is standing behind me.

Shelby still wanted to shoot him, of course. Beth suggested that we owed the Sorrow a say in his fate. Tarn said he wanted to discuss it with Mom. I don't know what they'll decide. I don't know what punishment could possibly be adequate.

"What do you want?" I say, my voice quieter than I wish it were.

"I want you to thrive," he says, without hesitation. "That's all I've ever wanted."

"Don't do that." My voice is almost a whisper now. I clear my throat and try again. "Don't do that. Don't make me spend the rest of my life thinking it's my fault that you . . . that you . . ."

"No, my dear," he says, hurriedly. "My mistakes, my hubris, those things are mine alone. But they don't change my intentions." He looks past me to the wall screens, where pioneers and Sorrow are mixing with each other. Talking. Planning. He shakes his head. "Please. Don't waste your life on this . . . fruitless daydream. Humanity needs you to *fight* for our future."

"No," I say, realizing the truth in the words as I speak them. "It doesn't. We aren't fighting for the future. We're fighting to live right now. For our families. For Tau. For Earth. If we do that right, the future will take care of itself."

With that, I step past him and walk out of the ship, without looking back.

"Took you long enough, Hotshot."

I turn to find Jay leaning against the landing strut.

"Haven't you had enough of being in a hurry for one

lifetime?" I say, letting my feet carry me to him of their own accord.

He tucks me close, our bodies shaping to each other. He rests his cheek on the top of my head. Then he makes a *what the hell* noise and straightens, lifting a piece of melted hair and sniffing at it. "Smells like . . . rotten apples," he says, leaning in to smell my head again. "And . . . aspartame?"

"I'm going to shower forever," I grumble, yanking my fried hair away.

"At least an hour," he agrees.

I kick him.

He kisses me.

"Guess what."

"Jay," I grumble, "I've used up every brain cell I possess canceling the end of the world. There will be no more guessing."

He grins so hard I think his face might split. "Oh fine. I guess I'll tell you."

"Tell me what?"

"Nothing much," he says, still looking like he's trying not to laugh. "Just something I forgot to say, a while back."

"You remember that thing about the shower?" I ask. "Cuz—"

"I love you too, Joanna Watson."

I blush. Instantly. He bursts out laughing.

"What's so funny?" I demand, pressing my hands to my burning cheeks.

"Nothing," he says, his voice still sparkling with joy. "Everything. Me. Us. We're alive. We pulled it off. And everything is pretty much just as screwed up as it was this morning but at least now tomorrow feels like, I don't know, a real thing. Which doesn't make any sense—"

"It does," I say, cutting him off. "It makes sense to me."

His stupid grin gets even bigger. "Which is just one of the many reasons I love you."

"Jay!"

"What, you started it."

He's right, so I kiss him. What choice do I have?

"Does that mean you still love me back?" he asks, against my lips.

"Come on, funny guy," I say, tugging him forward toward the others. The survivors of the *Prairie* squadron are clustered around Shelby, who is sitting on the grass while Doc examines her. Tarn and my mother are deep in conversation. Beth and Dad are standing a few steps from them, leaning against each other. Leela appears to be introducing Nor to her parents. Chris is talking to Dr. Howard at a million words a second. Dr. Howard isn't hearing any of it, I think. He's just drinking Chris in.

A rustle of movement pulls my attention from them. I look back and find a half dozen Sorrow in dim gray cloaks circling the *Vulcan*. Studying it. I should go find Chief G and have her give them a tour.

Grandpa stands a few meters away.

I meet his eyes. I don't want to. I can't help it.
He looks like he's watching his world die.
Maybe he is.
Maybe that's fine.
This isn't his world.
It's ours.

ACKNOWLEDGMENTS

To quote Joanna's dad, "unrealistic goals make us human." Writing a book definitely qualifies as an unrealistic goal. Turning ninety-thousand-odd words into a story is an adventure, and you can't make it from "Chapter One" to "The End" without a lot of help.

My parents taught me to write by listening. Without their infinite patience for my childhood ramblings (and the adult ones), I would never have learned to turn the worlds I saw in my head into books. My husband and daughter keep me fed and sane when I get lost in the creative weeds. They are my lighthouse. My guiding star. And I wouldn't be on this crazy writing journey without the guidance and friendship of Dennis Kim, who believed from the very beginning.

The Survivor and its predecessor, *The Pioneer*, exist in great part due to the determination of Petersen Harris. So, as always . . .

Thanks, Pete.

Thank you also to Wyck Godfrey, for brilliant inspiration, and to Marty Bowen and everyone else at Temple Hill for helping to guide this story on its journey. And, of course, many thanks to Alice Jerman at HarperTeen. A great editor is a gift. I am a better writer than I was when we started working together. I'm also deeply grateful for Simon Lipskar and Genevieve Gagne-Hawes at Writers' House, who have offered such passionate support for me and for this series.

But they aren't the only ones. So many brilliant and talented people have contributed their thoughts, feelings, and time to help me build this book and this world. Thank you, Menaka Chandukar, for your advice, friendship, and gentle frankness. And thank you, Tom Brady, for your sharp eyes and quick brain—writers co-op forever! Then there's Katie Lovejoy, Kaitlyn Wittig Menguc, Tina Gess, Dr. Kagan Tumer, First Officer Kevin Millard, and Dr. Manda Clair Jost. Thank you all for lending me your expertise to make this world, and this future, as authentic and accurate as possible.

And then, of course, there's you. The reader. Thank you for lending me your imagination to build Joanna's world. I hope you've enjoyed it.